BOUND BY BLOOD

TRACKING TROUBLE
BOOK 2

LINDSAY BUROKER

1

GRAFFITI ON THE BUILDING FACADE, SHATTERED GLASS ON THE sidewalk, and thugs in black leather made Arwen Forester wrap her hand around her bow as the car came to a stop. Their surly glares grew speculative as they considered her red-blonde hair, freckled face, and green eyes through the passenger-side window. One man with nose piercings smiled—or was that a *leer*?—as he tossed and caught a switchblade knife.

"This is a rougher neighborhood than I expected from North Lynwood," Arwen admitted.

"No cap," her sixteen-year-old driver, Amber, said. "Am I going to need my sword?"

"Hopefully not. Will your father be angry that you gave me a ride to such a dubious place at night?"

Arwen would have found another way here if she'd known there might be danger. She didn't worry that much about herself, but Amber was another matter.

"Not if he doesn't find out we're here."

"Will your *mother* be angry?"

"You mean, Val, the Ruin Bringer?" Amber asked. "She'll only be pissed if we don't kick those guys' asses."

"Your parents have high standards."

"It's hard being a teenager these days. At least we're in the right spot." Ignoring the thugs, Amber pointed at a neon-green sign over the building's barred front door. "Deep Root Tats. Inking since 1992."

"I don't sense anyone with troll blood inside." As a half-dark elf, Arwen could detect magical beings from a distance.

"Star Inker, the troll owner, comes in at nine. We've got two minutes." Amber held up her phone, tilting the display to show a Yelp review. "I did my research. Trust me. Five-star service between nine and midnight. Great art. Munchies while you wait. Magical tats off the *special menu* for those who know what to ask for. Cash only. You still got those hundreds Colonel Willard paid you?"

"I do have money left but not a lot. We put some aside for taxes, bought new tires for the tractor, and I put in a big order of pie tins and canning jars for the summer."

"You fought dark elves and shifters, and tires and pie tins were your prize?"

"We needed them, and I'm excited about the new Mason jars. For the first time ever, I was able to buy fancy ones with embossed flowers and bees on the fronts. It'll be perfect for our honey. Sigrid thinks we can charge a dollar more a pint because of the increase in perceived quality."

"Grandma isn't exactly a marketing CEO."

"You don't think we could charge more?" Normally, Arwen wouldn't take pricing advice from a teenager, but Amber had proven to be more business savvy than many, and the Lord knew Arwen wasn't experienced with much in the world outside of the forest and the farm.

"Yeah, you can, but not a dollar. *Five* dollars. And put words like *small batch, non-GMO,* and *thoughtfully composed* on the label."

"I'm... not certain that *batches* are an accurate way to describe honey." And what did *thoughtfully composed* imply? That the bees pondered the placement of the nectar in the comb while fanning it with their wings?

"Sure, it is. It's not like rando consumers know better anyway."

The thugs on the street took a few steps, moving closer to the front door of the tattoo parlor. Arwen was tempted to suggest leaving and coming back another night, but Amber reached into the cramped back seat to pull her sword out from under a gym bag.

"Those guys are going to be trouble," Amber said. "I can tell."

"This may not be worth picking a fight over." Arwen dearly wanted the magical spider tattoo on her forearm removed, but... "We don't even have an appointment."

"I emailed, but Star Inker didn't answer. The shop's Instagram says they don't take appointments." Amber shrugged. "We're here. You might as well talk to him. But I did wonder why that fire half-dragon couldn't help you out. He put his tattoo on you after all, right? He must know something about them."

"That was a magical mark, nothing done with ink, and it was temporary." Arwen winced, thinking of Azerdash Starblade, the half-dragon refugee hiding out on Earth from full-blooded dragons who wanted him dead because he was an *abomination.* She'd been trying to help him infiltrate a dark-elf lair to rescue his friend when she'd shot him in the thigh. Yes, she'd been magically compelled by an enemy, but that didn't make her feel any better about the situation. And it stung that he hadn't spoken to her when she'd gone out to his place to apologize to him. She didn't blame him... but it still stung.

"Perfect," Amber said. "Then he can make your ugly spider tattoo temporary too."

"I wish."

Forced to hold still and endure the tattooing at age seven, Arwen had lived with it for twenty-three years. Until recently, it hadn't been a problem, other than being garish and difficult to explain, but now that her mother's people had proven they could control her through it, it needed to go.

The last thing she wanted was to be compelled to attack Starblade again. In any normal situation, she wouldn't have a shot at hurting someone as powerful as he, but the dark elves could once again ensure she didn't face him on equal footing.

Realizing Amber was waiting for more of an explanation, Arwen said, "He's not talking to me. It's complicated."

"You didn't cheat on him with another guy or something, did you?"

Arwen mouthed, *cheat on him,* before realizing what Amber meant. "No, of course not. He's not interested in sex with me. He made that clear."

"Oh? You didn't come on to him like a simp, did you?"

"Of course not." Arwen hesitated. "What is a *simp*?"

"Someone desperate who tries too hard to get someone's attention."

"Then, no." As soon as the words came out, Arwen wondered if they were true. She *had* refused to take no for an answer when Starblade hadn't wanted to work with her against the dark elves. "Giving someone honey, pickled cherries, and tea isn't... *trying too hard*, is it?"

"Uh, what kind of tea?"

"An herbal anti-inflammatory."

"Sounds gross. You're probably fine."

Feeling indignant at the dismissal of one of her favorite blends, Arwen felt compelled to say, "It's good. It helps with cognitive function, muscle soreness, and, uh, erectile problems." Only after the words came out did she realize that wasn't something she should discuss with a teenager.

Amber's lips rippled back in distaste. "Ew. You didn't tell *him* that, right?"

"Since the tea was homemade and there wasn't a label with details, I did feel compelled to share the ingredients and benefits."

Amber stared at her. "You *did* tell him. OMG, talk about over-sharing."

Arwen shrugged.

"It's a real mystery about why he's not interested."

"I believe it's nine p.m. now," Arwen said stiffly, willing to battle brutes if it meant Amber would drop the topic.

"Yup. Good thing I practiced with Val yesterday." Sword in hand, Amber opened the car door. "I'm all warmed up."

Arwen slipped out, her quiver of magical arrows and bow ready. She hurried to make sure she would reach the door—or the thugs, if they tried to block the way—first.

"Are you sure Star Inker will be able to deal with my issue?" Arwen trusted Amber was a capable researcher, one far more computer savvy than she, but didn't know how extensive her experience with magic was. "I don't need another tattoo. I'm looking to get rid of mine."

Four of the thugs shifted to block the door. They smiled at Amber and Arwen, hooking their thumbs in their waistbands and nodding to them and each other. One fingered a leather collar around his neck.

"I'm not sure, no." Amber stopped, though she showed no sign of fear about the toughs. "The reviews didn't mention that, but if you've got a magical tattoo, then it makes sense that a magical tattoo artist would be the one to take care of it, right?"

Arwen didn't know. The first time she'd attempted to have it removed, she'd gone to a dermatologist. The magic in her tattoo had not only broken the laser machine but scared the person working it. Until that day, Arwen wouldn't have guessed it was possible to be banned from a dermatology office, but it was.

Amber flicked her fingers at the door-blockers. "Unless Star Inker hired you mob-movie extras to scare off his clients, you can wait over there." Her fingers shifted toward a broken streetlight where they'd originally loitered.

"This is a dangerous 'hood for a couple of hot girls to be alone," the collar-wearer said. "Why don't you come with us for protection?" He tilted his head toward an alley around the corner.

Amber rolled her eyes. "Has any woman *ever* gone with you into a dark alley? Move aside, or I'll fix your aesthetic. The hard way." She pointed her sword at the guy's chest.

"Sure you will."

"Step out of the way, please." Arwen didn't know whether being polite was called for, but Amber's words had only given them surly and mulish expressions. Arwen waved her bow, though she wouldn't draw an arrow unless she had to—these were mundane humans, and the laws were strict when it came to perforating people with arrows. With magical beings, Arwen might be able to get away with more now that she worked for Colonel Willard's special Army office in Seattle, but she didn't want to risk landing Amber in jail. "We have business inside."

"With a troll?" One guy sniggered. "What, humans aren't good enough for you? You want to get plowed by a green-and-blue dick?"

Amber strode forward with her sword.

Two of the men stepped aside, as if they would give way, but then crouched to spring at her.

Arwen leaped forward, using her bow as a blunt weapon. Thanks to its longer reach, she thwacked a man reaching for Amber before she could stab him. As he reeled back, grabbing the side of his head, Arwen swept the bow over to strike the other man angling for Amber, but the other two rushed her, forcing her to pull it back to defend herself.

The switchblade wielder swiped at Arwen. She smacked her bow against the inside of his arm, knocking the attack wide, then kicked, whipping the ball of her foot into his groin. He stumbled back, dropping the knife. Arwen cracked her second attacker in the nose before he could get close.

"Ow!" came a cry from the door.

Amber jumped back, her sword leaving a bloody gash in the guy's thigh. She pushed her blonde hair over her shoulder, issued an irritated *you-are-totally-inconveniencing-us* grunt, and pointed her blade at the next closest thug.

The two men Arwen had attacked crouched and seemed to be debating whether to try again when the door thumped open. A wreath of marijuana smoke framed the towering blue-skinned troll who stepped out. He had shaggy white hair, tattoos covering both bare arms, and a club bigger than Arwen slung on his shoulder. Star Inker had arrived.

"You kids quit roughhousing out here," he rumbled, his accent promising he hadn't been born on Earth. "I've got a business to run."

His baleful gaze included Amber and Arwen.

The thugs slunk away, the bleeding one grabbing his leg and limping melodramatically as he shot dark looks over his shoulder.

"We're here for business," Amber said.

The troll looked at them, grunted, and walked back inside, the door automatically closing behind him.

"I'm not certain if that was an invitation." Arwen looked wistfully toward her sleeve, wishing the troll *could* help her but growing more doubtful of that with each passing minute.

"None of the five-star reviews mentioned great customer service," Amber said.

"Just the art and munchies?"

"That's what people consider important." Undeterred, Amber opened the door, only wrinkling her nose at the smoke for a second before striding inside.

Arwen started after her but paused, something plucking at her senses. Or *someone*?

She looked back, but the toughs had disappeared. The businesses in the strip mall across the street were closed, windows and doors barred, lights out.

A stray cat wandered across the parking lot, but Arwen didn't see any people. She'd thought she detected a hint of magic—or someone with magical blood?—but it had only been for a second.

"Hopefully, this won't take long," she murmured and headed inside, but she had the uneasy feeling that someone was watching them.

2

"WHAT DO YOU FEMALES WISH?" STAR INKER WAS THE ONLY MAGICAL being in the back room with them, but a couple of human tattoo artists out front had customers stretched out in chairs and on tables. The troll, after regarding quarter-elven-blooded Amber for a second and Arwen for a much *longer* second, had led them into the private space.

"We *wish* you engaged regularly in sanitary practices." Amber pointed at gum stuck to a cracked floor tile and curled her lip at dust coating a bookcase and the frames of tattoo art mounted on the walls. "Are you sure you're qualified to do something quasi-medical?"

"Kazi... what?"

"Never mind." Amber looked at Arwen. "I see the reviews left out some key aspects. And what about that axe?" She eyed a rusty weapon mounted between the artwork, what might have been bloodstains darkening the blade. "Unsanitary."

"Sometimes, the club isn't sufficient when gangs come to oppress my establishment. Or customers don't pay." Star Inker gave them a toothy smile. "But you came in your own carriage, so you must have money. If you want a beautiful tattoo, I'm qualified for the project. I have owned this shop since I first came to this world ten years ago, and I have blessed many humans and mongrels with my work, even the mayor of this city."

Arwen had no idea who the mayor of Lynnwood was but imagined a man in a suit walking in, baring his butt, and getting a Pokémon on one cheek.

"Always, I do my work for a reasonable price. Just tell me what you need. You are in love with someone and wish to memorialize this on your flesh? With a little immunity magic to inspire good health? Or luck magic to help the relationship last?" Star Inker pulled a binder out of the bookcase to show them his portfolio, tapping a heart with a long-tailed dragon weaving through it like a worm eating an apple. "Dragons are popular this year."

Arwen could only shake her head, reminded again of Starblade. She'd thought they had fought well together in the dark-elf lair, but, now, she wondered if babbling about the benefits of tea and how to grow mushrooms had led him to believe she was a fool even before she'd betrayed him.

"We don't need a new tattoo," Amber said. "She needs to have one removed."

"Yes." Arwen pushed thoughts of Starblade out of her mind, though she couldn't help but wish she could make amends. Oh, she didn't feel she needed to apologize for her babbling, but the arrow in the thigh... *That* was an egregious insult. "It's magical, and I've tried to have it removed before, but it was problematic."

Inker grunted. "Problematic because the magic protected the skin from the laser tool, or problematic because the person attempting to remove it was struck down by lightning?"

"There wasn't any lightning." Was that truly a thing? "But, uhm, the machine he was using *did* stop working before it got hot, started smoking, and broke. Somewhat explosively."

Amber's eyebrows rose. Inker rested a protective hand on a piece of his equipment and frowned.

Arwen slid her sleeve up to her elbow so he could see the black spider, its legs curling around her forearm.

"This is dark-elven magic." Inker's frown deepened, but he pulled her arm under an articulating lamp to examine the mark more closely.

"Yes." Arwen resisted the urge to pull back. For her entire life, she'd hidden the tattoo because everyone who'd seen it had called it hideous or alarming, and she couldn't disagree. A neighbor lady had thought Father had given it to Arwen, and she'd lectured him vehemently on rearing children. Maybe it wasn't just Father's PTSD that kept him on the farm with little interest in interacting with others.

"It symbolizes Zagorwalek," Inker said.

"Yes."

"You are sworn to serve the dark elves' demons and follow the ways of their religion."

"No," Arwen said, "I most definitely am not."

"The tattoo says otherwise."

"That's why it needs to go. I'm my own person. I don't *serve* anyone."

"Except with pies," Amber murmured.

Arwen gave her a dark look.

"Hm." Inker probed the tattoo warily with his magic and didn't glance at them. "The ink infused in your skin is mixed with basilisk blood and more magical components I can't identify. They must all combine together to offer different elements to the tattoo. The blood, I know, offers protection."

"She's got some creature's blood embedded in her skin?" Amber asked. "Gross."

Arwen didn't disagree. As Inker rotated her arm, making the

tattoo itch with his careful magical probes, she tried not to feel like a specimen in a science experiment.

"Normally, I don't service your kind." Inker lowered her arm and walked to his bookcase. Below the binders were old tomes with faded covers, the words on some of the spines in languages other than English. Was that Elven on one? "Getting tangled up with dark elves is never a good idea."

"I'm not a dark elf," Arwen said. "My father is human, and he raised me."

Mostly, she amended to herself since she and her father had been her mother's prisoners for the first seven years of her life. She preferred not to think about those dark times—or admit to others that they'd happened. She wanted to be normal, to be accepted. Or at least not be shunned for something she'd had no control over.

"Blood is blood. It makes you and defines you."

"That's not true," Amber said. "Didn't they do nature-versus-nurture studies in troll school?"

"*Troll* school is where young trolls work with their parents and elders in their clans and learn from their wisdom. I know what I know."

"Homeschooled," Amber mouthed to Arwen and wrinkled her nose.

Since Arwen had also been taught at home, she didn't respond to the comment. From what she'd heard, public school could be torment for those who were different. She eyed the tattoo and had no problem imagining peers ostracizing her and teachers contacting her father to demand an explanation. No, it was a relief that she'd learned math, reading, and history from him, as well as skills for tracking and surviving in the forest.

"Hm." Inker returned with the Elven book open to a yellowed page that held a list and a few sketches. Tattoos? Small lines drawn around them might have indicated magic. Inker eyed the page, then her tattoo, and then the page again.

Could he read Elven? If so, he was a more worldly troll than Arwen would have guessed.

A book written in *Dark Elven* would have been better, but, as Arwen well knew, her mother's people didn't let their research and knowledge get out, at least not intentionally. The elves, however, having come from the same world as dark elves, might have some insight into their magic, so she leaned forward with hope.

"I have removed a tattoo left by a magical race before," Inker said. "Often, such magic does not *want* to be removed. It can be dangerous to me and the client, so I must charge a great deal."

"Uh, *how* great a deal?" Arwen worried she hadn't brought enough money.

"Two thousand dollars, plus tip." Inker turned the page. A diagram on that one *actually* glowed, slight magic wafting from the page.

Arwen stared bleakly at him. She *hadn't* brought enough. But maybe she could earn more by selling her goods at some of the upcoming fairs and festivals. Such crowded places always made her uncomfortable, and her twitching and nervous burbling prompted some potential customers to avoid her, but... if Inker could remove her tattoo, wouldn't it be worth it? If it would free her of dark-elven influence? Dark-elven *control*?

"I can pay five hundred now and the rest later," Arwen said. "Or five hundred and barter homemade goods for the rest. You're tall and muscular. You must get very hungry."

Inker lowered the book. "*Barter?*"

"Yes, how do you feel about canned foods? Truffle butter? Pickled asparagus? I can make body cleansers too. Goat-milk soap has great benefits. The Vitamin A makes skin vibrant, the fatty acids soften and moisturize, and do you have trouble with acne?

Or sensitive skin? I've had customers say the soap helped with both." Arwen eyed Inker's tattooed blue flesh.

"No barter. Two thousand dollars. *Tonight*."

"Her pickled food is really good," Amber offered.

Inker closed the book with a thump. "You are willing to pay the price, or not? As I said, this is not without risk for me." Inker frowned toward a window, shutters and iron bars over it ensuring he wasn't looking into the street, not with his eyes, but his senses would be stronger than Arwen's. "There is someone out there?"

"Just those thugs who like to waylay your customers," Amber said.

Arwen remembered the feeling she'd had of someone watching her. Though it could have been someone watching *the shop*. Given the location, it seemed more likely it had been an adversary of the troll than anything to do with Arwen. She didn't know how anyone could have followed her here when she herself hadn't known she would come until Amber called. Still, if the trouble *had* somehow followed Arwen, it would be her fault.

"They are common thieves. My *customers* should be able to handle such. It will be five hundred up front, and the rest upon completion. I will only ask for the rest if I am successful and the tattoo is fully removed."

"That... seems fair." Arwen reached into her pocket for the money she'd brought, prepared to promise him she would get the rest somehow.

Amber held up a hand. "What kind of magical tattoo did you remove before? Your Yelp reviews didn't mention it, and we'd like to know before letting you experiment."

The troll tucked the book under his arm and glowered at her.

"You won't answer?" Amber asked.

"A *goblin* tattoo," Inker said.

"Their magic is a lot less dangerous than dark-elven magic, right?" Amber asked Arwen.

"That's generally accepted as true," she said.

"It was a tricky tattoo sneakily placed and using machine oil as well as ink. It was a male shaman's attempt to claim a human female for himself. She did not want to be claimed, not by a *goblin*."

Arwen didn't know if Inker had the ability to remove her tattoo, especially with what sounded like limited experience, but she counted out the money, hopeful. When she tried to hand the stack of twenties to him, Amber intercepted her.

"You're not taking ten percent, are you?" Arwen asked, their last deal coming to mind. Amber *had* been the one to research this place and drive her over. Maybe she expected to be paid for the effort.

"No, I'm making sure you don't give *him* ten percent—or any percent—until he's successfully removed it. You don't put a down payment on tattoo removal that will take twenty minutes."

"Such a job will easily take an *hour*," Inker said.

"We'll wait and give you the full payment of five hundred when you succeed. *Not* two thousand. You only pay that kind of money to someone experienced and fast, and if you've only removed one magical tattoo before—one *goblin* tattoo—you're more like an apprentice than a master."

Inker squinted at her. "You are very pushy for a young female."

"Yes, I am."

"I am glad I will not give you a dragon tattoo. You do not *deserve* a dragon."

"I'm all angsty inside about that. Can you help my friend or not?" Amber waved to the twenties.

Inker grunted and opened the book again. "You are fortunate it's a slow night. And that I respect pushy females." He glanced toward the shuttered window again. "Clan Leader Higgoritha is female."

"Good for her," Amber said.

Arwen scanned the street out front with her senses, searching for whatever he felt, but if there was anyone magical outside, she still couldn't pick him or her out.

"Sit down." Inker gestured her toward a stool and tilted the light toward her arm again. He rested the book on the counter, open to the page with a list on it. "I may not be able to accomplish this without the formula mentioned here, but I do not have any of these ingredients. I will try the recommended generic incantation. That is all it took with the goblin tattoo."

Nerves teased Arwen's belly as she pushed her sleeve up. Would this work? Would she soon be free?

Inker reached for a tool kit but paused, his eyes growing glazed. He completely froze with his hand in the air.

"Did he have a seizure or something?" Amber whispered.

Arwen shook her head.

The hand dangling in the air reached for the book and tore the page in half.

Startled, Arwen lunged for his arm. Was someone *controlling* him?

Before she could grab him, gunfire rang out in the street. Something slammed into the shuttered window. A bullet?

"Down." Arwen sprang from the chair and grabbed Amber's arm, pulling her to the floor.

Belatedly, she reached for Inker, not wanting him to be riddled with bullets either.

But he sprang away from them, the life returning to his eyes as he grabbed the axe mounted on the wall. "The gangs *dare* oppress my shop again. Arms, my minions. Gather your arms."

With the axe gripped in both hands, he charged for the front of the parlor. More guns fired in the street, bullets slamming into the brick walls and going through the shutters.

"The reviews did *not* mention drive-by shootings," Amber whispered.

"They were an inefficient resource on many accounts."

Out front, a vehicle engine roared, tires squealing.

"You're telling me."

A bang came from the front of the parlor. Inker charging out the door with his axe? Or... someone charging in?

You will not escape your destiny, an unfamiliar male voice spoke into Arwen's mind. In Dark Elven.

Crap.

3

"ORCS AND OGRES," INKER BELLOWED FROM THE FRONT DOOR AS more gunshots rang out. He added something in Trollish before finishing with, "They will *not* destroy my establishment. To arms!"

Tires squealed again, closer now. Arwen sensed numerous magical beings out front, the orcs and ogres Inker saw, but that wasn't who'd spoken into her mind. Their kind wouldn't have used Dark Elven. Few on Earth spoke the language.

"What do we do?" Amber whispered from the floor.

She still had her sword, but Arwen gripped her forearm, forcing her to stay where she was. She couldn't let Val's daughter be killed.

An indignant roar came from the street out front. Inker must have rushed out to defend his shop.

Guilt swarmed Arwen. She couldn't be sure the orcs and ogres had anything to do with the dark-elf speaker, but she feared they did. If so, their presence here was her fault.

"I'm going to help him fight," Arwen said. "I want you to stay out of it."

A bullet slammed into the shutters, made it through, and

punctured an inner wall above their heads. Drywall dust flaked down into Amber's hair.

"*Far* out of it." Arwen looked at a dented door leading to the alley out back. Thus far, she didn't sense anyone out there, but whoever had spoken in Dark Elven was hiding himself from her. He might be in the alley, waiting for her to run out the back. "Hide there." She pointed Amber toward a desk beside the bookshelf before rising into a crouch with her bow in hand.

"*Hide*? I'm a capable warrior."

"There's nothing for you to gain from fighting orcs and ogres."

"Fire!" someone shouted in the street.

Inker roared.

"What's for *you* to gain?" Amber grabbed Arwen's arm before she could creep away.

"Nothing, but I'm obligated."

"*Why*?"

Arwen gently removed Amber's fingers, lifted her arm to indicate her tattoo, and said, "I just am. Stay." Arwen pointed to the desk.

Amber rolled her eyes. "I'm not a dog."

"Stay, and I'll bring you a treat."

Amber squinted at her. "Pickled cherries?"

"Watermelon too when it comes into season."

"Deal." Amber crawled on hands and knees to the desk, then pulled the chair in so she would be less noticeable. Anyone with the ability to sense magical auras would detect her by her quarter-elven blood, but Arwen crossed her fingers that nobody would make it inside.

After making sure the back door was locked, Arwen ran to the front room. The earlier occupants were gone. The front door stood wide open, flames brightening the street outside.

Arwen drew Swamper from her quiver, her magical arrow that had an affinity for trolls and ogres, and eased into the doorway.

Despite his earlier orders for people to fight, Inker stood alone on the sidewalk. A burly ogre rolled at his feet, blood dripping from a gash delivered by the axe.

Inker had conjured a magical barrier so the bullets that sped toward him from a dumpster in the parking lot across the street pinged off. Several were deflected into the walls of other buildings. One hit a lamppost.

Arwen didn't see the vehicle she'd heard, but she did spot fresh black tire tracks on the pavement. An orc rose from behind the dumpster and fired mechanically, no expression on his tusked face, his yellow eyes glazed. Arwen's gut twisted. He was under magical compulsion.

After Inker finished off the ogre at his feet, he raised his axe and stomped toward the dumpster. The orc, seemingly oblivious to the fact that his bullets weren't getting through the troll's barrier, started to fire at Inker's chest. But his gaze lurched toward Arwen. His expression never changed, but his aim did, and he shifted the gun toward her.

Though she believed he was being manipulated, Arwen didn't have any choice but to defend herself. She fired before he could, loosing her arrow.

Knowing it would arrive too late to stop the gunshots, she threw herself back from the threshold, rolling behind a tattooing chair.

Bullets hammered into the wall over her head, but a cry also came from the orc. Arwen peeked outside in time to see him fall to the pavement, her arrow protruding from his eye.

Axe raised, Inker stomped toward him, clearly intending to finish him off.

But the vehicle roared around the corner and came into view first. A black van raised up on huge tires with deep treads, it sped toward Inker.

Two orcs rode in the front, and the side door slid open,

revealing two more orcs with guns. A pair of crossed roses were painted brightly on the van above *Fiona's Flower Delivery* and a phone number.

None of those orcs looked like a *Fiona,* and the magical armor protecting the van promised it was used for more than flowers.

With swords or guns in hand, the marauders leaned out of the van. It didn't slow down as they took aim, instead accelerating toward Inker.

Arwen nocked another arrow. The orcs weren't looking at her, and she hesitated to shoot to kill. Instead, she targeted one of the tires.

When she fired, the arrow sank in. Despite its magic, it didn't tear enough of a hole that the tire deflated immediately. The van roared on.

Inker jumped out of the way while launching a swipe that took out the driver-side mirror. But the two orcs leaning out were able to grab him. They yanked him into the van.

Regretting her choice not to target *them*, Arwen nocked another arrow. But as she fired, the door slammed shut.

Had it been a regular vehicle, her arrow might have gone through, but enough magic protected the van that it bounced off. The orcs charged away with Inker trapped inside.

Arwen's first arrow stuck out of the tire, and she groaned, realizing she would lose it as well as the only person around who might be able to remove her tattoo.

Would the orcs kill him? And if so, why?

Keeping an eye out, Arwen jogged up the street to collect her other arrows. The orc behind the dumpster was dead, and she worried there would be repercussions. But it had been self-defense, right?

As she headed back, a scream came from the tattoo parlor.

Arwen cursed and sprinted inside. She should have checked on Amber before retrieving her arrows.

When she raced into the private room, the back door was open, the bookcase overturned with tomes all over the floor. Amber wasn't under the desk.

A weight thudded into Arwen's gut as she envisioned having to explain to Val that she'd lost her daughter—or worse. She sprinted into the alley as a, "*Hy-yah*" sounded.

Blonde hair swinging, Amber plowed her sword into the shoulder of an orc in a black leather jacket. He dropped two stolen books and ran after another orc lumbering toward the street.

"Are you all right?" Arwen blurted in relief as she raised her bow.

Looking more fierce than scared or hurt, Amber waved her sword. "I hit him once, and I'll hit him again."

The first orc wasn't hanging around for her to strike again. He'd already disappeared around the corner, but the second had his arms full—of stolen loot?—and ran more slowly.

Before he could escape, Arwen planted an arrow in his hamstring. The orc face-planted, a book and a small money chest tumbling from his grip. He drew a dagger as he rolled into a crouch and glared at them.

Arwen nocked another arrow and aimed it between his eyes. "Drop it, and put your hands up," she barked, thinking it would be good to question one of the orcs. She still didn't know if this had to do with her or the troll and his shop.

The orc snarled, knuckles tightening on the hilt.

Arwen didn't want to kill anyone else, but if he started to throw the dagger, she would do what she had to do to protect Amber.

But the orc froze, a strange expression coming over his tusked face. His eyes grew glazed.

"Not again." Arwen tensed, not sure what the compulsion magic would order him to do.

With a shaking hand, he lowered the dagger toward his own throat.

"No!" Arwen raced toward the orc to stop him. She couldn't sense the magical compulsion or where it originated, but if it was strong enough to force him to commit suicide, it came from someone powerful.

The dark elf who'd spoken to her had to be responsible. Deep down, she knew that.

She only made it halfway to the orc before he cut his own throat.

Arwen stopped, slumping in defeat. She doubted the orcs and ogres were wholesome, law-abiding citizens, but they might have been compelled from the beginning to this act of crime.

Amber, who'd been cool and collected during her battle, shrieked as the orc's lifeblood poured out onto the pavement.

"Why—" She pointed with the sword, then spotted the blood on her blade, and almost dropped it.

"It's not your fault." Arwen had battled enough people to be less shocked by the sight of death, but she was grim as she retrieved her arrow from the fallen orc, disturbed that she might have inadvertently been responsible for this.

"I don't get it," Amber whispered. "Why would he kill himself? Over some books. I wasn't even going to try to stop them, but they were taking the one the troll was reading. I thought he might need it for you." Amber swallowed and waved at Arwen's forearm.

"He might have."

If he hadn't been kidnapped...

"Thank you for the help." Arwen wasn't certain if Amber, who always seemed unflappable, wanted a hug, especially when they hadn't known each other that long, but she returned to her side and offered an arm.

"I'm all right." Face pale, Amber didn't *look* all right. She wiped off the sword, then hunched over and gripped her knees. "But I may throw up."

"The orcs kidnapped Inker."

"Meaning nobody will care if I upchuck in the alley?"

"Likely not." After assuring herself that Amber wouldn't faint, Arwen picked up the first two books the orc had dropped. Neither was the grimoire Inker had consulted. Figuring that was the third one, she turned, intending to grab it from the fallen orc's side.

But it had disappeared.

Arwen stared. It had been there seconds ago when she retrieved her arrow.

"We better tell Val about this," Amber said. "Or that colonel she works for."

"Willard," Arwen murmured. "I also work for her now."

"Yeah? You think she'll pay you to figure out what the hell happened tonight?"

Grip tightening on her bow, Arwen looked bleakly around, trying to sense the dark elf she knew was out there. But he remained hidden to her.

Arwen sighed. "I think she may *blame* me for what happened tonight."

4

The next morning, Arwen stood on the sidewalk leading up to an unassuming two-story building with a plaque out front that claimed the IRS had offices there. She'd only been inside once but knew better. The building held the offices, armory, and evidence vault for the Army unit that Colonel Willard commanded. It was responsible for stopping crimes perpetrated by refugees from other worlds as well as local members of the magical community, everyone from trolls and orcs to shifters and vampires. Since they and their magic didn't officially exist, as far as the US government was concerned, the office didn't officially exist either.

Before heading in, Arwen checked the smartphone that Willard had required she buy so it would be easier to communicate. After enduring a lecture from Sigrid about emergencies, Arwen's father had put in a new phone at the farm. Unfortunately, Willard had still insisted Arwen purchase a cell phone.

As usual, it warmed in her hand, threatening to overheat while launching warnings at her. For whatever reason, her aura negatively affected technological gadgetry. Sometimes, the phone spat static and turned off altogether. As someone who'd spent her entire life off the grid on her father's farm, she couldn't say she minded that much when it did.

Unfortunately, other than the excessive heat, it worked fine this morning. She had no trouble reading the message from Willard: *Report to my office at nine. I want to hear everything.*

Arwen was on the verge of going in when she sensed someone with a familiar aura approaching. Val Thorvald turned onto the street, driving her black Jeep. Her dragon mate, Lord Zavryd'nok-quetal, wasn't with her. Since he made Arwen nervous, she wasn't disappointed, but a dragon could have easily dealt with some orcs, ogres, and a dark elf. Assuming the dark elf was acting alone and didn't have a bunch of powerful magical artifacts that could nettle even dragons. After her last encounter with their kind, Arwen couldn't be sure of that.

Val parked the Jeep at the curb and got out, wearing jeans, combat boots, and a leather duster over a tank top. Her magical semi-automatic pistol was nestled in her thigh holster, and her big magical sword jutted from its scabbard over her shoulder.

"Hey, Arwen." Val waved as she walked up, her blonde hair back in a braid, her six feet in height equal to her daughter's. "How'd you get here?"

"I left before it got light out and walked."

"You walked from Carnation to Seattle? That's not exactly the next suburb over."

"No."

"Maybe Willard should have ordered you to get a car instead of a phone." Val waved at it.

Arwen, turning it off since it had grown alarmingly warm, jammed the device into her foraging bag. "I don't know how to drive."

"Wow, really?"

She shrugged. "I do okay on Frodo, but I don't think it would be legal for me to drive it on the streets."

"Frodo?"

"Our old tractor."

"Ah, yeah, I think they frown on those going over the 520 bridge at rush hour. In the future, text if you need a ride. I assume your regular driver is in school most mornings." Val arched her eyebrows.

Arwen couldn't read the expression but winced, suspecting Amber had told her everything—and that Val wasn't pleased that her daughter had ended up in a fight—*two* fights—at a tattoo parlor in a rough neighborhood.

"Sorry," Arwen blurted.

"About using Amber for a driver? I gathered she insinuated herself into the position."

"Oh, she did, but I meant about the tattoo parlor. When she found it for me... Well, I hadn't realized Lynnwood had sketchy parts. But when the hours were nine p.m. to midnight, I should have realized it wouldn't be safe for her."

Val had stopped on the sidewalk and was staring at her. "Amber was with you last night?"

"Uh, yes. She didn't tell you?" Arwen couldn't believe Amber hadn't blurted everything to her mother. Arwen knew Amber lived with her father, not Val, but still. Orcs, ogres, dark elves, and kidnapping and death were up Val's alley.

Her lips twisted wryly. "Of course not. I'm her mother."

"I... don't think I follow."

"That's because you don't have kids." Val glanced at the time on her own phone—*it* probably didn't hiss and huff and heat alarmingly in her hand. She had pristine and beautiful *elven* blood, not odious dark-elven blood.

Since Val, formerly known as the Ruin Bringer, assassin of magical beings who stepped out of line, had even more people after her than Arwen, Arwen supposed she shouldn't have envied her... but it was hard. How many times had Arwen perched in the branches of a tree, looking at the sky on a starry night, and wished she were the right kind of elf?

"Let's see what Willard wants." Val led the way through the front door, giving a security camera a cheery wave. "*She* hasn't told me anything either, though that's not unusual."

As they turned down the corridor toward the colonel's office, Arwen gave Val a brief summary. The night before, she'd texted the same information to Willard, reluctantly including the possibility of dark-elf involvement.

A loud buzzing came from the closed office door that said *Colonel Willard* on the plaque.

Arwen hesitated. "It sounds like there's a beehive inside. Possibly a wasp nest."

"Try a goblin secretary." Val knocked. "Gondo. He'll have built, disassembled, invented, or all of the above some new contraption."

"Come right in," came a high-pitched male voice. "The premises have been secured."

"Oh, I'm sure." Despite the invitation, Val opened the door warily and looked around before committing to crossing the threshold. "One time, there were floating fans ping-ponging around the office like balloons in a windstorm." She touched the back of her head at the memory. *Massaged* it, more accurately.

Before Val took more than a step inside, a four-wheeled, knee-high mechanical construct rolled past, a tape dispenser stuck to it —or... *part* of it?—rattling. A circular-saw blade whirred on the front. A *buzz-clunk* sounded before the contraption rolled past in the other direction.

Arwen peeked around Val, who had—wisely—halted. The construct plowed into a cracked ceramic flowerpot that might have been fished from a dump. The blade ground into it, pulverizing it and leaving shards all over the tile floor.

A gleeful cackle came from atop a desk, where a three-and-a-half-foot-tall goblin in overalls crouched with a remote control in hand. His wild white hair stuck out in numerous directions, as if he'd been electrocuted recently. Maybe he had.

He waved at Val, then spotted Arwen, squawked in surprise, and fell backward off the desk.

She gaped as he landed on the chair, bounced off, and hit the floor. A few seconds later, he peered over the desk at her with huge eyes.

"Gondo, why are you destroying innocent pottery in Willard's outer office? I'm positive she didn't okay this project." Val looked from the saw-wielding construct—which, without input from the remote, ran into a metal filing cabinet and got stuck—and toward an inner door.

"She did, Ruin Bringer." Gondo continued to hide behind the desk and look at Arwen as if she'd walked in with an Uzi.

She tried a friendly wave. As full-blooded magical beings, goblins had no trouble detecting her dark-elven half, and he wasn't the first to have gawked at her in alarm.

"Colonel Willard wants to improve the security now that there are known dark elves in the area," Gondo whispered.

"This is Arwen." Val waved for her to step forward. "Haven't you met before? She's a farmer, not a security risk. She cans vegetables for a living."

Arwen didn't mind being classified as a farmer, since it was true, but she raised a finger. "I'm more known for my tracking skills."

"That *can't* be true," Val said. "I've had your pickled cherries. They're amazing."

Arwen lowered her finger, deciding to accept the praise instead of objecting to the designation. "I hadn't heard you'd been able to try any."

"I talked Amber into giving me some. Well, *five* to be exact. She's a little hoarder."

"I believe Colonel Willard hired me to track bad guys, not can their vegetables."

"That's possibly true." Val gave the still-whirring construct a wide berth and knocked on the inner door. "Let's find out. Gondo, that's not going to secure anything from dark elves."

"Certainly, it will. It's an articulating, hallway-patrolling *battle bot*." His eyes gleamed as he hopped onto the seat. Maybe the talk of canning had convinced him that Arwen wasn't a threat.

"It's made from tape dispensers and staplers," Val said.

"*And* a circular saw. It slices, dices, and Ginsus."

"Dark elves will cower at the sight of it." Val looked at Arwen. "You're cowering right now, I presume."

Actually, Val's words had made Arwen think about pickling and the watermelon she'd promised Amber. Too bad the Crimson Sweet and Sugar Babies wouldn't ripen for a couple more months.

When Gondo looked hopefully at Arwen, she nodded. "Very much so, yes."

"*Excellent.*"

The door opened, revealing Willard in her camo uniform, her wiry salt-and-pepper hair recently cut, and her expression dyspeptic, *especially* when she looked at Arwen. That didn't bode well.

"Get in here, you two." Willard shifted the expression toward Val. "I've been on the phone with the mayor for the last half hour."

"The mayor of Seattle?" Val stepped in, waved for Arwen to follow, then shut the door.

"The mayor of *Lynnwood*." Willard skewered Arwen with her glare. "Early this morning, her police officers reported this to her." She pointed at her desk, where a number of photos had been printed out.

Arwen stepped closer to look at them. A dead troll with tattooed arms lay on the bank of a pond, his throat cut. She slumped.

"Anyone you recognize?" Willard asked.

"Nope," Val said.

Arwen stared glumly. "It's Star Inker, the troll who runs the tattoo parlor I was telling you about. When last I saw him, he was being pulled into a van and kidnapped by orcs. I didn't think— I'd *hoped* he wouldn't be killed."

"Why would anyone kill a tattoo artist?" Val asked.

"And why were you there *getting* a tattoo?" Willard asked Arwen. "It's none of my concern how my operatives decorate their bodies, but since there was a murder, you might end up being a suspect."

"Arwen doesn't slit throats." Val waved at the photos. "Now, if there were a dozen perforations left in the guy from arrows, it might be reasonable to make her a suspect."

"You don't think her foraging knife can do throats?" Willard asked.

"Isn't it for mushrooms? It has that cute little brush on the end for dusting them off."

"I was trying to get my tattoo removed." Arwen ignored the comments about her tool.

"The dragon one?" Val asked. "That one was kind of striking, though I can see why you wouldn't want Starblade tracking you through it."

"No, his mark disappeared on its own." Arwen pushed up her left sleeve to show them her bare forearm. "Or he caused it to disappear when he lost interest in keeping tabs on me."

"Should she sound *glum* when she admits a half-dragon lost interest in tracking her every move?" Willard asked Val.

"Probably not unless she has feelings for him."

"You have feelings for Zavryd, and I don't think you'd want him tattooing you and tracking you with magic."

Val shrugged. "He always knows where I am, regardless. Though you're right that I wasn't crazy when he *claimed* me and did it in a way that other dragons could sense it."

Not wanting to admit or even acknowledge having feelings for Starblade or his missing mark, Arwen pushed up her other sleeve. "*This* is the tattoo I hoped to have removed. The troll could supposedly do such things. He had an Elven book he was consulting when the drive-by shooting started up. Now, he's gone, and that book was also stolen."

Val waved at the photo again. "You think his murder has to do with you?"

"Don't you?" Arwen looked at Willard. "I assumed that was why you called me in, ma'am."

"Originally, I only wanted a more thorough report than the typo-mangled wall of text you sent me last night..."

"I'm not an experienced typer, ma'am. I'm sorry. The phone kept changing words too."

"That's called AutoCorrect," Val offered, aware that Arwen had only had a phone for a couple of weeks.

"It kept changing orc to orca." Arwen hadn't found the *corrections* helpful in the least.

"That happens frequently," Willard said. "Manufacturers of phone software don't acknowledge the existence of magic and magical beings any more than the authorities do."

"You'd think the kinds of geeks who program such things would have at least read Tolkien," Val said.

"Such as you have?" Willard raised her eyebrows.

"Yup."

The eyebrows remained up.

"What?" Val asked her.

"Just thinking of that old Southern expression about pots and kettles."

"We have that expression in the Pacific Northwest, too, and there's nothing wrong with being geeky yourself while pointing out the geekiness of others."

"I see. Look, Forester." Willard turned her attention back to

Arwen. "I'm not accusing you of anything and don't believe for a minute that you had anything to do with the troll's death, but the mayor of Lynnwood wants to know who did and for them to be dealt with."

"The mayor cares about a troll?" Val asked.

"A tax-paying troll with a Lynnwood business license, yes. Apparently, Star Inker not only did the tattoos for some of the well-to-do in town but donated regularly to Rotary Club."

"A troll cared about human youth and education?"

"We don't know if he *cared*, but he gave the organization money," Willard said. "It might have been to ensure the authorities didn't pester him, but he donated enough that the mayor is perturbed about his death."

"You want me to look into it?" Val touched her chest.

"Both of you."

"Did you look up the florist company that was on the van?" Arwen hadn't gotten a picture but she'd remembered the name and had included that in her text, painstakingly ensuring that *AutoCorrect* hadn't altered Fiona.

"I did," Willard said. "As far as the internet is concerned, it doesn't exist. I've got Gondo contacting his goblin acquaintances to see if it's some kind of service that only caters to the magical community."

"For all the shifters and vampires out there who want their romantic gifts delivered by tusked orcs wearing bandoliers of weapons?" Val asked.

"It's a *front* for something, Thorvald. Maybe they're professional kidnappers." Willard grimaced at the photos. "And cutthroats."

"I think they were being controlled by someone." Reluctantly, Arwen added, "A dark-elf someone."

"Not the female who compelled you in that building, right?" Val asked. "You and Starblade took care of her."

"He beheaded her," Arwen said.

"Yup, that'll take care of someone."

"She was only part of a larger clan. And she..." Arwen hesitated, again reluctant to admit this might all tie in with her—and that the tie might make the deaths her fault. Arwen wanted more than ever for her mother's people to disappear and never bother her again. "She mentioned my mother before she died. I'm afraid her clan may want me for something."

"I'll let you know when I figure out where these *florists* are operating so you can pay them a visit." Willard pointed at Val, then shifted her finger toward Arwen. "You better lie low for a bit. Not only was Star Inker connected in the city of Lynnwood, but he was well respected and regarded in the troll community. They'll also be looking for his murderer. Forester, did anyone else see you go into the tattoo shop?"

"Yes, there were other employees and customers in the front room. But they were mundane humans. They might not have paid attention to or remembered me."

Willard looked over Arwen, from her moccasins to her buckskin trousers to her foraging kit, her gaze lingering on her red-blonde hair pulled back into a bun with a pair of sticks. "Oh, you might be surprised at the details *mundane* humans can remember."

"Sorry, ma'am. I didn't mean to insult you."

Val picked a twig out of Arwen's hair and tossed it in Willard's garbage can. Damn, where had that come from? Arwen thought she'd remembered to brush her hair that morning, and she'd walked *mostly* through the city to get here. Admittedly, she'd deviated through parks whenever she could to avoid sidewalks crowded with people.

Val plucked a small leaf out of Arwen's hair and added it to the can.

"Just lie low." Willard waved her fingers to stop Val's ministrations. "Leave those there. They might help camouflage her."

The phone rang, and Willard sighed. "What close contact of the troll tattooer is pestering me now?" She turned her hand wave into a shooing motion. "Dismissed."

In the outer office, they found Gondo spraying his battle bot with WD-40 and oiling the saw blade with... was that a banana peel? He was too busy muttering to himself about improvements he planned to comment on their departure.

"Do you think he'll really be able to find out who's behind the florist orcs?" Arwen had heard that Willard's assistant had a lot of connections in the goblin world and that goblins were great information gatherers. People saw them as harmless pests and didn't hesitate to blather important details around them. Even so, Gondo was a touch distracted.

"Probably by lunchtime." Val clapped her on the shoulder. "Never underestimate a goblin."

Arwen allowed herself to feel encouraged. Maybe they could take care of this before the troll brute squad came after her.

The feeling of hope only lasted a few seconds before she remembered that she still had the dark elf to worry about.

5

Enticing scents wafted from the shortcake biscuits in the oven. Anticipation of a sample almost made Arwen forget her troubles as she sliced the first of the strawberries from the garden. Thanks to the magic she infused in the beds, they were already producing prolifically, so she had enough to make jam *and* shortcakes for the farmers market. And for herself.

Strawberry shortcake had been one of the first desserts she'd experienced after she and her father escaped the dark-elf tunnels, so she had fond memories of it. Its absolute deliciousness when smothered with fresh whipped cream helped along the fondness.

When she sensed a half-dragon soaring into the area, she dropped her paring knife in surprise. Starblade.

Even though she'd left him gifts of pickled cherries and used-coffee grounds for his mushroom trays, she hadn't expected to see him again. It had been weeks since she'd placed those items outside his home. He hadn't said a word to her then, nor had she encountered him since. Her first thought, as she stared out the window of her father's home, was that he was passing through, and his presence had nothing to do with her.

But who *passed through* rural Carnation?

"Nobody." Arwen put the knife on the cutting board next to her pile of strawberries and washed her hands.

Starblade wasn't visible through the window, but she sensed him gliding over the roof and coming in for a landing in the gravel driveway. Nervous, she wiped her hands and headed for the front door.

Her father was in Yakima visiting an old Army friend, so Arwen didn't have to worry about him charging out on the deck with his gun. That gave her some relief, as she'd never been sure how to explain the half-dragon to him.

When she stepped onto the porch, kiwi and goji-berry vines on trellises framing the doorway and running along the railings, she found Starblade in his dragon form. His black scales gleamed in the early-summer sun, and his violet eyes turned toward her, thankfully not *glowing*, at least not at the moment. From what she'd learned, that was usually a sign of irritation for him.

Seconds passed as he gazed silently at her, as if debating something. If he could trust her enough to shift forms and stick around?

Even if she'd had her bow close at hand, it wasn't as if she could have threatened him. From a dozen yards away, she had no trouble feeling the power of his aura, the raw energy he exuded, a warning to anyone who could sense magic that this was not someone to trifle with.

Whatever the debate, Starblade eventually shifted into his elven form, pointed ears thrusting up through his tidy, shoulder-length black hair. He was as handsome as always, jaw chiseled, eyes alluring, his muscular form hidden under...

"Is that... a high-school letter jacket?" Arwen had never seen him in Earth clothing before and gaped. Much like Matti's elven mate, Sarrlevi, Starblade usually looked like he'd stepped off the set of Lord of the Rings.

Today, he wore ripped jeans, high-top sneakers, and a black Slipknot T-shirt under the most garish school colors she'd seen together: purple and green. The gold highlights and tennis-racket and baseball-bat patches didn't do anything to add to the aesthetic.

"In my ongoing attempt to blend in with the natives of my new world, I have acquired this clothing."

"From... Goodwill?" Arwen guessed.

Since she shopped at the store herself, she had nothing against it or affordable secondhand attire in general, but she did wonder if these selections reflected Starblade's tastes or if a dubious clerk had steered him in the wrong direction. Since his usual browns and creams suited him, she suspected the latter.

"I observed a male human of approximately my height and age —or the human equivalent, since they are a short-lived species— pushing a grocery-acquisition cart alongside a street busy with your vehicular traffic. I was uncertain if he was a vendor, but there were many garments inside, more than I believed he needed, so I offered him a gold coin in exchange for providing me with wardrobe items that would allow me to better fit in with the indigenous peoples."

"You gave a gold coin to a homeless guy?"

The recipient must have been pleased to make that trade.

"I was unaware of his habitation status, but he proved well-informed on the sporting teams in the area and said this would allow me to interact with natives in a restaurant or tavern without appearing out of place." Starblade lifted the flap of the jacket. "As I informed you previously, I would prefer that neither mundane humans nor those with magical blood sense that I am a half-dragon or different in any way. Should reports of my existence on Earth reach the Dragon Council, the queen may send minions to slay me. Since I am—" his lip curled, "—an abomination."

"You're not that. You're very talented and useful and—" Arwen stopped herself from saying *handsome*, lest he think she was hitting on him, "—nice."

"Yes, I believe the scientist-general who made our kind wished us to be *nice* while we were marching into battle against the enemy troops." He forced the curl out of his lip, but it seemed an effort.

Not certain how to respond to his bitterness, Arwen switched to the subject she'd been considering the day before. "If there's a way I can help you get the dragons to change their minds about you, let me know. I regret letting myself be used, even if it was completely against my will and desire, against you."

Again, long seconds passed as he regarded her without speaking. Probably because a dozen sarcastic responses came to mind, such as that he didn't need her to fire arrows into the thighs of his enemies. But if he *was* thinking such things, he politely didn't voice them.

"That is not necessary. I have come on an errand. Actually, I have a *list*."

"A... list?"

"Yes." His mouth twisted, this time more with wryness than bitterness. "Perhaps, I should have also bartered with the owner of the grocery-acquisition cart for *it*."

"Oh, did you come for more pickled vegetables? And cherries?" Arwen brightened, always pleased when someone enjoyed her food. She wasn't above attempting to win the hearts and good regard of people with the contents of her pantry. "I won't have more cherries until the trees fruit later this summer, but I've done a number of the early-harvest vegetables from our gardens, and, if I have extra strawberries, I'm thinking of pickling some of them. I have a great recipe with white balsamic vinegar and champagne that everyone loves. I'm also making biscuits for strawberry short-cake right now. Would you like some?" She smiled, hoping his willingness to come to the farm meant he forgave her. At the least, he didn't hold such hatred and contempt for her that he felt compelled to spit in her direction while snarling *dark-elf mongrel* under his breath.

Through her monologue, he gazed silently at her, making her realize that might have qualified as burbling. Or, as Amber had recently called it, *oversharing*.

"My comrade gave me the list," Starblade said.

"Oh." Disappointment washed over her. Though Arwen was glad *someone* liked her food, it would have warmed her heart to know Starblade did. "Is he well?"

The last she'd seen the other half-dragon—Yendral, she recalled his name—he'd been half-unconscious in the dark-elf lair with a magic-nullifying mud crusted all over his naked body.

"Physically, he has adequately recovered from the torture and experimentation the dark elves inflicted upon him in their desire to magically remove remnants of his soul—*chi* may be the proper Earth term—and put it to use creating superior dark elves."

Starblade didn't glare accusingly at her when he spoke of the torture her mother's kind had inflicted on his friend, but Arwen couldn't help but wince, feeling responsible. Or at least guilty by association, which was silly, because she'd never *wanted* to be associated with dark elves.

"Emotionally..." Starblade shrugged. "We have endured much. It is simply another wound that will ache on cold nights and when the body is worn down." His shrug truly seemed indifferent, as if he accepted that the Cosmic Realms would torment them and that was just how it was.

"I'm sorry he had to go through that."

Starblade's nod seemed an acceptance of the apology. "During his recovery, Yendral found the foodstuffs you left at my home. He found and *devoured* them."

"Oh." Again, she tried not to let her disappointment show. She had hoped *he* would enjoy them.

"Yendral is ruled by his stomach. He is a superior warrior and an adequate officer, but I remain amazed that the enemy never infiltrated his ranks and assassinated him by sending a poisoned meal or perhaps a spy working under the guise of a personal chef. In addition to providing a *list* of items he wishes me to acquire from you, he suggested I pay you to prepare a meal for us. *Meals,* he said, but I told him you are already employed as a tracker."

His eyebrow twitch was the only thing to suggest he remembered how she'd originally accepted an assignment to track and tag him. Not that she'd ever seriously tried to carry that out.

Starblade tilted his head as he considered her. "Should you still seek a half-dragon to mate with, Yendral might be interested in such a proposal, especially if you feed him sweets beforehand."

Embarrassment flushed Arwen's cheeks. "Still? I'm not— I was *never* looking for a half-dragon to mate with."

He regarded her blandly, and her cheeks heated further. Supposedly, her tattoo kept him from reading her mind—it had before, anyway—but when she'd been in his enchanted lair, he'd been able to see her thoughts. And she distinctly remembered imagining having sex with him in his bed. She hadn't said anything out loud. How could she be judged by her *thoughts*?

Starblade opened his mouth but turned his nose toward the house before responding. His nostrils twitched, and he reminded her of the great predator he could become, more than the elf who stood before her. Though if he was smelling what she was baking, it had to be his elf half that was interested. Dragons didn't eat biscuits, as far as she knew.

"Regardless, females of many species find him attractive and enjoy his vigor." Starblade stepped forward, withdrew a piece of paper from a pocket, and offered it. The list. "We did not know if you would have the ingredients to create all these items, but I can pay for the portion of the order that you're willing to fulfill." He jangled a pocket that sounded heavy with coins.

Arwen hesitated before accepting the list. She didn't know if she was more chagrined that he wanted to set her up with his friend or that he wanted to pay her for a favor. She'd shot him with an arrow; she couldn't *charge* him. If anything, she was indebted to him and needed to pay him back somehow.

She read down the list. The first item, *pickled anything*, would be doable, as well as the *caramel apples,* but… "Devonshire clotted cream? Alfajores? Gâteau Fondant au Chocolat? Knafeh? I would have to get an international dessert cookbook. Maybe *multiple* cookbooks." Arwen didn't even know what all those items were.

"While I sought to improve my ability to fit in on Earth by acquiring suitable clothing and engaging in a project from the Study of Manliness, Yendral went to a bar. I believe there was a food program on the communications display device."

Arwen didn't know whether to ask what the *Study of Manliness* was or where they'd found a bar that ran the Food Network instead of sports. Before she could decide, the oven timer dinged.

"I need to take my biscuits out." Arwen held up the list. "I'll see what I can make. If not these, I can bake some other desserts. Do you want to try my shortcake? The biscuits I took out earlier should be cool enough."

"What are *biscuits*?" Starblade said the word carefully.

"I'll show you." She waved for him to follow her into the house.

He hesitated. Thinking of her betrayal? Or that he'd only come to drop off the list and pay her for desserts?

Maybe, but his nose lifted into the air. He sniffed again, then followed her up the steps and into the house.

6

THE OLD MANUFACTURED HOME HAD LOW CEILINGS COMPARED TO the airy cottage Arwen had built out back, and being inside made Starblade seem taller. Larger. His aura was more pronounced, too, or maybe it was only that he was closer to her now.

She didn't feel claustrophobic or panicked by his presence, as she so often did with others, but that sense of him being a powerful predator—and her the prey?—returned. For some reason, she thought about how nobody lived within earshot of the farm, and if he wanted to hurt her, she wouldn't have the power to stop him.

Feeling foolish, Arwen attempted to shove the notion aside. Starblade might be a half-dragon and a former military commander, but he was here on Earth as a refugee, trying to fit in. He wouldn't leave a pile of bodies in his wake.

Except she'd *seen* him kill. The memory of him slicing off Zyretha's head with a sword flashed into her mind. If Arwen threatened him or his comrade, he might do the same to her. She would be delusional to believe he wouldn't.

But she wasn't going to threaten him. She'd invited him in for strawberry shortcake. That was all.

As long as a dark elf with the power to control her through her tattoo didn't show up and force her to turn on him...

She gripped the edge of the kitchen sink, sick at the idea that such a thing could happen again. As long as that magical ink was embedded in her flesh, nothing would change.

"Is there a problem?" Starblade asked.

Was his tone wary? Impatient?

Arwen forced a smile, hoping he couldn't read her thoughts. "I'm daunted by that list."

She promptly felt bad about lying. But if she shared her actual concerns, he might realize she was a threat and leave. She didn't want him to go. She didn't know why, but she liked hearing about his attempts to fit in and wanted to ask about the *project* he'd mentioned.

"As I said, there is no need to make everything Yendral extracted from his anus."

Arwen blinked.

Starblade cocked his head. "Is that not correct? It is cruder language than I would usually use, but I have heard Earthers say something similar numerous times now and understood it to be a common idiom."

"Oh. You mean what he pulled out of his ass."

"Yes, I believe I said that."

The timer dinged again. Arwen grabbed hot mats and rushed to the oven, hoping the biscuits hadn't burned. Having a half-dragon arrive might be an understandable distraction, but she always hated to waste supplies.

After she'd taken the pans out and turned off the oven, Starblade withdrew his velvet pouch of coins. The last time she'd seen it, it had held gold coins. She hoped he didn't plan to pay for Yendral's baked goods that way. Arwen couldn't make change for an ounce of gold. But as she moved the cutting board full of strawberries aside, Starblade stacked three coins next to the sink.

"Is this a sufficient payment for the items on Yendral's list that you are able and willing to make?"

"It's too much."

"Though you did not accept my earlier payment—" a confused eyebrow lift suggested he didn't understand why she'd returned that, "—you were originally willing to take ten one-ounce gold coins in exchange for assisting me in infiltrating the dark-elf lair."

"Yes." Arwen didn't point out that he'd been the one to decide on the appropriate payment, not she. "That was a far more dangerous task than baking cookies and cakes for your friend. Unless he has a temper and will incinerate me if the food isn't adequate." She said it as a joke but, afterward, realized she didn't know Yendral in the least. Maybe he was known for having a bad temper.

"Our dragon blood *does* make us prone to incinerate things."

Arwen stared at him, afraid that was confirmation that Yendral might do that to her.

But Starblade's eyes twinkled. "He will simply tell you if he believes the food inferior. And if it doesn't put him in the mood, he may not be interested in recreational coitus with you."

"I'm *not* looking for that." Arwen started to say more, but his eyes were still twinkling. Hell, maybe he'd been joking about that all along.

"Then the consequences of a poorly received dessert will upset you little."

"That's right." She pushed the coins back to him. "Tell him he can pay if he likes what I bring. Just enough for ingredients. Normally, I wouldn't even take that, but that list is going to require a lot of items that I don't have on hand." She quailed inside at the thought of visiting multiple international grocers to find everything. A lot of those places had narrow, claustrophobic aisles, and it only took one other person coming down one to make her want to bolt.

Starblade might not have been able to read her mind, but he was watching her face. Before she could mask her feelings, he pushed the small stack of coins back toward her. "You *will* take the gold. To cover the cost of the ingredients, your time, and the presumptuousness of my comrade for believing you will set aside your work to bake for him."

His tone made it clear it was an order, not a suggestion or a request. For some reason, a little thrill went up her spine, as if she *wanted* to have him order her around like one of his troops. But she didn't want that. She was her own person. Still, she liked baking, and there wasn't anything unappealing about doing a favor for him. As she'd been thinking, she owed him. Technically, this would be a favor for his friend, but it might mean something to him.

"You will also compose these *short* cakes you have tantalized me with." His gaze—or maybe his *nose*—turned toward the biscuits.

"Your *comrade* might not be the only presumptuous one," she murmured, but she *had* promised him a dessert.

As she selected a golden-brown biscuit from the cooling rack, she watched him out of the corner of her eye to see if her words offended him.

"Perhaps not," he said with a faint smile.

"Does that come from the dragon half?" She selected a bowl and took the strawberry sauce and whipped cream she'd made earlier out of the fridge.

"From what I've heard, it comes from *both* halves." Starblade watched as she cut the biscuit in half, ladled strawberry sauce onto both sides, and dolloped whipped cream on top.

She suspected he was making sure she didn't poison anything —maybe he'd also been thinking about the possibility that she could be controlled again—rather than admiring the way she moved around the kitchen. A depressing thought. She allowed herself to feel some small pleasure that he was interested enough in her food to risk accepting something from her.

To finish the preparations, she placed freshly cut pieces of strawberry on top.

"Here." Arwen pulled a spoon out and offered the bowl to him.

Should she have made a portion for herself? He might not trust the food if she didn't eat with him.

He took the bowl and raised it to his nose. "It smells appealing."

"I hope you'll find it *tastes* appealing too."

He started to dip the spoon into the bowl but paused, pointing at one of the slices of biscuit. "You called this a short cake."

"Yes."

"You also called it a biscuit."

"Yes."

"One is not an error?"

"We use both words. Maybe you and Yendral can discuss the oddities of human food culture the next time you dine."

"Would that be... an appropriate conversation for males of this nation to have?" The furrow to his brow implied he'd heard contradictory advice somewhere else. Probably from the Study of Manliness, whatever that was.

"For the kinds of males that can find a bar broadcasting the Food Network, absolutely."

"Very well." Starblade took a precise spoonful of the dessert, making sure to get strawberries, whipped cream, cake—or *biscuit* —and a fresh strawberry all on board. He slid it in his mouth and chewed thoughtfully.

Arwen told herself to turn out the latest biscuits onto the cooling rack, not watch him obsessively, hoping for approval. His face was hard to read anyway. *Thoughtful* was the word that returned to her mind.

As she worked, he methodically ate every bite in the bowl. Well, that might not be a rave review, but it at least implied he liked it.

Once finished, he set the bowl in her sink, then delved into his pocket. He withdrew three more gold coins and placed them on the stack.

"*Starblade*," she said, flopping her hand down on the counter, torn between being stunned and exasperated. "You can't give me six thousand dollars for a strawberry shortcake."

"For the items on the list, as we discussed." He held her gaze, his eyes intent. Almost *intense*. "And you will come prepare a meal for my comrade and me."

His words and his eyes, that charged gaze, sent a hot tingle of pleasure through her. Because he liked her food and... she didn't know what else. He stood close enough that she was highly aware of him, not only the power that he exuded but the... *masculinity* that he exuded. The urge to step closer swept through her, but she didn't act, merely standing still, as if she might startle him away if she drew closer. As if he might remember that he didn't like her much.

"You're being presumptuous again," she whispered, the inane words all that came to mind.

"Yes." He rested his hand on hers. "But you *will* come."

Her body did *more* than tingle at his touch. Heat flushed her from the outside in, centering at her core, making her want... She didn't even *know* what she wanted.

"Okay." Her voice had an odd croak to it.

He stepped closer, his gaze holding hers. "I *did* eat your food." His chest almost brushed hers, and she could feel the heat from his body. His aura embraced hers, making her nerves buzz with awareness—and desire. "What I could pry away from Yendral." He offered a lopsided smile.

The gesture made his previously masked face achingly handsome and her brain short-circuited. She wanted to kiss him. Or for him to kiss her. *Not* for him to set her up on a date with his friend.

His thumb brushed the back of her hand as he held her gaze. Impulsively, she rose on her tiptoes, wanting to press her lips to his, to taste their warmth, to bask in the power and appeal of him.

But Starblade stepped back, frowning toward the ceiling and releasing her hand.

"What—"

"*He* comes," Starblade said in disgust, then looked at her.

The smile had dropped, his face hard now. He shook his head and walked out, leaving the coins stacked by the sink, and soon disappeared from her senses.

7

THE WAY STARBLADE LEFT SO ABRUPTLY, SNARLING, *HE COMES,* before stalking outside, made Arwen expect one of the shifters who'd attacked him or another heinous enemy. But as she stepped onto the porch, she sensed a familiar dragon flying in their direction.

"Ah."

Zavryd. He and Starblade had almost dueled once—over her, as surprising as that was—and didn't care for each other. It was a wonder Zavryd hadn't told his mother, the queen residing over the Dragon Council, that Starblade was present on Earth, not fifty miles from where he lived with Val.

Before the great black dragon appeared in the sky, Arwen also sensed her with him. Her and a second person with a less substantial aura. It was familiar, but it took Arwen a moment to place it. The quarter-gnome woman who owned a share of the Coffee Dragon and often worked in the shop. Nin.

A visit from Val wasn't that surprising, especially since she might be bringing an update from Willard, but why would Nin come out here?

Zavryd soared into view over the trees to the west of the property, his wings outstretched, his majestic black form standing out against the gray sky. When his head tilted to look at her farm—and find a landing spot?—his violet-eyed gaze skimmed over Arwen.

Not for the first time, she was struck by how similar in appearance he was to Starblade in dragon form. She'd wondered before if they might be related. Did Starblade have any idea what dragon or dragons had been chosen to donate genetic material to create him? But she wasn't an expert on how physical traits expressed themselves with their kind. Did scales and eye color have hereditary components? Or was it random?

Still, when those haughty violet eyes met hers, she couldn't help but think how similar they were to Starblade's.

Zavryd tucked his wings to land, alighting in the driveway, though his size made that a small target, and he ended up knocking branches off nearby hawthorn and quince trees.

"Guess those needed a pruning anyway," Arwen murmured.

Wearing the same weapons and outfit as earlier, Val slid easily off Zavryd's back. Nin, her hair dyed orange and swept up in a perky ponytail that made her look young, peered left and right before gingerly swinging one leg over and scooting sideways until gravity took her down. Her arms flailed before she landed beside Val, her bronze skin a touch green after the ride. Arwen assumed Nin didn't travel often on dragon-back.

Val steadied her before walking over. "Hey, Arwen. I have some good news and bad news."

"It's only been four hours since I last saw you," Arwen said.

"You don't think news can happen in such a short time? The world is a busy place."

Arwen looked at Nin.

"She's the *good* news," Val said. "Do you want that first?"

A touch wobbly, Nin walked away from Zavryd to join them.

"I have not yet agreed to your proposal, Val," she stated in a lightly accented voice, her English precise.

"Oh, you will. Trust me. Trust *Amber*. Have you ever known her to have poor taste?"

"In matters regarding fashion, no. I am less certain about her ability to assess quality culinary offerings." The wrinkle to Nin's nose was dismissive.

"You're just testy because she keeps telling you to add more menu items to your food truck."

"She also complains about how often I bring over my signature dish of *suea rong hai*, but Thad enjoys it very much and requests it multiple times a week."

"Thad enjoys *you* very much." Val smirked. "I'm sure he likes your food, too, but he also wants to make you happy. Amber doesn't feel as strongly about that."

"No. She does speak with me now and is relatively civil when I stay over, except if our morning shower uses more than our fair share of the hot water, as determined by Amber. This is a vast improvement from when I first started seeing Thad."

"I'm glad about that. And that she sussed out some wonderful new products that we'd be fools not to start selling at the Coffee Dragon." Val winked at Arwen. "I've vetted them too."

The nose wrinkle may have suggested Nin didn't think much of Val's taste in food either.

"You wish to purchase some of my canned goods?" Arwen guessed.

After stretching like a cat and shaking the leaves off his scales, Zavryd shifted into human form, appearing with short black hair with a slight curl and a goatee that accentuated a strong jaw. He looked less like the elf version of Starblade, but his eyes and hair color remained the same. Arwen didn't think the silver-trimmed black elven robe was anything Starblade would wear, nor the...

"Are those yellow Crocs?" Arwen studied his footwear.

"Yes," Val said. "They were a wedding gift, and Zav enjoys human whimsy, at least when it comes to footwear."

"With charms?" Arwen pointed at a T-bone steak charm sticking out of one of the holes. There were also racks of ribs and rotisserie chickens.

"*Whimsy*," Val said firmly.

Zavryd lifted his chin. "Yes. Also, they are more comfortable than the myriad other human footwear that I tried when I first came to this world. Earth cobblers create substandard work. It's a wonder they're not routinely flogged by your rulers."

Arwen decided Zavryd exuded even more haughty pompousness than Starblade.

"Tell her the good news, Nin," Val said. "I think we'll start there."

"It is not yet *good news*," Nin said, "but Val believes I should sample a few of your popular offerings to see if any would complement our coffee and now alcohol business. We serve numerous snack items to our guests, with baked goods and sweets doing well. We have never tried charcuterie trays with jams and toast— or pickled items—but it might be a possibility."

"Did you get to try any of the pickled cherries from Amber?" Val asked Nin.

"No. She keeps them in her jewelry safe instead of the kitchen. That is why I requested a tasting. Is that something you offer, Arwen?"

"Ah, I can give you some jars to take home and try."

"Home? I am staying with Thad this week, so I cannot do that. The items would disappear from the kitchen and into the jewelry safe."

Arwen scratched her head. "I've never heard of anyone putting my jam or vegetables in a safe."

"They do. They just don't tell you about it." Val gave her a thumbs-up.

Arwen didn't quite get the joke, if it *was* a joke. Maybe Val meant it as a compliment for her food?

"You can take them back to the Coffee Dragon, Nin," Val said. "Or your food truck. Amber doesn't show up in either of those places very often since we tend to put her to work when she does."

"Yes, I understand she's employed as a driver now." Nin looked curiously at Arwen.

Not wanting to explain how that had started, mostly because she'd recently put Amber in danger, Arwen pointed toward the front door. "Do you want to pick out a few things in the pantry that you might be interested in? It's just my father and me here, and he doesn't have much to do with the canning or baking, so we're a small operation, but I might be able to supply one coffee shop with a few items if you're interested. And you don't mind working within our limits. With the exception of some bartering we do with neighbors, we don't bring in a lot of outside produce, so what we grow here is what we have for base ingredients."

Nin pursed her lips as she gazed around the farm. The permaculture practice of growing myriad things together to complement each other, such as one might find in nature, made the place look wild to outsiders. Her gaze lingered on the beehives, the herb spirals, and the meandering orchard with honey locusts and other nitrogen fixers sprinkled among the fruit trees.

"I will make selections, yes." Nin nodded and headed for the house. "Thank you."

"How much longer will this errand take, my mate?" Zavryd's gaze took in the farm with bored indifference. "Perhaps I should go for a hunt while you discuss the troll problem with the tracker." He looked wistfully toward the west.

"If you go hunt, go *that* way." Val pointed to the east. "Not toward the cattle we saw grazing by the river. Those are domesticated."

"I am aware. Wild animals do not meander so foolishly in

open fields where they might be plucked up by aerial predators. Your cattle make for poor sport."

"Until recently, cows didn't have to worry a lot about *aerial predators*. They weigh two thousand pounds."

Zavryd gave her a blank look.

"Never mind. Sure, go hunt." Val pointed east again for emphasis, toward the foothills of the mountains and state land that was full of deer and elk.

"You are unlikely to need protection? Yetis *and* shifters have been known to assail this farm. Of course, you are a very capable warrior, but I would not wish the friends of my mate to be killed."

"I'm sure we can handle any assailments that come this way, but thanks for including my friends under your protection." Val clasped his hand and kissed him on the cheek.

"Certainly, my mate. That is the way of the clan. We protect our own."

Arwen gaped as a thought—no, an *idea*—popped into her mind. She'd heard Val say something similar before, that dragons protected their kin and the friends of their kin, but the ramifications hadn't clicked until that moment.

"What if Starblade was in your clan?" Arwen blurted before thinking things through. "A relative? Would you feel compelled to protect him?"

Arwen doubted Starblade *wanted* protection, especially from Zavryd. Against most enemies, Starblade could take care of himself, but if dragons found out where he lived and came after him, wouldn't it be ideal if Zavryd and maybe even others in the Stormforge clan stood at his side? Arwen couldn't help but feel wishful on Starblade's behalf.

Zavryd had been looking pleased by Val's affection, but he reared back at the question, horror twisting his face. "That mongrel *criminal* that dropped a flaming mountain on dragons attempting to arrest him and his kin for their own good? He does not have Stormforge blood in his veins."

"Weren't the dragons trying to *kill* him, not arrest him?" Val asked. "Because they consider half-dragons an abomination?"

Arwen didn't know about the event they were referencing, but she'd gotten the gist from Starblade that the dragons wanted him and Yendral dead, not behind bars.

"They *are* an abomination," Zavryd said stiffly, "born in an elven scientist's laboratory and *made* without permission from dragons."

"Are you sure it was without permission?" Val asked. "Didn't this all happen a thousand years ago? Who's still around who would remember?"

Zavryd looked in exasperation at her as he extracted his hand from her grasp. "Dragons have long lives. They remember. And we have historical records. After that scheme, the elves are lucky we did not permanently ostracize their people and deny them the honor and protection of being ruled over by the Dragon Council."

"Yeah, lucky. They'd hate to have to rule themselves."

Zavryd squinted at her. "My mate, you are a wonderful warrior, but you are ignorant when it comes to the politics of the Cosmic Realms. In regard to these matters, foolish words come out of your mouth."

"What can I say? My human blood makes me odd."

Zavryd nodded firmly. "You are fortunate to have found a mate as understanding as I who values your other qualities."

"Don't I know it."

Arwen, not sure if they were flirting or arguing—or both—was hesitant to interrupt, but her idea refused to remain silent. "Since it *was* so long ago that the half-dragons were made," she said, feeling weird referring to Starblade as being *made*, like a tool in a factory, "isn't it possible that the information about the dragon he came from has been lost? Isn't it possible he could be related to you? Created from a Stormforge dragon?"

"No," Zavryd said without hesitation.

"He does look a lot like you." Val pointed to one of her eyes.

"He is nothing like me. He has a *minuscule* size and was born a *mammal.* It is shocking that he has the ability to shift into dragon form. For all we know, he chooses his scale color, just as I choose how I appear when I transform into human form. It may reflect his tastes rather than anything genetic." Again, he nodded firmly. "Perhaps he, after seeing how magnificent I am in battle, deliberately chose to model himself after me."

"Oh, yes," Val said, "I'm sure that's it."

Arwen didn't want to pick a fight with Zavryd, but she questioned his hypothesis. If Starblade could alter what he looked like as a dragon, he would have *changed* his appearance after he met Zavryd. He couldn't want to look like a dragon he found so nettlesome.

"Could he be related to another Stormforge? Do your kin look like you, Lord Zavryd?" Arwen smiled, hoping he would answer her questions without being affronted. If some other Stormforge dragon learned Starblade was a relative, maybe he or she would feel compelled to protect him. Or even try to sway the queen to leave Starblade alone.

Zavryd looked at her like she was obtuse for continuing these questions when he'd so irrefutably denied the possibility of a relation, but he did answer. "Some of my siblings and cousins share my black scales. Some do not."

"Your mom has black scales," Val said.

"You are not being helpful in this discussion," Zavryd told her.

"Yes, she is." Arwen turned her smile on Val.

"Is there a way we could test Starblade's blood to learn his lineage?" Arwen imagined someone running slides of dragon cells through a DNA sequencer and the magic in their blood breaking the machine.

"No," Zavryd stated.

But Val nodded to Arwen. "Go see Matti and Sarrlevi when you get a chance. He had some kind of device that he used to test *her* blood after they met. That's how Matti learned her mom is a dwarven princess."

Even more excitement flowed into Arwen as she imagined being able to find out for Starblade who his dragon parent was. Maybe they could learn who his elven parent had been too. Did he know? He hadn't mentioned it before.

If she could learn that information, and if his long-lost relatives would protect him from dragons, wouldn't he appreciate that? Maybe he'd even forgive her for turning on him in the dark-elf lair. Maybe he'd do more than touch her hand the next time she fed him...

"A device that works on dwarves would not work on *dragons*. We know through our senses and auras who we are related to. We don't use magical gimmicks." Zavryd sniffed.

"So, who's Starblade related to?" Val asked.

"Nobody of significance."

"Because you don't know them?"

"Precisely. A dragon long dead, perhaps." Zavryd waved indifferently.

"Talk to Sarrlevi," Val told Arwen again, "but be careful going out and about. Be careful staying here too. After you left this morning, a troll came by Willard's office, wanting her to do something about you."

"Me?" Arwen pointed at herself.

"Those witnesses must have blabbed, because the trolls know you were at the tattoo parlor, and they think you were responsible for Inker's death. When Willard only neutrally said she would look into it, the troll showed up at the Coffee Dragon and tried to hire me."

"To do what?" Arwen asked, though the sinking sensation in her gut promised she already knew.

"Kill you. If I don't take care of it in the next two days, the trolls are threatening to put a bounty out, and it'll be open season on you."

"Why are they so sure *I* had anything to do with his death? Didn't those witnesses see the van and the ogres and orcs? They were there when the shooting started."

"Yeah, but someone figured out you had dark-elven blood," Val said.

"Thus condemning me even over the guys who shot up the shop and kidnapped Inker?"

"Someone thought they were under magical compulsion."

Arwen bent over and gripped her knees. The orcs *had* been under magical compulsion but not hers. She didn't know how to compel anyone. No, she admitted. That wasn't quite true. Long ago, when she'd been her mother's captive, she'd had lessons, and dark-elven magic like that came naturally to her. But she only used it to compel fruit to grow healthy and sweet, not force intelligent beings to attack one another.

"Obviously, I'm not going after you," Val said. "Willard finds it bad form to have operatives on her payroll assassinated."

"I'm so glad." Arwen continued to stare bleakly at the gravel at her feet.

"But I wanted to let you know about the two-day deadline. I need to fly up to Bellingham on another assignment, but I should be back soon. Maybe by then, Gondo will have learned where to find the florist-van orcs."

Arwen had less faith in the locating abilities of Gondo, last seen oiling his battle bot, but she kept the thought to herself. She was a tracker. She would return to the tattoo parlor and figure out herself where the orcs had gone.

If tracking people who'd driven away in a vehicle were easy, she would have tried it the night before, but she might be able to get a trail, especially since her arrow had driven away in the tire of the van. And if the orcs hadn't gone far...

"I'll figure it out," Arwen said. "When I find the killers, I'll make them confess to the truth."

"Well, don't go alone. I'll be back, and I can help."

Arwen nodded and said thanks, though she didn't know if she should wait. She wanted to resolve this as soon as possible, especially since she also had to worry about the dark elf that had been behind the attack.

Nin wandered out with bottles, jars, and a bowl of strawberry shortcake in her hands. It was half-eaten, and two of the jars had also been opened.

"Did you know there is a stack of gold coins by your sink, Arwen?" Nin asked. "This is not a safe way to store such a valuable currency."

"I know, but they're not staying. A, uhm, client overpaid."

"Huh." Nin popped a strawberry into her mouth and chewed contentedly. "Yes, your food is very tasty. And strawberry shortcake is one of my favorite American desserts. I thank you for allowing me to take these samples. I did not wish to wait to try them until I returned, lest they disappear into Amber's jewelry safe."

"I don't think shortcake keeps well in safes," Arwen murmured, though her mind was now far from baking.

"But canned goods might. I saw a list on your counter and added items I am interested in purchasing. Please let me know your rates at your earliest convenience and if you offer a discount for bulk purchases."

"Okay." Arwen didn't know when she would find time to fill all these orders, especially since she had pies to deliver that afternoon, but she made herself smile, glad her work might improve the farm's bottom line this year.

"You seem busy." Val must have caught the daunted expression on Arwen's face. "You could just text Matti, and she'll ask Sarrlevi about the device for you."

"Good idea. Thank you."

"All right, Zav." Val used a finger to make a couple of circles in the air—a gesture to request he shape-shift? Despite his talk about hunting, he hadn't left. "Thanks for waiting. We're ready to go."

Zavryd eyed Nin and her bowl and jars with distaste. "Sticky sugary desserts may *not* be consumed by my riders while they are on my back."

"No? If we stop at Matti's house, I'm sure Sarrlevi will clean your scales for you." Val's eyes gleamed at whatever past experience she was referencing.

"He cleans dragon scales with his *sword*." Zavryd's eyes flared violet. "It is unacceptable."

As he shifted into his dragon form, Nin's shortcake *and* Arwen's bowl went up in flames. Nin let out a startled gasp as she sprang back, dropping the jars.

Always hating to see her food wasted, Arwen lunged and caught them before they hit the ground.

"Are you okay?" Val looked at Nin in concern before she frowned at Zavryd and swatted him on a scaled forelimb.

Nin examined both sides of her hands, as if expecting to find them charred, but they appeared fine. "Yes. It didn't burn me. It just startled me."

"Because it was *startling*. And rude." Val glared at Zavryd.

No sticky sweets for my riders. He levitated Val and Nin onto his back.

"The lids were on tightly." Arwen held up the two jars she'd caught. "These aren't sticky."

Zavryd's big head turned on his long neck, one eyeball coming alarmingly close as he examined them. Arwen made herself hold the jars up instead of skittering back.

I will allow them to be carried by my riders. Zavryd levitated them out of Arwen's grip and into Nin's hands.

"You're in a bit of a mood today," Val told him, then looked at Arwen. "Probably because of the Starblade discussion."

"Sorry," she said, but she wasn't. As soon as she resolved her own problem with the trolls and the dark elf, she would do her best to help him.

Zavryd rumbled. It might have been a growl. Then he sprang into the air with Val and Nin.

Arwen waved goodbye as they flew away, and called, "I'll let you know what I hear about Sarrlevi's device!"

Another growl floated down from Zavryd. Arwen decided not to bring up the topic again when he was around. With all that she already had to worry about, she didn't need to add *being flattened by an irate dragon's tail* to her list.

8

ARWEN PEDALED DOWNHILL TOWARD THE SNOQUALMIE RIVER, A FEW boxes of strawberry-rhubarb pies remaining in the stack behind her bicycle seat. She'd done several deliveries already, and this was the last. Fortunately. She'd thought about bailing on the mission, but her clients had already made their payments. Besides, she wanted to wait until nightfall to visit the tattoo parlor and attempt to pick up the orcs' trail. Her power tended to be stronger after dark, and she would be less likely to run into the authorities doing an investigation of their own.

As she crossed the highway onto the road that ran past the farms along the river, Arwen spotted a number of cattle grazing in a floodplain area. They appeared undisturbed, so she trusted Val had succeeded in convincing her mate to hunt elsewhere.

A few goats bleated at her as she approached the Three Willows Farm, a communal property with a number of families living on and working it. They always ordered numerous pies and often gave her goat milk when they had extra.

Her phone rang, startling her. She hadn't learned to program in contacts, but she recognized the number. Not many people called her yet. With luck, not many people would call her *ever*.

"Hello, Amber." Arwen stopped her bike at the top of the farm's driveway, a cat-shaped flower basket hanging from the mailbox and lilac bushes to either side, a few late-season blooms lingering.

"Hey, Arwen. Val said you're doing research and asked a *goblin* to help you instead of me."

"Willard has him in her employ, and she asked him to do the research."

"Well, I'm good at finding things, you know."

"Such as a florist operation that's a front for orc mercenaries or possibly assassins?"

"Of *course*. I found you that job and got you an interview, didn't I?"

Arwen thought about pointing out that the job and interview had been bait for a trap, one she'd ambled right into, but that might not be polite. Besides, that wasn't Amber's fault.

"You did," Arwen said. "Does this call mean you're running low on funds and want to make another deal for ten percent? I'm afraid I'm trying to find the orcs for personal-preservation reasons rather than because someone hired me."

"Hey, I'm offended. I'm a capitalist, but not everything is about money."

"I apologize."

"I mean, if I found what you needed, *maybe* you could give me a couple more jars of pickled cherries, and did you say you'd have watermelon too? But I just want to make sure you figure out how to get the trolls off your back and nobody kills you." Amber must have chatted with her mother at some point. "I feel kind of bad about all that since I'm the one who found that tattoo parlor. I had no idea any of that would happen, but you know."

Arwen looked at the phone in surprise. She'd been upset that she'd gotten *Amber* into trouble there. It hadn't occurred to her that Amber might feel she was to blame for anything.

"I will have pickled watermelon later in the summer and can give you some," Arwen said. "Yes, if you find any information on Fiona's Flower Delivery, I'll be happy to take it. I have some orcs to question."

"I think you have some orcs to beat the crap out of."

"The questioning may involve that."

"It definitely would if Val went. Anyway, those orcs don't have an address or anything listed online or on any of the bulletin boards for the magical community, but I *did* go into a Discord where deals go down. Their business had some mentions. Apparently, if one wants to hire the florists for *flower delivery*, prices start at five thousand dollars, and a deposit and description of the type of *delivery* wanted can be left in a certain tree by Goodhope Pond in Pine Ridge Park in Edmonds. Arwen, do you know how creepy that is? That park is up the street from here. Like not even a whole mile away. And there are *delivery* deals being made."

Arwen scratched her cheek. "Does delivery mean..."

"Hiring *assassins*. I'm pretty sure, anyway. At first, I thought it might be about narcotics, but those guys weren't at the tattoo parlor to drop off TNT and Special K."

"I don't know what those are."

"Drugs, Arwen. Drugs. Don't you ever leave the farm?"

"Only to deliver pies." Arwen spotted one of her customers out in the field below the house and waved.

"So weird. Look, I can show you that park later if you want, but I have no idea how you'd find one certain tree out of the thousands there. The only thing I've ever seen there are ducks and squirrels."

"If the orcs go there to pick up their deposits, I could find the tree."

"All right. Let me know if you want to check it out. Like I said, it's close. Alarmingly so."

"Thanks."

"And let me know if you need any rides. I'm *not* out of money, but I'm always saving for the future. If nobody's paying you for a gig, I'll still offer the supreme luxury of my hatchback for twenty-five dollars an hour."

"A fair amount."

"I'll say. I got new fuzzy seat covers, so it's an extra posh ride now."

"I have no doubt. I'll—" Arwen broke off because someone powerful came on her radar. A dragon. And not one she was familiar with. "Uh-oh."

"What?"

A few seconds after Arwen sensed him, the dragon came into view. Blue-scaled and as large and powerful as Zavryd, the big male flew over the ridge across the river and arrowed toward a field on the other side. One where cattle grazed.

Guessing what he was after, Arwen wished she could telepathically warn the animals to run. But they were doubtless fenced in so they couldn't escape into the river or across roads. She could only watch as the dragon stretched his talons out and plummeted toward his prey.

As Val had pointed out, cows didn't usually have to worry about predators from the sky, and they didn't stampede until the last moment. Far too late.

The powerful dragon sank its talons into one, muscles bunching under his scales, and through a combination of magic and sheer brawn, he lifted the cow from the ground. Its alarmed cries of pain shattered the quiet of the valley, and Arwen reached for her bow. But she caught herself. Shooting at a strange dragon —at *any* dragon—would be foolish.

Instead, thinking of the camera capabilities of her new phone,

Arwen pulled it out. As the dragon gained altitude, heading toward the forest to consume his prey, she took a few photos of him. Though she doubted Willard's office tried to penalize livestock theft when extremely powerful magical beings from other worlds were involved, the colonel would want to know about unfamiliar dragons on Earth.

What was this one doing here, anyway? Weren't there more appealing wild worlds to hunt on? Zavryd had implied that catching domesticated animals wasn't challenging enough to be of interest.

As the dragon flew over Arwen, it banked abruptly, its head tilting so that one silver eye regarded her.

Aware that there were few trees near the road and she was out in the open, Arwen stuffed her phone into her pocket. Would the dragon know that she'd been taking pictures? Or care?

With a flick of its power, the dragon flung its captured meal away and flew toward Arwen.

Cursing, she jumped off the bike and grabbed her bow, selecting the arrow the dark elves had left for her, the one they'd forced her to use to shoot Starblade. Since the power of her bow had faded, she had few delusions about it piercing a dragon's defenses, but she would try if this one attacked. Which, as he descended toward the road with his silver eyes locked onto her, she worried he would do.

Hoping the dragon wouldn't destroy her bike—or her undelivered *pies*—Arwen took several steps away. She crouched between the mailbox and a lilac bush, as if they might provide protection from such a powerful being.

No sooner had the thought occurred to her than the bushes burst into flame.

Startled, Arwen leaped away, pointing her nocked bow at the dragon.

He landed in the road, facing her from ten feet away. With

wings spread and muscles bunched beneath those sleek scales, he towered above the pavement. His jaw parted enough to show off his sharp, sword-length fangs, and his aura emitted so much power that she wanted to drop to her knees and beg for her life.

Instead, she clenched her jaw, locked her knees, and kept her bow pointing at him. She chose one of his eyes for her target.

I am Darvanylar Silverclaw, his telepathic voice boomed into her mind, powerful enough to make her wince. *You have been in the presence of one of those deplorable mongrel half-dragons.*

"Uh." Arwen didn't know what to say. How could he know that?

I sense his aura lingering on you. Does he mate *with you?* The dragon's lips rippled, fangs still on display. *You are a mongrel yourself, dark-elf-human vermin. Disgusting.*

"No, no mating, and I haven't seen him in a long time." Arwen had no idea how the dragon could sense someone else in her aura, but there didn't seem to be a point in lying.

You saw him recently. *Where is he now? I knew some of their kind survived the confrontation at the elf mountain, but I didn't know they had come here. The cowards. They attacked and killed my kin, dragons in my clan, and then used subterfuge to escape. They did not face us bravely in the skies but lured our kind into tunnels where they were forced to take inferior forms to battle them.*

Arwen didn't point out that sounded smart, not cowardly. A half-dragon would be unwise to face a full-blooded dragon on equal terms.

For that, I will find any half-dragons that remain and slay them. Such abominations never should have been created, never allowed to live this long. Darvanylar stepped closer, his jaws parting further. *You will tell me where he is.*

"I don't know. I'm not his keeper. I don't think he's even on this world anymore." Arwen made herself stand her ground, though she wanted to flee. Unfortunately, there was nowhere to go. The last thing she would do was run down the driveway toward the house and endanger the farm. Besides, a house wouldn't provide any safety from a dragon.

His silver eyes narrowed to slits. *It is true that I do not sense him in this area. His mark ensures he is trackable even when he attempts to hide himself.*

Arwen remembered the dragon tattoo on Starblade's pectoral muscle.

Does he keep females on many wild worlds and alternate where he goes and ruts with them? The long neck extended, the head and eyes coming closer.

Even though he didn't have an obvious magical barrier around himself, at least not that Arwen could sense, Darvanylar showed no concern about her bow. No concern about her at all. After all, she was only a mongrel.

"I don't know," Arwen said again. "I'll be happy to ask him if I see him again."

I believe you will *see him again.* The dragon's nostrils flexed as he sniffed the air. No, he was sniffing *her*. Making note of her scent as well as her aura? *I do wonder if he's fond enough of you that he would come if your life were imperiled.* Darvanylar snorted, the hot air from his breath brushing her cheeks. *Though it's hard to imagine even one with sentimental* elf *blood being foolish enough to have feelings for a dark elf.*

"So I've heard," she muttered.

There was, however, a half-dark-elven half-dragon among his ragtag crew. She died when that mountain fell. They found her body. Did you know this?

"No." Arwen didn't know anything about any of that, but the news that one of the half-dragons had been part dark elf surprised her. Since Yendral and Starblade were both half-surface elves, she'd assumed they all were. Hadn't it been a surface elf who created their kind to help with their war?

Maybe he misses her and believes you an acceptable substitute. The head-to-toe consideration Darvanylar gave her was scathing.

Arwen told herself it was better to be dismissed as a non-threat than be killed.

Their elven blood makes them weak, Darvanylar said. *You will tell me where you believe Starblade is.*

"I don't know." A lie. Could he tell? "When he wants me, he comes to my home."

He had last time...

We shall see.

Tremendous power gripped Arwen's skull, and she gasped, her knees threatening to buckle. It was a mind scouring, and he didn't intend to kill her—at least she didn't believe so—but the pain made her self-preservation instinct kick in. She fired the arrow straight at his eye.

Her aim was true, but he snapped his jaws with amazing speed. Guided by his magic, he caught the arrow before it landed. He clenched down, and she expected it to shatter. Surprisingly, the shaft held under the crushing force of those great jaws.

The dragon growled and spat out the arrow. Its magic had kept it from being damaged, but it hadn't harmed him.

You dare *raise a weapon against a dragon!* Darvanylar roared into her mind. This time, the power *did* drop her to her knees. *I should kill you for such arrogant, disrespectful blasphemy.*

Mental talons ripped into her mind, evoking such intense pain that her back arched and she dropped her bow. He scraped through her thoughts as he inflicted his agony.

Would he kill her? She didn't know. Those cold reptilian eyes held no indication that a human—or mongrel—life meant anything to him.

Again and again, he tore into her mind, forcing her memories to the surface, all of Starblade. He saw them walking side by side into the dark-elf lair. He saw Starblade naked in his rejuvenation pool. And finally, he saw her trapped by the security vines in his tunnel.

Arwen tried as hard as she could to obfuscate any thoughts that had to do with the location of his home, but with such pain tearing into her mind, she struggled to do anything but drop to her side, curling into a ball and grabbing her skull to protect herself.

The tattoo on her arm throbbed, but she had no idea if it kept him from reading her every thought. As a full-blooded dragon, Darvanylar was more powerful than Starblade. Unfortunately.

A gunshot fired. Arwen couldn't tell where it came from, not over the sound of her raw gasps as she struggled to deal with the pain. More gunshots followed the first.

Darvanylar growled and looked away from Arwen and toward the farmhouse. With his focus elsewhere, the pain lessened, but she worried he only had a new target.

"Leave her alone!" someone cried.

Mrs. Keller. The lady who ordered her pies.

"Get off our property," a man yelled. Her husband?

You pathetic vermin dare shoot at a dragon? Darvanylar boomed telepathically. *Your place is on your knees before our kind, giving offerings of meat and serving us in any way you can.*

Arwen pushed herself to her hands and knees, hating that she'd been helpless in a ball before this asshole. He summoned power, not to lash out at her, but at Mrs. Keller and whoever was shooting.

Arwen hadn't wanted the dragon to notice them. Better that she, who could heal quickly from most wounds, take the brunt of his anger. Spotting her arrow on the road, she crawled toward it.

More gunshots rang out.

Darvanylar blasted power toward the Kellers. Arwen lunged and grabbed her arrow. She'd lost her bow. All she could do was scramble toward the dragon when he wasn't looking. She jabbed the point of the arrow into his taloned foot.

It didn't sink in as deeply as she would have liked, but it *did* pierce his scaly flesh.

He shrieked, yanked his foot away, and blasted *her* with power. Slamming into her like a hurricane gale, it hurled her into the air and twenty feet down the road. The arrows in her quiver flew free, scattering uselessly into the grass.

The dragon sprang after her, landing beside her as she struck down hard. Terrified, Arwen tried to roll to the side of the road to get away from him, but one of those taloned feet came down on top of her.

Darvanylar pinned her, trapping her helplessly on her back. His maw lowered, fangs dripping hot saliva onto her, and she saw her death in his furious silver eyes.

9

PINNED UNDER THE DRAGON'S TALONS, ARWEN COULDN'T ESCAPE, but she'd managed to keep her arrow. As Darvanylar's jaws lowered, the threat that he would tear her to pieces in his eyes, she stabbed him in his toe.

This time, the arrow didn't sink in. The dragon had erected a translucent barrier that protected him, even from her magical arrow. Frustrated, she stabbed again and again, hoping vainly to get through. On her back, she had no leverage, but she willed her own power to aid her blows, the power she'd inherited from her mother.

Her tattoo throbbed again and seemed to assist her, but not enough, not when Darvanylar was paying attention. He did pause, however, his jaws hanging above her but not snapping her in half. A drop of his saliva landed on her forehead.

You are frisky and defiant for a mongrel. He sounded *amused,* damn the bastard. *Perhaps that is why he enjoys your company, yes? Predators like spirited mates.*

Arwen stabbed him again, still trying to find a weak spot.

Darvanylar laughed into her mind. *I should slay you for your*

*impudence, but I believe you may be of more use to me alive than dead.
As bait. I have gained the location of your lair from your thoughts. I will
set a trap there. When he arrives to mate with you, I will be there, and I
will destroy him. I will lay his carcass at the feet of my queen to gain her
respect and to avenge the deaths of those the conniving half-dragons
slew.*

Darvanylar lifted his talons.

Not hesitating, Arwen rolled free. She sprang to her feet, gripping her arrow in both hands.

The dragon chuckled into her mind again, then leaped into the air, wingbeats stirring the grass to either side of the road. He retrieved his discarded meal before flying off to the east. In the direction of her home. To lay his traps?

Arwen slumped and rubbed her face with a shaking hand, afraid for herself, for her father, and for Starblade.

A groan came from the farmhouse. Remembering the Kellers, Arwen hurried back to their driveway as quickly as her battered body would allow. Her brain hurt more than the rest of her, but she'd also landed hard when he'd flung her through the air. Her back and hip twinged with each step, and she couldn't keep from limping.

She spotted the Kellers' grown son helping his parents to their feet.

"I don't know what you were firing at," he was saying as Arwen grabbed the pies—somewhat ludicrously, they and the bike hadn't been touched by the dragon or his magic—and headed down the driveway toward them. "But one of the cows from across the river... Uh, this will sound nuts, but I thought I saw it flying, like it was being sucked up—or sideways—by a UFO."

"Don't worry about it, Jason." Mr. Keller grimaced but lifted a hand toward Arwen. "Be glad you couldn't see what we were shooting at."

Dragons, Arwen recalled, usually weren't visible to mundane

humans on Earth unless they *wished* to be visible. Mr. and Mrs. Keller both had smidgens of magical blood. Arwen didn't know what species in their heritages accounted for it but assumed the little quirks they shared might have been what brought them together.

"Are you all right?" Arwen hoped they hadn't broken any bones when the dragon had hurled them about. Humans didn't heal as quickly as those with magical blood.

"More so than you, I think." Mrs. Keller must have noticed Arwen's limp, because she rushed forward to take the pies from her. "You don't charge *nearly* enough of a delivery fee." Though she'd already paid, she dug into a pocket of her apron and handed Arwen a wrinkled twenty-dollar bill.

"I don't charge a delivery fee at all." Arwen tried to hand back the money.

"*Exactly.*" Mrs. Keller stepped away, refusing to take it. "Jason, go get milk for Arwen. Add some extra."

"All right, Mom." Jason glanced toward the field across the river, a man still puzzling over a mystery.

"Do you need to call anyone?" Mr. Keller asked, waving toward their house.

"There's nobody you can *call* about dragons," his wife whispered.

"Isn't there an Army office in Seattle that deals with that sort of thing?"

Arwen snorted, wondering if she should tell them that she now worked for that office. But the questions made her remember that she'd been talking to Amber. She patted her pocket, but her phone had flown free.

"I'll report the sighting later," Arwen said. "Thanks for the help."

As soon as Jason came back with glass bottles of milk for her, Arwen thanked them again and returned to her bike. After tucking them in the basket, she looked for her phone while collecting her arrows. The one she'd pierced Darvanylar's flesh with had a smear of blood on the tip. She left it instead of wiping it off, wanting the reminder that she'd wounded him, however slightly.

She found her phone in the grass, the case battered, but it came on when she touched it.

"Uh, Amber? Are you still there?"

The line had gone dead, but Amber answered promptly when Arwen called back.

"What happened?" she demanded.

"A dragon."

"You're not tracking another one, are you? You said you didn't have any gigs right now."

"No, I learned better than to track dragons. This one... found me."

"That sucks."

"Yes. I believe I could use a ride, actually."

"To the park in Edmonds?"

"Yes, but, first, I need to head north, to warn... a friend."

Wait, dare she go to Starblade's home? Darvanylar had said he would look for him at *her* home. Maybe she'd succeeded at keeping him from learning where Starblade lived. But the dragon could have been misleading her. Maybe he intended to follow her in case she went to see Starblade. The thought of leading an enemy to his home made her cringe. It would be another betrayal, however inadvertent.

"The hot half-dragon?" Amber asked.

"I... How did you know?"

"Because you made a not-really-my-friend-but-a-guy-I-wish-was-my-*boy*friend pause."

How had Amber gotten all of that out of a slight hesitation?

"I need to warn him," Arwen said. "Or I need *someone* to warn him. Now that I'm thinking about it, I might not be able to go up there. I can't risk leading a dragon to him. Would you be able to go? Or maybe I should call Matti."

"*We* can go. I have a camouflaging charm if you need to borrow it."

"You do?" For years, Arwen had checked places where magical goods were sold. Mostly, she'd been seeking special arrows, but she would have snapped up a camouflaging charm if she'd found one. Powerful and useful trinkets rarely made it to Earth unless their owner was using them.

"Yeah, Val gave it to me for my birthday. It's pretty dope, and I would have given it a cherished place in my jewelry safe, but there was *blood* on it when she handed it over. It's hard to unsee that, no matter how many times you sanitize something. Val said she won the charm in a fight. I asked her if it really worked, given that some taco-breath bad guy hadn't lived to keep it for himself. She said it did, and I assume she would know."

"I would think so. If you can bring it for me to borrow, maybe it would be all right for us to go up there." From what Arwen knew about such trinkets, they could hide the wearer from even a dragon's strong senses. And, in case Darvanylar *had* seen in her mind where Starblade lived, she needed to warn him as soon as possible, not wait for someone else to be available. She crossed her fingers that the enchantment hiding the goblin sanctuary—and Starblade's home inside it—would fool the dragon.

"Great. You set up a Venmo account yet so you can pay me digitally like a civilized person?"

"No, but I have one strawberry-rhubarb pie leftover. I think you'll like it. The recipe has won competitions for me before."

"Just so you know, if your food wasn't so amazing, I wouldn't barter my services to you like we're in an emerging-world jungle without access to internet, cell service, or money."

"That's a yes, you'll come get me, right?"

"Of course. Where are we going? North is vague."

"The sanctuary northeast of Arlington. Starblade is kind of off the grid, but if you can get me close, I can walk."

"Where are you now?"

"By the Snoqualmie River in Carnation."

Amber issued a disgusted noise. "Can't you ever go anywhere *urban*?"

"Like the dark-elf lair in Bellevue?"

"Well, that place sucked too. Maybe next assignment, you can go to University Village or Bellevue Square."

"Those are shopping centers, aren't they?"

"Places where one can snag clothing, makeup, shoes, and purses while scoping out cute boys and slurping a shake. In short, a vast improvement over the places where you *usually* go."

"I've yet to be hired to track anyone in a mall, but I'll let you know when I receive an assignment like that."

"I'll hold my breath until then."

Eager to warn Starblade, Arwen asked, "How soon can you make it here?"

"I'm already on my way. Text me the address."

"Thanks, and don't forget the charm."

"I won't, but it's *thirty* dollars an hour for my services plus trinket rental."

Arwen thought about accusing Amber of exploiting her, but five dollars an hour for something as useful as a camouflaging charm was a good deal.

"And *two* pies," Amber added.

"I've only got one."

"I'll trust you're good for more. Be there soon."

Maybe it was fortunate that Starblade had left that gold. Arwen would have to start buying triple the usual amount of ingredients to satisfy all her obligations.

10

Neither Matti nor Val nor Colonel Willard answered when Arwen called, forcing her to leave voice mail messages. Their busyness made her glad that she'd bargained with Amber, who would be there shortly to pick her up. Arwen wanted to warn Starblade as soon as possible. If her father had been at home, she would have rushed there to make sure the dragon Darvanylar wasn't already at the farm, making trouble. Instead, she would have to trust that Horus the rooster could handle things.

When Amber drove up in her hatchback, Arwen stood beside her bicycle with her bow over her shoulder, her quiver again full of arrows, and her last pie in her hands.

Amber leaned over to roll down the passenger-side window, grimacing at the effort or maybe the awkwardness. More than once, she'd complained that the old car didn't have automatic windows. "You'd definitely look weird at Bellevue Square. Where are you going to put that bike? I don't have a rack."

"Will the back seat fold down?"

Amber huffed a sigh. "I suppose. I may need to up my fee though."

"It's very good pie," Arwen said.

"That's the only reason I'm here." Amber climbed out to fold down the back seat.

"I thought it was because you need funds for clothes and Matti doesn't have work for you right now."

"Oh, she has work." Amber grunted as she fiddled with the seats. "She and her half-troll business partner found some trash heap of a house in Shoreline and are demoing cabinets and clearing blackberry brambles as we speak." Amber took the pie, sniffed it through the box, and waved for Arwen to lever her bike into the car.

"Isn't she expecting her twins at any time?"

"In three or four weeks, I think. Right now, she's only hugely pregnant. Val said her half-dwarf blood means she'll probably swing hammers of one kind or another right up to the delivery day. Her kids are going to be so weird."

"Don't you think everyone is weird?" Arwen asked mildly, sliding into the passenger seat.

"Just everyone with magical ancestors. Here." Amber thrust a spyglass-shaped charm dangling on a keychain with two cute cat astronauts at her. "I cleaned the blood off for you. No charge."

"Thank you."

"If Val wasn't *weird*, she would have cleaned it before giving it to me. Proper protocol says you don't give bloody gifts to people. I don't think she even noticed. Blood is part of the biz to her." Amber mouthed, "*Weird*," again as she started the car, plugging Arlington in on her phone's GPS app.

"If Matti has started a new project, then you have multiple options for work. Thank you for taking the time to come get me." Though Arwen always felt a little exploited by Amber, it was nice to have someone willing to give rides. Oh, Sigrid was always willing and said, because she was retired, she didn't mind, but

Arwen hated to impose. She preferred to pay someone if she was going to inconvenience them.

"No problem. I like driving." Amber accelerated far past the speed limit, and a gleeful grin spread across her face.

Since Arwen was worried and in a hurry, she didn't complain.

"More than I like mixing cement, hauling lumber, and holding tools," Amber added. "I like doing research too. If I can't get a good job someday in the fashion business, maybe I'll become a P.I."

"A private investigator?"

"Yeah. Or I could be in fashion by day and a P.I. by night. My side hustle. It wasn't something I'd considered, but then Val gave me that charm, and I realized how epically I can spy on people now." The grin turned wicked.

"Is that why she gave it to you?"

"She gave it to me so I can hide when bad guys come around. Which happens way more than you'd like when your mom is an assassin, and all her friends are kooks." Amber gave Arwen a pointed look.

Arwen thought about pointing out that Val might not yet consider her a friend, but her phone rang. Another number she recognized.

"Hi, Matti," Arwen said. "Thanks for calling back." She'd already summed up what had happened when she'd left her voice mail, but as Amber drove them onto the highway, Arwen reiterated the need to warn Starblade. "I'm heading up there now."

"Okay. I let Val and Willard know about the new dragon—it's never good when they pop up in the Seattle area. And Val said you wanted to know about a blood-testing device from Sarrlevi?"

"Oh, yes." Thanks to the dragon chaos, Arwen had almost forgotten about her plan to learn Starblade's heritage. Now, more than ever, he could use a clan of full-blooded dragons on his side. Even one would be nice. Arwen didn't know how many dragons would feel as honor-bound as Zavryd to protect family. "I'm trying to figure out who Starblade's father was and if he's still alive." She explained her reasoning about getting him some protection.

"I'm not sure Zavryd would be willing to protect him even if we learned they were long-lost twins," Matti said.

"You don't think so?"

"Well, maybe he would, but he'd be snarky and haughty about it."

"He's that no matter what he's doing."

"True. Anyway, I asked Varlesh, and he said he lost the heritage-testing device along with his house when dragons destroyed it."

Arwen slumped in the seat.

"He knows where to buy them, though, and is willing to see if the gnome merchant has any more available for the small price of more of the sea-salt Concord jam and goat-milk truffle butter."

"*He* wants those things? I assumed he gave them to you."

"He did. He wants me to have more. For my contentment and happiness. He's a good mate."

Arwen was going to have to make a list of all the things she'd promised to make for people today. A *long* list. "Such a device sounds expensive, so I'm happy to pay or make whatever food you wish to gain access to it."

"All for Starblade? Or are you trying to test your own blood too?"

"I already know all about my heritage." Arwen grimaced at her sleeve, the spider tattoo hidden by the fabric.

"So all for Starblade. I hope he appreciates you."

"I... think he believes my food is okay."

"I guess that's a start. I'll let you know if we can get a device. Oh, but you'll need a sample of his blood for it to analyze. If he's anything like certain snooty full-blooded dragons, he might have a tantrum about giving it up. Alchemists can use dragon blood in lots of concoctions, so they're extra wary about letting it go. You'll probably need the blood of whatever dragon you want to test as a match too."

"Uh." That sounded daunting. Nothing about her conversation with Zavryd had suggested he would cooperate with what was essentially a paternity test, or maybe sibling test, and she had no idea how to find other dragons to ask them for blood samples.

"Yeah." Apparently, Matti could guess at her thoughts and agreed the notion was daunting. "You've given yourself quite the quest."

"It'll be worth it to help him."

"If you say so. Can you find the sanctuary again on your own? It tends to hide itself from anyone except the goblins who live inside and the handful of others my mom added to the enchantment."

"I think so." Arwen hoped she wasn't being arrogant, since she'd only gone to Starblade's home before with Val or Matti, but she could generally find anything in a forest. "I *am* a tracker."

She was glad she hadn't mentioned that to Darvanylar, or he might have thought to use her to hunt down Starblade. As powerful as dragons were, he wouldn't have needed a tattoo to magically compel her to do his bidding. She shuddered at the thought and hoped Darvanylar enjoyed his purloined cow so much that he forgot all about Starblade.

Wishful thinking.

"I guess I shouldn't have called you Chef Arwen to Nin then," Matti said.

"I don't mind, but I don't have any formal culinary training."

"You *should*," Amber interrupted, catching both sides of the conversation in the quiet car. "Cooking is way safer than hunting down bad guys. And with a little marketing and business help, you could be making a *fortune*." Amber gave her a shrewd, speculative look, dollar signs gleaming in her eyes.

"Is that Val's daughter?" Matti asked.

"Yes. She's driving me, and I believe she's also scheming."

"That sounds right. Tell her I have work digging out blackberry bushes if she's interested."

Amber made an aggrieved face.

"She's doing some research for me right now," Arwen said, "but I can let her know."

Amber gave a thumbs-up.

"I didn't know trackers made so much that they could hire driver-researchers," Matti said, "though I suppose Willard did give you that stuffed envelope with a combat bonus."

"Yes, and a... client insists on paying me in gold coins."

"For tracking?"

"Desserts, actually."

"I *told* you your food could make a fortune." Amber gave the pie box in the seat behind Arwen a longing look. Like she would rather be spooning some into a dish with ice cream than driving.

"Willard better entice you with some lucrative assignments if she wants to keep you," Matti said. "Once you're Mrs. Fields or Famous Amos, you might not want to track orcs."

"Oh, I will," Arwen said, reminded of her other mission to find Star Inker's murderers. Maybe, since her life was in danger, she ought to prioritize that, but she couldn't imagine not warning Starblade about the dragon threat.

"It is fun. Especially when you get to thump them at the end."

"You're going to be an interesting mother."

"The same as my mother, I think. I'll let you know if Varlesh finds a heritage tester. Don't forget to finagle a blood sample while you're there."

"I'll see what I can do."

Twilight crept over the increasingly forested sides of the highway as they drove north. When Amber took the turn for Arlington, Arwen started directing her the rest of the way. As they headed through town and toward the forests housing the goblin sanctuary, Arwen sensed a dragon again. Darvanylar.

"Damn," she whispered, horrified. She *had* inadvertently given him enough to know to look in this area. Had he already found Starblade? What if he'd been here long enough to *kill* Starblade?

"What?" Amber looked at her.

Remembering the charm, Arwen grabbed it and rubbed it as she willed it to camouflage her. "Does this need a command?" she asked a second before a tingle of magic washed over her.

"No, you just rub it like that. I can still see you, but Val said that's always going to be true if you get close to someone else. You need to stay at least five to ten feet away."

Arwen nodded, familiar with such magic. She'd heard of weapons that could extend a camouflaging enchantment around the wielder and had long wished for an arrow with such magic, but, as she'd been thinking earlier, such items were hard to find on Earth, and it wasn't as if she was powerful enough to make portals to other worlds.

"Here." Arwen rested a hand on Amber's arm, believing she could extend the magic to someone she touched.

Most likely, the dragon wouldn't think anything of someone with a quarter-elven blood driving on a road headed out of town, as there were plenty of other cars out here, but, just in case, Arwen wanted to hide them both from his senses.

"I'd be worried you were making a pass at me," Amber said, "but I'm pretty sure long-pause-friend and long-pause-client is a guy."

Arwen blinked. Had she also paused when she'd referred to Starblade as her client? "You're perceptive."

"Yup. That's why you're paying me the big money." Amber glanced at the pie with the wistful look again. Maybe she hadn't yet had dinner.

"I thought it was for the fuzzy seat covers." Arwen tilted her thumb toward the new addition.

"Those were to hide the rips in the seats. If I ever get a client who pays *me* in gold, I'll buy that Mercedes I was drooling over. With *leather* seats. Leather doesn't rip. Cows are sturdy."

Arwen grimaced, the poor cow that had been savaged by Darvanylar's talons coming to mind.

Though she couldn't yet see the dragon, only sense him, she watched the darkening sky through the windshield. He wasn't flying straight but back and forth, occasionally crossing over the road. In a search pattern?

With luck, that meant Darvanylar hadn't yet found Starblade. Maybe she'd only given him a vague sense of where the sanctuary was, and, with the powerful dwarven enchantment on it, he was struggling to pinpoint it. Arwen hoped so. She hated that she'd given the dragon even that much.

"Oh, shit." Amber slowed abruptly, both hands gripping the steering wheel as she peered upward through the windshield.

"You detected him?" Arwen guessed, assuming Amber's quarter-elven blood wouldn't grant her as keen of senses.

"A big freaking dragon? Oh, yeah. Is that why you're camoing us?"

"Yes."

As Darvanylar banked, soaring casually into view over the road ahead, Arwen worried that her guess that he was searching was incorrect. What if he was taking the dragon equivalent of a victory lap?

"Should I pull over?" Amber glanced in the rearview mirror and toward the shoulder of the road. "Or, uh, turn around?"

"*No.*" The word came out more harshly than Arwen intended, and she forced herself to more softly repeat, "No. We have to make sure he didn't find Starblade."

"What if he *did*?"

Arwen closed her eyes, not wanting to imagine that scenario, but her treacherous mind had no trouble conjuring up Starblade and his friend Yendral, bloody and dead on the floor of their home. She hadn't even gotten a chance to cook that meal for them.

"Arwen?" Amber said, a squeak to her voice. "He's flying this way."

11

"Keep driving," Arwen ordered, hoping she wasn't once again endangering Amber. "We're both camouflaged, right?"

"We should be." Amber glanced at the charm and Arwen's hand on her arm, making no further comments about being hit on. "Don't you dare let go of me."

"I won't."

Darvanylar flew closer, following the road—heading straight toward their car.

Since this was Arwen's first time using the camouflaging charm, she started to doubt it. Oh, she'd sensed the tingle of magic wrapping around her, but what if it *wasn't* a stealth charm? What if it was for luck or something else that would be utterly useless against a dragon?

No, Val wouldn't have been mistaken and wouldn't have told her daughter something inaccurate. Besides, Amber had said she'd used it.

The thoughts didn't keep Arwen from breaking out in a sweat as the dragon flew closer, clearly following the road. His silver eyes flared in irritation, standing out against the darkening sky.

Another car was on the road ahead, but Arwen didn't sense anyone with magical blood in it. They wouldn't see the dragon.

"Will he think it's weird that he doesn't sense or see anyone driving this car?" Amber whispered.

Arwen started to shake her head, but was she that certain? She didn't *think* dragons from other worlds cared how automobiles worked, but Darvanylar might know enough to find it odd that one would be driving without a person inside.

"Hopefully not." Arwen caught herself whispering as well.

Most camouflaging charms hid a person from view and masked their aura but didn't keep enemies from smelling or hearing them.

"That wasn't the most reassuring answer."

"Sorry."

"I want to live to eat your pie," Amber said.

"I want that too."

Darvanylar's eyes flared even brighter, and Arwen doubted the charm again and everything she believed. He was pissed, and he was continuing straight toward them. With trees hemming in the road from either side, there was nowhere they could go.

Arwen slid her bow and an arrow out of the back, though she already knew how ineffective her weapons were against the dragon.

Amber's knuckles shone white as she gripped the wheel.

The dragon disappeared from view as he flew over them. Amber pressed the accelerator, driving twenty over the speed limit.

Arwen couldn't blame her and braced herself, expecting the dragon to turn, descend, and grab the car the same way he had that cow. She keenly remembered watching Starblade utterly destroy a parked vehicle in Bellevue.

But Darvanylar continued past them, still following the road. Amber let out a long audible breath but probably only slowed down because they'd reached the car ahead and were tailgating them. She looked like she wanted to pass and continue away from the dragon at top speed.

"We're almost there." Arwen lifted a hand, hoping Amber would slow down. "There's a turn-off around the bend up there for an old logging road. It's got a gate across it." When she'd come on a motorcycle with Matti, they'd been able to continue around the gate and up the road for a few miles before heading into the undergrowth toward the village. "You can drop me off there."

"You're going into the woods alone, and you don't want me to wait for you?"

"I go into the woods alone all the time." Arwen smiled.

Amber gave her an exasperated look as she pulled over in front of the locked gate. "You're going into the woods alone with a *dragon* stalker in the sky above, and you don't want me to wait for you?"

"No, I'd prefer you go back home where it's safe." Arwen fingered the charm, debating if she should give it back to Amber to ensure she could drive home without the dragon sensing her. But Arwen needed to trek up to Starblade's home and couldn't risk leading Darvanylar there. She had to assume—at least she *hoped* —that his disgruntled search meant he hadn't been able to find his prey and was still looking. "Do you want your charm?"

"Hell, yes." Amber twisted to peer in the direction they'd last seen the dragon.

Unfortunately, Arwen could still sense him. He'd turned away from the road and was flying over the forest again.

When Arwen held the charm out to Amber, deciding she would have to hope for the best, Amber reached for it but paused.

"Never mind. You'll need it more than me. You're *rare*. A human with a little elven blood isn't that notable, right?" Amber bit her lip and glanced out the window again. She sounded like she was trying to convince herself.

"To a dragon, you're probably not notable, no. Dark-elven mongrels are rarer." Until the dragon had mentioned that one of Starblade's contemporaries had been one, Arwen hadn't believed there were any others in the world—the Cosmic Realms.

"Yeah." Amber retracted her hand without accepting the charm. "You keep it. Just give it back when you're done. I need to spy on my dad when he's talking to other kids' parents and deciding if I should be allowed to do something."

Arwen smiled. "Of course."

A part of her was tempted to leave the charm on the dashboard, whether Amber said to take it or not, but this was about more than her personal safety. She couldn't risk leading Darvanylar any closer to Starblade than she already had.

The thought made her wince. Would he blame her for the intruder circling the sanctuary? Of course he would. It was her fault. More than ever, she wanted her plan to learn his dragon heritage and find a protector for him to pan out.

"You sure you don't want me to wait here?" Amber asked, but her hand was on the gear shift, like she couldn't wait to tear out of there.

Arwen couldn't blame her. "I'm sure. I'll find a way home. May I come get my bike later?"

"All right."

Once Arwen climbed out, bow in hand, camouflaging charm in her pocket and activated, Amber backed the car onto the pavement. She did, however, wait until Arwen stepped around the gate and started up the road before leaving.

"I can't see you," she called softly out the window. "Charm's working."

Arwen waved, realized it wouldn't be visible, and called, "Thank you."

"I'll text you a rental document to sign for that. If you drop it off a cliff or into a dragon's gullet, I'm charging a huge lost-property fee."

"Understandable."

Arwen strode up the logging road and into the gloom, her muscles twinging from the beating she'd taken earlier. The hip that she'd bruised particularly ached. She thought wistfully of Starblade's rejuvenation pool, but he wouldn't have luxurious soaks in mind when she arrived.

Twice more as she climbed, she sensed Darvanylar. He was a determined dragon.

When the road took her through a clearcut area, the lack of cover made her uneasy, especially when he flew into view. Aware that camouflaging charms didn't work as well if someone was making movement—especially quick movements—Arwen paused by a stump to wait for his passing.

Remembering his twitching nostrils, she hoped her scent wouldn't give her away. How good were dragon noses? She didn't know but assumed their kind was as effective at catching scents as wolves and mountain lions and other predators. Luck put her downwind from him when he sailed over the ridge at the top of the slope.

As she crouched, it occurred to her that she didn't *need* to warn Starblade at this point. If he was home, he would have sensed Darvanylar in the area. He already knew everything she would tell him, that a Silverclaw dragon was looking for him.

What he probably didn't know was that it was her fault that Darvanylar knew where to search. She grimaced, wishing she could avoid admitting that.

It was only bad luck that had put her in the dragon's path when he'd been hunting. Why had he even been on Earth? As far as she knew, dragons had little interest in the world, with Zavryd the only regular visitor, and he only spent time here because of Val.

Shaking her head, Arwen veered off the road and into the undergrowth, trusting her memory to get her close to the sanctuary. There weren't any direct paths to it that she noticed. The last time she'd been here, she'd observed that the goblins, even though they hunted and foraged outside of its borders, were good at keeping trace of their passing to a minimum.

By the time she entered the old-growth forest near the sanctuary, she hadn't sensed Darvanylar for a while. She hoped that meant he'd given up his hunt, not that he'd caught her scent and camouflaged himself while waiting for her to lead him to Starblade.

She rubbed the charm again.

Clouds parted, and the light of a half-moon filtered through the forest. A bat flew past, and a frog croaked by a pond or stream. Not a hint of magic brushed her senses, no promise of a village or anything of interest.

She paused to rest a hand on the fir- and pine-needle littered ground, using a touch of magic to reach out to the trees and bushes nearby, accessing the collective memory of the forest to learn if any goblins had passed by recently.

Ghosts of the green-skinned creatures gathering branches, berries, and mushrooms came to her. They always headed back in a particular direction. She went that way as well, trusting she would sense everything once she found her way through the barrier.

It took longer than she expected, and she started to wonder if she'd veered off the road at the wrong bend. Then a faint buzz of magic whispered over her skin. The forest remained the same, old-growth trees that hadn't seen a lumberjack's axe rising in all directions, but she sensed dozens of goblins and some of their magical artifacts, as well. In the distance, a cook fire burned, and the air smelled of roasting meat.

Arwen thought about introducing herself, but she wasn't here for any of the goblins, and she doubted she would be welcome without Matti or Val along as her guide. Since she was camouflaged, the natives shouldn't notice her.

Bypassing their village, she headed up the hill toward Starblade's part of the sanctuary. The barest hint of a trail took her to the ridge overlooking the tree- and fern-filled gully and the hill on the opposite side. Overgrowth covered it as well, save for a stone bench and boulders at the top, and magical skylights in the earth that allowed light into the subterranean home. No full-blooded elf would have lived underground, but Starblade's dragon blood didn't mind such an abode.

She was about to descend into the gully when her instincts warned her of danger. She'd traveled far enough that she could no longer sense the goblins, but *someone* was out there with her. *Behind* her.

Hand dropping to her foraging knife, Arwen started to whirl, but a strong arm wrapped around her, preventing her from grabbing it.

Before she could react, she found her back mashed against someone's chest. Powerful magic wrapped around her, preventing her from reaching the knife—or anything else.

She tried to drive an elbow back into her captor, but the magical hold kept her from moving.

A blade came to rest against her throat, and she froze. Either the camouflaging magic of the charm had worn off or this person could see through it.

"Intruders aren't welcome," a cool male voice said.

It wasn't Starblade.

12

HEART HAMMERING AGAINST HER RIBCAGE, AND MEMORIES OF BEING trapped in dark-elven tunnels racing through her mind, Arwen blurted, "I'm a friend."

She hoped that was true and that Starblade had told his security guard that. No, she realized as she considered the power enrobing her. *Dragon* power. This wasn't a security guard. It had to be Yendral, his comrade.

"A friend?" he asked, his arm wrapped as tightly around her as his power. "We don't have any of those."

He was looking toward the sky instead of her. Tracking Darvanylar?

Arwen hadn't sensed the dragon for a while, but he could be out there. The more powerful half-dragon would have a much greater range for detecting such beings.

"Had you brought groceries," Yendral continued, his tone turning a little lighter, "I might have thought you our chef. But one doesn't expect the food preparer to come armed with a bow and magical arrows."

"I'm Arwen Forester."

"You *are* the chef." The dagger left her throat, though her captor didn't yet release her. "Azerdash didn't mention what a nice squish you have, more voluptuous than Gemlytha was, though the arrow fletchings trying to excavate my nostrils are a deterrent to physical familiarity."

Arwen's mouth drooped, and she didn't know what to say. Starblade had been joking when he'd said his comrade might be willing to *mate* with her, hadn't he?

What if he hadn't been? What if Yendral did have that interest and expected she would come eagerly to his bed? Or what if he shoved her against the nearest tree and wanted—

She didn't even know exactly. Her experience with sex was so limited. All she knew was she didn't want to have it with an over-powered stranger who could force her to do his will.

A touch of panic crept into her, renewing her urge to struggle, to try to reach her foraging knife and free herself.

"Easy, Arrows." Yendral released her and stepped back. "We're a little on edge here tonight, due to a pompous dragon flying about like a hawk in search of a titmouse. We didn't *think* any of their kind knew we were alive, much less on Earth."

Arwen lowered her arms to her sides and turned slowly so he wouldn't think she meant to reach for a weapon. Not that he had to worry about her. His aura was almost as powerful as Starblade's, and the muscled arm that had been wrapped around her promised he was physically fit too.

"I came to warn you about that dragon." Arwen hoped he couldn't read her thoughts and wouldn't find out that it was her fault Darvanylar was here. Again, she doubted the wisdom of coming here and worried they would be more pissed than grateful to her.

"You came to warn me? I'm touched." Yendral flattened a hand to his chest and bowed to her. Almost a foot taller than she, he had tousled short silver hair, pointed ears, and green eyes.

"Well, I came to warn Starblade. I know he rescued you from the dark-elf lair, but we never spoke, so..."

"*Rescued.*" Yendral shook his head in disgust. "You don't know how badly I'd like to deny that I needed his help—again—but you were there, weren't you? And saw me trapped in one of those chambers?"

"And covered in a nullifier, yes." Arwen hadn't meant to bring up a sensitive subject.

"That awful stuff. I'm still scrubbing it out of crevices where foreign substances are *not* meant to go. Especially *dark-elf* foreign substances." Yendral looked her up and down.

Arwen tensed, certain he was considering her dark-elfness and not her squish.

"He said you let yourself be taken over by them and shot him," Yendral said, "so I wasn't that inclined to like you, but he also said you made that *glorious* food. And it wasn't even poisoned. I'm willing to forgive you for your questionable loyalties."

"I'm not loyal to them. And I didn't *let* myself be taken over. I..." She, what? Wasn't that exactly what had happened? She'd been overpowered and betrayed by her tattoo. At least it didn't sound like Starblade had told Yendral that she'd *voluntarily* worked with the dark elves. "I didn't want to shoot him."

"No? Sometimes *I* want to shoot him. He can be sanctimonious when he's quoting dead generals. And melancholy and *moody* when he's not. One minute, he's talking about learning to fit in here so we can have pleasant lives of retirement, and other times, he's stomping around, bitter that the elves turned their backs on us and refused to give us sanctuary after we served them—well, their *ancestors*—loyally for decades. Maybe it was even a century. We were both over a hundred by the time the war reached its culmination and the betrayal came."

"Betrayal?" Arwen couldn't help but ask, though she should

have remained focused on Darvanylar, especially since Yendral kept glancing off to the east, as if monitoring the searching dragon.

"He didn't tell you about that? How it was one who should have been a loyal elf subordinate who sold us out to the dwarven spies? We shouldn't have been surprised. That one always hated following us and was bitter about our power. He thought *he* should have been leading the elven armies, but things didn't go well for our side after we were gone, so I hope he choked on his betrayal as an arrow took him in the throat." Yendral tilted his head, regarding her with curiosity, as if he was surprised Starblade hadn't already shared the whole story with her.

"No, he hasn't told me much. We're not..." Arwen caught herself from saying *close*. Since she'd opened their exchange claiming to be a friend, that might be a suspicious admission. "I haven't known him for that long. It's only been a few weeks since he showed up in the forest near my friend's cabin, hunting the same mushrooms we were foraging for."

"Mushrooms." Yendral laughed shortly. "The loathsome things. Now that his medicinal trays are growing so well—I understand your quirky acidic powder helped with that—he keeps foisting samples on me. I much prefer my meals to be meat-heavy and mushroom-light—or mushroom-nonexistent—but there's no accounting for Azerdash's tastes. Sometimes, I think he deliberately chooses vegetables and such, hoping an elf will see him eating appropriate fare and invite us to the capital." A wistful look came over his green eyes before they sharpened and refocused on her. "When you cook for us, I do hope you'll include copious amounts of roasted meat. Rotisserie meat. Smoked meat. Those are all acceptable. When it comes to non-meat items, I find that I quite enjoy desserts. Especially of the kind that you left as an offering."

An offering? Did he think she wanted to *worship* him? Or Starblade? Arwen hoped not.

"I can keep your preferences in mind," she said.

"*Wonderful.* You will have my heart." Yendral stepped forward, clasped her hand, and surprised her by leaning his face toward hers. Did he intend to *kiss* her?

Arwen froze with indecision. What was she supposed to do? Spring back? Punch him? He'd already proven he could overpower her with ease.

Yendral rested his forehead against hers and smiled, but he didn't press his lips to hers. He only held her gaze for a second before turning his head to the side, though his forehead remained touching hers.

Only then did Arwen sense that they weren't alone on the ridge. Starblade had joined them, camouflaged as he approached, waiting until he was a mere ten feet away before revealing himself. The moonlight gleamed on his straight black hair.

He carried his sword and had put away the purple-and-green jacket and other secondhand human clothing. Tonight, he wore elven garments, trousers, tunic, and a magical chainmail vest that gathered the moonlight without reflecting it.

Starblade's face was cool and unreadable as he regarded them. "Never would I have expected you to live so long when you give your heart to any pretty female who saunters into your camp."

Arwen stepped back, her bruised hip twinging and making her wince. She withdrew her hand, feeling like she'd been caught kissing someone her father wouldn't approve of. Or that *Starblade* wouldn't approve of.

But that was a silly thought. He wasn't interested in her and had implied Yendral might be. A bizarre notion since nobody appealing who'd known about her blood had ever been interested. And the unappealing ones, the ones who simply wanted to drag her into the woods to satisfy their urges... She'd never desired that. She'd always wanted romance. What the surface elves had—or what she'd always envisioned them having.

"Luckily, I had you to be the brains of the company." Yendral didn't appear chagrined or surprised at his friend's appearance.

Starblade snorted and stepped closer, joining them on the top of the ridge. Arwen shifted uneasily. Even though she didn't get a sense that either was a danger to her or intended her harm, her old instincts reared up, the panicked girl she'd once been warning her that too many powerful beings were near, that, if they wanted to hurt her, she wouldn't be able to escape. She should flee, put some distance between her and them...

"If my brains had been that capable," Starblade said glumly, "we wouldn't be here."

"We could have been dead on a battlefield centuries ago," Yendral said.

"That might have been for the best."

Yendral looked at Arwen. "He's going to treat us to melancholy and moodiness tonight."

"Melancholy suggests sorrow without an obvious cause," Starblade pointed out.

"Oh, I know we've got plenty of reasons for sorrow. But if you wished you were dead, you wouldn't be wandering around in that garishly colored jacket, trying to fit in with the locals. Though I can't imagine why you're bothering. If you wanted to *rule* this world instead of blending into it, I could understand that. The best use of the menial magic-deaf species here would be to serve those with power instead of squabbling amongst themselves. The verminous humans are ghastly." Yendral brought a thoughtful finger to his chin. "Except for their food. Some of it is delicious. It's their saving grace."

"I never had a desire to rule anything. You know that."

"Just serve our creators faithfully. Yes, I know you'd never consider forming your own army." Yendral sounded exasperated when he said that, as if he genuinely believed they should be angling to take over Earth or another world. "That the new elven king thought that is ludicrous. One wonders if he or any of his peers ever opened a history book."

"History isn't penned by those who were betrayed and ensconced in stasis chambers for centuries."

"That's the truth. In lieu of an army, I'll accept a fine meal." Yendral beamed a handsome smile at Arwen, some of the humor returning to his eyes. "Starblade, didn't you instruct your chef to bring groceries when she arrived? I don't smell an ounce of meat on her."

"I believe she was daunted by your *extensive* list of food demands and hasn't had time to acquire the ingredients."

"It is a long list, but I came tonight because I wanted to warn you." Arwen pointed in the direction Yendral kept looking. Though she couldn't sense the dragon, she trusted they knew who she referenced.

"Yes, we're aware of him." Starblade's aura and voice turned cold. He looked toward the sky, not at Arwen, but his abrupt chill made her uneasy.

"I was hoping to get here before him. I—" Arwen paused, her throat tight at having to admit her treacherous thoughts had revealed their hiding place. She didn't *want* to admit that and give Starblade another reason to mistrust her, but he would find out eventually. Better that she tell him. Besides, she didn't want to be dishonest with him. "It's my fault that he's here," she made herself say, looking at a tree between Starblade and Yendral instead of into their eyes. "I was delivering pies, and he happened to fly by— I have no idea why he was in the area or on Earth at all. For what-ever reason, he checked me out."

"Squish," Yendral said with a smirk.

"Be quiet," Starblade told him without looking away from Arwen.

"He said he could sense your aura on me. I didn't want to tell him anything. I wanted to *shoot* him. I did shoot him, but the arrow didn't go through." Arwen glanced at his leg, afraid she had reminded him of when she'd shot *him*. "He was too strong, and he read my mind. I don't know how much he got, but he talked about setting a trap. I'm sorry."

Starblade stepped toward her, lifting a hand.

His face wasn't angry, and she didn't *think* he meant to hurt her, but she'd already been on edge, and she jumped back. Unfortunately, she landed on a root, jarring her injured hip. She let out a gasp of pain, a sign of weakness she would have preferred not to show in front of the powerful half-dragons.

Starblade lowered his hand and frowned at her. "He hurt you."

It was a statement, not a question, but Arwen shook her head. "Not badly. I'm fine. I'm more sorry I wasn't able to keep him out of my head or avoid him altogether."

Yendral grunted. "We'd *all* prefer to avoid dragons altogether."

Jaw clenched, Starblade radiated anger.

A shiver went through Arwen. She couldn't tell if he was angry because Darvanylar had hurt her or because she'd been weak and betrayed him again.

"You could glower all night," Yendral said, "or you could heal her wounds and plop her into the rejuvenation pool."

"Relaxing while an enemy circles the area is not wise," Starblade said.

"*She* can relax. You can come back up here with me, and we can return to plotting how we'll deal with him if he finds us through the enchantment." Yendral smirked again. "Unless you'll be so distracted by her nudity that you won't notice an enemy razing the forest and laying waste to our latest refuge."

Starblade gave him a dark look. "That is *not* a concern."

"Well, if it is, *I* could take her to the pool." Yendral waggled his eyebrows at Arwen.

"You will remain outside and alert me if Darvanylar approaches."

"It's such a joy being your subordinate."

"I released you from your service when you came out of the stasis prison. Yet you are still here."

"I'm drawn by your wit and propensity for shoving medicinal mushrooms down my throat."

"I should have let the dark elves keep you."

Yendral shuddered openly. "Because you didn't, I'll stand watch for you while you enjoy female nudity."

"Your mind is singular, Yendral." Starblade lifted a hand toward Arwen again, but he didn't step closer this time, instead waiting for her to come to him. "We will go inside. I will treat your wounds while you tell me what he said to you."

Arwen nodded, wishing she hadn't overreacted the first time he'd reached out to her. He had every right to be angry with her, but he didn't seem to be.

Or so she thought, but as they headed toward the entrance of his home, his jaw was clenched, and when Darvanylar flew within range of her senses, his eyes flared violet. Starblade exuded dangerous energy. Even if she didn't feel it was directed toward her, if she said or admitted the wrong thing, might she draw his ire?

And what would happen if Darvanylar *did* find a way into the sanctuary? Would the two half-dragons be a match for him?

13

When they reached the bench on the hilltop, Starblade flicked a finger, prompting the hidden trapdoor to open. Arwen paused, her gaze drawn by something on the back side of the hill, something that hadn't been there before.

Nestled between trees and braced by boulders, the body of a small airplane rested, the cowling removed and the engine open to the elements. Magic protected it, however, and more magic emanated from various parts of the structure. Vines draped the wings, either because the foliage had quickly grown over them, or Starblade had used his power to coerce them to camouflage the craft from the sky. Or... from any scavenging goblins who wandered into the area?

The dwarven enchantment ought to keep anyone flying overhead from seeing anything but trees on the ground, but it wouldn't hide objects from those already within the sanctuary. Especially such *large* objects.

"Did someone crash?" Arwen asked. "Or did you feel the need to own an airplane?"

Starblade had already taken a few steps down the stairs, but he followed her gaze. "It is currently a derelict. I am teaching myself how to rebuild the engine."

"You can fly. *Without* an airplane."

"Yes."

"Are you interested in the mechanics?" Arwen remembered that he liked reading about engineering and had given a gnomish tunnel borer a loving pat.

"I am curious about such things, but, as I mentioned earlier, I am also following the suggestions in the Study of Manliness to better fit in with native males. Per the resource, it is important that I know how to build a fire, protect a female from the elements, trim a mustache, and *buy rounds for the boys*. I am still puzzling over that one, as I do not know which of the many definitions of round is referenced. One cannot, I believe, buy *squares* for the boys."

"No. It's a round of drinks. Like at a bar."

"Ah. An establishment I have little interest in visiting."

"Me either. Too many people." Arwen pointed at the airplane. He hadn't answered her question, had he?

"The resource suggests an appropriately *manly* hobby I might pursue is rebuilding an engine."

"Oh. I think it's talking about automobile engines." Though Arwen supposed there were guys out there who collected old airplanes and got them running again. Guys with very large yards.

"The text did not specify. This was of more interest." Starblade nodded for her to follow him and descended out of sight.

Arwen wondered what the magic in the airplane did besides protect it from the elements. There were a lot of different spells if only for that, but she knew little about enchanting.

"Will you infuse my bow with temporary power again?" Arwen asked as she followed Starblade through the kitchen area, his bedroom, the training room, and down the vine-laden corridor toward the steaming pool.

At the question, he halted and turned to face her. On the walls, the vines rippled, as if a conduit for his surprise. Or... his displeasure?

Suspicion drew his eyebrows together.

"In case Darvanylar finds his way into the sanctuary," Arwen hurried to clarify. "It'll be my fault. I want to fight with you and your friend."

Starblade gazed at her, and a slight itch under her skull announced he was trying to read her thoughts. Successfully, most likely. Last time she'd been here, he'd said something about the dwarven princess's enchantment overriding the protective power of her tattoo.

"I'm not being controlled by anyone." Arwen met his assessing stare, willing him to believe she intended him no ill will and that it devastated her that she'd hurt him before.

Starblade lowered his gaze.

At first, she thought he was looking at her chest, but she wasn't wearing anything revealing, and, unlike Yendral, Starblade wasn't sexually interested in her. So, she wasn't surprised when he gripped her forearm lightly, pushing up her sleeve. He hadn't been looking at her chest but toward her tattoo.

Arwen fought the urge to pull away from him. He probably wanted to see if the spider mark was glowing, as it had in the dark-elf lair, or doing something else to indicate that she was lying, that she *was* being controlled.

To her eyes, it looked like it always did and emanated the same faint magic, but she didn't know what he, with his keener senses, saw. It might be exuding something atypical, some displeasure or a greater degree of defensive magic because she stood close to him. In the dark-elf lair, the tattoo had seemed almost sentient.

"I understand why you don't trust me," Arwen whispered, "and I get it. Maybe I shouldn't have come up here and risked leading the dragon to you, but I was afraid he might already have found you and..." Her throat tightened as she remembered how she'd worried he would already be dead. "It would have been my fault. And it's my fault that he's out there now, a threat."

Starblade lowered her arm. "If he mind-scoured you and read your thoughts, it is not your fault. He, like all full-blooded dragons, is powerful. A mere human mongrel, even one with strong magic from her dark-elven heritage, could not resist doing his bidding."

Arwen clenched her jaw, wanting to deny that she couldn't *resist* some arrogant dragon, but it was true. She hadn't been strong enough. She *was* a mere human mongrel.

"I shouldn't have let him catch me. Or find me. It was a mistake."

"Being found by a dragon usually is." Starblade smiled ruefully.

As it had earlier, that smile caught her eye. What would it be like to see him happy? Was it possible to say something to make him laugh? He was, as Yendral had said, on the glum side. Maybe too much had happened in his life, too much death and pain, for him to laugh easily.

"I understand if you won't do it," Arwen said, "but I will ask one more time for you to lend my bow the power needed to strike a dragon. I'll make sure it hits the *right* dragon this time. I don't want you or your friend to be dragged back to the Dragon Council or *killed* because of my mistake. Also, Darvanylar pissed me off. I'd really like to pierce his scales more effectively the next time I stab him with an arrow."

"*More* effectively?" Starblade raised his eyebrows. "You managed to pierce his scales at all?"

Arwen lifted her arm slowly toward her quiver, not wanting him to think the move threatening, and selected the arrow she'd used on Darvanylar. She drew it out to show him the dried blood she hadn't removed from the tip.

"Impressive," Starblade said.

The word made Arwen want to swell with pride, but she'd been trapped under the dragon's taloned foot when she'd been stabbing him, so she sighed. There was little to be proud about.

"*Most* people, even those with full magical blood, drop to their knees, beg for their lives, and urinate on themselves when a dragon lands in front of them." Starblade's smile returned as he thumbed the tip of her arrow. "And *all* know it's unwise to attack one."

"I never claimed to be wise. My father says I have a penchant for seeking out trouble. It's just that I..." *want to prove myself,* she almost said, but it sounded hokey. And it wasn't exactly accurate. What she wanted was for people not to hate her for her heritage. She wanted to show them that she deserved a place in the world, that she wasn't evil. That she had worth.

Since Starblade was watching her, he might have read her thoughts, but all he said was, "You have gumption."

"Unwisely so?"

"As the great general Erstovar wrote, 'If not for the unwise, those who set aside self-preservation instincts and sacrifice themselves so that others may live, we all would have perished long ago.'"

She remembered Yendral's comment about Starblade being sanctimonious when he quoted dead generals, but she didn't agree.

He snorted softly—*definitely* following her thoughts. "Yendral is a paramount example of the unwise. Here." He handed the arrow back to her and pointed to her bow.

Would he channel power to it? Enough that she could strike the dragon?

Arwen gave her bow to him without hesitation.

"If Darvanylar finds us and attacks," Starblade said, sliding his hands along the shaft, "you will stay down here where you are safe. And where he cannot use his magic to compel you to attack us from behind with a weapon that draws dragon blood." He glanced at her quiver before giving her a significant look.

"That won't happen," Arwen said but realized it could.

Damn it. She shouldn't have made her request. If she betrayed Starblade again, she wouldn't forgive herself.

The thought made her reach for her bow, intending to take it back before he could infuse it.

But Starblade held up a hand. "Come."

With her bow in his grip, he continued down the tunnel. Whispers of steam and magic came off the warm pool, the air rich with the eucalyptus-like scent she remembered from before. She couldn't help inhaling deeply and wanting it to wreathe her body, to take away her pain.

"You will relax in the pool for one hour." Starblade stopped at the edge and pointed her bow toward the water. "I will be outside with Yendral so that nobody will remark on your *squish*." He glanced at her chest.

Embarrassment crept through her. Even though he was being polite, she felt mortified.

"Your wounds are not great," he said, setting his sword and her bow across one of the two lounge chairs by the pool, "so I don't believe you need one of the healing pads."

"No, I'll be fine."

"But you limped earlier. I saw your pain." Starblade stepped closer and rested a hand on her hip, the one that had been twinging since Darvanylar hurled her down the road.

"It's fine," Arwen repeated, though she liked having him close and wanted him to do whatever he intended. "I stepped wrong on a root; that's all."

"Because of your injury." Warmth and power flared from his fingers and penetrated her skin. It soothed and invigorated at the same time, and her discomfort disappeared, as if absorbed by his magic.

Her lips parted, such relief coming at the cessation of pain that she almost moaned. But, conscious of Starblade standing close and watching her, she managed to refrain. She wished there weren't a threat outside, that he would stay here with her instead of leaving. Maybe he would join her in the pool.

But Arwen sensed the dragon flying close again, and Starblade did too. All too soon, he stepped back, the warmth of his hand leaving her hip. He eyed the ceiling with distaste. When his magic faded, she couldn't help but feel disappointed, but the pain didn't return, so that was a relief. She rested her hands on her hips and did a few experimental hip rotations. It didn't hurt.

"Oh, that's so much better." Arwen closed her eyes, luxuriating in the ease of movement. She hadn't realized how tight and tense that hip had been. "Thank you."

When Starblade didn't answer, she opened her eyes. He wasn't looking at the ceiling but at her—at her hips—and she felt silly throwing them around. She'd probably been jutting out her breasts and butt and everything else she had. He would accuse her again of wanting to seduce him.

"You will still soak in the pool," was all Starblade said when he lifted his gaze.

His eyes weren't glowing, but they were intense and sent a heated charge through her.

When she said, "Okay," it came out squeaky.

He picked up her bow and gripped it in both hands, power swelling around him before he channeled it into the weapon.

"Wait," she blurted. "You said it's not wise, that it's too dangerous if I'm... if I can't keep Darvanylar from compelling me." Her mouth twisted with bitterness at the thought.

"It is a danger."

"Why are you enchanting it then?"

"Unwisdom abounds. Should he get past us and for some reason go after you, I want you to be able to protect yourself." More magic swelled around Starblade, his energy making the air come alive around him.

With the palpable power emanating from him, he seemed as great as Zavryd and Darvanylar and the other dragons. The thought crossed her mind that *he* could force her to do his bidding if he wanted. Being around such powerful beings wasn't good for her ego—or her longevity. It would be better to avoid them all and go back to harvesting vegetables and selling them at the market.

Yet, as she had the last time he infused his power into her bow, she found herself drawn closer to him, wanting to bask in that power, to be his ally not his enemy. Maybe *more* than his ally.

The energy around him faded, though his aura remained strong and appealing. Now, her bow almost hummed with magic. Arwen caught herself standing closer to Starblade than he probably wished.

"Thank you." She nodded to the bow and started to step back, but he lifted a hand and rested it on her shoulder.

She halted.

He gazed into her eyes. "I see that you feel you betrayed us. That is not true. It was I who, in spending time in your proximity, left a hint of my aura on yours. As the dragon pointed out, his kind are sensitive enough to detect such things. Even we can. If I had not been outside when you arrived, I would have known that you'd been near Yendral, that he'd had his arm around you." His grip tightened slightly on her shoulder. Not painfully but almost... possessively?

No, that wasn't the right word. He didn't want her. He'd been the one to suggest she could be with Yendral.

"He thought I was an intruder," she said.

Starblade snorted. "He did not. He enjoys companions of all

types and will hold them if permitted. He isn't deterred by blood if said female is attractive. He'll mount anything."

Arwen shrank back, wincing at being lumped in with *anything*. Like she was some monster that only intrepid adventurers would dare embrace. Her mind brought forth her memory of being a teenage girl when a neighboring goblin had been dared by his buddies to kiss her.

Starblade lowered his hand. "I apologize. I chose my words carelessly. What I meant is that he's not daunted or deterred by much. He propositioned the fae queen once and also a minor but still powerful female dragon."

She tried to smile, though she wasn't sure his words had improved anything. "Did his propositions work?"

"The fae are lascivious, and I believe that encounter went the way he wished. The female dragon tried to bite off his head. He is fortunate that's *all* she did." Starblade shook his head, though he smiled again. "He is a strange and overly libidinous comrade but loyal."

"That's good, I think."

"Yes. Loyalty cannot be bought or bartered for, but it is invaluable beyond riches."

"Yeah." Arwen wondered what it would be like to have someone loyal to *her*. Oh, her father would do anything for her, and Sigrid was a good friend, but to have a relationship with a man she cared about and shared loyalty with... She'd only experienced such things through books. Books with heroines who were never like her.

Starblade stepped back, and she sensed that he would depart. Even though he'd insulted her, it had seemed inadvertent, and she didn't want him to leave. Especially after he'd healed her and improved her bow. She wanted to thank him for both, though she didn't know how she could.

"Who was Gemlytha?" she blurted before thinking better of it.

But Yendral had mentioned her, and Starblade had also spoken the name back when they'd infiltrated the dark-elf base. It had sounded like she was someone similar to Arwen—someone half dark-elven?

Starblade's face grew distant and stiff. "She is dead."

14

As Arwen stared at Starblade, a realization struck her. A dead dark-elven half-dragon. This must have been the same person Darvanylar had mentioned, one of Starblade's "ragtag crew," one who died when a mountain fell on them.

Curiosity made Arwen want to ask more, to learn about someone who'd been a half-dark elf, like her, but Starblade had masked his face. It wasn't enough to fully hide the pain in his eyes.

"Yendral mentioned her?" His tone was clipped with displeasure.

"Only in regard to, uhm, squish."

Starblade laughed without humor. "He would."

"I was curious, but you don't have to answer." Arwen groped for a way to apologize about bringing up the subject.

He sighed. "She was one of us, a half-dragon. But she was half-*dark* elven instead of half-surface elf. And she was..." His mask faltered, doing little to hide his feelings. Regret. Caring. Love? "She was a subordinate."

Subordinate didn't convey the kind of emotion in his eyes.

"And more," Arwen whispered before realizing she'd spoken aloud.

"No." His gaze met hers again. "*Because* she was a subordinate and we had to go into battle together and lead troops, she was not."

Arwen wasn't sure she understood, maybe because she'd never served in the military. "But you cared for her."

Starblade hesitated.

Arwen lifted an apologetic hand for prying, but it was so hard not to.

"More than I was supposed to." It was almost a whisper. An admission.

"Even though she had dark-elven blood." Arwen couldn't help but wonder about this person. Never had she heard of another like her. Oh, a half-dragon would have been far more powerful, but Arwen immediately felt a kinship to the woman and regretted that she'd passed. "Did you not worry that she would betray you?"

"No. She grew up on Veleshna Var and trained with us. She was never among the dark elves, except later when she sought to learn about her power. Even then, she was not gone for long and came back to us."

"You trusted her."

"Fully, yes."

"Ah."

Unlike Arwen, a half-dragon would have been too powerful for a dark elf to manipulate, to turn against the other half-dragons or elves. Arwen, on the other hand... She shook her head sadly.

If Starblade followed her thoughts, he didn't comment on them. He nodded to the bow to change the subject. "If Darvanylar tries to use you as bait or a tool, you will employ that on him. Vigorously."

He pantomimed stabbing an arrow into something—a dragon's foot perhaps.

Arwen managed a smile. "I'll do my best."

"Yes." He nodded again, then turned to walk away. Before departing, he pointed toward the stone-and-dirt wall on the far side of the pool. Through the steam, alcoves were visible, holding rolled towels and a few other items. "Should you wish it, there are scented soaps and healing ointments meant to be used in the water. Yendral acquired them. He is a hedonist."

"Because he likes soap?" Arwen supposed such luxuries weren't discussed in the Study of Manliness, unless to be outright forbidden.

"For *many* reasons."

"He doesn't sound like a military officer."

"He has his moments. Earlier, he suggested I mobilize the goblins in the village and create a great army to take over this planet for the use of refugees from other worlds."

"That's... not an army many would see coming."

"No. How would your world leaders react?"

"To hordes of goblins stealing their staplers and building things? I'm not sure."

Starblade grunted and walked away.

The vines in the tunnel rippled, some detaching from the wall, leaves unfurling. His magical security system, he'd said when they'd ensnared her. He must have been arming them, because even after he disappeared from her sight and senses, they remained stretched across the tunnel.

Had he trapped her down there to make sure she wouldn't wander off and snoop? Or come running outside with her bow, compelled by an enemy to shoot them?

She shook her head again, deeming the latter most likely.

The warm magical vapors from the pool wrapped around her, inviting her to shuck her clothing and take a dip, to forget any embarrassments or faux pas and relax.

It seemed foolish when an enemy might find his way into the

sanctuary soon, but Starblade *had* instructed her to get in and enjoy the healing properties. Though his magic had left her feeling invigorated, the pool might ensure she wouldn't be sore in the morning.

Besides, if his vines *were* trapping her, what else could she do?

"Nothing," Arwen whispered, stepping closer to the edge and inhaling the soothing scent.

When she leaned her bow on a chair, she spotted Starblade's sword. Had he meant to leave it? Or forgotten it?

Probably because she'd flustered him by asking about his dead friend. His *subordinate* who'd been far more than that.

Arwen thought about calling out telepathically to Starblade, but she didn't sense him or Yendral. They had to be camouflaging themselves in case their enemy found a way into the sanctuary.

Well, she'd seen Starblade levitate her clothes out of his home from the air above. She trusted he could magically retrieve his sword without trouble if needed.

As she soaked, the warm scented water as soothing as she'd hoped, she let her head loll back against the edge. She realized she hadn't brought up the subject she'd originally wanted to talk to Starblade about. The heritage analyzer and finding out what dragon had lent its blood to the elven scientist's experiment.

Would he be insulted if he learned she wanted to find a dragon protector for him? Would he agree to give her a drop of his blood for analysis? Was there any point in asking before she knew if Matti's mate could acquire a new device for the testing?

Probably not. Besides, she worried Starblade wouldn't appreciate her idea as much as she did. He might be too proud to accept the help of a full-blooded dragon. Of *anyone*. He might be offended that she thought he *needed* help.

But wouldn't it be logical to accept assistance if most of dragon-dom wanted him dead? And some, like Darvanylar, were actively seeking to kill him? Even a full-blooded dragon would need assistance to defend against so many.

Arwen *wished* Starblade would be grateful or at least appreciative that she wanted to help him, that he would be moved to touch her again. She wished his healing had morphed into something else, that she had invited him to join her in the pool, and he had eagerly done so...

"Sure. *Yendral* might."

Yendral wasn't unpleasant, despite him greeting her with a crushing arm around her waist and a knife to her throat, but she didn't think she wanted to get naked in a pool with him. If Starblade's words were true, he would be like so many of the other men she'd met who were interested in sex but little else. Yendral was handsome and quick to smile, and she supposed curiosity might prompt her to accept an offer if it were given without malice or pity or condemnation, but... she was much more drawn to those who wanted a relationship. Those who understood and approved of the idea of loyalty. *Mutual* loyalty.

Reminded of the soaps and ointments Starblade had mentioned, Arwen rose, the water lapping at her hips, and waded toward the nooks on the far side. The steam wreathed her lovingly, but a nip in the air made her body tighten and goosebumps rise. She would submerge again as soon as she checked everything out.

The sponges, bottles of concoctions, and promised scented soaps *did* seem more designed to appeal to feminine preferences than male, but one of the containers smelled like pine trees, so maybe not. An ointment labeled in a language she couldn't read emanated slight magic. A concoction meant to help with healing?

Though she felt better after Starblade's ministrations, Arwen opened it out of curiosity. It smelled of lavender and another floral scent she couldn't name. A plant from another world? It was different from but as enticing as the eucalyptus aroma wafting from the pool, and she had the urge to slather it all over herself.

Trusting nothing dangerous would be stored in a bottle next to towels and sponges, Arwen poured some into her palm. Surprisingly cool against her skin, it tingled pleasantly, reminding her of tea-tree oil.

She was about to rub it on herself, especially the hip that had been injured, when a whisper of magic made her look around, startled. Nobody else could be down there, could they? Starblade had raised the possibility of Darvanylar using her as bait, but there wasn't another way out of the pool area. He couldn't have sneaked past the half-dragons.

Starblade's sword lifted from the chair and floated toward the tunnel. Ah, no need to be alarmed. As she'd assumed he would, he had realized he'd left his weapon behind and was levitating it outside.

Or *was* he outside? Maybe it was her imagination, but some instinct made her believe she wasn't alone in the chamber. She couldn't *see* Starblade in the tunnel, but were the vines parted where they hadn't been before? To allow someone to have returned?

The sword disappeared from her sight and senses. She couldn't tell if he had grabbed it, camouflaging it along with himself, or if it had floated up the tunnel and outside. He might be sitting on the hilltop with Yendral, discussing goblin armies.

Which wouldn't be disappointing, Arwen told herself. She didn't want anyone peeping at her while she bathed.

But was that true? Or would she be titillated to find out Starblade was interested enough in her to *want* to peep?

He probably wasn't, but on the off chance that he was keeping an eye on her, she rubbed the ointment luxuriously over herself, imagining him appreciating her nude body. She didn't want to seduce him to get him to forgive her betrayal, but she wanted... Oh, she didn't know. For someone like him—someone polite and handsome and appreciative of her food—to want her.

The tingle of the ointment spread across her skin, somehow stimulating and soothing at the same time, and she remembered to rub some on her hip, leaning against the edge and thrusting it out of the water. It was a more provocative pose than she'd intended, and she almost laughed at the idea of someone watching her. It probably looked silly, not sexy.

Two violet glows flared from the shadows inside the tunnel.

Arwen froze. Her instincts had been right. She wasn't alone.

15

WITH HER HAND ON HER HIP AND THE WATER LAPPING AT HER thighs, Arwen stood utterly still, not sure how to react.

The violet flare of Starblade's eyes disappeared so quickly she wondered if she'd imagined it in the deep shadows of the vine-draped tunnel. She couldn't see or sense him, so if he was there, he was camouflaged. Had that little flare slipped out? Usually, his eyes glowed when he was incensed, but she couldn't imagine he was angry she was using the bath items, not when he'd directed her to them. Maybe he was—

A far more dangerous aura registered to her senses. Darvanylar.

Arwen looked toward the ceiling, sensing the dragon flying overhead. *Directly* overhead.

She couldn't tell if Darvanylar had seen through the enchantment or not—chance might have taken him over Starblade's home —but a swell of magic came from outside. To her, it felt like defensive magic. Yendral? Or some device the half-dragons had installed for protection?

"Starblade?" she called softly, looking toward the tunnel.

It remained dark, no eyes glowing, no suggestion that anyone was there. Her instincts made her believe she was alone again. If he'd been there—and she was already doubting herself, thinking she'd imagined his eyes—he was gone. He would have sensed Darvanylar too. That might be why he'd come back for his sword.

A distant roar sounded, muffled by the ground between Arwen and the surface but unmistakable. It was the roar of the dragon.

Something told her Darvanylar *had* flown through the enchantment. And once he'd passed through, he must have sensed the goblins and the magic of this dwelling. Even if Starblade and Yendral were camouflaged—and her senses told her they were—there might be enough traces of them for the dragon to know they were nearby.

Though Starblade had ordered Arwen to stay below and soak for an hour, she couldn't do that while they fought for their lives. Abandoning the ointment and soaps, she pushed herself out of the water and grabbed a towel. As she jogged for the chair where she'd left her clothing, another roar sounded. Closer this time.

She toweled off quickly but not so fast that she missed seeing the sheen to her skin. It wasn't oily, and nothing unpleasant came off when she rubbed her finger over her stomach, but it made her look like a female bodybuilder on a stage, modeling for the judges. Maybe she'd inadvertently put on more of a show for Starblade than she'd intended.

The thought that he'd enjoyed watching her would have been more appealing if she didn't now worry that she'd been distracting him from preparing for a battle.

A third roar sounded as she dressed, hurrying to stuff her feet in her moccasins and wishing she had armor. The noise came from directly above, removing all doubt about whether Darvanylar had found them or not.

Between one eye blink and the next, Yendral and Starblade popped into her awareness, both atop the hill. Or flying above it?

Had Darvanylar torn away their camouflaging magic some-how? Or maybe it had dropped when they'd started flying.

Arwen grabbed her bow, the fresh power infused in it startling her before she remembered Starblade's enchantment. She vowed to put his magic to use against his enemy.

But when she tried to run into the tunnel, the vines didn't give way. They stretched from side to side and floor to ceiling, most of the gaps between them too small for her to fit through. Some of them *weren't* too small, but she well remembered being caught last time, held helpless by the security magic until Starblade came down to release her. And there had been a sedative in the vines, something that would have knocked her out if she'd hung there long enough. The last thing she wanted was to be dangling limp and helpless if Darvanylar made it down there.

Although, judging from the roars and fast-moving auras of all three dragons, he was thoroughly engaged in trying to kill Yendral and Starblade.

"Let me pass." Arwen touched the earthen wall next to a vine. "Please."

She rubbed Amber's camouflaging charm, hoping the vines would loosen if they no longer sensed her, but it didn't work.

A pained shriek reached her ears. Starblade? Yendral? She couldn't tell, but she worried for both of them. Compared to Arwen, the half-dragons were immensely powerful, but compared to another dragon? Darvanylar had twice their size and power. They might not be a match.

Forcing herself to stay calm and think rationally, Arwen willed her magic into the vines. An impatient part of her was tempted to try to destroy them, but she didn't. With dark-elven power she'd often twisted to use like surface-elven magic, she attempted to coerce the vines into flattening themselves to the wall. Telepathi-cally, she shared with them that she wanted to help Starblade, that she would use her arrows to pepper the dragon intruder. She also infused them with the same kind of magic she used to make the trees and plants on the farm healthier, letting them derive more nutrients from the soil and resist diseases and frost.

"Underground frost, sure," she muttered to herself, wondering if the vines would see her ministrations as buttering them up. Manipulation. How intelligent were they?

The tips of one of the vines unfurled and reached for her wrist.

Arwen drew her arm back before it could grab her. "Way *too* intelligent."

The vine waved a leaf at her. She thought it might be giving her the botanical equivalent of a middle finger, but the growth blocking the way loosened, providing enough room for a person to pass through.

Not positive it wasn't a trap, Arwen walked slowly, ready to spring back out of the tunnel. But when another pained shriek came from above, she sprinted through the passageway.

The vines didn't stop her. A few even waved, as if urging her on.

Nocking an arrow as she went, Arwen charged through the home and up the stairs. She paused before bursting out, rubbing her charm again in case she'd broken the magic by running.

When she stuck her head through the open trapdoor, she almost tumbled back down the stairs in surprise. A silver-scaled dragon rolled through the air like he'd been launched from a cannon. Yendral.

He tumbled past so close that he almost hit the bench. But nothing impeded him as he flew all the way across the gully, barely getting his wings out and flapping them in time to stop himself from crashing into a tree. Before he could recover, a second attack struck him. This time, he *did* hit the tree. *Hard.* The wood cracked as he tumbled to the ground, and numerous branches broke, falling onto him.

A shriek came from the other direction, from the ground near the airplane. Starblade, with his black wings spread, crouched atop it as Darvanylar fumbled under a magical silver net, its strands glowing as they enrobed him. Blood saturated the earth around him, but it also ran from gashes in Starblade's scaled hide.

Neither dragon had magical barriers up, not that Arwen could sense. They may have started out protected by their power, but they must have torn away each other's defenses.

Starblade breathed fire at Darvanylar, trying to roast him through the net. The dragon shrieked in pain—had he been the one crying out all the time?—but he also summoned a whirlwind of magic and hurled it at his attacker. Starblade crouched, talons digging into the top of the airplane for purchase, but the power struck him so hard that he couldn't stand against it. Not only did he fly backward, but the magic ripped several nearby trees from the ground, dirt flying from their roots as they were wrenched free.

Starblade struck hard and rolled down the slope.

With another surge of power, Darvanylar blasted the netting entangling him. The strands broke into a thousand pieces, silver glowing threads fluttering in the air. The dragon roared in fury, his eyes glowing.

Irreverent mongrel filth, Darvanylar bellowed telepathically, the words so powerful they struck Arwen's mind like daggers. *You and your piddling traps are no match for the might of a* real *dragon.*

Starblade staggered slowly to his feet, appearing on the edge of defeat. Then his eyes flared with defiance, and a torpedo of purple magic blasted from the airplane, from one of several integrated weapons that Arwen hadn't recognized as such earlier. The torpedo struck Darvanylar square in the chest.

Though his armored scales deflected the brunt of the blow, he staggered back and snarled in what might have been pain. Pain and anger. When his head turned toward Starblade, Arwen sensed Darvanylar summoning his power to attack again.

But she was faster. She loosed the arrow she'd already nocked, aiming for the side of his neck. If his barrier had been torn away, maybe she could get through.

Without the extra power Starblade had infused into her bow, she wouldn't have, but the arrow blasted from the weapon, as if she'd launched it from a Howitzer instead of a bow. It plunged deep between two scales, sinking almost a foot into the dragon's neck. His head jerked upward in surprise.

Before Arwen could feel any satisfaction, Darvanylar whirled, turning his angry glowing eyes onto her. If the arrow had bothered him more than a splinter to the skin, he didn't show it, and the intensity of his fury and his power made her knees weaken. Starblade's words popped into her mind, that most people wet themselves when a dragon looked at them.

"Tempting," she whispered but locked her knees and fired again, aiming for his eye.

This time, Darvanylar saw the attack coming. He blasted her arrow with fire.

Arwen winced, afraid she would lose one of her precious magical projectiles. But his battle with the half-dragons might have used up some of his power, because her arrow sailed through the inferno undamaged and struck him. Not in the eye, since he'd moved his head, but it caught him in the cheek, sinking in as the other had.

Darvanylar shrieked in pain and stomped toward her. *Impudent mongrel!*

Realizing she was out in the open on the hilltop, the charm not able to hide her through her attacks, Arwen crouched, intending to spring through the trapdoor for cover below.

But his power wrapped around her, pinning her in place. She tried to reach for another arrow and found she couldn't move her arms any more than her legs. Standing helpless in the open, she realized that joining in had been a bad idea. But she couldn't regret it, not when the others had needed help.

She sensed Starblade leaping into the air to fly up and assist her. Would he reach Darvanylar soon enough to stop him? The dragon had hurled him far down the hillside.

Darvanylar must have sensed Starblade, because he glanced back. His glowing eyes grew calculating.

You will not battle me, mongrel, Darvanylar told Arwen. *You will serve me. Shoot the abomination. End his unwanted existence in this world, and I will reward you with your life.*

Arwen shook her head, but the dragon's power flowed into her. Her bow jerked up, and she reached for an arrow.

Panic clutched her heart. Just as Starblade had feared, she was vulnerable to compulsion. Darvanylar was using her against him.

As Starblade flew toward the dragon with murder in his eyes, Arwen's treacherous arms shifted her bow's aim to target him.

No, she growled to herself, calling upon all the magic within her to resist the compulsion. She even glanced at the spider tattoo, her sleeve fallen back so that it was bare to the night. *Help me*, she urged it. *Dark elves have no love for dragons.*

Later, she might feel like a hypocrite for calling for help from the very tattoo she wanted to remove, but she didn't care. All she knew was that she *couldn't* shoot Starblade, not again.

Darvanylar stomped around to face his approach. Starblade had to have noticed Arwen's bow—her treacherous aim—but he kept coming, battle lust burning in his eyes. Driven by his desire to destroy his enemy, he wasn't aware of the threat she posed.

Help me, Arwen commanded the tattoo again.

The spider glowed purple, as it had in the dark-elf lair. For the briefest moment, the power of the dragon's compulsion lessened. Gritting her teeth, Arwen shifted her aim.

But she didn't have a good target. With his back to her, his tail rigid and up in the air, Darvanylar breathed fire as Starblade arrowed toward him with talons outstretched.

With few other options, Arwen shot the dragon in the ass.

When the arrow landed, sinking in a few inches, it was far from a killing blow, but the violent twitch of the tail promised it startled Darvanylar. His fire faltered. He still managed to spring into the air, stretching his talons outward and opening his fanged maw to meet Starblade, but it didn't matter.

Even though he was physically smaller, Starblade crashed into him with magic as well as physical force. Darvanylar struck down hard enough to make the hilltop shake.

Starblade landed on top of him, his jaws sinking into the big dragon's neck, his talons raking into the exposed belly. It was as scaled and armored as the rest of Darvanylar, but it didn't matter. While pummeling him with magic, Starblade tore chunks from Darvanylar.

When the dragon tried to shake him off, to free his neck, Starblade only bit down harder, his long fangs more deadly than swords. His power kept Darvanylar pinned on his back. The big dragon's own power was waning, growing diminished compared to Starblade's. Darvanylar thrashed and fought, but he was no longer a match for his foe.

Arwen kept her bow at the ready, but she didn't think Starblade needed her help. Not now.

Eyes still glowing with fury, he broke Darvanylar's neck. The snap rang out through the forest.

When Starblade lifted his head to look at her, blood dripping from his fangs and his violet eyes still alight, fear and uncertainty charged through Arwen. She remembered the dark-elf lair, the look he'd given her after killing Zyretha, how Arwen had believed that he might kill her.

This time, she'd helped him, not hurt him, but with the battle lust surging through his veins, did he know that? Or did he simply see someone with dark-elven blood? Another possible enemy.

She hadn't been aiming her bow at him but at Darvanylar. Afraid Starblade wouldn't recognize that, she lowered it to her side and spread her arm.

"Good fighting," she told him.

The words sounded inane. Inane and inadequate. Arwen still felt guilty over having inadvertently allowed that dragon to find him.

Long seconds passed as Starblade stared at her, not moving, but his eyes gradually calmed, their glow fading, and he closed his jaws. He stepped off Darvanylar's unmoving body and shifted into his elven form.

His clothes were ripped, his hair mussed, and dirt and blood smeared his face, but he strode toward Arwen without a limp or any other sign of major injury. His aura was strong, almost intense. Even though his gaze had turned from a stare to something softer, he hadn't yet spoken, and Arwen worried he was angry with her. She'd helped, but he'd told her to stay below, not endanger herself.

She set her bow on his bench, not wanting him to think... Well, he wouldn't see her as a threat now, but she wanted to remove all doubt.

"You would have used it when the dragon compelled you, if you were going to." Starblade stopped close to her.

"I'm relieved that didn't work." Arwen didn't glance toward her tattoo. Her sleeve had fallen over it again, so she didn't know if it was still glowing, but she hated to acknowledge that it had helped her.

"Yes." Starblade lifted an arm. "You resisted his power."

He looked pleased. Even... proud?

Oh, how she wished she'd done it completely with her own

willpower and not the tattoo's help, but that didn't keep her from leaning into him and letting him wrap his arm around her.

"Were you injured?" he asked.

"No. You were though. Do you need help with anything?" An image popped into her mind of Starblade naked in the rejuvenation pool and her rubbing that oil over his bare chest, followed by him pushing her against the edge and kissing her.

A rumble came from his chest, reverberating into her. A growl? She wasn't sure, but she blushed at the idea that he might have seen that thought.

If he had, it must not have bothered him, because he didn't move away from her. Instead, he brought his other arm around her, one hand shifting to the back of her neck to rub her muscles. That felt wonderful. She leaned more fully against him, resting a hand on his chest, wishing they were in that pool now and that she could touch more than his chainmail armor.

"You didn't stay where I told you," Starblade murmured.

"Sorry." She wasn't.

"And you suborned my vines."

"I told them I needed to help you."

"While bathing them in extra energy and healing nutrients," he said dryly.

"Uhm." She didn't know what to say to that.

"I'm fine too," came a call from across the gully.

Arwen twitched. She'd forgotten about Yendral and immediately felt like a heel.

Starblade didn't twitch in surprise or even stop rubbing her neck. *He* hadn't forgotten his comrade. He'd probably already used his senses to check on Yendral and determine that he was all right.

"I am aware," Starblade called back.

Arwen sensed Yendral, now returned to his elven form, picking his way down the gully and toward the hill. He must have been injured, or he would have flown over before shifting shapes.

Certain Starblade would release her any second, Arwen pressed her chest into his, wanting to enjoy this before he remembered he had no interest in her.

She slid her hand up to touch his jaw and whispered, "You were amazing."

"Someone has recently improved the health and potency of my Mushrooms of Stamina." The corner of his mouth quirked up as he telepathically shared an image with her of the trays, the glowing fungi more robust now, the substrate sprinkled with used coffee grounds.

"And that was the secret to your success?"

"Also the traps, Yendral, and you." Starblade sighed, lowering his hand and loosening his grip on her.

Disappointment swept into her. She didn't want him to let her go. He didn't entirely, and she didn't step away. Maybe she should have with Yendral approaching, but she liked being close.

"Defeating a dragon is not a simple matter, and there will be repercussions for this." Starblade looked toward the body of his fallen enemy. "When he does not return, his clan will seek him. If they know he was on this world, they will begin their search here. I wish I had my old sword, though even it didn't even the odds completely."

"I wish you had your galaxy blade too." Yendral crested the hill and came into view. "That sword was brilliant. Ass-bad as the natives here say." He gave Arwen a friendly nod.

She thought about correcting him, but Yendral added, "Speaking of asses, is it my imagination or does Darvanylar's backside have an arrow sticking out of it?"

"It does." Starblade gave Arwen that proud look again.

Her insides warmed, not from embarrassment this time.

"Also the cheek and neck," Starblade added.

"Not bad shooting." Yendral's next look was more appreciative, but then he seemed to notice how close they were, and he raised his eyebrows at his friend. A question?

If Starblade saw the silent look as an inquiry, he ignored it, instead lifting a hand and using his magic to extract the arrows from the dead dragon.

"What are we going to do about the body?" Yendral asked.

"The Rules of War and the Dragon Code," Starblade said, "dictate that we should bring the corpse to the Dragon Council, explain what happened, and state that the battle was honorably engaged in and we were victorious."

"Uh-huh. What are *we* going to do?"

Starblade frowned at him.

"We're refugees now, not soldiers, and we don't have a nation willing to back us up. Not even the one that created us and that we served for so long. If we did what the Code dictates, we'd be dead before dawn."

Starblade sighed again. "I am aware."

"To kill a dragon, even in self-defense, is a major crime in their eyes."

"I know that too."

"I think we need to stab holes in his body, tie boulders to it, and throw it in the ocean, so it'll sink and nobody will ever find him."

Starblade winced. "Yendral... even if I believed that would work, that the Dragon Council's magic wouldn't allow them to discover the body—and the truth—it would not be an honorable way to treat a fallen enemy. As the philosopher Syrinar Serth said, 'If we do not treat our enemies with the same respect we give our allies, we deserve the ire of their kin and clan.'"

"I know, I know."

"Go see to your wounds."

"What about *your* wounds? You're dripping blood all over our chef."

"It's all right," Arwen said. Besides, he wasn't doing that. He'd probably already started healing.

"I'll take care of them soon," Starblade said.

Yendral gave them another long look, then shook his head and headed for the stairs. "Glad you were here to help, Chef Arwen, is it?"

"Yes. Just Arwen."

Yendral gave her an elven salute, a hand to the chest with a slight bow, before descending out of sight.

Starblade stepped back from Arwen, handed her the arrows he'd retrieved, then dropped his arms to his sides. "I need to apologize to you."

"For what?" She'd come here to warn—and apologize to—him.

He flexed one hand, put it in his pocket, then drew it out and clasped it behind his back. She couldn't remember seeing him hesitant to speak his mind before. Was this about the pool? Maybe he knew she knew he'd been there and felt he'd been inappropriate for watching her.

If so, she was surprised that a dragon, even a *half*-dragon, would feel chagrined about something like that. They seemed to believe the lesser species weren't their equals and that they would have every right to ogle one of them if they wanted.

No, she admitted. She hadn't gotten the vibe that Starblade was like that. Oh, he could be pompous and had that dragonness inside of him that he'd admit gave him urges, but he was also honorable.

"Earlier, before the battle..." Starblade trailed off and looked toward the south, then cursed. "Another dragon is coming."

16

STARBLADE'S ANNOUNCEMENT THAT ANOTHER DRAGON WAS COMING at first made Arwen believe Darvanylar's clan had somehow already found out about his death and that they were about to be in a lot of trouble. But the dyspeptic expression that twisted Starblade's face told her before she sensed the visitor that it was Zavryd. Of course, that didn't mean they wouldn't be in trouble.

Starblade looked at Darvanylar's body and grimaced. "He may feel obligated to report the death of a dragon to his queen."

"Should we, uhm, hide the body?" Arwen asked.

Starblade had already vetoed that, but he probably hadn't expected to have to figure out what to do with it in the next two minutes.

"By kicking dirt over it?" Starblade cocked an eyebrow as he gestured in the air, outlining the dead dragon's size.

"Well, maybe some boulders."

He gave her a frank look.

"A *lot* of boulders."

"I will deal with the repercussions," Starblade said. "It is likely Yendral and I will have to leave this world."

Arwen stared bleakly at him. Even though she hadn't known him for long, the thought of losing him when she'd just started getting to know him depressed her.

She should have said something serious that let him know she cared. What came out was, "Before I've gotten a chance to bake the things on Yendral's list?"

"*That* could be the work of years." Starblade managed a smile.

"I haven't even gotten to make your dinner yet."

His smile turned wistful. "Perhaps there will be time at least for that." He looked toward the sky again. "Another comes with him. The half-dwarf enchanter."

"And Val?" Arwen wouldn't expect Zavryd to fly anyone around without Val also on board.

"His half-elven mate? No, she does not accompany him."

Zavryd flew close enough for Arwen to sense. Soon, she also picked out Matti and spotted them soaring over the trees in their direction. They headed straight for the hilltop, not stopping to visit the goblins along the way.

She could tell the moment Zavryd noticed the dead dragon, because his eyes opened wide and flared violet. They were so similar to Starblade's that she once again couldn't help but believe they might be related. Would Matti have come up here to personally tell her whether Sarrlevi had found a heritage device?

"How offended is he likely to be over the death of a Silverclaw dragon, I wonder," Starblade mused. "Their clans are rivals."

What evil, murderous, treacherous backstabbing has taken place here? Zavryd's voice boomed into their minds.

"Fairly offended, I think," Arwen said.

"I believe he's more offended that we puny beings killed a full-blooded dragon when he doesn't think it should have been possible. Not without *treachery*. But laying traps is not dishonorable, not when defending one's position in an openly declared conflict. It is the only way the weaker may triumph over the greater."

"I don't disagree with you."

When Zavryd landed on the hilltop, one taloned foot gripping the bench, as if he might hurl it to Canada, steam seemed to waft from his ears.

"He does, I fear," Starblade murmured.

Mongrel half-dragons. Zavryd shared the words with all, but he pinned Starblade with his stare. *You will explain exactly what has happened here. To kill a dragon is forbidden, except through a mutually agreed upon duel.*

It was not a duel, but he intended to kill me, and I defended myself. Starblade lifted his chin.

Arwen noticed he didn't look at her or say *we* to implicate Yendral had helped him. Did he intend to take all the blame on himself?

On Zavryd's back, Matti gazed down at the dead dragon. She didn't appear irritated so much as curious and maybe a little concerned. She slid off Zavryd's back, landing less easily than she might have if not for the extra weight she carried, but Zavryd was too distracted to levitate her down.

You will tell me everything that has transpired here. You and the other half-dragon. I sensed him and know he is present.

"You are not my keeper." Starblade, arms folded over his chest, glared defiantly back at Zavryd. "But I will tell you what happened."

Arwen nodded to him, thinking Zavryd would be the one dragon who might give him a fair hearing. After all, he'd known Starblade was here for months and hadn't reported his presence to the Dragon Council.

"Arwen?" Matti waved, then nodded toward the other side of the hilltop. "You're the one I came to see." She touched her pocket. Indicating her phone? "You didn't reply to my texts or calls." She smiled, though it had an exasperated tinge. "Do you carry the phone Willard insisted you buy?"

"I do. I've been distracted." Arwen pulled it out, not remembering it ringing or buzzing at any point. When she tried to activate it, a warning about the temperature came on, along with a promise that she could turn it on when it cooled off.

"Did a dragon breathe fire at you?" Matti asked.

"Not me, no. I don't think I was in any heat, but technological things don't perform well for me." She slipped the phone back into her pocket. It *was* oddly warm. Maybe some byproduct of the tattoo's magic?

"I may have worse news for you than I thought, then." Matti opened what Arwen had originally thought was a purse but turned out to be a tool kit. She withdrew a magical box with bent wires sticking out of it, a small hole in the top, and a panel on the side that opened to reveal a bunch of puzzling mechanical innards.

"Is that..."

"A heritage detector, but it's on the fritz. Varlesh threatened to maim the proprietor trying to sell him a broken device, as all good mates on a honey-do errand should, but the gnome had only this one to offer. He *did* give Varlesh a substantial discount, recalling that he was an assassin before he became a noble. Varlesh would have preferred a pristine and unused device, always willing to pay more for quality, but such items are apparently on the rare side. I gather gnomes don't mass-produce their magical goods in factories."

"I've heard that." Arwen looked toward Starblade and Zavryd.

They'd taken their telepathic conversation private, and Starblade had transformed into a dragon—in case he needed to fight or flee? She couldn't tell how it was going, but Zavryd kept grinding his talons into the rocky slope, so likely not well. Starblade didn't lower his head or give any sign that he was cowed. After a moment, they both took to the air.

"I took a look at it myself." Matti waggled her fingers to indicate she'd used her power, not only her eyes. "But it's more techno-logical magic than enchanting magic, and I'm kind of mystified when it comes to gnomish stuff. I feel less bad about that than I used to because my mother admitted *she* finds gnomish devices mystifying too. But I thought since you're off-the-grid and presum-ably handy—and you know how to use your dark-elven power—you might be able to fix it, so I brought it even though it's defunct. I also thought Starblade might know how to fix it since he knew how to extricate people from gnome-built stasis chambers, but that may only have been because he had intimate knowledge of them."

Arwen nodded, having gotten most of that story by now.

"If you don't know anyone who can fix it," Matti added, "we could try Gondo."

Arwen gaped at her. "I'm sure bolting *staplers* to it won't make it work."

"No, no, I meant that he has a lot of acquaintances, so he might know someone who could do it. Admittedly, he has a lot of *goblin* acquaintances, but you never know."

"I can try Imoshaun, the gnome." Arwen accepted the quirky device. "I've been meaning to check on her and her husband anyway. They both had their essences depleted by the dark elves."

"I'm glad *my* essence—all of my essences—" Matti rested her hand on her abdomen, "—stayed away from that assignment."

"Like alcohol and cigarettes, dark elves are best avoided when pregnant, yes."

"All the time, I've heard. No offense."

Arwen shook her head ruefully.

"I have something else for you, but, uh, do you want me to call Willard about that?" Matti pointed at the dead dragon. "It's a little large for her corpse mobile, and I doubt anyone could drive up here, anyway, but she usually handles the disposal of bodies of magical beings."

"I'm... not sure." Arwen stopped because Yendral had climbed into view. "Starblade's friend suggested stabbing holes—*more* holes—into the body and tying rocks to it before throwing it in the ocean to sink, but that may not be acceptably honorable."

Yendral grinned. "Still an option if my noble commander changes his mind."

"That's a big dragon," Matti said. "You'd need a *lot* of rocks."

"Is incineration a possibility?" Arwen didn't know if that was an acceptable funeral practice for dragons, but it would be a way to destroy the evidence, if that was what they decided to do.

"Dragon bodies are magical," Yendral said. "Tough if not impossible to incinerate."

He considered Zavryd and Starblade for a moment. Arwen thought he might shift into his dragon form and stand—or fly— beside his comrade, but he yawned, not appearing too worried about the argument going on overhead.

"What's that?" Yendral pointed to the magical box as he joined them.

"A heritage device," Matti said.

Yendral tilted his head. He squinted at them, and a slight itch under her skull was Arwen's only warning that he was reading her mind.

"You want to find out which dragons offered up genetic mate- rial for the scientists to smash together with elf blood to make us?" Yendral curled a lip. Because he didn't want to know? Or he didn't want to acknowledge his dragon side? "Azerdash," he called. "You might want to see this."

Nerves tangled in Arwen's stomach. Would he disapprove?

Starblade had continued flying as he discussed—or argued about—the situation with Zavryd, but he landed and shifted back into his elven form. Back stiff, he walked over.

I must report the death of a dragon, even a Silverclaw dragon, on this wild world, Zavryd announced as a portal formed in the air.

"Is he also going to report who did it and where it happened?" Worried anew, Arwen looked at Starblade.

His jaw was set, his eyes flinty.

"I did not say that either of you assisted me." Starblade nodded toward her and Yendral.

That wasn't what she'd been worried about, though maybe it should have been a concern. The dragons ruled the Cosmic Realms with an iron fist and didn't give a pass to crimes, which was what they would consider the killing of one of their kind, that happened on the wild worlds.

"You don't think the Dragon Council will notice the arrow hole in Darvanylar's ass when they come to collect the body?" Yendral smirked.

Starblade gave him a flat look.

"How will you get home without Zavryd here to fly you?" Arwen whispered to Matti.

"I have my portal generator with me. It needs to take me to another world before it can open a portal back to Green Lake, but that's not a problem. My mom is always happy when I visit."

Arwen couldn't help but feel longing for the existence of such a mother—and the ability to flit to other worlds on a whim. Despite her magical heritage and the power to do many things normal humans couldn't, she couldn't make portals and had never left Earth. She'd never even left the Pacific Northwest.

Yendral pointed at the box again. "Did you know about this, Azerdash?"

"I do not know what that is." Starblade eyed it, more curious than suspicious. "It is gnomish technology."

"Yes." Arwen, remembering he was a fan, wondered if his interest in the workings of the device might override any disapproval he felt about her plan. "It's not operable now, but I think Imoshaun can fix it. Unless you have the aptitude to repair it." She glanced at the airplane project before smiling at Starblade.

Before he could answer, Yendral said, "She wants to test our blood and figure out what dragon we owe our existence to."

The curiosity disappeared as Starblade's face grew closed.

"To what end?" His tone was flat. Wary.

Arwen took a deep breath. "My understanding is that dragons feel compelled to protect those who share their blood or marry—mate—into their clan. If we could find out who your father is or was—I assume your mother was an elf—maybe the dragon or his descendants would be honor-bound to help you out. To keep other dragons from hunting you down. If word about this gets out—" Arwen waved to the fallen Darvanylar, "—a *lot* of them might come looking for you, right? Like the whole Silverclaw clan?" She had no idea how many dragons that represented but assumed it wasn't insignificant.

Starblade didn't answer right away, but his jaw remained tight. Yendral merely shook his head, as if he knew nothing good would come from this.

"You do look a lot like Zavryd when you transform into a dragon," Matti offered.

"I am *nothing* like that self-righteous, arrogant blowhard." Starblade glowered up at the sky, though Zavryd had disappeared through his portal.

"Just in coloring. Is that an aspect you can change or does it indicate a trait you inherited?" Arwen remembered Zavryd's argument that it might be a personal choice for the half-dragons.

"*Many* dragons have black scales," Starblade said. "Among many different clans. It means nothing."

"He didn't answer my question, right?" Arwen whispered to Matti.

"Nope."

Starblade glared at them.

Arwen peered into his eyes, reminded of Zavryd's fiery gaze. His were the exact same hue of violet.

"This coloring is also not uncommon." Starblade pointed to his eyes.

"What I'm gathering is that the color of dragon they change into isn't a choice," Matti said, "but something determined by their genes."

"We cannot shift into whatever we want," Starblade said. "We could use illusion magic to appear different to those with weak senses, but what you have seen is what I am. I am *not* related to that pompous Stormforge dragon, and it wouldn't matter if I were. Nobody has ever defended us, and nobody ever will." Back still rigid, he walked to the other side of the hill and glowered off into the night.

Earlier, he'd been warm and even affectionate as he held Arwen and rubbed her neck. Now, he was cool and distant. Maybe she never should have concocted this plan.

"And Moody Azerdash returns," Yendral said.

"I just want to help," Arwen said.

"Then you'll have to bring him something to lighten his dourness. Sweets, perhaps."

"From your list?"

"That would lighten *my* dourness." Yendral flattened his hand to his chest.

He didn't seem like someone who was ever dour for long.

"You could also bring him parts for his project." Yendral waved toward the airplane. "He said he needs a... carburetor, I believe it is."

"Sweets are more in my wheelhouse."

Yendral brightened. "Good. I'll admit the weapons and traps he built into that wreck came in handy, but I can't imagine wanting to fly in the contraption. What would the point be when one has perfectly good wings? And the noise those things make. I've seen—*heard* them roar by above. I considered incinerating one that was particularly noisy and low-flying. It was also flinging chemicals onto fields over that way." He waved toward the south.

"The pilot appreciates you *not* incinerating his airplane," Matti said.

"Hm." Yendral eyed the box again, then headed toward the corpse. "I will levitate this body somewhere before it starts to stink."

Left alone with Matti, Arwen rubbed the back of her neck and considered whether they should leave or she should explain herself further to Starblade. He seemed to get the gist—and believe there was no point in pursuing this. If someone repaired the device, would he deign to give her a blood sample for testing?

"Are you still going to try to get it fixed?" Matti asked.

"Yes. I believe it's possible they're wrong, that if someone like Zavryd *was* proven to be related to them, he would feel compelled to stick up for them."

"Maybe," Matti said neutrally and fished in her pocket. "Here's the other thing I mentioned." She handed a scrap of torn paper to Arwen. It looked like part of a page from a book. "One of Willard's operatives got to search the troll tattoo artist before his clan claimed his body for whatever funeral rites they perform. I don't think he did an autopsy, but he *did* find this in his pocket."

Arwen rocked back. It was the page Star Inker had torn out of the Elven book on tattoo magic. The partial page.

"We translated it," Matti said. "It's part of a recipe. Not for apple tarts, but we don't know what."

"It has to do with magical tattoos."

"Is that it? We wondered. The header and top third of the recipe were on the missing part of the page. These are instructions for the preparation and some of the ingredients, but they're quirky magical items. I took the translation by Zoltan's laboratory—he's our outrageously overpriced alchemist—but he wasn't familiar with the recipe. He did say that some of the ingredients are hard to acquire, and one of them can only be found in the tunnels of dark elves, where they cultivate it. It's something particular that they use their magic to grow."

"I think this is the formula that's required to remove my magical tattoo." Arwen hated the idea of having to venture into dark-elf tunnels to acquire ingredients, but it would be worth it.

"You saw the book it came out of?"

"Yes. Inker was consulting it when the attack happened. If this really could remove my tattoo, I'd do a lot to make that happen. To make sure the dark elves couldn't compel me again to attack allies." Arwen looked sadly toward Starblade.

He still had his back to them, his arms crossed over his chest, but he had turned his head slightly. To listen to their conversation?

"Not easily anyway," Arwen added, remembering that Darvanylar had almost compelled her. In that instance, her tattoo had *protected* her from manipulation. Even so, she would rather have it gone. Today aside, she believed she was more likely to run into dark elves again than dragons who cared about compelling her to do anything.

"I'd want to get rid of it too." Matti deposited the gnomish device in her hands. "I'll give that to you, but Willard wants me to remind you about the mercenaries trying to hunt you down and that you yourself pointed out possible dark-elf involvement."

Starblade's head turned toward them again.

"Meaning I should prioritize my own problems over half-dragon genealogy?" Arwen asked.

"It's just a suggestion. Since the half-dragons aren't enthused by the genealogy project, it seems a wise one."

"I suppose."

Too bad. That project was less daunting. A strange thought since a dragon had tormented her twice that day. But, as crazy as it seemed, she would rather risk crossing dragons than dealing with her mother's people.

Matti removed a magical globe from her tool kit. The portal-creating device? "Do you want to come with me? To Dun Kroth and then back to my place? It'll be closer to wherever you're going than here, I'm guessing."

"Dun Kroth is the dwarven home world, right?"

"Where my mother and my father live together, yes."

"Your human father?"

"Yeah, they're inseparable now. Making up for lost time. Vigorously, sometimes. As Mom has no shame telling me about. She's the reason Dad doesn't mind Dun Kroth. And now that he remembers to duck going through doors, he hardly ever hits his head anymore. Though it sounds like he doesn't know what to make of King Ironhelm constantly suggesting he grow a decent beard."

"How long will you stay there?"

"Well, it's getting late here, so not too long, but I do feel I should visit for an hour or two when I stop by."

"Ah. Let me see if I can get a ride from someone else first."

Matti looked to Yendral, who was levitating Darvanylar's corpse down the hillside toward a portal that he'd formed, and then Starblade.

"Is he... talking to you, right now?" Matti touched a finger to her temple to indicate telepathy.

"No."

"Are you sure he'll help you?"

Arwen smiled sadly. "No."

She headed over to Starblade to ask anyway.

17

On the edge of the hilltop overlooking the forest, with moonlight casting shadows from the trees, Arwen approached Starblade. He didn't turn to look at her or acknowledge her presence.

"Are there any famous dead generals with advice on treating women well who want to help you, even if you don't entirely agree with their methods?" Arwen stopped beside him, not too close, though a part of her wanted to grip his hand and offer support.

"Few generals spoke about women, that I recall. One did say that troops with someone to return home to would fight harder to survive."

"It's possible your reading material was too limited."

"When we were young, our commanders were strict about the books we were given access to. Philosophical musings from civilians who'd never faced the point of a blade were considered useless fluff."

"Your library must have been small."

"The subject matter was somewhat limited. The number of tomes available... Well, those were turbulent times."

"Did your commanders not mind books by gnomish inventors? From what I've heard about gnomes, they don't seek out many confrontations at blade point."

"They do not." Starblade gave her a sidelong smile. "I sneaked engineering manuals into our barracks."

"You must have been considered rebellious for enjoying such degenerate reading material."

"I wasn't, but only because I wasn't caught. Did your instructors—or did your human father teach you?—put no limitations on what you could read when you were young?"

"My father did homeschool me, yes, and didn't forbid much when it came to reading material. Though I remember some condemning remarks about romance novels and approving nods at anything nonfiction that taught useful skills. Since there weren't any libraries or bookstores near the farm, my options were limited. We did have a mobile bookseller come through once in a while. I used to get bloody fingers picking extra raspberries and blackberries to peddle door-to-door for money. As an introvert, I cannot emphasize enough how much more painful trying to sell things to neighbors was than enduring the thorns, but I was determined to pay for the books I wanted. Classics such as The Baby-Sitters Club series and *Twilight*."

"These were... romances?"

"Not entirely, but they were a window into the world of public school and normal kids—more normal than I, at least."

"I believe I would side with your father on what is considered appropriate material for a youth."

"Is that so?" Arwen smiled, glad he was talking to her. The lightness of the topic was promising, though he hadn't unfolded his arms from his chest or stepped any closer to her. She had a feeling hugs and handholding were off the table now. Too bad. "Maybe you two can watch Jeopardy together sometime."

"A human television show?"

"A gameshow, yes. There are trivia questions."

"Gnomish engineering is covered?"

"Well, engineering in general. American media doesn't acknowledge the existence of magical beings."

Starblade tilted his head. "Even when such beings now proliferate on your world?'

"Yup. The media is controlled by the government and big corporations, and they only want us told what they think we should know. Anything else is considered *misinformation* and is squelched."

His eyes narrowed thoughtfully as he considered this. "Yendral may be wiser than I suspected."

"Yendral, who was last seen preparing to stab holes in a dragon corpse before sinking it into Puget Sound?"

"He has a—what is your term?—out of the cube way of looking at things. I believe an insurrection employing goblin armies *could* work on this world."

Arwen snorted. "It might." She lifted a hand but didn't presume to touch him. "You don't owe me anything, but would you consider doing me a favor? I need to visit Imoshaun the gnome— hopefully, she's still using that workshop in Bellevue, because she didn't tell me where in Renton her home is—to see if she can fix..." She hesitated, tempted to say some useless doodad, but he already knew what she intended. And she didn't want to lie to him. "The heritage detector."

His face hardened again. "Your plan will not work."

"I want to try it. Even if we can't gain you a stalwart big brother who will drive off any dragons who want to kill you... wouldn't you find it interesting to learn your heritage? To find out what dragon clan you came from?"

Starblade looked away from her, his chiseled face toward the forest again. As long, silent seconds passed, Arwen worried he'd decided not to speak further with her on this matter. Or *any* matter?

But he finally said, "Our instructors used to promise us that if we won the war, they would tell us our origins—the names of those who contributed the genetic material so that we could be created. As a boy, I was curious. Many of us were. As time passed, and I heard whispers and caught stray thoughts from unguarded minds, I came to suspect that the dragons were either tricked or stolen from, their blood used without their permission. Even the elves, those who birthed us... We were originally told they were powerful mages or great hunters, but hints suggested they might have been downtrodden souls who were willing to risk death to birth us, either to increase their status in society or because they had nothing to lose."

"Death?" Arwen gaped at him.

"For the first round of births, of which I was one, it was not known if the mothers would survive. In nature, dragons cannot breed with warm-blooded mammals, such as elves or your own humans. In this... *science experiment*, it was not known what kind of offspring would emerge. Had we been born as dragons with talons, we might have shredded our mothers' wombs without ever knowing better. Or the births might simply have been too difficult for them, resulting in the deaths of both mother and child." He hesitated. "There are rumors that some of the mothers *did* die during the births. The more I learned, the more I gave up the idea of loving parents who would be delighted by our existence and who would... care for us."

He closed his eyes, but not before she caught the wistfulness in them. Growing up in barracks with strict military instructors for caretakers couldn't have been that pleasant. She remembered enough of her first seven years in the tunnels with only dark elves around to know the feeling. Had he longed for a normal childhood? The kinds of parents that some had?

"I eventually came to the conclusion that it would be better not to know the details," Starblade said. "And the war... the war was never won. Eventually, there was a truce that led to an alliance, but that was after our fall, after we were imprisoned in those stasis chambers. What I've learned about how things ended comes from books. Strange, you can imagine, to read history about yourself. The experience has made me doubt the veracity of many of the tomes that I treasured in my formative years and that I accepted as truth."

"They say history is written by the victors."

"Yes, and by scribes, rarely by those who fought on the battlefield. However accurate they strive to be, their biases filter what they write. Only by being there can one know the truth."

"Though one's perceptions and beliefs also affect what is seen as truth, even when witnessed, don't you think?"

He smiled at her. "That is an argument to take into consideration. Neutrality is an illusion. We see that which reinforces our beliefs."

She liked it when he was smiling at her and wanted him to understand why she longed to seek out his heritage.

"I do understand," Starblade said, reminding her that he could read her thoughts when they were in the sanctuary. "My pride makes me affronted that you believe we need help, and my cynicism and experience make me certain no dragon will offer it, regardless."

"Aren't generals supposed to be optimistic so they can rally the troops?"

"They must be pragmatic so they can keep the troops alive. Being clever doesn't hurt, either, though that was never as much my forte as I wished."

Thinking of the traps he'd laid, anticipating Darvanylar or another attacker, Arwen didn't agree with that.

"There was another, a contemporary of mine, whom I admired

a great deal. He was a brilliant strategic thinker, adored by our elven tutors, and they believed *he* would be the great general who led our troops to victory."

"But?"

"I had more raw power than he, and the other half-dragons, wanting to be led by the strongest rather than the cleverest, wished me to be in charge. That is not the elven way, but it is the *dragon* way, and even though we were raised on Veleshna Var and indoctrinated with elven culture, the dragon existed in all of us. He and I ended up dueling for the right to command our troops. I would have been content to follow, but we were goaded into deciding it with fang and talon."

"And you won."

"I killed him."

"It was a duel to the *death*?" That surprised her—if so much time and effort had gone into training the half-dragons to be great warriors and defeat the enemy, why pit them against each other?

"It was not, but we both chose to fight as dragons. In that form, the... beast, I shall call it, is close to the surface. It is always there, lurking in our blood, and in battle, it emerges. You're engulfed by the primeval drive of a predator who must win, must dominate at all costs, and you can lose your rational mind. Sometimes, you return to awareness only when the battlefield has grown quiet, the bodies of your enemies littering the ground around you, and you can barely remember slaying them."

Arwen remembered the looks he'd given her after killing Zyretha and Darvanylar. Starblade *had* seemed like a beast who didn't recognize her and might attack, the battle lust fully engulfing him.

"That is what happened to us, with what should have been only a duel for the leadership of a company." Starblade shook his head. "I regret that I allowed myself to be talked into fighting him. I believe our instructors regretted it as well and never quite forgave me, though they'd had enough demonstrations by then of our nature. Of the propensity for the beast to override the elf. It was unfortunate. He was the best of us and would have been best *for* us. He would have foreseen the treachery that resulted in our fall. We may even have won the war if he'd lived."

Arwen lifted her hand again, wanting badly to take his, to comfort him in whatever small way she could. Or maybe just to commiserate. She certainly knew what it was like to have a dark half and to have been raised, at least for a time, for someone else's ends.

Starblade gazed at her, but she couldn't tell if he was reading her thoughts or agreed that they had similarities even if he was.

"I will take you to see the gnome, and you may employ her in fixing that if you wish." He pointed at the heritage device. "But more important, before I go, I will assist you with putting a stop to those who wish you dead, be they orcs or dark elves."

Arwen started to nod her appreciation, but her mind snagged on three of his words. "Before you go?"

"This refuge was discovered by one dragon. Soon, others will come. It was never ideal that Zavryd'nokquetal knew of it."

"Where will you go?"

"Another world. It is best that you do not know where."

Arwen winced. Right, since she could be forced to blab his location to any dragons who happened across her, she was a weak link for him.

"It is not your fault," he said firmly. "It is simply the way of the universe. Dragons are too powerful for anyone to repel."

"Will you at least let me make that dinner for you—you and Yendral—before you go? And what about his list? You can't leave Earth without desserts from at least fifty nations in your pack." More emotion than she wanted to admit to filled her words, and they didn't come out as light as she wished.

"Perhaps if you made three or four, that would be more reasonable."

"You paid enough for fifty. And then some."

"The coin is not important. When we uncovered the remains of our ancient barracks, a chest of gold remained. Once, it would have been for supplies and a salary for all our kind fighting for the elves, but with almost all of us long gone, I felt no compulsion to return it to the king. The king who rules now is not even *our* king. We were strangers to him, strangers it was clear he would have preferred to remain forgotten in those stasis chambers for all eternity." Starblade shuddered. "I will, however, do as I promised before we faced the dark elves."

Not remembering any promises, Arwen looked curiously at him.

"Build you a rejuvenation pool. One in a private locale where people are unlikely to watch you." He shook his head ruefully, and she remembered the apology he'd been on the verge of giving earlier. He bowed to her. "You are ready to depart?"

"Uhm." Arwen looked around.

Yendral and the dragon corpse had disappeared. Matti remained, now lying on her back on the bench, watching something on her phone. Arwen had forgotten she was there and waved apologetically when Matti looked over. She hadn't meant to speak with Starblade for so long while Matti waited to see if she needed a ride.

Is everything okay? Matti asked her telepathically.

Nothing is okay, but he said he would take me to see Imoshaun.

If it helps, I don't think Zavryd will rat him out. That was a Silver-claw dragon. Based on the stories Val has told me, those are the scheming nemeses of the Stormforges, Zavryd's clan. He's definitely not going to weep over that guy's death.

I hope not, but if one dragon found Starblade and Yendral, others might. They're planning to leave the refuge.

Ah. Matti didn't sound that broken up about it. Maybe she'd assumed this wouldn't be a long-term home for the half-dragons.

But they'd built it out of nothing and brought in an airplane to work on. Had they truly intended it to be so temporary?

All right. Matti sat up and picked up her portal generator. *Be careful. You may want to reach out to Willard later. She asked Gondo to look up other people who may be able to remove magical tattoos and also see if there's a duplicate of that book on Earth so we can find the full recipe.*

I'll be glad if something comes of his research. That wasn't Arwen's priority at the moment though. She had to figure out how to fix things so Starblade could stay on Earth and be safe. She nodded to him. "I'm ready to go."

18

IS THERE AN IDEAL LOCATION ON YOUR PROPERTY WHERE A POOL MAY BE located? Starblade asked telepathically as he flew Arwen toward Bellevue.

She rode on his back, the lights below growing more numerous as they left the rural lands behind. "That's not my priority right now."

It is a promise I wish to fulfill before I'm forced to leave. I may not have much time.

Even though Arwen would love to have a magical rejuvenation pool with healing power, she wished she hadn't made the request of Starblade. She'd been half-joking at the time, especially once she learned it took three days of meditation and working with an artifact to build such a place. Even though a magical pool would be special and a way to remember him after he was gone, Arwen wanted to fix things so he could stay.

The ideal location? he prompted.

"Would it have any deleterious effects on the ground around it?" Arwen thought of hot tubs and swimming pools and all the chemicals people put in the water to keep them sanitary. Even though the elven pool had smelled nothing like chemicals, it was possible it would alter the soil around it.

Deleterious? Certainly not. If anything, the installation of an elven rejuvenation pool would benefit the nearby soil. Your plants may creep down and root themselves near its edges to bask in the healing magic.

Arwen imagined an overgrown jungle cropping up and her not being able to reach the water. Since they'd left the sanctuary and he might not be able to read her thoughts anymore, she attempted to share the image telepathically.

That is a possibility. Shall I also leave you a machete?

"That's okay. My magic ought to be sufficient to nudge the plants aside to make a path."

As they flew toward Lake Washington, the skyscrapers of Bellevue coming into view, Arwen reached into her pocket to rub her camouflaging charm. Even though Val, Zavryd, and some of Willard's people had cleaned out the twenty-story building the dark elves had claimed and returned it to the insurance company —and the employees who'd survived—Arwen worried that her mother's people might linger in the area.

I am also camouflaged, Starblade told her as he banked, angling toward the building where Imoshaun had her basement work-shop. *I have not sensed other dragons, but they may be in the area. Darvanylar might not have come to this world alone.*

"Why do you think he came at all?"

During our encounter, he neglected to do more than berate me for being born an abomination and call me a coward for defending myself when his kind sought to destroy us on Veleshna Var.

"So his vacation plans weren't covered."

They were not.

As Starblade glided toward the flat rooftop of the building, apparently finding that an appropriate dragon landing pad, Arwen peered into the alley that held the door to Imoshaun's workshop. She hoped for sign that the gnome remained in the area. What she didn't expect was a line-up of half-gnomes, goblins, half-elves, quarter-dwarves, and more magical beings in the alley. There had to be twenty people standing along the brick wall next to the door.

"Uhm." With so many beings with magical auras present, Arwen couldn't tell if Imoshaun was in the area or not. Seeing such a crowd gathered didn't make her want to go down and knock on the door. She shrank at the idea of being packed into an alley with all those strangers.

The door opened, and three more mixed-bloods walked out of the basement workshop. Starblade landed on the rooftop, his talons barely making a sound as he touched down, and leaned his long neck over the edge to peer down into the alley.

Did you expect these persons?

I did not, Arwen said, switching to telepathy so she wouldn't be overheard.

The hodgepodge of people didn't look like they were together. Most didn't carry any magical items that Arwen could detect, but the three who'd exited were an exception. Each wore a medallion that emanated a small amount of power. Had the gnome workshop been taken over by some cult?

As one, the three medallions emitted a high-pitched beeping. The owners gripped the devices and whirled, peering all about in the alley.

Did you expect our arrival to prompt that noise? Starblade shook his head like a dog irritated by a smoke detector going off.

I did not, Arwen repeated. *Are you sure* we're *the reason for the alarms triggering, if that's what those are?* Arwen's hand strayed to her pocket, but she'd already activated the camouflaging charm.

Perhaps someone invented a dragon detector.

"I don't see anyone." One of the medallion wearers had drawn a handgun and was pointing it at the dumpster, but he glanced uncertainly at both ends of the alley and a doorway on the opposite building. "Are they invisible?"

"Conniving dark elves are stealthy," someone else barked.

Arwen blinked. *Dark elves?*

She also caught herself looking up and down the alley and at the rooftops. She'd been worried some of her mother's people might be in the area...

"Come inside where my defenses can protect you," a familiar voice called from the doorway. Imoshaun.

Not only did the three people with the medallions run back inside but everyone in the alley did. The metal door slammed shut.

Arwen scratched her jaw. *Not a dragon detector but a* dark-elf *detector.*

Was the alarm bestirred because of your blood?

Oh. Arwen hadn't considered that. Maybe it wasn't fussy about the purity of the dark elves it detected. *That's possible.*

You are camouflaged. Whatever enchantment is on the medallions is effective if it can detect you through such magic. Considering I do not sense any other dark elves in the area...

Yeah. Well, at least we know Imoshaun is home. Arwen slid off Starblade's back.

She would have climbed down the building to the alley—the brick wall offered sufficient handholds for one with elven blood—but Starblade used his magic to levitate her to the ground.

Thank you.

He sprang down beside her, changing forms in the air to land as an elf. He created a defensive barrier around them. "I believe you may be greeted with weapons if you attempt to enter."

"I should have brought a pie."

He gazed blandly at her, and she thought he might not get her attempt at humor, but he nodded in agreement. "Yes."

Arwen deactivated her charm so Imoshaun could sense her and would recognize her.

"In the event of your death, would you like me to build the rejuvenation pool for your father?" Starblade asked.

"Is that a joke?"

"Yes. It is unlikely the gnome has weapons that can defeat my magic and reach you."

"Father probably *would* like a magical hot tub. And I think it should go behind my cottage near the melons and cruciferous garden beds. The cantaloupe and cauliflower can be challenging to cultivate in our climate, especially in the years when the summers aren't hot. I think the warmth of the nearby water would extend the growing season without the need for cold frames. Oh, and maybe the wasabi would do well by such a pool. Wasabi sells well in the market, but it's hard to grow outside of its native Japan. The roots like constant moisture but don't want to be waterlogged. Very fussy."

"You've put a lot of thought into this quickly."

"Well, you made me. If *you* die, do you want me to have something done with your airplane so the goblins don't scavenge it?"

He gave her an aggrieved look. "That *would* be egregious. Perhaps there is room on your property for it."

"We... technically have the *room*. Getting it there would be a problem. Even if it flies, we don't have a runway."

"It is not yet operable. My understanding of the manly project of rebuilding an engine is that it may take many years to complete, during which time the female spouse will complain about the conveyance's presence in the driveway or on the lawn."

"That sounds right. But you don't have a female spouse tucked away somewhere, do you?"

"I do not. The Study of Manliness suggested locations where a suitable mate could be sought, but I am not looking for one."

Maybe it wasn't only that he had no interest in her, because of her dark-elven blood, but that he wasn't interested in *mates* at all at this time. Arwen didn't know whether to find that heartening or not.

"Your life is a little unsettled now for long-term relationships, I would think," was all she said.

"Indeed. You *will* need a dragon to levitate the airplane to your property. If I die and Yendral lives, he will do this task for you." Starblade nodded as if he'd already gotten his friend's agreement.

"Poor Yendral gets stuck with the dirty work often, doesn't he?" Arwen wondered if he was stabbing the dead dragon full of holes and tying rocks to the body, even as they spoke.

"*Poor Yendral* volunteers for the work that doesn't require him to think overmuch."

"Do you two squabble often? He called you, uhm, sanctimonious and moody."

"He obeys my commands despite his tendency toward impudence." Starblade nodded toward the door. "I believe the procedure is to knock or ring a gong, but I do not see the latter."

"Doorbells are more typical in America but not for basement workshops." Arwen knocked and braced herself, glad to have Starblade at her side.

Several long seconds passed, making her wonder if the gnome had forgotten her aura and didn't recognize her.

Is the half-dragon your ally or your captor? Imoshaun spoke into her mind.

Earlier, we battled an enemy together, and he rubbed my neck afterward, Arwen replied, then felt silly. Why had she shared that? Because she wanted Imoshaun to believe she was capable of gaining the regard of someone powerful?

I am uncertain if that answered my question.

I don't accept neck rubs from captors.

Yes, I frown on such activities as well. Especially since I am married. The door opened, and four-foot-tall Imoshaun peered warily through her spectacles at Starblade before saluting Arwen with a set of pliers.

Soft murmurs drifted up the stairs from below. All those people were jammed into the workshop. The beeping continued, though not as loudly as before. Several grunts, bangs, and clanks also floated up.

"Are *you* the reason the dark-elf detectors are going off?" Imoshaun peered left and right in the alley, as if an army of demon worshippers might be poised to spring.

"Possibly." Arwen spread her arms. "I was camouflaged when those medallions started beeping."

"Well, that's *wonderful* then. What proof that it works. Gruflen didn't think it would, but it did, and for a *half*-blood. It's brilliantly sensitive. Even more so than I thought."

"Why are you building dark-elf detectors?" Arwen worried the project meant that more of her mother's people had been sighted in the area. Sighted or *worse*.

"Because there's a market for them now. Many in the magical community were disturbed by the reports of dark elves perpetrating nefarious schemes in the bowels of that building. *More* than reports, as I can attest." Imoshaun clutched her chest, no doubt remembering the device she'd been attached to, the pain it had inflicted while stealing her essence. "And there have been rumors of more of their kind around. They haven't been seen, as far as I know, but people in the magical community have claimed to sense them."

"Just tonight, I did," a man called up from below. "I was eating dinner at the teriyaki place by Mark's Marks and sensed one skulking under the street in a stormwater tunnel. When I went out to my car, I even thought I saw him ducking into an alley."

"Mark's Marks?" Unease burrowed into Arwen's belly. Could it have been the same dark elf that she'd sensed at Star Inker's parlor?

"It's a tattoo place," someone else said. "Magical Mark—he's a half-troll—can do enchanted inkings. Amazing work. Tell them Randy sent you if you go."

Arwen looked at Starblade. *I hope this isn't related to me somehow.*

Hm? He'd been gazing thoughtfully at the brick wall while she and Imoshaun spoke.

The dark elf sensed near this other tattoo place. Arwen squinted at him. *Were you using your senses to monitor the area for threats or thinking about your airplane?*

My barrier ensures no threats will reach you.

That hadn't answered her question, she noticed.

He gave her a half smile. *I might have been determining where on your property would be a suitable place for the airplane. So I can give Yendral instructions before my death.*

How about you just don't die?

Always a worthy goal. He looked a little wistful.

Hell, he didn't think he was going to be killed by a horde of dragons before he could finish the pool and leave Earth, did he?

"You did not come for a dark-elf detector, did you?" Imoshaun was peering curiously at Arwen.

"No, sorry." Arwen pulled out the heritage detector and explained her problem.

Unfortunately, Starblade's face grew sour again when she touched on her plans to test dragon blood with the device. Maybe she shouldn't have distracted him from his daydreaming.

"Interesting." Imoshaun accepted the box and examined the sides and poked the wires before opening the lid. "The magic is familiar. I believe I have encountered the work of this inventor before. Back on the gnomish home world."

"So you might be able to fix it?" Arwen asked.

"It is a possibility. You do know that unless it is preloaded with the results of many kinds of blood that it has already analyzed that you would need to collect samples from all you wish to compare, yes?"

"That makes sense."

"And dragons are notoriously disinclined to offer up blood samples."

"Half-dragons as well," Starblade murmured.

"Gruflen," Imoshaun called over her shoulder.

The banging and clanking didn't stop, but the murmurs of the people below fell silent, making it possible to hear a male voice grumbling to himself in the gnomish language.

Imoshaun rolled her eyes and called again. "Gruflen, the new reactor crystals are here."

The banging halted, and a male gnome wearing welding goggles came into view, a glowing soldering gun in his hand. He set the tool aside and rushed up the stairs, almost tripping twice. Grumbling, he shoved the goggles up to his forehead and made it the rest of the way.

His short white hair stuck out in all directions, stiff and pale, as if he'd electrocuted himself recently. He wore a leather apron, a diamond-shaped whirring gizmo that emanated magic attached to the front.

"My crystals?" he asked in English, peering over Imoshaun's shoulder hopefully. "They've arrived from our home world?" His expression shifted to wariness as he took in Arwen and Starblade, his gaze lingering much longer on Starblade. He gripped Imoshaun's shoulder. Since Arwen had grown accustomed to Starblade, she didn't always notice the power of his aura, but she hadn't forgotten it was there and that others could sense it. "These aren't our usual delivery agents, my wife."

"You're right. I was mistaken. Here." Imoshaun offered him the heritage device. "I believe I can repair this, but you are the scientist. Are you able to determine if the results of any previous analyses are retained inside the *fyorka?*"

Staring at Starblade, Gruflen didn't take the device right away. "I can certainly look at it, but why is there a *dragon* on our doorstep? A dragon with... elven blood?" His gaze shifted to Starblade's pointed ears. "Is that possible?"

"It is possible," Starblade said, "through elven science and magic."

"Elven science." Gruflen scoffed but, when Starblade's eyes closed to slits, added, "It is not without its merits."

"Especially if you wish to genetically alter a plant," Imoshaun said.

Gruflen released her shoulder but only so he could poke her in it. "He is not a plant."

"That is true. Though, knowing the elven kind, he may have bits of plants engineered into him." Imoshaun looked over her shoulder. "Are you aware that you're hiding behind me again, Gruflen?"

"Yes, but I think that's a fair thing to do when a half-dragon stands on the threshold. And one's wife has lied most heinously to one."

"You don't hear me unless I mention your crystals, power cells, or a threat to your workshop."

"The last time I stepped boldly out in front of you, I was taken by the dark elves." Gruflen shuddered, ducking his head behind hers. "And the female has some of their blood."

"She helped rescue you. You remember her from the underground lair, don't you?"

"I was so woozy and weak that I remember very little."

If this errand has concluded, Starblade spoke telepathically to Arwen, *we may engage in the next. I intend to end the threat to you. We will go to the tattoo place the mongrel mentioned and seek the dark elf to find out if he hired the orcs who attacked you.*

I don't know where that shop is. Arwen pulled out her phone and looked doubtfully at it. It was no longer hot to the touch and came on when she brushed the surface, but the myriad images that one might activate made her pause. Amber had shown her how to check the internet and look at maps, but the lesson had been swift and had already grown fuzzy in Arwen's memory.

I saw its location in the mongrel's mind. I also saw the male spy that he glimpsed. Starblade inserted the image of a strip mall into her thoughts, a hooded and cloaked figure ducking into an alley.

Between the night's shadows and the hood, only a hint of the person's chin had been visible. The pale skin *might* have been albino, but Arwen wasn't certain the figure was a dark elf or even male based on the memory.

He believes it was a dark elf, Starblade assured her. *He sensed as well as glimpsed him.*

All right. Out loud, Arwen said, "We need to check on something else."

Imoshaun and Gruflen had continued to argue while she conversed with Starblade, but they stopped at her words.

"One moment," Imoshaun said. "I have repaired and improved the human garment that you left behind. I also have a gift to thank you for helping us escape the dark elves."

"Oh." Arwen hadn't forgotten that she'd left Amber's jumpsuit in the workshop, but since it had been ripped and bloodstained, she hadn't been certain it would be salvageable and hadn't thought to rush back for it. "I'll gladly return the jumpsuit to its owner, but gifts aren't necessary."

"Unless they are schematics of gnomish war devices or even the tunnel borer that we visited," Starblade said.

"We went into that passage to sneak into the dark-elf base," Arwen whispered to him, "not *visit* the tunnel borer."

"I made you an arrow," Imoshaun told Arwen. "And I didn't realize the garment wasn't yours. I... the owner may not desire the improvements I made. Because of your dangerous life—" she glanced at Starblade as if he were the reason for Arwen's dangers, "—I armored it slightly."

"I am certain the owner won't mind such a gift. If her college interviews are fraught or she's attacked on the way, she may appreciate armor."

"It is *you* that I hoped would put the garment to use, due to your woeful lack of protective gear."

"She is protected currently," Starblade said.

"Yes, but I assume you are not always with her. Unless..." Imoshaun eyed their closeness. "You have not become mates, have you?"

"No," Starblade said with depressing firmness.

Arwen made herself add an agreeable, "No," though wistfulness went through her at the memory of him hugging her after the battle. "We're working together for a time."

"Ah." Imoshaun turned back down the stairs to where her guests were speaking again. Another dark-elf detector went off, beeping indignantly.

Starblade curled his lip at the noise.

Gruflen, perhaps realizing he'd been left alone on the steps with them, spun as if to run back to his project.

"Wait." Starblade halted him with a whisper of his power as well as the command. "Is that an *ingorate dal*?"

Turned back by Starblade's magic, Gruflen rotated toward them again.

Arwen frowned. Why was Starblade using his power on an ally? Or at least a friendly gnomish scientist? He *liked* gnomes. Or gnomish engineering, anyway.

"This?" Gruflen touched the gizmo attached to his leather apron. It whirred softly, pulsing magic. "Yes."

"It has more enchantments layered on it and more features than a typical *ingorate dal,* does it not?" Starblade gazed raptly at the gnome's chest.

"Ah, yes." Gruflen flipped open the top of the diamond-shaped device as if it were a pocket watch, but instead of the time being represented inside, numerous cogs and springs and tiny moving parts glowed and whirred back and forth. "We've made improvements."

"You have the schematic?"

"My wife has some drawings, yes."

"With notes?"

"I believe so, yes."

"You will make a copy of them for my perusal," Starblade stated.

"Ah." Gruflen scratched his head with a screwdriver, looking more puzzled than affronted by the command.

"Please," Arwen said anyway.

"What?" Starblade asked.

"He isn't one of your troops. You should *request* a copy of his notes. Politely."

"Were it not for us, he would have been sacrificed to the dark elves. He should be honored to share his work with me."

"Oh, I *am* honored," Gruflen assured him. "It's just that we don't have a copying device, so there are only originals of our notes."

"It would be a simple matter for one with your talents to make such a device to create copies."

"There's probably a Xerox machine somewhere around too." Arwen waved in the direction of the office buildings surrounding the area.

"Is it that you do not wish to share your secrets with a stranger?" Starblade asked.

"Gnomes often *are* hesitant to let their schematics and notes escape. We don't want our devices being made by those from other races with unfriendly intent." Gruflen's voice grew aggrieved. "Or goblins who will malign our brilliance by inserting *substandard* materials."

Arwen suspected that latter was the more egregious insult.

"I will not craft the items," Starblade said, "only read your notes. It is a hobby of mine. However, if you have a human contraption called a carburetor, I am working on a project of my own."

"*You,* one with dragon blood, are engineering? Instead of simply making with magic? Or *taking* what you desire?"

"I enjoy crafting siege engines and other items with martial merit. Many such devices were used against me in the war."

"Which caused you to appreciate them?" Arwen asked.

"To some extent. As one can appreciate the cunning of a strong enemy, one might admire the mechanics of a weapon catapulting flaming projectiles at one's troops."

"I haven't found that to be true," she murmured.

"Because of your dark-elven blood." Starblade nodded to her. "It makes you odd."

"Yes, *I'm* the odd one here."

"Let me see what I can find." Gruflen held up a finger and trotted down the steps.

"General Herathdor the Great said, 'It is wise to be polite to the ally whose castle walls you seek to shelter your troops behind.'" Starblade gave Arwen a pointed look.

"Are you implying I should kiss your ass because you're sharing your defenses with me?"

"Herathdor did not mention *asses* at any point in his writings. In truth, the word he used was not *be polite* but *genuflect,* but I believe you are too proud to adopt such a behavior with me."

"That's right," Arwen said.

"The mongrels below are conferring, believing you are a threat and considering banding together to attack. Three possess weak human firearms, and two have daggers."

Arwen grimaced. Was that true?

"I will not let them harm you. And *you* will not presume to criticize me in front of lesser beings."

"Asking you to say *please* isn't a criticism. It's a correction."

"It is presumptuous to *correct* a dragon or one with dragon blood."

"You're kind of a pill sometimes, you know."

Starblade mouthed *pill* with some uncertainty but must have gotten the gist, because he nodded in agreement.

Imoshaun and Gruflen returned, she with Amber's green jumpsuit, the entire garment now shimmering with a metallic overlay and endowed with multiple enchantments.

"It's very nice." Arwen appreciated the sentiment, though her limited awareness of fashion trends suggested Amber might not find the new version of her garment *snatched*, as she'd once described her clothing.

"Yes." Imoshaun also held out an arrow. It, too, had been enchanted. "Unlike the one you were tricked by the dark elves into finding, I crafted this one using the blood that was left on the garment."

Arwen had started to reach for the arrow, excited to have a new one to add to her quiver, but she froze. "That was *my* blood. From when the security guard threw a dagger at me." Horror blossomed in her at the idea that this weapon might have been crafted to be especially effective against her.

"Yes, which is half *dark-elven*." Imoshaun clasped her hands together. "I also used it to make the dark-elf detectors."

"Uh. Its human part didn't mess up your inventions?"

"Oh, not at all. It was a simple matter for Gruflen to siphon out that genetic material. He is *quite* the scientist." Imoshaun might have been arguing with him earlier, but she beamed pride at her husband now.

You still believe one should be polite *with gnomes?* Starblade smiled smugly at Arwen.

One should be polite with everyone.

The Study of Manliness suggests being firm with strangers and to take control when it comes to females and children. Gnomes are like children.

Maybe you should stop reading that book. It's a bad influence.

It will not help me fit in on this world?

It will help you be a dick, which may help you fit in with some humans, *but not the kind anyone likes.*

Nobody likes dragons. Or half-dragons.

Because they're haughty and arrogant and use their power on others without asking.

Hm.

Still smiling, Imoshaun extended the arrow toward Arwen again. "This is now enchanted to have greater efficacy against dark elves and dark-elven magic."

Arwen accepted it, though she couldn't help but think it might end up being used against her someday.

"An offering for one with dragon blood who appreciates gnomish technology." Gruflen touched the gizmo on his chest, then swept something out from behind his back. A roll of toilet paper.

Writing in black ink all over the top layer—if not *all* the layers —suggested he didn't expect Starblade to wipe with it.

"Gnomish notes?" Starblade accepted the roll and looked at the writing.

"When we were being chased, before the minion the dark elves sent captured me," Gruflen said, "we were forced to hide in a lavatory in a human recreation area."

"A park," Imoshaun said.

"Yes. We used our magic to secure the door, but then we were trapped inside with few tools other than a pen..." Gruflen shrugged. "When we find ourselves in such a state, we mull on future projects."

Arwen, while wondering how often gnomes found themselves trapped in public restrooms, watched Starblade to see if he would be delighted or offended to have been given scribbled-upon toilet paper.

"There are also a few poems," Gruflen said. "They are not our original work but were something we copied down to remember due to their insight into what humanity considers art and culture."

Arwen rubbed her face, imagining Starblade offering up, *Here I sit all broken-hearted...,* the next time he wanted to quote something.

"I will accept your gift and not grow affronted that you've taken and used the blood of my..." Starblade extended a hand toward Arwen but didn't seem to know what to call her. "Of this female without her permission. *She* may, however, grow affronted."

"It's okay," Arwen said, "especially if your, ah, detectors keep others from being caught by dark elves. Nobody wants that."

"No, indeed. I would give *you* one—" Imoshaun pointed at her, "—but your own blood would set it off, so it would be of little use."

"I'll accept the arrow then. And thank you for the armor."

"Use it well. From all that we've heard, we believe that more dark-elf plots are afoot."

Arwen glanced at her sleeve, the tattoo hidden beneath. "I'm aware."

19

"I will enter with you," Starblade stated after flying Arwen across Bellevue toward a strip mall with a neon-blue arrow directing them to an alley entrance for Mark's Marks. They stood in a parking lot, motorcycles and trucks taking a few spots. "I sense shifters and half-bloods within the structure."

A window on the front side of the strip mall let them see men and women playing air hockey and pool, but they appeared to be mundane humans. Fortunately, few customers were outside, so Arwen didn't have to worry about encountering crowds, at least not until she visited the tattoo parlor. She thought the magical beings were in there. Starblade was right. There were a number of them. Was a tattoo parlor an appealing place to hang out? Or was the wait to be inked that long?

"I appreciate you flying me around, but you don't have to be my bodyguard." Arwen lifted her bow. "I can handle myself."

Starblade looked up from the partially unrolled toilet paper that had reappeared in his hands when he'd shifted form. "You are competent with the bow, but you are not wearing the armor the gnome gave you, nor do you carry a weapon sufficient for close-quarters fighting."

"My foraging knife works in a pinch."

"It is not magical. And the blade is small with hair sticking out of the hilt."

"Those are boar bristles. They're for dusting off mushrooms."

He gazed at her for a moment before asking, "Was your statement meant to refute mine?"

"Just educate. You could put some power into it for me if you'd like me to be better armed." Arwen didn't expect that and said it as a joke, but right afterward admitted that a magical foraging knife would be a dream tool.

"It is not a sufficient vessel for my power."

"Does that mean you think it would blow up if you poured magic into it, or your ego objects to you enchanting something meant for foraging instead of killing people?"

"What I choose to use my power on has nothing to do with my ego. Items not built to hold magic are poor receptacles for it." He shared an image with her of power entering her knife and it exploding, as if it had been zapped by lightning. The boar bristles flew off, and pieces of the charred wooden handle tumbled to the ground.

"Ah. My apologies. I didn't mean to insult you."

Starblade rubbed the material of the jumpsuit. Before, it had been silky. Now, it was closer to a fine mesh that lent it a slinky look. Arwen wondered if it would pinch her skin if she wore it. It wasn't anything one would want to wear without a bra, but she did find its new sheen appealing. She considered putting it on, but she felt obligated to return it to Amber without fresh holes or bloodstains.

"You would be wise to wear this armor. Gnomes aren't as practiced of smiths as dwarves, but their work is sometimes more clever and can be effective at deterring claws, arrows, swords, and other weapons. I believe the magic in this garment would protect you from mundane human weapons of many kinds." He looked at her shirt, then nodded at the armored jumpsuit and at her.

"What, you want me to put it on right now? I don't think it's loose enough to go over my clothes. I'd have to change, and we're in the parking lot in front of strangers." Arwen looked toward the window, though nobody was paying attention to them.

"Even though I can protect you, it is always wise to be armored, and you do not know how to create a magical barrier around yourself. That is a deficiency. You should find a tutor who can instruct you on such defensive magic."

"Thanks so much for the tip. I hadn't thought of that."

He cocked his head.

"I *have* thought of that before, but I'm not going to the dark elves to find a tutor, and I wouldn't want to use dark-elven magic anyway. I've told you why."

"Yes. You worry that drawing upon your dark-elven power will lure you to embrace that heritage, as I've worried, not without proof that it's possible, that spending too much time as a dragon might cause me to forget my elf half and lose myself to the beast." Starblade touched her shoulder, as he had when they'd discussed the topic in the dark-elf lair, and gave her the same we-have-more-in-common-than-it-seems-like-we-should look. At least, that was how Arwen had interpreted it then. His touch sent a warm tingle through her. "I understand this, but you have learned to improve the health of the plants on your farm with your power."

"Because I found a book on elven plant magic and taught myself. Books on creating magical barriers haven't fallen into my lap."

"It is difficult to learn magic from a book."

"Tell me about it."

"I am doing so."

"No, I mean... Never mind."

"When I am constructing your rejuvenation pool, and I must take breaks from the meditation, *I* will instruct you on creating a personal barrier around yourself. Even though you are a mongrel with inferior human blood, I believe you have the power to learn such an ability."

"You really know how to compliment a girl."

That earned her another puzzled head tilt.

She waved away her sarcasm. "I would be grateful if you could teach me that."

"Yes." Starblade twitched a finger at the garment. "Until then, you will don the armor. If you wear your camouflaging charm, none will be able to look upon you as you do so."

"I guess that's true." Arwen eyed the parking lot, feeling out in the open and vulnerable, even with nobody except Starblade looking in her direction. "Hold these, please." She handed him her bow and quiver.

"I am pleased that you accept the wisdom of my advice." The sour look he turned on her weapons suggested he might be less pleased to be used as her personal shelf, but he did hold them. He also stepped back to give her privacy.

Arwen would be sad when she had to return the camouflaging charm to Amber. But if Starblade could teach her to make a protective barrier, she would feel more confident in her ability to defend herself even if she couldn't hide from those who could detect magic.

Changing clothes while holding the charm was awkward, but the thought of showing her underwear to the people in the bar made her do it. At first, she tried putting on the jumpsuit over her regular clothing—armor often went *over* clothes, after all—but it wasn't loose enough in the shoulders or hips to manage that.

As she lowered her buckskins, she realized she had nowhere to put her clothes. She'd carried the jumpsuit from Imoshaun's workshop, but would a tattoo artist find it odd if she wandered in holding pants and a shirt? The pavement was damp from a recent rain, with litter scattered about, so she didn't want to set them on the ground.

"Will you carry these, too, please?"

When Starblade looked over, Arwen lobbed her clothes, hoping he wasn't startled by having them appear out of the ether and sail at him.

He caught them without comment and draped them over his arm, but his head swiveled toward the cloudy night sky. "Yendral comes."

Since she was half-naked, that alarmed Arwen until she remembered he wouldn't be able to see her either. "Not with a dragon body floating along behind him, I hope."

"That is unlikely." Starblade watched as the silver dragon flew into view, angling toward the parking lot.

Yendral shifted form before he reached the ground and landed in a crouch in his elven form. He smiled, gripped Starblade's forearm, gave the toilet paper roll and weapons a puzzled look, then looked around the parking lot. "You have permitted our new female to wander off?"

Well, that reaffirmed that he couldn't see her.

"*We* do not have a new female," Starblade stated.

"Ah, yes. You have no interest in mating with anyone on this wild world." Yendral shook his head. "Such a strange commander I have. As refugees being hunted, we have so few joys left, and she defended us against that dolt Darvanylar. An unexpected delight. Before, it was only her food that interested me, but *now...* Aren't you in love with her?"

Arwen, one foot through the leg of the jumpsuit, almost fell over.

"No," Starblade stated. "And neither are you. Also, she is present, hidden by camouflage."

"Oh? You are playing a game in which you must find her?" For the first time, Yendral noticed the clothes in his arms. His lips twitched as his eyes gleamed with amusement. "Are you playing a game in which you must find her *naked*?"

"I do not remember you being this juvenile when we fought in battle together."

"The stasis chamber must have addled your memory. I always sought to enjoy the small freedoms we were permitted between campaigns."

"Juvenilely," Starblade stated.

"Naturally. We're not *that* old. Not by elven standards and certainly not by dragon standards."

"I do not feel that young."

"The weight of command and your inability to relax and have fun are prematurely aging you. You're lucky your black hair hasn't turned gray." His eyes gleamed again as he looked around and raised his voice to say, "You're also lucky you don't need the benefits of the tea that our new female left."

Startled, Arwen fumbled and dropped the charm. It clanked several feet, and both half-dragons looked over at her. Yendral's lips quirked with amusement.

Pants half-pulled up, Arwen hopped over, grabbed the charm, and activated it again. As if they hadn't already seen her.

She rubbed her face in embarrassment, less at being seen half-naked and more because Yendral's comments reminded her of how she'd informed Starblade of all the benefits from her honey-lemon-herb tea. Had he *shared* that information with Yendral? She winced as she imagined them laughing as he recounted how she'd invaded his home to snoop, then tried to win his friendship with food. And herbal tea.

"Her name is Arwen," Starblade said, looking back at Yendral, "though you're odious enough that she won't invite you to use it. I do not know why I sought so hard to free you from the dark elves."

"Because of my inherent appeal and the utter loneliness you felt when I was gone."

"I do not recall mentioning loneliness. You brought news? Or to report on the disposal of Darvanylar?"

"He's been suitably taken care of. I *did* run into someone who had interesting information." Yendral glanced toward where he'd seen Arwen, then must have shifted to telepathy.

As much as he supposedly loved her, he wouldn't speak of some things in front of her.

Starblade nodded, presumably responding in kind.

As she finished pulling on the jumpsuit, Arwen told herself it didn't mean they didn't trust her just because they wanted to speak in private.

Strange company you keep, an unfamiliar male voice spoke into Arwen's mind in Dark Elven. No, it *was* familiar. It was the same person who'd spoken to her outside the other tattoo parlor.

She scanned the area with her senses. Little had changed. The shifters, half-troll, and a few other magical beings were in the back of the strip mall. She couldn't detect anyone with dark-elven blood and wished she'd asked Imoshaun for one of her devices. Though if it would have gone off constantly because of *her* blood, it wouldn't have been helpful.

Who are you? Arwen risked asking.

You don't remember me? Harlik-van?

The name didn't stir up any memories.

I suppose I wasn't the facet in your life that She Who Leads was.

Arwen swallowed. That was the name the dark elves had given her mother when the demons had supposedly chosen her to be head of the clan and represent them.

The voice hadn't been warm to start with, but it turned icy when he added, *Did you also not remember Zyretha? I saw her decapitated body. There was also an arrow hole in her heart.*

The male dark elf is speaking to me, Arwen thought to Starblade, attempting to make her telepathic words pinpoint for him alone.

She didn't think the dark elf—Harlik-van—was that close, but it was hard to tell when he was camouflaged. He had to be close enough, however, that he'd seen her arrive and knew roughly where she was, or his words might not have reached her.

I have not sensed a dark elf in the area, Starblade replied without looking toward her.

Nor have I, but he's speaking to me, and I don't think he's pleased with me.

I thought you didn't seek to please *your mother's people.*

No, I don't, but I mean, I think he knows what happened in their lair.

We killed all the dark elves who were present.

Not we, *he.* Oh, she'd shot Zyretha, but he'd annihilated the rest before Zavryd and Val reached the basement lair. This Harlik-van wouldn't care though. He clearly believed Arwen had been involved.

You will not *remove your tattoo,* Harlik-van stated. *She Who Leads does not wish it.*

It made Arwen uneasy that he—and her mother?—knew what she was up to. Was the tattoo itself spying on her somehow? And reporting her errands? Even if it had shared that she'd been at the troll's parlor, how could her mother have sent a minion to reach her so quickly? And he'd had time to hire those orcs. How? Had they simply been in the area and available for gigs?

I am indifferent to the lives of half-bloods and trolls, Harlik-van said. *Should you attempt again to have it removed, I will kill the owner of that parlor, even though it is unlikely he would be able to remove our magic. It is not a simple matter, certainly not something a book could advise on.*

If that's true, why did you steal the books in the other shop? Arwen asked him, even as she told Starblade the dark elf was threatening to kill the shop owner.

We will lay a trap and catch and slay him, Starblade told her. *Yendral and I will camouflage ourselves while you approach the shop alone. If he attacks, we will spring out at him.*

As much as I love being bait, that wouldn't work. He knows you're ten feet away from me. He said I keep strange company.

Demon-worshipping vermin called us *strange?* Starblade shot a scathing look around the parking lot.

Sorry.

Starblade nodded slightly to Yendral.

"Our female hid herself quickly instead of allowing us to gaze upon her," Yendral said aloud. "Did you offend her? Perhaps she is taking advantage of having a charm to flee your boorish company."

"She is not," Starblade said aloud while speaking telepathically to Arwen. *You are correct. In order to convincingly perpetrate this ruse, we may need to open a portal and blatantly leave. We would have to travel to another world before returning to this one, then come out in a location far enough away that a dark elf would not sense our arrival. Then we could camouflage ourselves and fly back here.* Out loud, he added, "My company is refined and exquisite."

"Oh? Did you speak to her of your engine project and show her the grease on your hands?"

"No." Starblade whirled toward the east, his eyes scouring the sky.

Arwen looked but didn't sense anything. Harlik-van hadn't answered her last question. Because he was busy creeping close to attack her?

No, he wouldn't dare with two half-dragons next to her. Maybe he hadn't answered because he'd been lying, and he didn't want her to figure that out. Maybe the recipe in her pocket *could* do something—if she could find the rest of it.

Who are you? Arwen asked again.

I have given my name.

Yes, but why would I have known you?

I am someone who does what the family requests. I am not ungrateful or tainted by the daylight denizens of this magic-bereft world.

"A dragon comes," Starblade said. "I knew it wasn't safe for us here."

Arwen couldn't sense a dragon and didn't know if this was part of the ruse he'd suggested or if he, with his greater range, had detected one.

Yendral also looked to the east as he dropped into a fighting crouch. "We shouldn't have gotten involved in the female's affairs. Such a mongrel is beneath our kind."

"Yes," Starblade said coolly, tossing down Arwen's weapons and clothing. "The dark-elf blood makes her unappealing."

"The dragons she keeps leading to us make her *especially* unappealing."

For a stung moment, Arwen didn't know what to do or think. But when Starblade lifted an arm and magic swelled, a portal forming, she realized they were trying to fool Harlik-van, to make him believe they were leaving. She *hoped* they hadn't decided she was beneath them.

Stay hidden, and take no risk for fifteen minutes, Starblade spoke into her mind as he and Yendral jogged toward the portal. *We will return.*

They disappeared, leaving Arwen alone in the parking lot. She was tempted to ask more questions of Harlik-van, to try to learn more about who he was, but if she continued to speak, he might be able to use her telepathic voice to triangulate her position.

A chill went through her as she worried that he might *already* have done that. If he'd been lying and had come to kill her, he might have a weapon aimed at her.

Careful to move silently, Arwen crept forward and grabbed her clothing, bow, and quiver so they would disappear along with her, then moved a couple dozen yards down the parking lot.

A female scream came from the back of the building. Her heart sank as she realized she'd worried about the wrong target.

When a second scream sounded, she sprinted toward the alley. She couldn't wait for fifteen minutes.

20

AWARE THAT RAPID MOVEMENT COULD BREAK HER CAMOUFLAGING magic, Arwen changed from sprinting to jogging around the strip mall. Until another scream ripped through the night, followed by shouts.

A door slammed open as she reached the back alley, another neon sign reading Mark's Marks over it. Two mixed-bloods ran out, glancing over their shoulders as they went. They sprinted down the alley in the opposite direction from Arwen.

She still didn't see or sense the dark elf but worried he was attacking the tattoo artist.

The door banged open again as she reached it, and a bare-chested ogre with tattoos on his pecs almost crashed into her. Close enough to see through her charm's magic, he halted on the threshold and lifted a hand, as if to shove her aside. He paused as his eyes widened—because he recognized her heritage? He backpedaled, tripped over a tattoo chair, and landed on his back.

A roar filled the room as a wolf leaped at a female half-orc with her jeans around her ankles. She threw a tattoo gun at her gray-furred attacker as she tried to leap aside.

Something else hurtled toward Arwen, and she ducked. A bucket hit the doorframe before bouncing to the pavement behind her.

Opposite the wolf—the *werewolf*—and half-orc, two human women alternated clawing at each other with throwing punches. Blood dripped from a deep scratch in one's cheek.

Arwen gaped at the chaos, not sure what to do.

Straight back from the entrance, another ogre pounded at a metal door with a sign that read *office*.

"Go away!" a man shouted from inside.

The ogre grabbed the knob, yanked, and ripped the door off the hinges.

A long stream of swearing in the Elven language came out of the office as the ogre flung the broken door toward a tattoo table. A gun fired from within, but that didn't keep him from stomping through the doorway. A crash and more shouts in Elven followed.

Bow in hand, Arwen looked around the parlor, trying to figure out what was going on. Only when she glimpsed the glazed blue eyes of the werewolf did she realize someone was using a magical compulsion to control these people. Harlik-van?

"Who else?" Realizing she might be vulnerable in the doorway, Arwen eased inside and put her back against the wall.

She rubbed her charm again in case its magic had faded, but in the small parlor, half the people would be able to see through it anyway. Not that they were looking at her. The fighting human women tumbled past, gripping each other's shoulders as they fell to the floor, wrestling and thrashing.

More gunshots fired, followed by the clang of metal.

Arwen picked her way past the women and headed for the office, guessing the half-troll she needed was inside and being threatened by the ogre. Though Elven curses were what kept flying out, and she sensed... Ah, was the tattoo artist's other half elven?

An utter scream of pain came from the female half-orc. The werewolf's jaws were wrapped around her shoulder.

Arwen lifted her bow, tempted to come to the half-orc's defense, especially since she looked like a human not that different from her, but the wolf's blue eyes remained glazed as he bit down. All of these people were fighting because of the compulsion, not because they wanted to.

Arwen spotted binders of tattoo designs on a table and threw one at the werewolf. It wasn't the deadly deterrent that an arrow would have been, but it struck the wolf between the shoulder blades.

He released the half-orc and whirled toward Arwen. Shoulder bleeding, the woman managed to yank up her jeans, half a tattoo on her butt visible, and staggered toward the doorway.

"Thanks," she yelled at Arwen.

Unfortunately, the glazy-eyed wolf didn't appear as grateful. He leaped onto a table and sprang for Arwen.

With another table at her back, the fighting women to her side, and the ogre in the office, Arwen didn't have room to dodge. She loosed an arrow, aiming for the wolf's shoulder instead of chest, then ducked.

A yip of pain assaulted her ears as the arrow landed, sinking deep. The wolf sailed over her head, his attack faltering, and crashed into a wall decorated with guitars. Several tumbled to the floor with him, strings twanging in protest.

Arwen scrambled through the doorway and almost tripped over a huge body. The ogre was sprawled on the floor.

"One of *you*," came a snarl in accented English.

The half-troll, green-skinned and shirtless but with pointed ears and blond hair, pointed a huge revolver at her.

"Dark-elf bitch!" His finger tightened on the trigger.

Arwen dove over the ogre, hoping to reach an upturned table for cover, but she wasn't fast enough. The bullet thudded into her shoulder. She felt the jolting thump, but, surprisingly, it didn't stab her with the agony she expected. Thanks to the armored jumpsuit?

In the limited space, she couldn't roll to lessen the impact of the landing, but the magic in the jumpsuit must have protected her, because it again didn't hurt as much as it should have.

"I'm not with them." Arwen stayed low behind the upturned table. She didn't have any armor to protect her head, and she didn't want to shoot the guy she'd come to see. "I came to warn you that there's a dark-elf out there who's killing tattoo artists, and he's after you."

"I think *you're* after me, mongrel dark elf, loyal servant of their kind." The gun fired, bullets thudding into the table. One splintered and went through, skimming past Arwen's side, the armor deflecting it. "You killed Inker."

"I didn't. I—"

A roar came from the doorway as the werewolf sprang through it and landed on the unmoving ogre's chest. The *dead* ogre's chest? Arwen's arrow protruded from the werewolf's shoulder, but it didn't slow him down.

Crouching awkwardly behind the table, she nocked another arrow, this time grabbing Tangler, the one enchanted to do more damage to shifters. She feared she would have to aim for a more vital target to stop the werewolf. She also feared the half-troll would shoot her while she dealt with the other threat.

The werewolf didn't leap toward her but toward the tattoo artist.

Cursing again, he fired three more times, bullets thudding into the werewolf's chest. Eyes glazed, his lupine assailant snapped his jaws, barely reacting to the wounds. Coming from a mundane weapon, they weren't enough to kill him, not right away, not with the compulsion controlling him.

Arwen sprang up and fired Tangler.

Even as the wolf snapped his jaws at the half-troll's throat, her arrow slammed into the back of his skull. Bone crunched as it sank deep.

The wolf's jaws didn't reach their target. As the half-troll dodged to the side, his attacker crashed into a wall. Framed art tumbled down, landing atop the wolf as he slumped to the floor.

Arwen shook her head, knowing that had been a killing blow. But what choice had she been given?

Nocking another arrow, she faced the half-troll, but she didn't aim the weapon at him.

He'd landed in a crouch and looked from the downed were-wolf to his gun to her. He glanced at a desk with a box of ammo open on the top, but he eyed her bow and didn't reach for it.

"You say you're here to warn me?"

"Yes," Arwen said as the fighting women out front crashed into furniture and knocked down something that shattered. "If you're in charge—the one who does magical tattoos."

"That's me. I'm Mark."

Arwen blinked at the common human name on someone with pointed ears and green skin.

"Originally Markyseel from Veleshna Var and other parts." He waved vaguely.

"Well, I'm not with the dark elves. I came to see you."

"Because... you want a tattoo?" He eyed her arm, though the loose sleeve hadn't fallen enough to show the spider. He had the strong aura of one gifted with magic and doubtless sensed it.

"I want a tattoo removed. That's why I went to see Star Inker, too, but then he was killed. I *didn't* do it." Arwen hesitated, torn between wanting to be honest and not wanting to admit that he'd been killed because of her.

"Who's responsible for tearing up my shop and killing my

customers?" Mark frowned at the ogre and the wolf. "Ten minutes ago, we were inking these guys' asses."

Literally, Arwen thought, remembering the half-orc woman in jeans who'd fled. "A dark elf, I think. At least one."

She *hoped* there was only one, but it sounded like Harlik-van was on a mission for her mother, who still led her clan, so he might have a lot of allies, all hidden by magic, out there.

"Those bastards. I'll—" Glass shattered—a window breaking. Mark cursed and picked up a short sword on the floor.

"Be careful," Arwen urged as more glass broke. "The dark elf is still out there."

"I'm not letting him bust up the rest of my shop." Sword in hand, Mark strode over the ogre and toward the front door.

Hoping if she stuck with him, Harlik-van wouldn't attack, Arwen followed with her bow drawn.

Numerous people had shown up in the alley outside, many carrying long sticks. One struck another window, breaking more glass.

Snarling, Mark leaped through the doorway to confront the vandals.

Not vandals, Arwen corrected as she stepped into the alley behind him. More than a dozen glazy-eyed humans had converged on the parlor, wielding pool sticks.

She kept her bow down, not wanting to hurt them. Mark sprang into their midst, slicing his sword through the sticks. At least he didn't aim for more vital targets.

Arwen peered up and down the alley. She had to find Harlik-van. Until she stopped him, people under magical compulsion would keep attacking. Why the dark elf was using others to do his dirty work instead of attacking himself, Arwen didn't know, but *he* was the one she needed to deal with. Especially if all this was happening as a result of her quest to remove her tattoo. How many would be killed because of her desire?

Since none of the pool-hall humans were armed with anything deadlier than the sticks, she risked moving down the alley away from Mark and the chaos. She still couldn't sense Harlik-van, but if he'd been by here more than once recently, maybe she had a shot at tracking him.

At the end of the alley, Arwen crouched and rested a hand on the grimy pavement. It didn't hold tracks, nor were there any nearby trees she could appeal to for information on passersby, but this was an emergency, so she reluctantly called upon her soul-tracking ability.

First, she camouflaged herself, though she doubted the charm would keep her hidden when she was using power. Then she checked on Mark, to make sure nobody more dangerous than the humans was targeting him. Finally, calling upon the magic of her mother's people, Arwen siphoned her power into the pavement and the alley walls, hoping to find traces left by the dark elf's soul.

Since this wasn't his home or anywhere he'd likely spent a great deal of time that day, it wasn't as simple as tracking Imoshaun's essence in her workshop had been. As Arwen's eyesight shifted slightly, letting her see a realm where souls were visible and left traces, she glimpsed the remains of numerous glowing prints on the ground. They were all faint, left by people who'd passed through but not lingered.

Those with more substantial auras left brighter tracks, and she saw the traces of several magical beings who'd come through recently. Everything was a tangle since this was a thoroughfare for visitors to the parlor. She detected Mark's soul traces most prominently, then an ogre, the shifters, and she even sensed traces of Starblade's essence, though he had only flown over the alley.

Finally, she picked up very faint tracks close to a cement wall. Was that hint of malignance to them her imagination? Her gut told her they belonged to the dark elf.

They led away from the alley, and she looked back toward

Mark again, afraid to leave him. Harlik-van had said he would kill the tattoo artist. If she moved away, he might take advantage and do it while she was hunting him.

These tracks had been left hours ago. By now, Harlik-van could be anywhere. He might be crouching on the roof and watching the chaos he'd created.

Mark landed a punch that sent one of the humans tumbling away, a pool stick flying from his hand. As a couple more men came at him, he backed into the doorway of his shop.

Starblade? Arwen called softly with telepathy, imagining his face and hoping Harlik-van wouldn't catch the words. *Are you back yet?*

She didn't know if fifteen minutes had passed. It had to be close.

Arwen resolved to wait and track Harlik-van when Starblade returned, but then she sensed the dark elf out front. Only for a second, as if he'd accidentally dropped his camouflage while he activated some other magic, and then he disappeared again. But she knew where he was.

Grabbing the dark-elf arrow Imoshaun had made for her, Arwen nocked it and jogged toward the parking lot, hoping her camouflage wouldn't drop.

When she rounded the corner, she spotted someone on the ground on her back. The half-orc woman she'd helped in the parlor. Her legs twitched as she lay dying, her throat slit.

Damn it, Harlik-van had *just* done that.

Arwen ran toward the woman, but she gave one final twitch, then lay still. It was too late to help her.

Furious with Harlik-van, Arwen scanned the ground, calling upon her magic again. There ought to be *fresh* tracks now.

Yes, the same malignant prints, brighter now, led her back around the strip mall toward the alley from the opposite end. She swore under her breath. Harlik-van was circling back toward Mark.

Abandoning stealth, Arwen ran after the tracks, afraid she had only seconds to save him.

21

BEFORE ARWEN ROUNDED THE BUILDING, SHE SENSED HARLIK-VAN on the roof and jerked to a halt. She'd been certain he was going for Mark in the alley, where the blows and shouts from his battle with the pool players continued. But maybe the dark elf intended to shoot him from above?

Making sure her camouflage was active, Arwen put her bow on her back and hurried to the side of the building. She sprang toward a lamp mounted on the wall, caught it, and swung herself up to the roof. As she twisted in the air and landed on her feet, an orc registered on her senses. Someone else with camouflaging magic.

From five feet away, he charged her. Arwen didn't have time to pull her bow off her back—she barely had an opportunity to dodge, but she managed to skitter aside and bring her knee up. The orc must have thought he would catch her by surprise because her counterattack startled him. He didn't get a defense in place, and her knee slammed into his side. When he stumbled, Arwen twisted, hooking his leg with hers, and pulled him further off balance.

It wasn't enough to topple the orc, but he flailed and tottered. That gave her time to yank her bow off her back and swing it like a staff. He flung his arm up but too late, and she struck him on the side of the head. Too bad the weapon didn't have enough heft to crack a thick orc skull.

Her opponent stepped back and pulled a dagger, but he glanced to the side before attacking. Another orc, a burly female with spiked green hair and a black leather jacket, sprang at Arwen with a sword.

She backpedaled away from both of them and darted across the roof while nocking an arrow.

"Get her!" one orc barked in English.

With space between them, Arwen whirled back and took aim. The female charged after her, sword raised.

Arwen released her arrow, and it pierced the orc's thigh. She screeched in pain and anger, stumbling to a stop.

Not hesitating, Arwen fired at the other orc. After her arrow flew away, she glanced around, expecting to find Harlik-van on the roof, but she no longer sensed him.

Had she sensed him at all? Or had he somehow tricked her to make her believe he was up there?

Her arrow struck the male orc in the shoulder, spinning him around. Cursing, he dropped his dagger.

Still shrieking, the female yanked the arrow in her thigh free. She flung it at the roof, then threw her sword at Arwen as if it were a hatchet.

Arwen ducked aside only to almost crash into a third camouflaged orc. Were these the same mercenaries who'd attacked the other tattoo parlor?

A male with painted tusks and wild white braids, the orc swung a spiked club at her head. She ducked again, feeling the turbulence as it swept over her head, and jabbed the tip of her bow into his gut.

When the orc yanked his club down to protect himself, she leaped out of the way, then back in, landing a kick to the side of his shin. His knee buckled, and she whipped her bow at his head.

Footfalls sounded over the chaos in the alley as the other orcs ran closer. Second-guessing herself for not aiming at lethal targets, Arwen dove to the side and rolled away.

As she jumped to her feet, an explosion roared in the alley, fire blasting away the night dimness. The rooftop shook, and two of the orcs pitched over.

Arwen kept her balance, but realizing she might have failed rocked her as much as the explosion. After cracking the closest orc on the head one more time, she ran to the edge of the roof.

In the alley, the fire continued to roar, magic fueling it, making the flames seethe and writhe. That had been more than a grenade or bomb.

Squinting against the intense light, she peered into the flames. They burned for several yards in all directions in front of the parlor's doorway. The neon Mark's Marks sign shattered and went out.

Movement at the entrance to the alley drew her eye, and she spotted the hooded dark elf. Harlik-van pumped his arm three times, throwing projectiles. Metal glinted, reflecting the orange of the flames.

"Look out," Arwen yelled in case Mark somehow lived in the inferno.

She grabbed her special dark-elf arrow and fired at Harlik-van. He sprang to the side, but her arrow grazed his shoulder just before he reestablished his camouflaging magic and disappeared from her sight. She'd intended to shoot the murderer in the chest, but he was fast. Unfortunately.

You would harm your own kin? Harlik-van asked indignantly into her mind. *When I have not harmed you?*

You're not my kin. Arwen fired again, but now that he was invisible, it would have been dumb luck if she hit him.

Oh, I am.

You sicced the orc gang after me!

They have not harmed you. I'm only here to ensure you do not leave the clan.

I left the clan more than twenty years ago.

He laughed into her mind. *You have never left, and you never will. You'll take your place serving She Who Leads, as I have.*

Her tattoo itched.

Arwen glowered at it and shot again, but her arrow only skipped off empty pavement before landing near the other in the street.

Below, the flames slowly died down. Arwen braced herself, expecting to see a dozen charred bodies, but she sensed an aura she knew in the middle of the dwindling fire. Starblade?

Either he'd been camouflaged to hide from Harlik-van, or the great magical fire had been enough to drown out his presence.

Movement to Arwen's right made her whirl toward the roof with her bow raised. But the injured orcs shambled away instead of taking advantage of her distraction. They leaped or swung down from the roof on the far side.

That dark elf is well-defended and excellent at hiding, Starblade spoke calmly into her mind. *He also has a plethora of dangerous weapons.*

He murdered people.

It is what their kind do.

When Arwen peeked over the edge again, the flames had fully disappeared. The walls on both sides of the alley were charred, but she didn't see the horde of dead that she'd expected.

Starblade stood calmly in his elven form, gripping Mark by the upper arm and holding the half-troll's sword with the other. Starblade's magical barrier wrapped around them, and neither was singed, so it must have saved Mark from the heat of the fire.

Three magical projectiles had partially pierced the translucent barrier, however, and hung embedded, as if they'd struck a log. Throwing stars. The placement of two of them indicated they would have hit Mark in the chest or even face if not for Starblade's protection. The tattoo artist must have recognized that because he was alternately gaping at the throwing stars and at Starblade. He also glanced up at Arwen.

She shimmied down from the roof, broken window glass crunching under her moccasins. Glancing through the parlor's doorway reminded her that not everyone had gotten away. The ogre, the shifter, and that woman out front... They'd all died tonight because a damn dark elf who thought she was his *kin* hadn't wanted her to get her tattoo removed. No, because her *mother* hadn't wanted it. She had no trouble believing Harlik-van had spoken the truth about that.

You did not wait the fifteen minutes that I suggested before engaging in battle. Starblade frowned at her.

It was an order, not a suggestion, wasn't it?

Perhaps, which makes it all the more egregious that you disobeyed.

I'm not one of your troops, remember, but I couldn't wait because he attacked people. Arwen didn't go into more detail, feeling chagrined that Harlik-van had lured her into his trap. If Starblade hadn't returned in time, Mark would be dead as well.

Starblade released the half-troll. "My associate is in need of your services."

"Uh." Mark rubbed a hand over his face. "I'm a little shaky right now, but if you let me brace myself with a few shots of whiskey, I could probably find my artistic touch."

"She needs a tattoo removed, not placed."

Mark looked curiously at Arwen.

Though her instincts were always to hide the damning spider mark, she pushed up her sleeve.

Mark eyed it and then her face. "You *sure* you're not with them?"

"She is with *me*," Starblade said.

"Don't take this the wrong way, but I don't know who the hell *you* are."

"Clearly, not a dark elf, and I protected you from certain death."

"Yeah, I got that." Mark rubbed his face again. Sweat gleamed on his bare tattooed chest. "And I do appreciate it." He nodded at Arwen as well as Starblade. "I'll be happy to give you a freebie, but removing magical tattoos, especially *dark-elf* magical tattoos, isn't easy."

"I have part of a recipe torn from a book that I think references removing them," Arwen said. "Do you want to see it?"

"I guess, but *part* of a recipe isn't that helpful. And the ones I've heard about for making magic-diluting ink involve a lot of hard-to-find ingredients and the talents of an alchemist. Unless you've got the ink, I wouldn't be able to do anything."

"But if we found the ingredients and had an alchemist make the ink," Starblade said, "you *would* be able to accomplish this task?"

"I've removed magical dwarven tattoos before. And trollish ones. I might be able to do a dark-elf tattoo if someone lent me extra power for the job."

"I can funnel power into you."

"You do have plenty." Mark eyed him. "But you're not a dragon, are you? You seem kind of like it, but..."

"I am half dragon."

"That's not supposed to be possible."

"Yet I am here." Starblade nodded to Arwen. "Show him the recipe."

"Is that an order or a suggestion?" she murmured, but she did remove the torn page from her pocket.

"An instruction that would be wise to heed."

Mark stepped into his parlor, grimacing at all the broken glass and upturned tables—not to mention the *bodies*—and considered the page under the light.

As he read, Arwen wondered if she should call Willard. This had been a crime against beings in the magical community, and the colonel didn't typically get involved unless magical beings committed crimes against humans, but she might make an exception for this. Also, Arwen felt she ought to confess that she'd inadvertently played a role in the carnage rather than waiting for word to get back to Willard.

"You're right. This is only part of a recipe." Mark pointed to the air where the ripped portion of the page would have been. "I'm positive there are more ingredients on the other half."

"I know," Arwen said. "The rest of the book, and presumably that page, disappeared."

Into Harlik-van's hands.

"That'll make things tough on the alchemist," Mark said. "Can you bake a cake with half a recipe?"

"I am quite familiar with typical cake recipes and could likely guess the missing ingredients, yes."

That earned her a sour look. "This isn't a *typical* recipe. If you find the other half, get all the ingredients, and have the magic-diluting ink made, I may be able to assist you. If I can be certain it won't get more dark elves pissed at me."

"Your aura is insignificant, your power scant," Starblade stated. "It is unlikely they care about you."

Mark blinked, then faced him, his shoulders bunching. "My *aura* is fine. And they cared enough to try to take me out tonight. Me and my poor shop." Mark jerked his arm out to indicate the trashed parlor. "Some jealous rival must have hired them."

Arwen was tempted to let him believe his hypothesis, but her integrity wouldn't let her. "It's my fault that you were attacked. The dark elves don't want me to remove my tattoo."

Mark scowled, frowned at her arm, and then glowered at the floor. Arwen worried he would rescind his offer to assist her. She couldn't blame him, but who else could she go to? Should she even pursue the quest now that her mother's stooge was keeping tabs on her? She badly wanted the tattoo—and the dark elves' ability to control her through it—gone but not at the cost of more lives.

"They want to keep you in the clan?" Mark asked.

"Yes. I fled a long time ago, when I was a little girl, but they have some use for me now and want me to work for them."

"With those wicked bow skills?" Mark nodded at her weapon. "I, and the rest of the vulnerable-to-magical-arrows world, would prefer you *not* work for them."

Starblade squinted at him.

"I don't want to," Arwen said. "I promise."

"That they're trying to force you to pisses me off on your behalf." Mark managed a smile for her. "That they destroyed my place pisses me off on *my* behalf. If I can remove that tattoo for you, I need you to promise to shoot that bastard in the ass."

"Asses aren't what I usually target. I did shoot a dark elf in the heart not that long ago."

"*Good.*" Mark laughed shortly and handed the torn page back to her, brushing her fingers as he did so. "I wouldn't like to see you on their side."

He smiled at Arwen again.

Starblade's squint deepened. *Is this mongrel troll flirting with you?* he asked her telepathically.

I don't think so, and he's half-elven, the same as you.

He is nothing like me. His aura is weak.

A crime, no doubt.

A deficiency caused by his weak heritage.

"Let me know if you find the rest of the recipe and the ingredients. In the meantime, I'll be..." Mark looked around his shop. "Uhm. Where *will* I be?" He scratched his head. "Is that guy going to come after me again?"

"I'm afraid he might," Arwen said. "It would be a good time for you to take a vacation. I hear Aruba is warm, exotic, and sun-drenched."

Mark snorted. "My business isn't so lucrative that I can afford tropical vacations."

"Maybe Tacoma, then."

"Tacoma is *not* warm, exotic, and sun-drenched."

"But it is, the last I heard, dark-elf free," Arwen said.

"Tacoma it is." After another look around and a rueful head shake, Mark walked into his office.

Weariness seeped into Arwen as she stepped into the alley with Starblade. The battle hadn't been that exhausting, but... the deaths of the innocent? She blamed herself for them, and that would weigh on her for a long time.

"I'm sorry to keep imposing, but will you give me a ride home, Starblade?"

"Yes." He helped her collect the arrows she'd fired, then led the way back to the parking lot so he had room to shift shapes.

Seeing the woman's body again made Arwen wince. She couldn't bring herself to call Willard, but she did send a text, explaining what had happened. Not wanting to have a conversation about it, not yet, she hoped the colonel had gone to bed and wouldn't respond until morning.

Grimly, Arwen wondered if anyone else—any relative of those who'd died here tonight—would try to hire Val to kill her.

Power wrapped around her, levitating her into the air. She almost dropped her phone.

Starblade, who'd turned into his dragon form, must have gotten tired of waiting for her to type.

Where is Aruba? His magic settled her onto his back.

Arwen pocketed her phone as he launched himself into the air, wings flapping. *In the Caribbean Sea. I've never been, but I've heard of it in, uh, a song, and seen pictures.*

Dragons like warm climates.

And swimming in the ocean?

A warm *ocean, yes.*

She supposed that meant the Washington coast didn't count. People wore wetsuits to surf out there. *You'll have to check it out sometime.*

A text came in from Willard. *Send me a thorough report in the morning. No, come to my office, and give it in person.*

Arwen made herself reply with, *Okay,* but she didn't want to do either. She needed to figure out how to get Harlik-van off her back so he wouldn't hurt anyone else. But, right now, all she wanted was her bed, and she was relieved that Starblade flew straight across Bellevue and Lake Sammamish toward Carnation.

Thank you for your help tonight, Arwen told him, realizing she hadn't shared that she appreciated his assistance. He didn't owe her anything—she might have helped in some small way with Darvanylar, but she'd been the one responsible for leading that dragon to his home. It also hadn't been that long since she'd shot Starblade. *You've earned another strawberry shortcake. And that dinner Yendral wants.*

Yes.

What happened to Yendral, by the way? What did he come to tell you about?

Starblade banked and headed toward the dark rural area where the farm was located. *After he disposed of the body, he went to an establishment where shifters congregate.*

Is that wise?

Yendral does little to deserve that adjective, but he did hear something useful. It's not surprising, but it is good to be aware of. You may recall that, before we infiltrated the dark-elf lair, the tiger shifter and his allies threatened to tell dragons that I am hiding on this world.

Arwen shifted uneasily on his back. *I do.*

I'd hoped the shifter hadn't had an opportunity to do that, but he or another of his kin did. That Silverclaw dragon may have accidentally chanced across you, but he was here on Earth looking for me.

Oh, no. I'm sorry.

There will be others.

Do you think Darvanylar had a chance to tell his clan where you live? Or where he believed you lived? Based on, uhm, his mind reading of me?

I do not know, but it doesn't matter, because Yendral and I will, after assisting you, leave and find another world to hide on.

Arwen sagged on his back. He'd already said that, but she'd hoped he wouldn't have to go, that if she found his dragon relatives, they would be compelled to protect him. But maybe that was naive.

I'll miss you. She leaned forward and rested her cheek on his cool, smooth scales, the weariness she'd acknowledged earlier deepening.

You will, he agreed.

She snorted softly. *Maybe you'll miss me too.*

He landed on the roof of her cob cottage. *While you sleep, I will consider appropriate locations for a rejuvenation pool.*

Thanks. She supposed she couldn't expect him to admit that he might miss her. Maybe he would be relieved when she and her treacherous arrows were out of his life.

Starblade levitated her to the ground in front of her door, then settled on his belly, as if he meant to stay for a while. Even though he wasn't as large as a full-blooded dragon, her cob home also wasn't large, and he took up the roof space and then some. His back end and tail dangled off, and his shoulder was mashed against her chimney.

"Are you going to contemplate the location of the pool from the roof all night?"

His head shifted to hang over the side, his gaze holding hers. *Yes.*

"It's not that large a property."

Maybe he did care, the tiniest bit, and was sticking around to keep an eye out for her. Was that possible?

There are many factors to consider. You yourself said that it must be an appropriate place to grow wasabi.

"Do you have any idea what that is or where it likes to grow?" Arwen asked in amusement.

He hesitated. *Japan. It likes roots that are continuously moist but not waterlogged.*

"*I* told you that."

I deem you a reliable source.

"A pool back there would be nice." She pointed downhill from her home and beyond the pumpkin patch.

I will consider that area tonight. You will rest and not overly concern yourself with deaths that are the fault of the dark elves, not yourself.

Arwen swallowed. He'd said he couldn't read her mind when they were out of his sanctuary, but maybe he'd come to know her well enough to get the gist. For a pompous half-dragon, he wasn't that bad a guy. Too bad he would soon leave Earth forever.

22

Arwen woke to birds chirping outside, the dull light of a cloudy morning filtering through the window. The memory of a dream flitted away. Unfortunately. Starblade had been in the tattoo parlor, holding her hand and examining her spider, his touch sending tingles of pleasure up her arm as he made the loathed mark disappear.

Her body ached from hurling herself all over and being shot at —no, *shot*—the night before. It could have been a lot worse. Imoshaun's improved jumpsuit hung over a chair, and Arwen lamented that she had to return it to Amber. Would it be presumptuous to ask the gnome to make Arwen something else? Maybe if she offered to pay...

Arwen would need every advantage she could get to find and handle Harlik-van. The idea of killing someone working for her mother made her uneasy, but she couldn't let *him* keep killing people.

Her gut churned at the memory of all who'd died the night before. As Starblade had said, it *was* the dark elf's fault, but she couldn't help but feel responsible. If she hadn't been trying to remove her tattoo, Harlik-van might not have hurt anyone. Certainly not those particular people.

As she swung her legs out of bed, Arwen used her senses to check the roof for Starblade. He wasn't there. Even though she hadn't expected him to hang out on her roof all night, his absence disappointed her. Having him around was comforting. Pleasant.

Remembering that she'd seen her father's truck in the driveway the night before, she checked the rest of the property with her senses to make sure nothing inimical lurked. Not that Harlik-van would show up during daylight hours. Or that she would sense him even if he did.

Surprisingly, she sensed Starblade on the other side of the property. He seemed to be...

"In the barn?"

That puzzled her until she remembered that she'd once told him about the antique apple press in there. Maybe he'd decided to check it out. Too bad it was too early in the season for apples, so she couldn't demonstrate it.

After washing and dressing, Arwen headed outside. A few clangs drifted out of the barn, and she frowned. Starblade wasn't taking apart the press, was he? Did the Study of Manliness suggest applying tools to the equipment of female acquaintances?

As she drew closer, she heard voices. Starblade's and her father's.

"Uh." Arwen quickened her pace.

Though they'd met before—at the least, they'd been in the same area while driving off shifters—and she didn't *think* Starblade would attack or otherwise threaten her father, she couldn't help but worry. Starblade *had* magically put her father to sleep and read his mind.

Horus, the rooster, squawked from the grass beside the barn. Maybe it was Arwen's imagination, but he seemed to be squawking in Starblade's direction. He also shooed the hens out of the area.

"You're a good guard chicken, Horus," Arwen told him. "Big predators *are* a danger to your brood."

Admittedly, Starblade would be more of a danger to larger livestock. He'd mentioned the appeal of *ungulates*.

When Arwen walked through the open barn door, she almost stepped on a hydraulic pump. It was one of *many* tractor parts disassembled and spread across the cement floor. The apple press in the back of the barn appeared undisturbed. Starblade crouched opposite Father in front of Frodo's innards.

"Good morning," Arwen said when they looked at her.

She carefully set her foot down to avoid hoses and valves while wondering what had prompted the disassembly. Their permaculture farm didn't require use of the tractor often, but this would usually be a winter project.

Starblade opened his mouth, but Father only glanced up from the engine he was tinkering with and grunted at her. Starblade looked thoughtfully at him, then at Arwen, and then *he* grunted.

"If you're using my father as a role model on how to fit in as a human," Arwen told him, "he's not the most standard representative of our species."

"He seems to embody many of the attributes praised in the Study of Manliness," Starblade said.

Her father grunted again and wiped his hand on his jeans, leaving a smear of grease. Rolled-up sleeves revealed his faded tattoos and sinewy arms.

"Oh, I'm sure," Arwen said. "I didn't realize you'd changed your policy about letting strangers onto the farm, Father. Do you, ah, know what Starblade is?"

"I haven't changed any of my policies." Father spat on a bolt and cleaned it with his greasy cloth. "I was fixing to throw him off the property—"

Arwen almost choked on the idea of anyone throwing a half-dragon anywhere.

"—but he said he was *seeing* you." Father squinted at her.

"Uhm." Arwen couldn't tell if that squint conveyed disapproval, concern, or a warning. Her father hadn't forbidden her from dating, not since she'd turned eighteen, but he had always been protective of her. Instead of asking him for clarification, she looked at Starblade. "You said you don't have a romantic interest in me. *Multiple* times."

"Correct. I have, however, seen you on numerous of the previous days."

Father turned his squint on Starblade.

"He's not from around here." Arwen remembered telling her father about her mission to track Starblade and that he was a half-dragon, so she supposed he knew that, even if his human blood didn't allow him to sense such things.

"I gathered that when he suggested I replace the drivetrain with a gnomish *flikopdedorik*." Father looked to Starblade. "Did I pronounce that right?"

"You did not."

Father only grunted again and returned his attention to the engine.

"A gnomish version of your *drivetrain*—" Starblade said the unfamiliar word with care, "—would improve the equine power equivalency."

"*Horse*power."

"Yes."

Arwen scratched her jaw, not sure whether she should leave them to their project, offer to make breakfast, or see if they wanted help. *She* needed to solve her dark-elf problem, but she hadn't yet figured out how to do that.

Starblade tilted his head as he considered her. "You have removed the armored tunic and trousers."

"Yes, the jumpsuit is a loaner. I need to give it back to Amber."

"Did you not say it stopped a bullet?"

Father lifted his head, concern replacing his previously calm expression. "You were in a battle last night? And were *shot*?" He looked her up and down.

"Yes, but I'm fine." Arwen held up her hand. "And I'm figuring out how to deal with the responsible party." It irked her greatly that she hadn't managed to *deal* with Harlik-van the night before.

Father stood. "I'll get my gun and *help* you deal with the party."

"It's a dark elf."

He curled a lip but didn't appear any less resolute. "All the more reason to deal with him. Fatally."

"I think he might be... working for my mother."

"That doesn't change anything. Makes me want him dead even more."

Starblade rose. "I am assisting Arwen with this problem. I will not allow the dark elf to harm her."

Father squinted at Starblade again. "You sure you're not seeing her?"

That prompted another puzzled head tilt. "I see her presently." He extended a hand toward Arwen. "She is not employing the camouflaging charm, which *also* should not be given away."

"Returned to its rightful owner," Arwen corrected.

Her phone rang, a familiar number popping up.

"Speaking of the rightful owner," Arwen murmured and answered. "Hello, Amber."

"Hey. It's a holiday."

"Not from battling dark elves, unfortunately." Arwen wondered why Amber had called to relay that information.

"I can take you to that park if you want to look for the stash spot of those mercenaries."

Arwen had almost forgotten about her plan to do that. Now that she'd met, in a manner of speaking, the person she believed had hired them, she didn't know if tracking down the orcs mattered. It was doubtful they would know where Harlik-van was hanging out.

Though she supposed it was possible they had that information. They'd shown up to do work for him again the night before. Might they have an arrangement about meeting him for the rest of their payment?

"Actually, I would be interested in checking it out," Arwen said.

"Excellent. Do you need me to pick you up? I won't charge a higher holiday rate. Traffic won't be as bad."

"That's generous of you, but I think I can get a ride up there." Arwen looked at Starblade. "Will you take me to Edmonds?" Maybe she shouldn't have presumed that he would stick around and taxi her wherever she wished, but he did seem determined to help her solve her problem before leaving Earth. A thought that still made her glum. She wished she could dedicate this time to solving *his* problem.

"Yes." Starblade must have heard Amber's side of the conversation because he added, "I also will not charge a holiday rate."

"You haven't charged me for anything yet."

He smiled slightly. "I am tallying the number of jars of pickled fruits Yendral and I will require for our services."

Arwen almost pointed out that *Yendral* hadn't provided any services yet, other than calling her *our female*, but if he had disposed of the dead dragon, she supposed that counted. And, the night before, he'd warned Starblade about more dragons possibly coming.

"I'm short on cherries until more ripen this summer," Arwen said, "but you can have whatever you want that's in the pantry."

"I will accept that. Also more shortcakes." Starblade stepped toward the doorway. "I will retrieve your armor, which you *will* wear, and change into my dragon form."

"It's not my armor, remember?" Arwen waved the phone. "We're going to meet the person whose jumpsuit that is."

"She will wish to give it to you. I will ensure it."

"You can't threaten a sixteen-year-old. It's against the law."

Starblade opened his mouth, as if he might refute that, but glanced at her father again and only grunted before walking out.

"I'm not sure you're a good influence," Arwen told her father.

"I'm a great influence, but where are you going? If it's to face a dark elf, I want to help."

"The dark elf won't come out during the day. I'm looking for some orc mercenaries next."

Judging by his sour expression, Father wasn't tickled about her facing *them* either, but he did say, "I suppose you can handle them. Especially with that one's help." He nodded in the direction Starblade had gone.

He'd disappeared from sight, but she sensed him nearby. He was probably levitating the jumpsuit up to the driveway, which he considered his landing pad.

"Yes, he's handy."

"And he likes your food." His eyes glinted. In approval?

"Are you okay with that? We really aren't, uhm, involved."

"No? Men don't usually jump through hoops to help women they don't want to be *involved* with."

"He's assured me that's not the case."

A black tail rolled into view, flopping down on the portion of the driveway visible from inside the barn. Was that Starblade's way of saying he was ready to go?

"I'd say you could do worse, like the smarmy werewolves who sometimes hit on you at the farmers market, but I don't know." Father eyed the tail. "That's a little alarming."

"Was it alarming when he helped us deal with the shifters who were magically compelled to attack us?"

"It was alarming to *them*, I'm sure. Especially when pieces of their truck flew all over the place." Father appeared far more appreciative than alarmed himself, even if the tail earned a wary eye. "Be careful, girl." He gripped her shoulder. "Let me know if you need help."

"I will, but do me a favor and don't open the door if any strangers show up. Especially at night."

"If any strangers show up, I'll introduce them to Aragorn." That was his rifle.

"I don't think mundane weapons will do much against a dark elf with powerful magic. Better to hide."

"Will *you* hide?"

"I... don't think I have that luxury."

23

Starblade didn't object when Arwen tucked the armored jumpsuit into a pack with a few jars from the pantry instead of donning it for the ride. His powerful wings flapped majestically, flying them north of Lake Washington on the way to Edmonds and Amber's house overlooking Puget Sound.

The newly armored garment is most appropriate for you, Starblade said telepathically.

"Because it stops bullets, I know." Arwen rested her hands on his scales as they flew, his muscles rippling with each wingbeat. She found him most appealing in his handsome elven form, but he made a beautiful dragon too.

It also has a striking sheen and accentuates your form.

Arwen blinked. Was that an indication that he'd *noticed* her form? And... appreciated it?

Yendral mentioned it, Starblade added.

Did he? Maybe I should ask him on a date.

You will not. It sounded like an order rather than a foretelling of the future.

Why not? A couple of days ago, you mentioned he might be available if I wanted to, uh, mate with a half-dragon.

Oh, he is very available. Starblade's telepathic words radiated disapproval. *To many.*

Even a mongrel that nobody else wants.

Maybe not *nobody,* she amended silently, not wanting him to think she felt sorry for herself or was fishing for compliments. Just few who wanted romance and a relationship. Most with magical blood avoided her altogether. Though some, as her father had brought up, came up to her at the farmers market to hit on her. They usually said something to imply they wanted to know what it was like to *bag* someone with dark-elven blood. Regular humans weren't as bad, since they knew nothing about her blood, but one who'd glimpsed her tattoo had drawn back in horror, his expression changing from interest to the certainty that she was a freak.

I have observed that many other males have interest. Not only Yendral. Starblade's tone still held disapproval. *The half-troll artist desired you.*

He told you that?

His mind was simple to read. Despite having elven blood, he was not trained to mask his thoughts.

Oh. He was kind of handsome. Arwen hadn't been thinking of romance or sexual interest, but the half-troll had been nicely put together. Since so many considered her strange, she wouldn't automatically rule out a mate whose skin had a green tint.

He was not, Starblade stated.

You don't think so, huh?

No.

He angled downward to take them in for a landing, opting to alight on the roof of Amber's house instead of in the street. Arwen hoped there weren't many in the neighborhood with magical blood who would spot him and be alarmed.

Amber sat at a table on the back patio, reading on her phone and enjoying the sun that peeked through the clouds. *She* had no trouble seeing him. Her mouth gaped open.

"We have an HOA," she called up to the rooftop.

Arwen had heard of homeowners associations, though her rural neighborhood had nothing of the kind, but didn't understand the statement. "Are... dragons not allowed?"

"No roof ornamentation of any kind. Not even at Halloween."

This is the female you will give bulletproof *gnomish armor to?* A displeased rumble—or was that a *growl*—reverberated through Starblade.

I'm going to return what's rightfully hers.

Offer to give her the coin the garment was worth before it was enhanced.

Are you upset that I'll lose its protective qualities or that Yendral *won't be able to admire it accentuating my form?*

Another growl reverberated through Starblade. That was the only answer he gave, instead levitating Arwen into the backyard.

"At least he didn't destroy our mailbox. Apparently, mailboxes in Val's neighborhood go up and down like clown heads in a carnival booth. The property values on that street have plummeted. And that was *before* the goblins moved in." Amber wrinkled her nose in distaste.

"Maybe those who live there appreciate the lesser taxes that come from lower property values."

"I doubt it."

"Thanks for agreeing to show me the park." Arwen could have found it on her own, but the need to return Amber's jumpsuit had compelled her to come here first. Besides, the park was close. She reached into her pack. "I think I mentioned this was ripped and bloodstained and that I didn't know if I'd be able to get it back to you."

"You mentioned that you *lost* my cute little briefcase completely."

"Yes, I'm sorry about that. But a friend was able to repair and magically enhance the jumpsuit." Arwen shook it out and held it up. "The bloodstains are gone, and so is the rip." She didn't mention that the blood had been used to make dark-elf detectors.

Amber stood up, horror blossoming on her face. "What *happened* to it? It's *glittering.*"

"It's armored now. I wore it last night, and it stopped a bullet."

Amber gripped the edge of the table. For support? "Arwen, clothes are supposed to make you look hot or professional or support you in sports, not stop bullets. What is *wrong* with your life?"

"You've asked that before."

"Because your previous answer wasn't acceptable. Why are people *shooting* at you all the time? You're not an assassin, like Val. You make *pies.*" Amber's horrified expression for the jumpsuit turned to an affronted one for Arwen, as if she was offended on her behalf.

Arwen grimaced, reminded of the beings she had shot the night before. She hadn't *wanted* to be an assassin, but was she any different from one? It had been self-defense, not for money, but the end result was the same.

"I don't know what... *tailor* you took that to—" Amber pointed at the jumpsuit, "—but it looks like the outfit of a magician's assistant now. Is your dragon going to saw you in half?" She looked up at the roof.

Unconcerned by the regulations of the homeowners' association, Starblade not only remained on the roof, but he'd settled onto his belly in a sunny spot, his tail dangling over a gutter and in front of a window.

"No," Arwen said. "He's keeping other people from sawing me in half. And less desirable things."

Amber gave her a you're-so-weird look but only said, "I guess that's one good thing. Dragons are usually—"

Starblade lowered his head over the roof to pin her with his violet eyes. They flared briefly.

Amber might have been about to voice something like *pains in the ass*, but she finished with, "—aloof."

"He's very helpful," Arwen said. "And he likes the new version of the jumpsuit."

"Then I'm going to be super magnanimous and gift it to you." Amber had already stuck her hands behind her back, refusing to accept it.

Maybe Arwen should have been chagrined that she'd allowed the outfit to be altered in a way that Amber didn't like, but... she was delighted. She would gleefully wear tinsel and sequins if it meant her torso was bulletproof.

"Thank you. Can I give you something in return?" Arwen smiled. "Pies?"

"*Obviously.* I'm distressed you didn't bring a couple over this morning." Amber looked hopefully up at Starblade, as if he might be wearing the dragon equivalent of a bicycle basket stuffed with pastries.

"Life has been fraught since my last pie delivery, and I haven't had time to make more, but I can add you to my list." With all that she needed to bake after her life settled down, Arwen would be in the kitchen until Christmas. Maybe Easter.

"Deal. I'll get my keys. Do you want a ride to the park?"

"How much will it cost me?"

"It's five minutes away. I'll throw it in for free, though if you want me to wait while you track bad guys, the meter goes on."

You prefer to ride in the conveyance of that one instead of with me? Starblade asked.

No, but she knows the area better than I do. And you look pretty comfortable up there. Do you want to tan yourself a little longer?

Dragons do not tan. They do, however, crave sun, especially on the

chillier of the wild worlds. And in climates where it rains a great deal.
He gave the remaining clouds in the sky a baleful look.

"Is, uh, your friend coming?" Amber asked.

"I don't think a dragon will fit in your vehicle."

"I know *that*, but can't he change?" Amber made the same
circle in the air with her finger that Arwen had seen Val give
Zavryd.

"Yes, but he's enjoying the sun."

"He looks like a cat on a windowsill."

"He finds our usual Seattle weather chilly."

"Who doesn't?" Amber led Arwen through the house, grabbing her keys and purse on the way.

When they passed the bathroom, Arwen paused. "Maybe I should
put on the armored jumpsuit. In case we run into trouble at the park."

"You'll be fine." Amber gripped Arwen's arm and pulled her
away from the bathroom and toward the front door. "It's a good
neighborhood, a trouble-free park."

"Aren't we visiting it because there are rumors of a mercenary
gang meeting there?"

"At *night*. Nobody's ever mentioned vans of marauding orcs
during the day."

"Are you saying that because it's true or because you don't want
to be seen in public with me in the altered jumpsuit?" Arwen
followed her through the front door, trusting Starblade would fly
in to help if he heard gunfire.

"You're pretty swift for a farmer."

"I'm used to people not wanting to be seen with me, or around
me in general, because of my dark-elven blood."

"It's your *fashion* sense that's the problem. Next time you're
feeling rich, hit me up. I'm still willing to be your personal
shopper for a reasonable fee." Amber shot a dark look over her
shoulder as she descended the steps toward the driveway. "Just

promise me you won't *alter* any of the clothing I choose. Definitely don't add shimmery whatever that is. I—" She stopped with a surprised squawk when she reached the driveway.

Starblade had changed into his elven form and stood with his arms folded by the dented red hatchback. "Her *fashion* is most adequate. She battles magical beings and tracks enemies in the forest."

"You think the raccoons and squirrels are into that weird glimmer?" Amber asked.

Starblade's eyes glowed. "Yes."

Amber stepped back and lifted her hands. "Fine, fine. All the more reason for her to keep what *was* a perfect jumpsuit for college interviews." Amber looked wistfully at the garment.

That made Arwen feel guilty, and she vowed not to borrow more clothing from Amber. If she someday needed to attend another job interview—Arwen shuddered all over at the thought —she would purchase her own outfit.

"Uhm, you're blocking the door." Amber jangled her car keys in Starblade's direction but didn't presume to step closer. She had some wisdom for her age.

"I will accompany you to seek the location of the orc mercenaries."

"You can't fly over to the park and meet us?" Amber raised her eyebrows toward Arwen.

As if *she* could tell Starblade where to go and what to do. She hadn't even managed to get him to say *please* to someone.

His eyes slitted as he stared at Amber. "I will accompany you to ensure no more insults to Arwen are given."

"I was insulting her *clothes*, not her. She's fine."

Starblade's eyes remained slitted. Arwen didn't know whether to be touched that he was defending her or exasperated that he was borderline threatening a teenager, one whose mother had a dragon mate, a huge dwarven sword, and an even huger magical tiger.

Amber looked at Arwen. "I don't know if you've got an over-protective boyfriend or a big brother."

Before Arwen could shake her head and say neither, Starblade curled his lip.

"I do *not* have dark-elven blood," he said.

Maybe Arwen should have been offended by his reaction, but she wasn't crazy about her dark-elven blood either.

"Boyfriend it is," Amber said. "Make sure to buy her plenty of jewelry."

Arwen snorted, certain *that* wouldn't happen. And Starblade had already made his stance on their relationship, or lack of a relationship, clear.

"Jewelry," Starblade said slowly, "such as... dangling ear and neck decorations." Elves had to have such things—the Lord of the Rings assured it—but maybe, as a military commander who'd spent his life in soldier-filled barracks and on battlegrounds, he didn't have a lot of experience buying jewelry for girlfriends.

"Yeah," Amber said.

"Unless such items are enchanted to have useful magical attributes, they are not practical."

"They're not supposed to be *practical*." Amber rolled her eyes. "Just pretty."

"The tractor of Arwen's father is old and functions sub-opti-mally. A superior gift would be a gnomish *flikopdedorik*." He looked to Arwen. For verification?

"Maybe for her *dad*." After issuing another eye roll, Amber jangled her keys again. "If we're going, let's go, though you may have to ride on the hood. There's not much room in the back, and you're tall."

"I'll take the back," Arwen volunteered.

Though her five-foot-nine height didn't make her short by

most people's standards, she was the shrimp in this trio. Besides, sitting with his knees squashed up to his chin in the compact back seat wouldn't improve Starblade's mood.

Arwen opened the door, shifted the seat forward, and crawled into the back, only banging her bow on the frame two or three times. Amber pointed Starblade to the passenger seat. He walked slowly around the vehicle, opening the hatch to consider the back storage area before continuing to the indicated spot.

Amber slid in and put the key in the ignition. Starblade passed the passenger-side door, strolled to the front of the car, and tried to open the hood.

"What is he doing?" Amber asked. "I was *joking* when I said he had to ride up there. I wouldn't be able to see around him."

"It may be his first time getting in a car."

"Does he think people ride in the engine compartment?"

"He may want to know how it works."

"I'm not popping the hood for him."

Starblade waved a hand, a trickle of magic opening it, regardless. "This vehicle has a carburetor, yes?"

"Uh, maybe." Amber gave Arwen a peeved look. "I'm twenty seconds from changing my mind about this being a freebie."

"Sorry."

Amber rolled down the window and stuck her head out. "Look, I don't need an oil change for another two thousand miles. I'm pulling out in ten seconds, whether your butt is in the seat or not." She turned the key and started the engine.

Starblade gazed around the hood at her. "You are not properly respectful toward one with vastly more power than yourself. The predominantly human blood in your veins makes you weak."

Amber stared at him for a long moment before looking back at Arwen. "He'd better get you a *lot* of jewelry."

"He's not my boyfriend," Arwen said.

"Doesn't matter. He's a dumbass. He needs to make up for that to everyone he meets."

Starblade lowered the hood and opened the passenger-side door. Even the front seats weren't that roomy for someone over six feet, so he folded himself carefully inside, pausing to probe the fuzzy seat covers. "This mimics the fur of an animal but is made from an inferior material."

"Uh-huh." Amber put the car in gear. "Close the door."

He did so, his knees against the glove compartment.

"I suppose dragons don't know about seat belts." Amber pulled the car out of the driveway.

"I am half-dragon and half-elven." Starblade opened the glove compartment and poked around inside.

"Which half makes you a nosy snoop?"

Instead of answering, he pulled out a Leatherman multitool and opened the blades and prodded the tiny scissors. "The design of this item is clever. I would assume it of dwarven make, but it lacks a hammer."

Arwen thought it would have been difficult to craft a hammer that folded out of a knife.

"It came from a factory." Amber glanced back at Arwen. "My dad got that and a jack for me for my birthday. *He* should have gotten me jewelry too."

"But he chose a practical gift, yes?" Starblade nodded as if she'd proven his point.

"It's in case the car breaks down on a dark freeway some-where," Amber said. "Like I'd fix the problem with a folding screwdriver instead of calling my insurance for a tow."

Arwen smiled. "Fathers want their daughters to be able to take care of themselves."

"I know. It's *horrible.* When we came home with the car, he made me learn to change the oil before he'd let me take it out. He doesn't even do that on his own car. He's a professional computer geek. He can format and partition your hard drive, but that's the limit of his handyman skills." Amber turned the hatchback onto the main road. Either because she loved driving fast or she wanted Starblade out of her car as quickly as possible, she ripped up the long hill of Main Street.

"If it helps, my father usually gives me garden tools and baking supplies for my birthday."

"You kind of like those things though, don't you?" Not slowing much, Amber hit the curb twice as she swung them through the roundabout at Five Corners.

Starblade found the oh-shit handle and wrapped his fingers tightly around it. His narrowed eyes hinted that he might be two or three seconds from taking control and levitating the car to the park.

"I do," Arwen admitted, "but something frivolous and impractical would be fun now and then. Something meant to be enjoyed. Last year, I got him a jerky-of-the-month club membership."

"He's not part dragon, is he?" Amber whipped the car down residential streets before slowing down and signaling for a parking lot.

"No," Arwen said. "Lots of fully human men like meat."

"Yes." Starblade nodded. "It is covered in the Study of Manliness. As well as appropriate meat-preparation methods for males of the species to engage in."

"Smoking and barbecuing?" Amber guessed.

"And turning a carcass on a spit over an open fire," Starblade said.

"Yeah, all the guys in the neighborhood get excited when my dad pulls the carcasses out."

Arwen, sensing something magical ahead, frowned and leaned forward. A van—the same van that she'd shot at in Lynnwood—was parked in the small lot. Tree branches hung over it, casting it in shadow. No other vehicles were present, and, despite the sun, the area felt closed-in and ominous.

"Wait here," Arwen told Amber, worried about threats.

She didn't sense any orcs, but the ones who'd attacked the night before had all worn camouflaging charms.

"No problem," Amber said.

Starblade returned the Leatherman to the glove compartment and unfolded himself from the car.

Pack slung over her back and bow in hand, Arwen approached the van. The windows were up, the front seats empty, but a dark droplet on a rock on the ground outside the sliding door caught her eye. Blood.

She knelt and touched it. It was dry. She eyed the area for prints, but the park was in the core of the suburbs and popular with walkers. She would be hard-pressed to pick out specific tracks on the gravel parking lot or packed-dirt trails.

When she knocked on the van door, Starblade raised his eyes.

"Do you typically announce your presence to enemies?" he asked.

"Well, it's polite to knock on a door before presuming to open it without permission."

His eyelids drooped. "You entered *my* domicile without acquiring permission."

"It's hard to knock on a stone bench or a trapdoor covered with dirt." Though Arwen expected to find the van door locked, she tried to slide it open.

Surprisingly, the handle obliged. As she slid the door aside, the scents of pot and beer filling the air, a blue-skinned arm fell out.

It wasn't attached to a body.

24

THERE WERE FOUR ORC BODIES CUT UP INSIDE THE VAN, BLOOD saturating the shag carpet.

Arwen had seen enough death not to be alarmed by it in most circumstances, but she drew back at the macabre scene. Two decapitated heads were also visible among the bodies. Guns and daggers lay where they'd fallen, having been of no use in saving the lives of their owners.

"This was done with a sword," Starblade said. "By someone very swift—or with powerful magic."

"The dark elf?" Even though Arwen hadn't physically battled Harlik-van, she had seen evidence of his power. But she looked to the sky, the morning sun long since up. "It would have to have happened during the night. And if it was him, why would he have attacked the very mercenaries that he'd hired?"

"To keep them from confessing that which you seek to know? His location? Where he sleeps during the day." Starblade's eyelids drooped. "And where he may be found to kill."

Amber rolled down her window. "Everything okay?"

"Yes." Afraid she would get out of the car, Arwen hurried to shove the detached arm back inside and close the van door. But the arm bumped one of the torsos and didn't go all the way in. The door caught with the wrist and fingers hanging out.

Amber leaned her head out the window. Wincing, Arwen shifted to block her view. Amber had been distressed by the taxidermy elk head mounted in Father's home. Decapitated orcs might traumatize her.

"I'm going to look around," Arwen continued. "You can go back home. Thanks for bringing us to the park. Starblade enjoyed the ride."

His flat expression did not connote agreement.

"And the advice on gift giving," Arwen added, waving for Amber to go.

"Uh-huh." Amber saw his flat expression too. "What's in the van that you don't want me to see?"

Arwen thought about lying but doubted it would work. "Dead orcs and a lot of blood."

"Ew. I'll be at the house until noon if you need a ride anywhere else. FYI, I charge double for multiple passengers if one of them is a dragon."

"That's a new rule."

"Yup." Amber grimaced at the van, then waved and drove off.

Arwen reached for the arm, intending to throw it all the way in this time, but hesitated. This was a crime scene. Maybe she shouldn't have touched anything.

The blood spatter on the rock drew her eye again. Could it indicate that one of the orcs had gotten out at some point during the fight? And maybe escaped?

She walked around, looking for more signs that the dark elf hadn't gotten them all.

"Someone approaches." Starblade nodded toward one of the trails that emptied into the lot.

A woman with a panting black Labrador retriever walked into

view, skirting the van and starting for another trail. She eyed Arwen's bow and quiver. As if *they* were the most alarming things here.

Arwen moved again to block the view of the arm caught in the door but didn't know if she succeeded. She should have stuffed it back inside, crime scene or not.

"Ma'am?" Arwen asked. "Did you see anyone on the trail? We're looking for the owner of this van." Or one of the riders in it, at least.

"No, but that van was there when I came through at dawn. I thought it belonged to homeless people. It wouldn't be the first time they've camped here." She grimaced toward the van door as the dog paused to snuffle the ground, then tugged him toward the other trail.

Another introvert who didn't care to chitchat with strangers. Arwen understood perfectly.

"If the van was here last night, Harlik-van could have killed the orcs." Arwen still thought it strange that he would have taken out his putative allies, but Starblade's hypothesis might be correct. All along her journey, he'd somehow known what she was up to and been a step ahead of her. She eyed her tattooed arm with distaste.

"Yes," Starblade said.

Arwen's search didn't reveal any more bloodstains, but the dirt could have hidden droplets. "Let me see if my tracking magic can help."

"Very well."

She trickled her power into the earth, toward the roots under the parking lot. She also placed a hand on a thick fir near the van and closed her eyes, trying to grasp what it had recently sensed.

Trees didn't see the way humans did, but she'd learned they could feel the world around them and even had a memory of sorts. Reputedly, they had more of a sentience on the worlds with greater magic in the ground than Earth, but Arwen had never traveled elsewhere and couldn't say from personal experience. Here, she'd often been able to get a feel for what had happened in the woods, especially if the trees deemed it a threat to their kind.

When she used her magic to tap into the fir's awareness, she caught one of its memories, its roots sharing the disturbing vibrations in the ground that had taken place when a nearby lot had been cleared for a house to be built. It took a moment before Arwen could nudge the tree to share something more recent.

It gave her the far subtler reverberations caused by the footfalls of a large person. Even without sight, the fir had sensed the being carried an axe. Since such blades were a threat to the woods, it had noted it, but the wielder had continued past without striking any trees. Its gait had been uneven.

Such as if the being were limping? Might it have been an orc with a battle-ax?

The tree shared the sense that the being had headed into the park toward a pond on the far end.

When Arwen opened her eyes, she found Starblade watching her from the opposite side of the fir, his hand also on the bark.

"It is interesting that you are able to twist your inborn dark-elven magic in elven ways to emulate what we do with our power," he said.

"I do strive to be interesting. Maybe someone will write a paper on me one day."

He tilted his head in consideration. "You would be amenable to such an activity?"

"I was joking. Nobody wants to write about me."

"You might be surprised what scribes like to note. I was once interviewed by a bard who wanted to know about our battles and what it was like being a half-dragon and flying."

"Did he write a flattering song about you that people adored?"

"He created a tale with more emphasis on rhyming than accuracy."

"Our media is iffy too."

"Because of rhyming." Starblade nodded.

"Yeah, it's a big problem." Arwen pointed down a wide trail. "I want to check the pond."

"Yes, I also saw what might have been the tree's interpretation of an orc."

"You were trained as a tracker?" Arwen asked as they headed down the trail through the trees.

That wasn't surprising, but learning he might have similar abilities as she, in addition to much greater versatility and power, made her feel less useful. What could she do that he couldn't?

"When I was a boy, we trained in outdoor survival skills. Some battles take place at the gates of cities. Some are in pivotal wild areas where resources must be acquired or defended."

They didn't have to go far before reaching the pond. It was fenced only partially, with trails leading to the water in places where the banks weren't overgrown. In other spots, the ground was marshy with reeds choking the shoreline. They walked around the pond but didn't see much more than ducks.

Since Arwen didn't sense any orcs, she worried they were wasting their time. Then she spotted a place where the fence had been broken. Someone had cut the top rail, then bent back the chain links. An orc with an axe?

Arwen pushed through, spotting freshly snapped foliage and tracks in ground that grew muddier closer to the water. The wild gamy scent of orc reached her a moment before she spotted a boot —no, a whole leg—thrusting out of a broken bush. At the same time, she drew close enough to sense the orc. He was indeed using a camouflaging charm or the equivalent. His aura was weak, but he was alive. For now.

Starblade walked behind her as she approached and wrapped a magical barrier around her.

With the orc sprawled on his back in broken foliage, Arwen

doubted he was a threat. He must have been fleeing from the dark elf or whoever had killed his comrades. Maybe this was as far as he'd made it before his legs gave out.

No, not his legs, she corrected as she pushed aside branches for a better look. One of the magical throwing stars that Harlik-van wielded stuck out of the side of the orc's thick neck. Another was embedded in his chest. His leg was also twisted so greatly that it had to be broken. The axe the tree had sensed lay fallen next to him, but the orc stirred and gripped the haft as his yellow eyes opened.

"*Throk dak lu morgarki*," he rasped in a weak voice, struggling to lift the axe.

Arwen slung her bow over her shoulder and held up her empty palms. "We won't kill you. We want to figure out where the guy who did this went. Do you know where he lives?"

The orc stared mulishly at her. She assumed he understood at least some English, since he and his fellow mercenaries had a business in the area, but he only said, "*Throk*," again and spat.

"I know you said you're not a healer," Arwen said to Starblade without risking looking away from the orc, "but you've helped with my injuries before. And those elven regeneration pads are wonderful. Do you have any with you?"

"You wish me to heal an enemy?" Starblade asked. "One who has joined others in attacking you and slaying those who could help you with your problem?"

"I'd prefer he not die before we can get the information we need out of him." Arwen didn't particularly want the orc dead, regardless. He might be the equivalent of a soldier following orders. It wasn't as if the orcs who came to Earth had a lot of job opportunities. Becoming mercenaries and bouncers and the like were typical ways they made money here.

Starblade let out a low rumble that would have been a growl in his dragon form. He showed his teeth, then said something in Orcish.

The orc showed *his* teeth.

Starblade pointed back toward the parking lot—toward the van full of bodies—and spoke again.

The orc slumped and grunted a short response.

"What are you discussing?" Arwen asked.

"I said I'd heal him if he swore his allegiance to me and promised to never harm you."

"His allegiance? I didn't know you were recruiting troops."

"Besides the goblins?" Starblade poked into an inner pocket in his tunic—it might have been an *interdimensional* pocket—and pulled out a tiny case that held miniature versions of the regeneration bandages she'd seen.

"I thought Yendral wanted the goblins," Arwen said.

"He wanted *me* to assemble them into an army. Yendral is capable of leading troops but will be the first to declare that it's a lot of work and he prefers following to being in charge." Starblade stepped past her and opened the case to show the moist green squares to the orc, who should have had the power to sense their magic. "This troop would be more formidable than a goblin. I suppose I shouldn't toss aside the idea of gathering an army. Wherever we locate ourselves next may be more dangerous than this world. Extra men may be necessary for adequate defense."

Arwen shook her head at the reminder that he would leave soon.

When the orc didn't object to the bandages, Starblade crouched and tugged out the throwing stars. His patient swore and grunted in pain but didn't try to stop him. Removing the stars caused blood to flow again and, as Starblade wiped the neck wound and flattened a bandage to it, the orc passed out.

"I was monitoring his thoughts when you questioned him." Starblade shifted to apply another pad. "He understood you.

When you asked him where the dark elf was, a memory of a waterfall with a cave behind it came to mind. He and his clan leader first met the dark elf there when they were hired. He believed it wasn't the dark elf's home but a temporary place where he is staying while he does his work here."

His work. Making sure Arwen didn't find a way to sever her tie to her mother's people.

"It's possible he is still staying there," Starblade continued, "sleeping in the dark cave during the day. The orc did see evidence of a camp."

"There are a lot of waterfalls with caves behind them in Western Washington. I've seen more than a few myself, and I'm aware of popular hiking trails that lead to others."

"It is unlikely a dark elf would be camped in a popular location."

"True, but..." Arwen debated how one might research such places, eliminate unlikely candidates, and home in on others that would be worth checking. The internet? Might Amber be helpful in learning such things? Or perhaps Arwen could ask Colonel Willard. She had many resources and wanted Arwen to report to her office anyway.

Starblade lifted a hand toward her face but paused before touching her. "If you wish, I can share what I saw in his thoughts."

Since he'd read her mind before without asking for permission, it amused her that he paused and waited for it now. Maybe that meant something. That he had come to believe she was worth treating as an equal. Or at least someone whose feelings on such topics mattered.

"Okay," was all Arwen said. "Thanks for asking."

Nodding, Starblade touched his fingers to her temple. The image he placed into her mind was in line with what he'd voiced, but the cave was deeper than she'd imagined, enough that the back half was very dark with little light making it through the curtain of water falling over the entrance. So little light that she guessed the cave mouth faced another rock face or had numerous trees towering opposite the falls, something that diminished the amount of sun reaching the water.

In the vision—the *memory*—the orc and his leader knelt with their foreheads to the ground, despite their armor and array of weapons. They listened as Harlik-van spoke. Just as when Arwen had seen him, he wore a cloak and hood, his albino face not visible other than the barest hint of a smooth jaw.

Starblade lowered his fingers, touching her cheek before drawing them back. That prompted a zing of awareness in Arwen, along with the urge to step closer to him. Maybe he would like her to brush *his* cheek. Was that tenderness in his expression or her imagination?

A pained sigh escaped the semi-conscious orc, and Starblade shifted his attention back to his patient.

Arwen's phone rang, and she pushed away thoughts of cheek touching.

Not recognizing the number that popped up, she stepped back and answered with a wary, "Hello?"

"It's Imoshaun."

"You have a phone?"

"Certainly. I'm not a troglodyte. I called to inform you that we have repaired the heritage detector. You may come by to pick it up when you wish."

"That's good news. Thank you." Arwen wished they could go right away to retrieve it, but Willard was waiting. Also, Starblade's face grew closed, any hint of tenderness gone. She might have imagined it.

"Yes," Imoshaun said. "The results of previous analyses were stored in the device's memory, but, not surprisingly, none from dragons. There are many elves, however. In fact, there are *only* elves. It's likely the device was used on their world."

"Elves are into genealogy, huh?"

"Many species are, especially if there is a heredity aspect to their rule and—"

The wail of a siren—a *loud* siren—made Arwen jump, and she didn't hear the rest of the sentence.

Starblade stepped away from the orc and toward the fence as he raised his barrier around them again.

"Police," Arwen guessed, wincing at the sound of the sirens. Her ears weren't as keen as those of full-blooded elves, but she'd always heard more than humans. "The dog walker may have spotted the arm sticking out of the van and reported it."

Another vehicle with a siren roared by on a road parallel to the park as it headed toward the lot.

"This may be an opportune time for us to leave," Starblade said.

Arwen nodded but looked to the orc, afraid the police would find him and shoot him. Magical beings, when their existence was acknowledged, weren't subject to the same laws as humans and were rarely treated well by the authorities.

But the orc had disappeared. He must not have been as unconscious as they'd believed.

"Your new loyal troop is gone." Arwen waved at the crushed foliage, certain she could track the orc if she wished, but Starblade only nodded. He'd probably sensed him leaving and didn't care that much about his *troop*.

Barks came from the parking lot. A K-9 unit? The police might intend to search the park for the killers.

"Come." Starblade started for the broken fence but reconsidered and, instead, waded into the water where he shifted into his dragon form, having the room above the pond to spread his wings. His power wrapped around Arwen, and he levitated her onto his back.

As he sprang into the air, wingbeats stirring the branches, she glimpsed police running down the trail with German shepherds. The dogs barked, perhaps sensing a dragon in their midst, but Starblade wrapped camouflaging magic around them as he flew higher.

"You're handy to have around." Arwen rested a hand on his scales.

Yes.

"I don't suppose you'd like to stop by Imoshaun's shop on the way to Willard's office?"

No.

"It's hard to help someone who doesn't want to be helped."

General Mysolysar once said that the wise commander funnels his resources toward protecting those nations that desire the aid of foreigners. He doesn't attempt to house troops where they are unwanted.

"I guess it's a good thing I'm not that wise." Arwen patted his scales and wasn't surprised when he didn't respond.

Maybe she was stubborn and naive, but she refused to give up on her idea of helping him, not when he was doing so much to assist her.

25

Zavryd'nokquetal is present in the military leader's office, Starblade said with distaste as they flew over the suburbs toward Willard's building in Seattle.

"Maybe she ordered him to report in too." Arwen rode with her eyes closed, enjoying the wind on her face, the sunlight warming her skin, and the salty air wafting in from Puget Sound.

Unlikely. A dragon does not take orders or report to anyone from a lesser species.

"Maybe he's informing her that her office building has insufficient landing spots."

A more likely scenario.

"I know you're not excited about my quest to learn your heritage, but will you give me a sample of your blood for the device?"

You should focus on eliminating the dark-elf threat to yourself.

"A small sample? I may only need a drop."

His head turned enough for a single violet eye to skewer her as he flew.

"Maybe it doesn't even take blood. Earth DNA tests only need a cheek swab." Arwen smiled stubbornly at him, though Imoshaun had mentioned blood, so she assumed the gnomish device had different requirements.

Starblade angled downward to take them in for a landing. *I believe nothing will come of your ancillary quest, but I will give you a drop of my blood to satisfy your curiosity.*

"Thank you. Do you think Zavryd would give me a drop of his blood?" Of all the dragons Arwen had seen, Starblade looked most like Val's black-scaled and violet-eyed mate.

I do not. I also sense the elven assassin present in the military building.

"Sarrlevi? Are Matti and Val there too?"

I do not sense them.

That was disappointing. Arwen would have preferred to face the stern Colonel Willard with backup. Thus far, Val and Matti had proven willing to stand up for her, at least on minor occasions. Of course, Starblade had defended her wardrobe. Maybe that would be enough for this meeting. She imagined him justifying her *shimmer* to Willard.

Starblade alighted on the grass in front of the building without trouble, so maybe the landing pads here were sufficient. Instead of shifting to his elven form, he remained a dragon, his tail and neck rigid and his wings outstretched as he glared at the building. Or maybe *through* it to those inside.

Now that they were closer, Arwen could also sense Zavryd and Sarrlevi. In addition, she picked up the much smaller aura of Gondo.

"Everything okay?" Arwen asked.

The pompous Stormforge tyrant lectures me.

"So, it's going to be one of your normal meetings?"

Again, Starblade skewered her with his gaze. Then he snorted, inasmuch as dragons made that noise, and shifted into his elven form.

"He is insufferable. There is no chance that I could have been bred from such uptight and sanctimonious genes."

"Yeah, you're nothing like him." Arwen headed for the front door, hoping he would follow. "I didn't clean the blood off the arrow that poked Darvanylar, so we can test him too."

"I am not related to a *Silverclaw* dragon." Starblade sounded as affronted by that as the notion of having Zavryd for a brother. Maybe more. "In my time, they were conniving and scheming, and I've heard nothing has changed."

"Are there *any* dragons you would find acceptable, uhm, donors?" Arwen had no idea if that was the right term. She was positive dragon anatomy was different enough from humans—and elves—that sperm hadn't been involved. It had sounded like test tubes, science, and magic had been required.

"No."

"Maybe you came from a wyvern. Or a hydra. They have scales." Arwen held the door open for him. "Do you ever get the urge to sprout more heads when you shape-shift?"

Starblade halted, giving her a surprised look. Or maybe that was a scathing look. "You are *teasing* me."

"Yes." Impulsively, Arwen kissed him on the cheek.

His flummoxed expression suggested it surprised him as much as the teasing. Chin up, he strode through the door.

She was more amused by his disgruntlement than sympathetic to it. Given who *her* mother was, she couldn't imagine things being any worse for Starblade.

The mongrel dark-elf has arrived late for the important meeting on orc mercenaries and dark-elf plots, Zavryd's voice boomed in Arwen's head as they reached the outer office door.

Maybe she could understand why Starblade didn't want to be related to him.

Before opening the door, he shared an *I-told-you-so* look with her.

Inside, Gondo was talking on the phone and scribbling in a notebook instead of working on inventions. Maybe he actually performed secretarial duties for Willard from time to time.

He bowed to them and waved them toward the inner office door. On the way past his notebook, Arwen read the header: *New recipe for a world-shattering delightfully dense FORTY-pound cake.*

Well, maybe the phone call was at least for Willard. Gondo was answering questions about the process for dealing with chimeras in Bellingham.

Willard sat at the desk in her office, Sarrlevi facing her from one corner with his arms folded across his chest. Zavryd stood in the corner opposite him, his arms also folded across his chest as he glowered not at Willard but at Sarrlevi.

"Is it okay for us to come in?" Arwen asked from the doorway.

Gondo had waved them in this direction, but maybe she should have knocked.

"Yes," Willard said. "I'm giving Sarrlevi an assignment while I wait for your report, and trying to suggest that he would find the help of a dragon useful since he needs a ride to Eastern Washington. Twisp has become a hotbed for yeti activity, and we believe something more inimical than goblins is behind their appearance this time."

"My purpose here," Zavryd said, "is not to allow myself to be pressed into taxi duty for a supercilious elf with a penchant for cleaning my scales with his *sword* when he rides on my back."

"I only did that one time," Sarrlevi said, "because magical goblin pitch adhered to them."

"A simple solvent would have sufficed, not that I would have asked *you* for help maintaining my cleanliness, regardless. You presumed much because of your pathological fastidiousness."

"I'm responsibly fastidious, not pathologically."

"Enough." Willard held up a hand while glaring in exasperation at them. "Lord Zavryd, I have noted your request for more lenience in scheduling Thorvald's missions so that you may observe the anniversary of your meeting with time away from Earth. It wasn't necessary for you to come in person to let me know about the anniversary mating flight and ritual in the nest." Willard grimaced. Deeply.

"I believe it *was* necessary. You say you've noted it, but you have written nothing in your journal." Zavryd pointed to a notepad and laptop on one side of Willard's desk. "The *cake* recipe that your assistant is scribbling down does not count."

"Oh, the details are indelibly imprinted in my memory." Willard touched her temple. "Trust me."

Zavryd squinted at her. Untrustingly.

"I must also report a need for an absence from my Earth duties," Sarrlevi informed Willard.

"You have work on Veleshna Var that calls you again?" Willard asked.

"No. The date that Mataalii anticipates the birth of our children approaches, and I wish to ensure I am not distracted or away during this vital period. Also, as a mother in a stressful state, Mataalii must have the most exquisite of exotic foods from various locales. In addition, elven babies are often fed droplets of *yeklak* milk as a supplement to their mother's milk. It is not only nutrient-rich but helps infuse the newborns with sensitivity to the magic of the world. I will need time to gather these supplies. Further, the season for collecting the wild *arthmorak* milk required for making kobold *amylorthak* cheese soon approaches."

Willard deciphered all this as, "You want paternity leave so you can pamper your family?"

"Yes."

"Isn't Puletasi still a month out?"

"Our children will be one-quarter dwarven, which will make them stubborn, impatient, and prone to temper tantrums. It is possible they will insist on being born early. Also, the wild *arth-morak* milk—"

"Yes, yes, you've got a grocery list that Instacart can't handle. I've got it. Deal with my yetis, and then you can take all the time you need. I will, however, note that *Puletasi* has not requested *maternity* leave."

Arwen imagined Matti happily hammering shifters, yetis, and other troublemakers right up to the delivery date.

Zavryd looked over at Sarrlevi. "Considering the lowly limitations of her species, the human military leader is *not* properly respectful to superior beings."

"I am aware," Sarrlevi said in what was probably a rare moment of agreement for those two.

Willard frowned at them, and then at Starblade, as if wondering if he was also going to be a pain in the ass. He said nothing.

Willard shifted her focus to Arwen. "I'll take your report now."

"Yes, ma'am." Aware that her text message had been brief, she shared everything that had happened the night before, the dead orcs they'd found that morning, and what they'd learned about the waterfall cave.

"I was going to let you know about the mercenaries' meeting spot in—" Willard glanced at her notepad, "—Pine Ridge Park and also that their supposed flower-delivery company is located in a duplex in South Everett, but I suppose you've gotten what you need from them."

"More precise directions to the waterfall would have been nice," Arwen said.

"Let me bring in Gondo and see what I can learn about that. There are goblin clans all over the national forests and BLM land. If there's an off-the-beaten-track waterfall cave out there, their people know about it. I agree with you that a popular hiking area is an unlikely place for a dark elf to set up camp. If he had, we'd have heard of people being sacrificed along the trail left and right, I'm sure." Willard grimaced again.

"More likely, they would have disappeared from the trail and been sacrificed in the depths of the cave," Arwen said.

Willard flicked her hand dismissively. "Either way, I'll see what I can find. Your dark elf sounds powerful. If I can get you the address of his cave, you'd better not go alone. Is your, ah—" she waved to indicate Starblade, "—acquaintance going to assist you?"

"Yes," Starblade said promptly.

"Didn't she shoot you recently?" Willard asked.

"Yes."

Arwen winced.

"Since then," Starblade said, "she shot the dragon Darvanylar in the backside while I crushed his neck with my great maw."

"So, you've bonded."

Starblade considered that. "Her assistance in that matter made me wish to assist her in return." After a pause, he added, "I have also promised to build her an elven rejuvenation pool."

Willard's mouth drooped open.

Sarrlevi, who probably knew exactly what Starblade was referencing, looked at him with interest. "A *yavasheva*?"

"Yes," Starblade said.

"You have a *raishay yavasheva tee*?"

"I do."

"Fascinating. They are not made any more and were believed to all be lost. The rejuvenation pools are rare and highly valued."

"I am capable of making them."

"If the dragons knew that," Sarrlevi said, glancing at Zavryd, "they might leave you alone."

Arwen expected Zavryd to scoff, but his expression grew wistful. "The *yavasheva* are amazing. Better than a goblin water box."

Sarrlevi was the one to scoff. "*Many* things are better than that."

"Do not be jealous, assassin, that goblins never give *you* gifts. Elves are not as worthy of offerings as dragons."

"I am not—"

"Enough." Willard jerked her hand up and gave *everyone* in the office an exasperated glower that time.

Arwen didn't think she'd done anything to earn that, but she attempted to look attentive and cooperative. If it was possible Gondo, through his goblin network, could find that cave, she wanted that information. She wanted resolution to her problem.

"You—" Willard pointed at Sarrlevi, "—yetis. You—" her finger shifted to Zavryd, "—elf taxi. You—" her finger moved toward Arwen.

But Arwen, realizing she might not get another chance to speak with Zavryd again soon, blurted, "Wait. I need a drop of dragon blood. *Your* blood, Lord Zavryd. I know you said it's impossible that you could be related to Starblade, but we won't *really* know that until we run a test, right? The heritage device is working now, so we can do that." She gave him her most imploring and—she hoped—persuasive smile, though the glower he directed at her would have wilted the sturdiest, most invasive weed on the farm. "Might I prepare an all-meat dinner for you one night? In exchange for a tiny drop of your blood?"

"A dragon does *not* give up his blood to alchemists, wizards, scientists, or anyone else who wants to *experiment* with it. It is *not* dignified."

"I'm not any of those things," Arwen said, "and there won't be any experimentation. You just put the sample in the box, and it spits out your lineage."

Zavryd's eyes flared violet. "I *know* my lineage. I am not some motherless riffraff left in an eyrie in the wilds to fend for himself. My mother is Zynesshara. My father was Araknator the Just, a great scholar, warrior, and law enforcer for the Cosmic Realms."

"So uptight and sanctimonious," Sarrlevi said.

"An opinion widely held." Starblade nodded to Arwen with another I-told-you-so look.

Zavryd's eyes glowed again, but his focus shifted from Arwen to Sarrlevi. Surprisingly, he didn't include Starblade in the glare. "You insult me to no end, assassin. Do not think I will forgive these transgressions simply because your domicile is now located across from mine."

"Oh, I don't. I expect you to challenge me to a duel any second. You are as one-note as every dragon in existence."

"Now, you presume to insult my entire race? A race *vastly* superior to lowly elves?"

Willard lifted a hand, and Arwen expected her to demand they stop again, but she picked up her phone. "Gondo? We're going to have words later about your scheduling tendencies when it comes to booking my appointments."

"A truly superior being would not be so insecure about giving up a drop of blood," Sarrlevi said.

"It is not *insecurity* that makes me refuse that odious request. It is pride."

"Or is it pomposity?"

"No." Zavryd reached to his hip, as if for a scabbard, though no weapons were visible on the silver-trimmed black elven robe that he wore. Nonetheless, he produced a fiery magical sword out of nowhere and pointed the flaming tip at Sarrlevi's chest.

Arwen, who was closer to him than the elf, backed out of the way. She sensed Starblade creating a magical barrier around her, but Zavryd wasn't looking at either of them.

"I *do* challenge you to a duel, elf," he said.

"I assumed." Sarrlevi drew the twin longswords that he always wore in scabbards on his back. "*I* will acquire a sample of your blood and give it to the dark-elf mongrel."

"You haven't the talent to make a dragon bleed."

"You've bled every time we've dueled."

"Only when I have battled you in *this* inferior form." Zavryd jerked a hand to indicate his human body. "And with less-than-optimal footwear."

"Which you are wearing now while in that form. I will make you bleed before you've taken three steps."

"You can make him bleed outside." Willard pointed toward the door. "This office isn't large enough for dueling."

"Very well." Zavryd nodded curtly.

"Why don't you save the mongrel some time and give her a sample of your blood now?" Sarrlevi asked. "You know your fate is inevitable."

"And you call *me* pompous, elf. You will bleed before I do."

"The small wounds you can inflict on me do not prompt fear in my being. Nor do I quail at the thought of others experimenting on my blood."

"I neither fear *nor* quail. Ever."

"Then let her take a sample. Let us find out who is or is not a relative of the half-dragon." Sarrlevi squinted at Zavryd, who squinted right back at him, their stares locked.

Arwen, who hadn't expected Sarrlevi to help her, held her breath, wondering if this would work.

"*Very well.*" Zavryd lowered the fiery sword. "I will show you that I fear nothing, and we will see for certain that the scaled mongrel is neither a Stormforge dragon *nor* any kin of mine." He stuck out a finger toward Arwen.

Startled, she stared at it, realizing she had no idea how to collect blood samples. Did she need to get a syringe? A cotton swab?

"Use one of your magical arrows," Sarrlevi advised. "A mundane knife will not pierce his skin even when in he is in his lesser form."

Zavryd's squint deepened. He probably objected to anything about him being called lesser.

After drawing an arrow, Arwen crept toward him, half-expecting him to change his mind and prong her with the fiery sword. Maybe Starblade had the same concern, because he didn't lower the barrier around her.

Zavryd noticed and turned his exasperation on Starblade. "I will not spring upon your female with my talons, mongrel."

"She is not my female."

"You are building her a *yavasheva*, and you expect me to believe you have not claimed her as your mate?"

"I am fulfilling a request she made and that I agreed to."

"It takes three days to build a *yavasheva*." Zavryd stuck his finger farther out toward Arwen. "No male would undergo such an endeavor for a female he did not wish to *tysliir* with in the nest."

Starblade opened and closed his mouth, but he didn't seem to have a response. If anything, he appeared flustered.

"She made food for me," he finally said.

"Ah. Food." The way Zavryd nodded suggested the answer might be a believable alternative to sexual interest.

Shaking her head, Arwen poked him gently with her arrow. Its magic cut through his skin, drawing blood. His lips rippled, but he didn't pull back.

Arwen hesitated, not certain how best to transport the blood. "Do I need a vial?"

Willard came around the table and handed her a tissue. "This should suffice."

"Right." Arwen wiped some onto it but also left a smear to dry on the arrow, just in case.

"I hope your ability to duel won't be hindered greatly by that wound," Willard told Zavryd.

"Certainly not."

"Do you need a bandage before we engage?" Sarrlevi asked. "I wouldn't want you to later claim the grievous injury was the reason for your defeat."

"I do *not*." Zavryd lowered his hand, the poke already healed, from what Arwen could see. Still carrying the fiery sword, he jerked his head toward Sarrlevi and strode out the door.

Sarrlevi inclined his head toward Arwen as he departed, murmuring, "May you find what you wish."

She didn't know why he'd helped her when he barely knew her, but she nodded back, glad he had. "Thank you."

"I have inserted into the goblin's mind the memories of the waterfall cave from the orc," Starblade told Arwen, his focus more on *her* troubles than his own. "We will find the one that plagues you."

"Thank you as well." Arwen smiled at him, resisting the urge to kiss him on the cheek again. "Maybe we could take a trip to Bellevue to visit Imoshaun while we wait to see what Gondo comes up with."

Starblade sighed deeply.

"If you stay here," Willard said, "you run the risk of being flattened by the duel I expect to start any moment."

A roar came from the lawn outside. Zavryd had decided to do battle in his dragon form. Either that, or he could make his human vocal cords do impressive things.

"That would be unappealing." After sighing again—somewhat melodramatically—Starblade extended his hand toward the door. "We will go to the gnome."

Though Arwen had a lot to worry about, a zing of anticipation went through her. If she was right, and Starblade was related to Zavryd, they might find out within the hour.

26

On the way to Bellevue, Arwen peeked in her pack, glad she'd thought to grab what might serve as gifts from the pantry earlier. After helping with the heritage detector, Imoshaun deserved pickled goodies.

This time, when Starblade landed on the roof above the gnome's basement workshop, there wasn't a line of people in the alley. Arwen didn't sense anyone except Imoshaun inside and let out a relieved breath. Until she sensed Starblade camouflaging and creating a barrier around them.

"Are you expecting Imoshaun to get feisty with us?" Arwen slid off his back, checking her pockets to make sure the samples hadn't fallen out. Before leaving Willard's office, she'd also gotten blood from Starblade.

No. But I sense another dragon flying around the city. Yendral is away, attempting to learn how much the Silverclaws know about our location, and I would prefer not to fight a full-blood by myself.

"I'm here with my arrows to help."

Arwen thought he might dismiss her ability as being of no use, but he said, *I would prefer not to fight a full-blood even with a diminutive but fierce ally.*

Though tempted to object to being called *diminutive*, Arwen admitted that applied in comparison to him in his dragon form. Besides, he'd also called her fierce. That was complimentary.

Go see the gnome. Starblade levitated her from the rooftop toward the alley. *I will monitor the dragon and remain hidden.*

Still hopeful that determining Starblade's lineage would result in other dragons helping him—*protecting* him—Arwen hurried to the door and knocked. It opened promptly, remotely activated, and Arwen descended the steps three at a time to the workshop.

"I have been waiting for you," Imoshaun said brightly, putting down tools and grabbing the heritage detector. All the wires were on the inside now, and when she held it up, a soft conical glow beamed through a hole in the top. "Did you, by chance, bring any blood samples?"

"Yes. Will these do?" Arwen offered the wrinkled, bloodstained tissues from Willard's office.

"I believe so. Hold one above the hole. I have the device in data-collection mode."

Arwen stretched the tissue with Zavryd's blood through the glow.

The device beeped softly. Indicating it had analyzed the sample? Or at least recorded it?

"I also have another dragon's blood dried on one of my arrows," Arwen said. "Will it accept something a couple of days old?"

"I believe so, but how ever did you get dragon blood on an arrow?"

"By shooting him with it."

"And that worked? Was it the arrow that *I* gave you?"

"No, but I can try that next time if you like." After loading Starblade's sample, Arwen fished in her quiver for Darvanylar's.

"My arrow, as I told you, is specially formulated to harm dark elves, but I am curious if it can penetrate a dragon's scales. If it can, I could add that to my marketing materials. Imoshaun the Inventor, creations capable of defense against even dragons."

"You have marketing materials?" Arwen looked for evidence of brochures on the workbench but saw only tools and projects.

"Of course. Word-of-mouth is delightful, but you cannot depend on it wholly, especially when you are new in an area."

"All those people looking for dark-elf detectors didn't find you through word-of-mouth?" Arwen held the arrow over the hole until the box beeped.

"No. I put an ad on the internet."

"I guess it worked."

"Indeed. Do you have any more samples?" Imoshaun looked toward Arwen's quiver, as if every arrow inside might be smothered with a different dragon's blood.

"Not unless you want one from me."

"I will accept that. More data is always better."

"But I already *know* who my parents are and that they don't have anything to do with Starblade."

"More data is always better," Imoshaun repeated cheerfully.

Arwen poked herself in the finger with her knife. Not seeing a tissue, she held it directly over the box. It beeped happily in agreement with Imoshaun about data.

"It would take hundreds of samples if it could." Imoshaun rested the device on her workbench, then placed her hand on the side.

The conical glow shifted to an interface of some kind, words in Gnomish. And was that Elven as well?

Imoshaun tapped a couple of options. The interface disappeared, and a soft hum, almost a whirring, came from within.

"It's processing the data," Imoshaun said. "I instructed it to look for links to Starblade's blood."

"Will it take long?"

"I don't believe so. The database isn't as large as in some of these devices I've heard of. That is unfortunate, however, since the odds of finding a match go up with more analyses stored inside. Though I doubt many heritage detectors in all the Cosmic Realms have much *dragon* data. One does not walk up and poke a needle into one of their kind." Imoshaun eyed Arwen's quiver again. "Though perhaps a particularly cheeky archer might."

"Yes. And it was an arrow not a needle."

"That would make a poking more grievous, not less. How did you survive shooting that dragon?"

"Starblade and the defensive weapons he'd constructed finished Darvanylar off."

"Oh, dear. It's not healthy to *finish off* dragons. Their kind are vengeful. If the dragon's clan finds out…"

"I know. So does Starblade. He and Yendral are planning to leave Earth soon." Arwen wondered if they would ever come back to visit. Or if there was some way she could visit Starblade on another world. Matti had a portal generator. Would she use it to take Arwen on a trip?

But Starblade couldn't tell her where he was going, not if he didn't want to risk another dragon reading her mind and finding out. That meant the odds were against her ever seeing him again.

Arwen stared glumly at the whirring box.

Use your charm, came Starblade's telepathic instruction from the rooftop. *From this far away, I cannot include you in my camouflage, and the dragon approaches. I believe it is another Silverclaw.*

Arwen jammed her hand in her pocket, glad she still had Amber's charm. She hoped she hadn't waited too long to activate it. The last thing she wanted was to be mind-scoured by another dragon. Or risk Starblade's life since he might spring to her defense to prevent that from happening.

"Oh, dear." Imoshaun looked toward the brick wall. "Another dragon."

"Starblade knows."

"He is here?"

"Camouflaged on the rooftop."

Imoshaun pulled a tree-shaped charm off a shelf and murmured a command to it. "We will *all* camouflage ourselves. As is wise when large strong predators fly overhead. Unless you intend to prong another dragon with an arrow, which I do not recommend, even with your new armor." She pointed toward Arwen's backpack, no doubt sensing its magic. "Should you not don it?"

"I have no further pronging plans, but if that dragon comes down here, I definitely will. Thank you for making it, by the way. The original owner let me keep it. Last night, it stopped a bullet."

"Of course it did." Unlike Amber, Imoshaun showed no surprise that Arwen had been shot at. "Mundane human weapons are easy to deter."

The dragon flew close enough to register to Arwen's less powerful senses. Another big male that radiated power like a sun, he soared across Lake Washington and over Bellevue. It wasn't a straight flight but one in which he swooped north and south as he continued east. A search pattern.

Arwen's heart sank. He could be searching for evidence of his missing comrade or for Starblade and Yendral. Neither scenario meant anything good.

As the dragon flew over the area, Arwen and Imoshaun made no noise, scarcely breathing. The insulated basement was quiet, no hint of traffic or other city noise reaching them. Thus, when the heritage device beeped three times, they both jumped.

Starblade's elven face appeared in the air above the hole like a hologram. A line angled upward and to the left from his head, pointing to an empty oval. Another arrow went diagonally downward from the oval and farther to the left. It pointed to another empty spot. Another arrow heading downward from it pointed to a row of small heads, a number of male and female elves, all with long silver hair and green or gray eyes. They were similar enough in appearance that Arwen thought they might be siblings. Since Starblade had black hair, she struggled to see his likeness in any of them, but if the intermediary empty ovals indicated unknown ancestors, the elves might be distant relatives.

A line angling to the right only went up one level to a single empty oval, with no ovals or heads beyond it.

"Interesting. It must be using the elven data I mentioned is in there." Imoshaun pointed at the row of heads. "That makes sense."

"It does?" Arwen waved at the empty ovals. "Does this mean it doesn't know who his parents are?"

"Correct. Or his siblings. But his... I believe these may be his cousins or perhaps nieces and nephews. You said he was in a stasis chamber and asleep for centuries, didn't you?"

"Yes."

"Not many generations of elves would have passed during that time since they're such a long-lived species. It is likely his nieces and nephews could still be alive. In fact..." Imoshaun leaned closer to squint at one of the silver-haired males.

Arwen scratched her jaw. It hadn't occurred to her to research who Starblade's elven relatives were, but she didn't think they would matter in the way the dragons would. Starblade had suggested that the downtrodden had been used, elven females who had been willing to take the risk of birthing the half-dragons to improve their position in society. Their people, at least those who studied history, probably knew all about the half-dragons and where they'd come from.

"I believe that's Eireth, the elven king." Imoshaun leaned back. "I am not familiar with the others."

"They don't look much alike," Arwen said dubiously, picturing

Starblade's black hair again. It was an admittedly atypical coloring for an elf. Maybe it had to do with his dragon side? "Other than... sternness."

"I'm not certain that's conveyed by the blood. As for the dragon side—" A couple more empty ovals and arrows appeared, and Imoshaun trailed off. This time, they were off to the right. "Hm, it wasn't done thinking."

Arwen held her breath, eager to see if a dragon would appear in one of the ovals. The *right* dragon. Even though she didn't adore Zavryd and thought him obnoxious, he was on their side—or at least *Val's* side—and he might feel obligated to help if evidence proved he *was* related to Starblade. But if the Silverclaw dragon showed up... Arwen was a lot less certain how that clan would react, especially after Starblade had killed one of them.

The heritage detector whirred more loudly. It sounded indignant, as if they'd given it an impossible task.

Finally, the most distant oval filled in with a black dragon head, but it was more faded than the elven heads.

"That's Zavryd," Arwen said.

Imoshaun touched the device, assessing it with a trickle of magic. "I am not certain what the fading indicates, but I would guess a lack of certainty. It probably needs more data, more samples from dragons. Do you suppose his parents would give you a blood sample?" She looked toward Arwen's quiver.

"Zavryd spoke about his father in past tense, and his mother is queen over the Dragon Council—over all dragondom, I think." There was no way Arwen would get a ride to her world to try to poke her in the butt with an arrow.

"I believe if the queen or Zavryd's father had spawned—or donated genetic material to the creation of—Starblade, the device would have deduced that link from Zavryd's blood sample."

"But this may suggest one of Zavryd's relatives participated in Starblade's creation?"

"I think it may. This evidence may not be, however, as humans say, admissible in a court of law."

Arwen snorted, imagining Starblade wandering into a dragon courtroom to make a paternity case to a scaled judge.

Imoshaun opened a drawer and pulled out a smartphone to take pictures.

Realizing she could do the same thing, Arwen activated hers. But who would she send them to? Willard? Val? She doubted dragons had phones but imagined Zavryd promptly deleting her text and reporting it as junk.

"I'll send it to Willard and Val and ask them to let Zavryd know." Arwen took photos of the dragon holograms and texted them. "Maybe it'll be enough for him to want to help Starblade." She hoped so but doubted it. She'd longed for a stronger link. "I wonder if the elven *king* would help him."

"Against dragons hunting him?" Imoshaun looked toward the ceiling as the Silverclaw flew over Bellevue again. "I do not think elves interfere in such things. In truth, there are not any races that will openly stand up to the dragons. Only in secret do some brave souls seek to improve the Cosmic Realms and lessen their *draconian* hold over it. That English word is most excellent."

"Yeah." Only after Arwen sent the photos did she realize she should have asked Starblade before doing so. He'd been understandably quiet since the Silverclaw dragon had shown up.

Starblade? Arwen asked telepathically, almost a whisper since she worried the other dragon would overhear. *Are you still up there?*

Yes. His response was also quiet, as if he worried about the same thing.

The phone rang before she could respond, Val's number.

"Hello?" Arwen answered.

"I got your pictures, and I'll let Zav know about it when he gets back, but we've got something bigger to worry about. He's off warning the queen about a Silverclaw dragon that appeared in Seattle. Another one."

"If it's the same one we're sensing now, he's flying over Imoshaun's workshop, looking for Starblade."

"He's doing more than that. He tore the water tower off a building and hurled it into a pond."

"Is every dragon in the Silverclaw clan an ass?"

"Every one I've encountered, yes." Val hesitated. "Look, Arwen, I know Starblade is a friend or something to you, but Willard wants to know if you'll ask him, for the sake of Seattle, if he'll move his refuge to another world."

"The dragon is in Bellevue now."

"They don't want their water towers annihilated either."

"Starblade is already planning to leave Earth soon. He's just been helping me, because... Well, I'm not entirely sure why, but it's been nice."

"I'm sure, but dragons don't belong on Earth. They can knock over buildings by accident with their tails."

"You're married to a dragon who lives with you."

"I know, but when Zav is the only one here, only mailboxes and patio chairs are at risk. It's relatively low stakes."

"Not to the mailboxes."

"Arwen..."

"I know, I know. Like I said, he's not planning to stay much longer, but will you ask Zavryd if his clan will stand up to the Silverclaws? Because Starblade is a relative?"

"The results there looked kind of inconclusive. Doesn't that box only have blood samples from two dragons in it? It might only have been saying that the half-dragons are loosely tied to the Stormforge clan. I don't think that will be enough to get Zav's kin to drop everything to come defend Starblade. Besides, we don't want dragons having a war in the skies over Seattle. *Or* Bellevue. Let them duke it out on another world."

"Val… Starblade has had a rough life. He could really use an ally."

Val sighed. "I'll show Zav, but please tell Starblade to beat it, okay? It doesn't have to be forever. Just until the Silverclaws stop looking for him on Earth. Until Zav gets back, which will hopefully be soon, we don't have a way to get rid of this guy."

Arwen stared glumly at the phone, not giving a definitive answer. The call ended.

"She is right," came Starblade's soft voice from the stairs.

Though still camouflaged, he came into view as he walked into the basement, stopping at Arwen's side. He glanced at the heritage device, the holograms still floating in the air, but returned his gaze to her.

"Yendral and I should have already left. I did not wish to abandon you when you may need an ally, but it is our fault that the Silverclaw is here, wreaking havoc on the human metropolis. He is close enough that he may be tracking me by my mark—" Starblade touched the pectoral muscle that held the dragon tattoo, "—even through my camouflage. It would explain why he's looking here instead of near the sanctuary. I need to go. You have allies and will be able to complete your quest to deal with the dark elf?" He looked at Arwen's phone and at Imoshaun.

Arwen clasped his hand, wanting to ask Starblade to stay, but he didn't owe her anything, and it would be safer for him as well as the city if he fled before the Silverclaws homed in on him. "I'll be fine. Yes, I do have allies."

"Good." He squeezed her hand before stepping back, drawing it from her grip.

Her feelings made it hard for her to let him go, and she caught herself impulsively stepping forward to hug him. Hard. "Be careful."

She expected him to pull out of her grasp, but he returned the hug, bending his head to rest his cheek against hers. "I will attempt to do so. And, if I am able, I will return one day to build the pool I promised you."

She didn't care about the pool but didn't say so. She wanted him to have a reason to come back. If not for her, then she would accept him coming for his obligation.

"I hope you shoot the dark elf in the leg." His hand drifted to his own thigh.

"I hear that really waylays people."

"*Yes.*" He smiled against her cheek.

When he stepped back again, Arwen made herself let him go. He touched a finger to her cheek before disappearing up the stairs.

27

ARWEN DIDN'T SENSE STARBLADE AFTER HE DISAPPEARED UP THE stairs, but a few minutes later, Val called again.

"That was impressive," she said.

"What?"

"The Silverclaw dragon was destroying more buildings when Starblade appeared out of nowhere and threw something magical at him. It exploded and made all of downtown Seattle shake. It didn't kill the dragon, but it definitely got his attention. Starblade made a portal and flew through it. I appreciate that he made a point to let the pest dragon know he was leaving. I hope the Silverclaw leaves too."

"Me too."

It wouldn't have been worth it to send Starblade away if the other dragon remained.

"There's Willard," Val said. "I'll call you back."

"The Val you spoke of is the Ruin Bringer, yes?" Imoshaun asked after Arwen hung up.

"Yes."

"There is a rumor that she is the daughter of the elven king."

Arwen nodded. "I think so."

"Did you ask her to show him this information?" Imoshaun pointed to the lineage diagram.

"No. I sent her the dragon half. Even if the information changed King Eireth's feelings about the half-dragons—from what I've gathered, he's not pleased they appeared on his world after being gone for centuries—it doesn't sound like the elves would do anything to piss off dragons. I don't know what they could do against such powerful beings even if they *didn't* mind pissing them off."

"The king might offer the half-dragons refuge, but perhaps more pertinent is that this implies the *Ruin Bringer* is related to Starblade."

"Distantly." Arwen didn't know what the offspring of a nephew would be in relation to someone. And vice versa.

"But related nonetheless. They should attend family gatherings together."

"I'll see if Val wants to invite Starblade to her next neighborhood barbecue."

"Yes, but also see if she wants to help defend him from the Silverclaw clan. The Ruin Bringer has slain dragons before. She has a great tiger and a dwarven sword. Also a dragon for a mate."

"I'm aware." Arwen had seen all three. "Even Val hesitates to pick fights with dragons. I do see your point, however."

"If she is like many mates, she may also have sway over how Lord *Zavryd* interacts with Starblade. Even if he is unimpressed with his possible relation to the half-dragon, would he not feel compelled to protect a relative of his mate?"

"I'm not sure, but you're right. I need to send Val the other half of the lineage chart."

"Yes." Imoshaun nodded. "Then perhaps Starblade can return and assist you with your dark-elf problem. Did you say why exactly this particular dark elf is harassing you?"

While Arwen took another photo to send to Val, she explained her tattoo-removal quest.

"You are aware," Imoshaun said, "that Earth is not the only place where magical tattoos can be acquired—and removed—correct?"

"It's the only place *I* have access to."

"Is it? You know dragons, half-dragons, and the Ruin Bringer."

Arwen paused, looking up from her phone. Actually, she knew *Matti,* who had that portal-generation artifact.

"Further, it is highly unlikely that the dark elves could sense you through your tattoo after you pass through a portal. The various worlds in the Cosmic Realms are spaced all over the galaxy. Portals are like magical wormholes that offer shortcuts from world to world, defying the common understanding of time and distance to allow nearly instantaneous travel. There are some who can track via portals but only if they are in the area when one is used and only if it's done very soon after it disappears. My point is that the dark elves will have no idea where you go if you leave Earth, and your stalker won't know what tattoo artist you're going to see—or be able to threaten him."

"Those are good points that hadn't occurred to me."

"Because you are a tracker and a farmer. Those are simple occupations that don't require brain brilliance. Not like science and inventing."

"Is that so?" Arwen asked.

"Yes."

"Even though you're insulting my occupations, I am grateful for your help and that you've given me something to think about."

"I encourage you to think at all opportunities."

"I will." Arwen shrugged off her pack and removed jars of jam and pickled vegetables. She wished she had pies and other baked goods to pile onto the gnome's workbench as well. "These are for you."

"Food?" Imoshaun picked up a jam jar and read the label.

"Things I made. They're good. To human tastes, anyway. And half-dragons. Do gnomes have a favorite food?"

"Yes. *Ukdekoran.* They are like your snails, but they gather the sweet syrup dripped from the *hyka* tree, so they are extra delicious when you bite into them. We make a soup that also uses the syrup. It is sweet and savory. Perfection."

"I don't think I can get those in Seattle." Nor did Arwen know what dish she could make from a sweet snail. "Do you have a favorite *Earth* food?"

Imoshaun touched a finger to her chin. "I like mochi. Cinnamon-raisin mochi, yes. Also mochi ice cream."

"That's quite different from snails."

"I do not think mochi snails would be tasty. First, you eat the snails and *then* the mochi. Yes, that sounds like a delicious meal." Imoshaun opened a jam jar, poked a finger in, and licked it. Her eyes brightened. "Maybe you can make *jam* mochi. Or serve mochi with jam."

"I'll keep your preferences in mind the next time I get a chance to bake."

"Yes. Excellent." Imoshaun opened a jar of pickled asparagus.

Arwen sent Val the second half of Starblade's lineage chart along with a text mentioning she might be Starblade's long-lost great niece or something like that. As she finished, her phone rang again, startling her.

Her father's number popped up. Even though it had been weeks since he'd installed the new phone at the farm, he'd never called Arwen, and worry immediately burrowed into her gut.

"Father? Are you okay?"

What if Harlik-van had gone there and threatened him?

"Yes, but a goblin messenger on a bicycle came by and delivered an envelope for you. There's writing on the front in Dark Elven."

Hell, Harlik-van *had* threatened her father.

"The flap wasn't sealed, and I was worried, so I opened it. The only thing inside is a photo printed off on computer paper that shows what I believe may be a half-troll—he has pale green skin but pointed elf ears."

Arwen sagged. "Mark. I've met him." And she'd told him to leave town. "Is he... dead?"

"In the photo, he's alive, but he's bound and on his knees in front of a pool of water in a cave."

"Can you read the writing?"

Her father had picked up some of the spoken language during the years he'd been a prisoner, but Arwen didn't know if he'd learned to read it. Her mother had tutored her—or *had* her tutored by others—but rarely with him present.

"Enough. It says this one dies if you remove your tattoo."

Arwen rubbed her face. She'd tried so hard to keep Mark alive. "Does it say that he wants me to do anything? That I can trade my life for Mark's?"

"No, and I hope you're not planning to do *that*. I'm relieved their kind didn't come for me, especially since they obviously know where we live."

"Yeah." Arwen frowned. Now that her father mentioned it, she was surprised Harlik-van hadn't tried to use *him* as bait, delivering a photo of him trussed up in that cave.

But it didn't sound like he wanted anything from Arwen except for her to leave her tattoo alone. Whatever the reason, she was relieved Harlik-van hadn't gone after her father, but she didn't want to see the poor tattoo artist killed either. She also hated being strong-armed.

"Arwen, why don't you leave the tattoo issue be for now?" her father asked. "Someday, when the dark elves aren't paying as much attention to you, you can figure out how to have it removed."

It was logical advice, but... "Their recent *attention* makes me think they're not going to stop watching me, that things might get worse. They want me back with them for some reason, to use me somehow. They were only waiting until I grew up by dark-elf standards, which means turning thirty, I gather. And now... I don't know what they want, but I'd prefer to escape their power before finding out."

"How are you going to do that?" The wariness in his tone suggested he didn't want her to go off into danger.

Arwen couldn't blame him. She wouldn't be foolish enough to tackle Harlik-van alone. Last time, he'd gotten the best of her. If not for Starblade returning, Mark would already be dead.

"Surprise him in his lair while he's sleeping and take care of him," she said.

"Do you know where his lair *is*?"

"I hope to soon. I have someone researching it." She didn't mention Gondo, doubting her father had much faith in the research abilities of goblins.

"Let me know when you find out. I'll go with you."

"I won't go alone."

"Because you'll take *me*," he said firmly. "Or at least Starblade," he relented. "I'll allow that he's more powerful than I am."

"You'd trust him to keep an eye on me? I didn't know you'd bonded that thoroughly over Frodo's innards."

Imoshaun, one finger slathered with jam while she held asparagus spears in her other hand, raised her eyebrows.

"Our tractor," Arwen mouthed.

"I wouldn't say we *bonded*," her father said, "but he kicked the asses of those shifters, and he also incinerated oil stains on the floor of the barn."

"A clear demonstration of his power."

"He incinerated them flamboyantly."

Arwen managed a smile, remembering the inferno Starblade had used to reveal Imoshaun's trapdoor.

"If you won't take me," Father said, "even though I *know* I could help, I hope you'll at least take him."

Arwen wished she could. Not wanting her father to worry, she didn't say that Starblade had left Earth.

"I won't go alone," was what she repeated, hoping it reassured him.

He sighed and told her to be careful again before hanging up.

Arwen looked at Imoshaun, who'd sampled all the offerings by now and was continuing to sample them.

Her eyebrows rose above the rims of her spectacles. "I cannot be your backup. I am an inventor, not a warrior. Remember, I use my *brain* and not my brawn. Besides, I have already given you an arrow designed to impale dark elves." Her gaze shifted toward Arwen's quiver.

"I know. I wasn't going to ask you to come. I don't even know where that cave *is* yet. I'm just contemplating my options."

A great roar sounded in the distance, and she sensed the Silverclaw dragon. Damn, he hadn't followed Starblade? Had he not been able to tell where that portal went? Even if he couldn't track Starblade, the Silverclaw had to know he'd left Earth. Why was he still flying around Bellevue?

"A good option is hiding," Imoshaun said. "It is one gnomes enjoy pursuing."

"I gathered from the schematic-filled roll of toilet paper."

Arwen's phone rang again. This time, Willard's number popped up.

"Yes, ma'am?" Arwen answered warily, hoping she wouldn't be blamed for the dragon trouble.

"Gondo found your waterfall cave."

"Oh?"

"It's up near North Bend. There are a lot of hiking trails in that area, but there's not one that goes to it. It's fairly inaccessible on foot, at least to humans. There's a goblin clan in the area though, so that's why they know about it. They don't go there anymore, due to bad mojo."

"Mojo?"

"That's not the word Gondo used, but it's how I translated it. Do I understand correctly that your half-dragon ally left Earth and you don't have a way to fly up there?"

"Not unless Zavryd is willing to give me a ride. He sounded busy when I spoke to Val."

No, he'd sounded like he wasn't on *Earth*.

"He's still busy," Willard said. "He's in the area, but there are now *two* Silverclaw dragons flying around Seattle, causing trouble."

"But Starblade left," Arwen said.

"Tell *them* that."

"I thought *he* did. With an explosion followed by a portal."

"All I know is that I'm getting calls from people all over the city who can see dragons—and others who can't but know they exist and can see the damage they're doing. I'm hoping Zavryd can talk them into leaving. I don't want to divert him from this problem, but Thorvald can help you, especially if you think getting rid of the dark elf might fix the rest of the trouble in the city." Willard sounded hopeful.

"I... don't think the two problems are related, ma'am."

"Well, I want that dark elf taken care of, regardless. He's killed numerous humans as well as members of the magical community. That makes him a criminal in my book."

Arwen didn't point out that Harlik-van might not have made any trouble at all if she hadn't started her quest. In truth, she didn't know that. And someone like that... he'd probably killed a lot of innocent people before her mother had sent him on this mission.

"Where are you?" Willard asked.

"Imoshaun's workshop."

"I'm sending Thorvald to pick you up. You two can figure out how to get to that cave and make sure that dark elf doesn't murder anyone else."

"The inaccessible-on-foot cave?"

"You two have elven blood. You're agile. Swing from vines if you need to. Willard, out."

"There aren't a lot of *vines* in the Pacific Northwest," Arwen murmured, but the colonel had already hung up.

"The Ruin Bringer is very good backup," Imoshaun said. "Your father will be pleased."

Arwen had a feeling her father would prefer she take backup with the power to incinerate oil stains—and enemies—but she nodded. Val *was* a capable warrior. Arwen would be glad to have her assistance—assuming they could find a way to that cave.

"You will want to put on your armor," Imoshaun said.

"Oh, I will." Arwen dug into her pack to do exactly that.

"With luck, traffic will be good, and the Ruin Bringer will arrive quickly." Imoshaun looked at a clock mounted on one wall. "You will want to encroach upon the dark elf's lair *before* the sun goes down and he wakes up for the night."

"Good point."

It would be to her and Val's advantage to face Harlik-van when the sun was out. Once it was dark, all the advantages would be his. Unfortunately, evening wasn't far off, and it would take a while to drive out to North Bend. Arwen hoped they could find the cave quickly.

28

THE SIDE MIRROR REFLECTED THE SUN DROPPING TOWARD THE horizon as the Jeep headed east on I-90. In the passenger seat, Arwen fidgeted with her borrowed camouflaging charm.

"Plenty of time 'til dark. And if he's awake when we get there, it'll be more fun." Val patted her gun in its thigh holster.

She hadn't remarked on Arwen's shimmery new armor other than to agree it wasn't Amber's style. If she worried about being seen in public with someone wearing such a thing, she didn't mention it. Of course, they weren't heading anywhere *public*.

"He dodged a gnomish arrow enchanted to have an advantage against dark elves." Arwen sensed the magic of Val's firearm, but it was far less substantial than that of her dwarven-crafted sword.

"It's harder to dodge a bullet than an arrow. Trust me."

So that was where Amber got that phrase.

"We'll see." Arwen wanted to be optimistic, but it wasn't in her nature. Not when dealing with dark elves. "This is his lair. Even if it's temporary, he'll have traps set up around it."

"I have a charm for finding snares, deadfall traps, pits full of snakes, dungeon entrances, and oubliettes. Though nobody's ever tried to lure me into an oubliette. They're more popular in Europe than America, I understand."

"We're a heathen nation that lacks the finer things."

"Zav tells me that a lot, but it's in regard to our whole planet. Anyway, Matti made me the charm for my birthday." Val touched the leather thong tied around her neck, various magical trinkets dangling from it, including the feline head that she used to summon her tiger. "One of the best presents I ever got. *Much* better than the edible panties Zav gave me. He didn't read the box carefully, so he was surprised and displeased when they turned out to be made from candy instead of beef jerky."

Arwen blinked slowly. "Was there a *reason* he thought they'd be made from meat?"

"The ones he got me for Christmas were. He doesn't have a sweet tooth. He has a *meat* tooth."

"I've observed that."

"Dragons are wonderful allies in battle and can be loyal and loving companions, but their singular interest in food—in their preferred type of food—can make them a little..."

"Quirky?"

"Yeah." Val smiled fondly as she took an exit, heading toward the Rattlesnake Lake Recreation Area. "It's understandable since they have large bodies and burn a lot of calories."

"This is a popular area with a lot of trails." Arwen didn't know the forest here as well as the state lands north of I-90, but she'd visited a few times for Search and Rescue training. The number of people meandering up and down the mountain's paths and chatting loudly, especially in the summer, ensured she would never seek the area for recreation. If a hiking trail had more people on it than in the farmers market, it was far too busy for her.

"I know. We're supposed to go up a forest-service road, past a locked gate, and then veer off into the wilds." Val fished her phone out and brought up a photo of a map with a spot along a river circled. Someone had drawn a stick figure with pointed ears on it.

"Exactly how Harlik-van looked when I saw him," Arwen murmured.

"That's Gondo's artwork. He said he would try to arrange a guide for us."

Arwen sensed a dragon in the sky behind them. "Uhm."

"Time for another handy charm." Val rubbed one that looked like it was made from used gum and paperclips. Not surprisingly, it emanated goblin magic. "For a while, I had this on my keychain, because it's hideous and I didn't want it around my neck, but stealth magic is too handy to tuck away. I hear you're borrowing Amber's?"

"Yes." Arwen activated the charm, though she hoped the dragon had no reason to look for either of them, not with Starblade gone. "Can Matti make camouflage charms?"

"I'm not sure, but she's getting quite versatile. She's been working on her enchanting recently since late-stage pregnancy has slowed her down. Don't tell her I said that. She'll deny it completely while trying to thump me with her hammer."

"I wouldn't think of it. My birthday isn't for a while, unfortunately."

"Keep bringing her tasty pickled vegetables while dropping hints about your desires. She's a sucker for cheese too."

The dragon's aura grew stronger as he flew closer. He seemed to be heading in the same direction as they, and Arwen shifted uneasily in her seat.

"Your guy doesn't have a deal with the Silverclaws or anything, does he?" Val asked.

"I hope not."

The concerned frown Val slanted her suggested she didn't like that answer.

"His name is Harlik-van." Arwen didn't care what Val called

him but didn't want the pronoun *your* attached to it.

"I'd ask you to write that down for his tombstone, but I think Willard has the bodies of deceased criminals incinerated."

As the Jeep continued farther from the interstate, turning off the main route and onto gravel and eventually dirt roads, Arwen kept glancing in the sideview mirror. The dragon wasn't bothering to camouflage himself, so it wasn't long before she glimpsed him above the trees, his green scales bathed by the setting sun.

"He's only a half mile back," Arwen said.

"I know." Val continued driving, but she kept an eye toward her side mirror, too, adjusting the tilt to show more of the sky. "We're both camouflaged, but he'll be able to see the Jeep. And I'm not sure these charms are a hundred percent solid at hiding people in moving vehicles. I know running and fighting—fast movements— will break the spell."

"We aren't going that fast," Arwen said as Val maneuvered around a pothole. Now and then, they passed another SUV, but the traffic had thinned considerably.

"True. I'm going to be pissed if he attacks my Jeep. This is technically *Willard's* Jeep. She found me a loaner after Zav destroyed my first one."

"He *destroyed* it? Did you not get him the right kind of meat for an important feast?"

"All kinds of meat are the right kinds, and no. Haven't I told you the story of how we met? Of how Zav threatened my life and hurled my old Jeep into the branches of a tree? It's a classic tale of *not*-love-at-first-sight."

"I guess Starblade reading my mind at our first meeting isn't that great an offense after all. Though he did incinerate your mother's gun."

"Dragons are rude until you get to know them." Val fell silent as the aerial stalker flew closer. "I think he knows we're in here. Matti once used her magic to hide us *and* her motorcycle, but that was from the police, not dragons. And she's an enchanter, so she's gifted in that area. I've only learned a few elf-magic tricks for fighting and about my sword's powers."

Verminous mongrels, the dragon boomed into their minds, *I know you are allies of the half-dragon dung sniffer. You will tell me where he went. To what world did he flee when he saw our numbers and our great might?*

Val turned up a new dirt road, the grade so steep and boulder-filled that a vehicle with a lower clearance couldn't have navigated it.

"We don't answer him, right?" Arwen whispered.

"I wouldn't. Do you know where Starblade went?"

"No."

"Normally, I'd say that's good, so we can't betray him, but I doubt this guy will care. He might mind-scour and torture us even if he sees that we don't know anything." Val navigated them over and around rocks and through ruts that tossed Arwen into the door and dash, even with her seat belt on and one hand firmly around the oh-shit handle.

"Yeah."

"Silverclaws don't hold themselves to the same standards as Stormforges when it comes to the laws of the Cosmic Realms," Val said.

"Those laws don't seem to say much about mind scouring and torture, not when it comes to lesser species."

"Another truth."

Do not think that because you are the weakling mate of that fool Zavryd'nokquetal that I will not reach into your mind and extract what you know, the dragon continued.

"I'm trying to telepath to Zav," Val said. "He's outside of my range, but he sometimes knows I'm in trouble and hears me even when my power shouldn't be great enough to reach him."

"Willard said he's back on Earth, right?"

"He said something about getting allies, so I'm not sure. If he's not, all bets are off."

Ahead, a blue metal bar across the road came into view. Val gunned the accelerator to find the power to ascend the final incline to the gate. Arwen couldn't imagine this had once been a logging road, not at this grade. Maybe there was a fire lookout tower at the top of the mountain.

"Okay, he heard me," Val said. "He says to get out of the Jeep so we can hide more effectively. Thanks, Zav. So helpful. If we get out of the Jeep, Mr. Grumpy up there might tear it to pieces."

The dragon flew ahead, landing on a cedar that overlooked the gate from fifteen feet away. The top of the tree swayed under his weight since he was ludicrously large for the perch.

"You don't think he'll do that anyway?" Arwen removed her seat belt, envisioning having to fling herself outside any second.

The dragon had yellow-green eyes that glowed as he peered down at the Jeep. He flexed his wings, like he might jump off and dive-bomb.

"If he does, he's going to get a sword up the ass." Val stopped the vehicle and cranked the emergency brake hard. "Normally, I'd turn us sideways to the hill, but I don't think he's going to stay still and let me find the perfect parking spot."

A screech came from the dragon, and he sprang from the branch.

"Get out!" Val yanked out the keys and threw her door open.

Arwen grabbed her weapons and leaped into ferns to the side of the road. As the dragon plummeted toward them, she nocked an arrow. But she hesitated. It would be safer to do as Zavryd had suggested and hide, not do anything to goad the dragon.

But Val leaped onto the hood of the Jeep with her sword raised as silver mist gathered in front of the fender, the shape of her tiger coalescing. "You stay away from my rig, you overpowered asshole!"

So much for not goading the dragon.

Though Arwen sensed a magical barrier around him, as well as the natural armor of his scales, she fired toward his long neck. Hopefully, one of her arrows would have the strength to pierce his defenses. Most of the extra power Starblade had infused into her bow had faded, but some remained. Maybe it would be enough.

The dragon stretched his talons toward Val as he plummeted toward her. Arwen's arrow pierced the barrier but clinked against his scales and bounced off.

As talons slashed toward Val, she leaped to the side and swung her blade. Her dwarven sword sliced through the barrier and clipped one of those talons before she dropped away, landing in the ferns.

The tiger leaped to the hood, then the roof of the Jeep, and finally after the dragon, slashing in the air with his claws. But their foe jerked his feet up before they struck. Val had drawn blood, however, and a drop fell onto the roof as the dragon flapped his wings, heading back upward. No doubt so he could dive again.

He struck branches, knocking needles and cones to the ground as he gained elevation.

"Got another blood sample for you," Val called as she climbed back onto the Jeep, sounding calm until she raised her voice and added, "But I hope the half-dragons aren't related to any *inferior* Silverclaws!"

Their foe screeched, probably more furious at the insult than the tiny hole she'd cut in his foot.

I do adore it when you bring me abruptly into this world to face dragons you've taunted into extreme ire, a male voice sounded in Arwen's mind. It took her a moment to realize it was the tiger. When she'd seen him before, he hadn't spoken to her.

"You love a good hunt, Sindari." Val crouched on the Jeep, waiting for the dragon to attack again.

Even a mighty Del'nothian tiger does not hunt predators twenty times his size.

"Only ten times?"

Rarely even that. Predators do not have an appealing taste.

"Yeah, that's my problem with dragons too."

The *predator* banked to turn back toward them, but, instead of diving again, he blasted magical power down at them. Val was his target, but the Jeep jolted, almost tipping, and she flew backward over the hood. She twisted in the air to try to come down on her feet.

Clipped by the power, Arwen didn't see if she succeeded. She tumbled backward, slamming into a tree. Several other trees either snapped or were ripped free from the earth by the great blast. Thanks to the armor, the blow didn't hurt badly, but it was still jarring.

Sindari roared at the dragon from all fours in the road behind the Jeep. Arwen nocked another arrow and ducked behind a still-standing tree. The fallen ones littered dirt from their exposed roots.

The dragon roared back at Sindari, or maybe all of them. *To attack one of our kind is a great crime. Do not think your status as Zavryd'nokquetal's mate will save you from the wrath of the Dragon Council. And from the wrath of the Silverclaw Clan.*

"This guy is going to wake up the dark elf, even if he's sleeping," Val grumbled.

"I'm not sure that's our main problem right now," Arwen said.

"I got in touch with Zav, but he's stuck in town dealing with other Silverclaws. They're threatening him because they think he's been hiding the half-dragons."

Arwen grimaced because there was some truth to that. At the least, Zavryd hadn't told the other dragons where Starblade and Yendral were.

"They've figured out that one of their brothers was killed," Val added, "and they're not happy with the situation."

The dragon roared again.

"I gathered." Arwen pointed her nocked arrow at him.

With his magical barrier reinforced, the dragon dove toward them again.

Val must have activated her camouflage charm, because she disappeared. Arwen didn't hear a sound but trusted she'd moved off the road.

The dragon kept aiming for that spot—with the trees to either side, he couldn't easily swerve. Branches cracked as he struck some while coming down. He landed where Val had been and blasted power all around him as he tore into the ground with his talons, flinging dirt and rocks.

Ugh, Val grunted into Arwen's mind.

Did the power get you?

Val didn't respond, and Arwen worried she lay crippled and in pain, camouflaged but unable to continue the fight.

When the dragon didn't find Val, he whirled toward Arwen. His yellow-green eyes pinned her, making her realize the shots she'd fired had caused her camouflage to drop.

With little choice, Arwen shot another arrow, aiming for one of those glaring eyes, then jammed her hand into her pocket to rub the charm. The dragon's maw opened, and fire spewed forth. The flames kept her from seeing if her arrow had landed, but she doubted it.

As Arwen darted to the side, heat crackling in the air and fire almost scorching her, she worried she was moving too quickly for the camouflage to reactivate.

With few other options, she ducked behind a stout tree and drew another arrow. The dragon's head moved, flames continuing to spew, like water from a hose. Branches and entire trees caught fire.

Arwen shot one more arrow, but her cover burst into flame. Startled, she dove behind a pile of boulders.

Sindari roared from the road, but Arwen didn't know if the

tiger could do anything effective. The fire continued to pour into the forest all around her. No, it focused on her boulders, forcing her to stay where she was lest she burn to a crisp. Doubting the armor could stop that, she pressed her back to them.

One of the rocks overheated and snapped in half, shards pounding her between the shoulder blades. Arwen grunted as she dropped to her knees.

Trapped, with the heat wrapping around the boulder pile to scorch her cheeks, she couldn't risk leaning out to shoot again. Nor could she run.

Val? Arwen asked hopefully.

A screech cut through the forest, and the fire halted, though trees burned all around. When another screech sounded, Arwen risked poking her head over the top of the boulders.

Across the road, Val drew her sword out of the dragon's tail—it had been on the ground between the trees. She backed away as he whirled toward her, jaws snapping. Only a thick fir kept him from reaching her.

Arwen fired at the dragon's back. Thanks to Val's work, his barrier was down, at least for a few seconds. The arrow landed, finding a less armored spot between two scales and sinking in.

Sindari leaped over the back of the Jeep, landed on the hood, and sprang off as if it were a diving board. His jaws snapped around one of the dragon's wings, and he bit down hard.

Roaring, the dragon used his power to blast the tiger away. He caught Val in the magical blow, and she and her sword, along with several trees, flew backward. With a taloned forelimb, the dragon batted at Arwen's arrow, tearing it free.

Instead of pressing the attack, he leaped into the air, wings flapping. *Do not think you mosquitoes have deterred me. You will tell me where the mongrel half-dragon scum went, and we will find and slay him.*

Knocking more branches to the ground, he flapped his wings

until he ascended above the trees.

Expecting him to dive at them once more, Arwen readied another arrow. But the dragon flew off toward the west—toward the city—and she realized those had been parting words. At least for now.

Val staggered out of the woods, a hand to her side and soot blackening her face and blonde hair. Flames crackled in the trees all around her.

She rested her hand on the tiger's back as she came onto the road. "There are claw marks on the hood of my Jeep, Sindari."

Those are talon *marks.*

"Oh? I didn't notice the dragon using the hood as a launchpad."

Would you have preferred I let him chomp on you?

"I guess not. You okay, Arwen?"

"Yes." She eyed the burning trees, hoping this wouldn't start a forest fire, and collected her arrows. "Where do you think he went?"

"Zav's sister and another Stormforge came through a portal. I'm *hoping* they'll settle things without a fight, but Zav will be pissed that one of the Silverclaws attacked me." Val grimaced.

"It was at least polite of him to rip my arrow out so I didn't lose it." Arwen waved the one that had pierced his scales before returning it to her quiver.

"Yeah. I was thinking what a polite dragon he was as he hurled me through the forest and into a rock. I..." Val frowned and looked around.

It had grown later, twilight descending on the forest. Now that the dragon was gone and they weren't talking, something plucked at Arwen's instincts. The crackling of wood was the only sound, but she sensed someone watching them.

Val pointed between two trees beyond the gate. A pair of eyes glinted, reflecting the flames.

29

THE EYES WIDENED AS ARWEN AND VAL SPOTTED THEIR OWNER IN the gloom. Arwen started to raise her bow, afraid another enemy had arrived, before she sensed the aura of a goblin.

"Hello," Val called. "Are you our guide, by chance?"

"I am Tuttuk," came a quavery male voice. "Gondo said you seek a dark elf. I thought this was terribly horrible and that nobody would wish to be guided to a *dark-elf* lair. And then you showed up with a dragon. Even worse." The goblin glanced up the mountain behind him, as if considering ditching the crazy trouble attractors that had shown up in his neighborhood.

Arwen wouldn't have blamed him for fleeing, but she hurried to delve into her pack. "We're sorry about that. We brought you a gift."

The goblin's head turned toward them. In the gloom, it was hard to see much, but his pointed green ears might have perked with interest. "A gift?"

"Delicious food." Arwen held up the last of the goods she'd brought from home, a jar of honey. Since she knew numerous goblin recipes called for the sweet substance, she believed it would be well-received.

"Delicious food? Like rotisserie raccoon? Or squirrel stew?"

"Honey crafted by bees foraging among sweet elderberry and strawberry blossoms."

"Oh." The goblin trotted toward them. "I will accept your gift and take you as close as is sane to the dark-elf lair."

"So, you'll ditch us a mile away?" Val asked.

"*Two* miles away." Tuttuk took the jar, opened the lid, and stuck his tongue straight into the honey.

"Guess he's not sharing that with the rest of the clan," Val murmured.

"Let's hope."

Val must have decided the burning trees were a threat to the Jeep, because she moved it farther down the hill. She didn't park it parallel to the slope, as she'd mentioned earlier, but facing downhill in the middle of the road. To facilitate a quick escape, Arwen trusted. A rock shoved under a tire as a chock block would hopefully keep the Jeep from a premature departure.

The goblin had eaten a third of the honey by the time she rejoined them.

"This way, mighty warriors." Tuttuk thrust the jar into the air and headed away from the road and into the woods.

"Maybe he'll get us within a mile and a half." Arwen hurried to catch up with the goblin.

"If you'd brought a pie, he might have taken us to the front door of the cave."

"Like a rotisserie raccoon pie?"

"Yum yum."

Val kept her tiger out for the trek, probably expecting more trouble as they trod through dense undergrowth, clambered over logs, and maneuvered up and down steep slopes. The scent of charred wood hung in the air long after they left the gate, and as they climbed higher, glimpses backward revealed flames still burning. Arwen hoped they could convince Zavryd or someone else with enough power to come put out the fires later. Assuming they all survived the night.

"Do you get worried when Zavryd fights other dragons?" Arwen asked after an owl hooted at their passing. Insects buzzed, and a frog croaked nearby.

"Yes. He's a badass, but those Silverclaws are treacherous, and they've got a feud with his clan going way back."

"The Silverclaws accused *Starblade* of being treacherous. They looked down upon him for setting traps and not openly facing them."

"Like... suicidally?"

"Yeah."

"They don't openly face the Stormforges either. Trust me."

Val issued a command that prompted her sword to glow blue, illuminating the way as night deepened. They might have lost their guide if not for his aura—and the way he hummed happily, pausing now and then to slurp from the jar.

The goblin easily skimmed through tight spots, and he fearlessly led them across a ravine by tucking his honey away and swinging hand under hand across a rope. Arwen might hate her dark-elven blood, but she was glad for the agility and athleticism it lent her as she followed him. Their route had turned into an obstacle course, and she could see why there wasn't a hiking trail to the waterfall. Sindari, without the thumbs necessary for ropes, scrambled down into the ravine, finding his own route to the other side.

"I hope the dragon doesn't come back while we're dangling." Arwen struggled to keep her bow on her back as she swung along the rope.

Val, who'd been forced to sheath her sword, grunted in agreement. "My latest update is that they're all busy fuming at each other in town. Starblade's name keeps coming up. For a guy who's supposed to be hiding out, he's drawn a lot of attention to himself."

"I don't think he's the type of person who's good at hiding and doing nothing."

"It's hard to retire when you're only two or three hundred years old."

On the far side of the ravine, Tuttuk swung to the ground and scurried down a slope. Sindari rejoined them, grumbling about sticker bushes, and Val picked a few thorns out of his silver fur. When they caught up again with the goblin, he pointed across a valley toward the opposite ridge.

"Go down there, up there, and back there is a river that you can follow downstream to the waterfall grotto. My people have not gone into the cave behind it for many moons, not since the dark-elf invaded it, but we believe it is the place you seek."

"Thank you," Arwen said.

"Thank *you*." Tuttuk stuck his tongue in the jar again before saluting them with it and trotting back the way they had come.

"As an adept woodswoman, you can find your way back to the Jeep, right?" Val asked Arwen.

"Yes."

Do you mean that the great claw gouges in the hood are not so vast and deep that you can see them from here? Sindari asked.

"Surprisingly, no," Val said.

"Is your tiger being snarky with you?" Since this was Arwen's mission, she took the lead, descending into the valley.

"More often than not, yes."

By the time they reached the ridge, the first hint of rushing water reaching their ears, the insects and wildlife had fallen silent. It might have been because of Sindari, but Arwen doubted it. Earlier, the owls had been unconcerned by him. More likely, the forest creatures were uneasy at the presence of a dark elf and his magic.

A hint of that magic brushed Arwen's senses, and she paused. They weren't yet close to the river.

"Do you feel that?" she asked.

"Yeah, some kind of artifact?"

"Or a trap."

"I have something for that." Val rubbed one of the trinkets on her thong.

"The oubliette charm?"

"Nah, this is a different one, specifically for locating magical traps. I like to be prepared for any eventuality."

Since Val had the charm, Arwen let her take the lead. They walked along the ridge to a rocky outcropping high enough above the forest that they had a view all the way back to civilization, the lights of North Bend visible. What looked like a mundane telescope was set up on a tripod, but it was the source of the magic. Dark-elf magic.

Val pointed. "How much do you want to bet he's not using that to stargaze?"

After checking to make sure the telescope didn't register as a trap to Val's charm, Arwen peered through it. And straight at—a tree?

A tingle of magic emanated from the device, and her tattoo itched.

"Yes, it's dark-elven magic," she murmured to it.

On a hunch, Arwen pictured the Space Needle in her mind. The device's power fluctuated, and the view blurred until it focused on downtown Seattle, the city lights bright against the deepening night. The Space Needle appeared in the center, the elevated restaurant so crisp and detailed that she could see the diners through the windows. A man stuck a roll into his mouth.

"Uh."

"Are you being enlightened?" Val asked.

"Horrified, maybe." Arwen imagined Val's and Matti's houses in Green Lake, and the view blurred, refocusing on them. "I know how he's been keeping tabs on me." She was positive there were hills in the way that would have made it impossible for a normal telescope to have a line-of-sight view of Seattle, but the magic made it anything but normal.

"Yeah." Val didn't sound surprised.

Arwen was about to back up when she glimpsed something flying in the sky beyond the houses and out over Green Lake. It was too large to be a bat or bird. Then yellow-green eyes glowed, and her stomach sank. One of the Silverclaw dragons.

"Are they all there?" she asked the telescope, envisioning Zavryd.

The view rose higher and grew broader, showing the sky over the entire lake and the surrounding park. Zavryd, a lilac-scaled dragon, and another black-scaled dragon flew—paced—back and forth at one end. One blue and two green dragons did the same on the opposite end of the lake. The sharp magnification let Arwen see a gash in the side of the lilac dragon. The two clans weren't fighting at the moment, but they must have been before. Had the green one who'd attacked Val and Arwen returned to Seattle to even—or *skew*—the odds?

"Val?" Arwen stepped aside and waved for her to look.

"That's Zav and his sister, Zondia, and I don't know the Silverclaws. The other black dragon... I'm not sure. Probably a relative of Zav's. I can tell it's not the queen. There's some gray around the muzzle. It reminds me of his uncle, Ston-something-or-other, but I've only met him once. Shit. A portal just opened."

"Reinforcements?"

And for which side?

"I think that's Starblade. Someone must have forced him to

come back. The portal is over the lake. He's going to end up right in the middle of it and—"

Worry made Arwen nudge Val aside so she could look again. Why would Starblade have come back?

She spotted him flying out of the portal over the lake, his eyes glowing violet. Val was right. He had appeared in the middle of both parties.

"What are you *doing*?" Arwen whispered, but he was too far away for her to reach telepathically.

"Get back!" Val grabbed Arwen and pulled her from the telescope. One of the charms on her thong flashed green three times.

They scrambled away, and Val tugged Arwen behind a tree. None too soon. White light flashed, and great power blasted outward from the telescope.

Even with the tree for cover, they felt the blast. The ground shook, and they fell to their knees. Brush and rocks flew over the edge of the ridge.

Sindari snarled and sank low for balance on the quaking ground. Rock sheared from the side of the ridge and cracked and banged as it plummeted down the steep slope.

"Shit," Val whispered.

Arwen was on the verge of running, afraid the whole ridge would collapse, when the power faded, and the ground stopped shaking. With trembling hands, she pushed pine needles out of her hair.

In the aftermath, the telescope lay dormant, no longer offering up its views.

"Do you think it's smart enough to realize non-dark elves were using it?" Val wondered. "Maybe it didn't object to you, because of your blood, but it didn't like me."

Given how long they'd used it before the *objection* had started, Arwen didn't think that was it. "I have a feeling... the dark elf is awake and knows we're here."

30

Pitch darkness smothered the forest as Arwen and Val carefully picked their way down a nameless river without a path. The roar of a waterfall and Val's glowing sword guided them. Her charm alerted them to two magical traps that they were able to avoid without triggering them. She'd taken the lead, and Arwen was glad, because her own focus was split as she worried about Starblade.

"The Silverclaws are again accusing the Stormforges—Zav, in particular—of hiding the half-dragons," Val reported, communicating telepathically with her mate. "I haven't figured out yet what brought him back. The two sides are testing each other's forces from across the lake with magic, so Zav can't talk that much. We'll finish up here so we can go help them, if need be."

Though Arwen couldn't imagine joining in a battle that involved six dragons, she didn't object.

The roar of the waterfall grew louder, the river water frothy and white as it churned over rocks ahead. After squeezing past a few bushes, they came to the rim of a cliff. No, it was more of a huge hole than a cliff, with the river tumbling over the edge and filling a great pool below. Bound by vertical rock faces on all sides, the waterway ended, or maybe it continued underground after plunging down?

It reminds me of a cenote, Val said, switching to telepathy. They would have had to shout to be heard over the roar, and neither of them wanted to do that, not when they were above a dark elf's lair. *Though those are made by rock collapsing and exposing groundwater. They're not carved out by rivers.* She leaned over the ledge to peer down the rock face. *That's a long drop.*

I'll remind you that Del'nothian tigers only swim in placid waters on hot, sunny days, Sindari stated.

I think Earth tigers have a similar policy, Val replied.

Do you have a levitation charm? Arwen asked.

Sadly, I haven't come across one yet. I usually have a dragon to help me with that.

This would have been much easier to get to with one of them.

Yeah, but they're busy having a pissing match. Val waved toward the west. *I think it's all about Starblade, and who's the other one? Yendral?*

Yes.

They may get defenders, after all. The Silverclaws are infuriating Zav, and maybe his kin too. He may be inclined to offer his protection to spite the other dragons.

Would his protection be enough to keep Starblade and Yendral safe? Arwen didn't care how help came, only that Starblade would get it. And she wanted it to mean that he wouldn't need to leave Earth.

I don't know. It may depend on how many more Silverclaws show up tonight. Right now, the odds are even if there's a fight, but... Like I said, I want to finish so we can go help. In case arrows and a big dwarven sword would make a difference.

I'm agreeable to that. Since they couldn't levitate, Arwen dropped to her knees far enough from the waterfall that the rocks weren't slick, and eased one foot over. Even in daylight, the hundred-foot-drop would have been daunting, but what choice did they have? At least Arwen and Val had elven blood to grant them dexterous fingers and agility.

You sure you want to be that vulnerable when he might be camouflaged down there with weapons pointed at us? Val asked.

Arwen paused on the edge. *No, but we have to get down somehow.*

I know. Val drew her gun and pointed it toward the pool below. *You go first, and I'll cover your back.*

Okay. Thanks.

As Arwen started down, her fingers finding crevices and narrow ledges to use as handholds, Val added, *I have rope in the Jeep. If we hadn't been attacked by dragons, I wouldn't have been distracted and forgotten to bring it. That was a rookie move.*

It's fine. A hundred feet of rope would have been hard to carry over that ravine.

True. The goblin managed his load without trouble though.

His load of... the honey jar? Arwen hadn't seen Tuttuk carrying anything else.

Yeah. He didn't have pockets. Where do you think he kept it?

Clenched between his legs, maybe. Arwen's hand slipped, and she told herself to focus. If she fell, she might land in the pool, but she had no idea how deep it was or if there were boulders under the churning water.

Halfway down, something flapped to her right, startling her. Her foot slipped, and she gasped and leaned into the rock, gripping tightly with her hands. Dirt and pebbles slipped away, though any noise they made was drowned out by the roar of water.

It's a bat, Val told her.

Heart hammering, Arwen got her foot back on a solid ledge. *Scared me.*

Me too. I almost fired. I'd rather not do that, just in case the dark elf hasn't noticed us yet.

Arwen doubted they were that lucky, but she said, *I know. I've got a— Look out!*

Red beams shot out from holes in the rock face all around the pool.

One cut into Arwen's hand, and she couldn't keep from screaming at the pain. She jerked her hand away as the beam continued, blasting into the rock. Shards hit her face, and she ducked her chin, trying not to let go with her other hand. But another beam struck the rock above her, and a huge chunk tumbled down. It slammed into her shoulder and knocked her free.

Arrows flew from her quiver as she tumbled. Terrified she would land on rock instead of in the pool, she tried to use her magic in a way she never had, to shift her body out over the water.

Val fired from above, but her bullets couldn't stop the attack. More beams shot out, one buzzing past, searing off the tip of Arwen's moccasin. She couldn't keep from shrieking and jerking her limbs in, all thought of using her magic vanishing.

She hit the water shoulder-first, plunging in deep. The current caught her immediately, sweeping her around in the pool. Her head clipped a submerged boulder, and she scrambled, paddling and hoping to find the surface. Her hand hurt, her shoulder hurt, and her lungs already demanded air.

Red light flashed—more of those beams? She let it guide her toward the surface and came up with a gasp.

Arwen sensed Val plummeting down toward her and swam to the side, pain lancing her hand with each movement. When she ran into another boulder, she latched onto it. This one, at least, was above the water, and she used it as an anchor.

Val landed in the pool, a splash washing over Arwen, and disappeared below. Had she dived voluntarily? Or been struck by a beam?

Silver blurred past, and another splash erupted as Sindari

landed paws-first in the water. He came up before Val, yowling like a Siamese caught by a vacuum cleaner. Dog-paddling fiercely, he swam to a narrow ledge to the right of the waterfall.

Arwen clawed her hair out of her face and peered warily toward the rock face. The beams had stopped. Had that been the automatic security system, or were they guided by Harlik-van's hand? His power.

Val finally came up, her blonde hair bright in contrast to the dark rocks and water.

Who makes a lair in such a crappy location? she demanded telepathically. *How does he even come and go without getting soaked? And blasted to smithereens by his ridiculous sci-fi lasers?*

Arwen eyed her scorched hand, not thinking the "lasers" had been ridiculous. Just painful. *I'm sure they don't target him. And he may know how to levitate. For that matter, he may be powerful enough to create portals.*

Ugh. I hate bad guys who are stronger than I am.

After reaching the cramped ledge, Sindari planted his paws and shook himself vigorously. *Val, this visit to Earth has been abysmal. Point me to a nefarious evil-doer on whom I can sate my aggressions.*

I may be able to do that. Val crawled out of the pool beside him, and they crouched, eyeing the waterfall. The ledge looked like it might lead behind it and into the cave the orc's memory had promised.

Preferably not a dragon.

Her hand aching with each stroke, Arwen made herself swim out to collect the arrows she'd lost. Fortunately, their magic let her find them in the dark and kept the water from damaging the fletchings. The armored jumpsuit dragged at her but not any more than regular clothing. Still, by the time she swam to Val and Sindari, she was relieved to climb out.

Val stood behind Sindari, observing the waterfall while wrapping a makeshift bandage around one hand. One of the lasers must have caught her too.

Once Arwen stood, Val handed her a couple of arrows she'd grabbed.

"Thank you."

"You'll need those for our friend."

One of them had been Imoshaun's dark-elf arrow, so Arwen nodded firmly. "I will."

Sindari shook himself off again, splattering them both with fresh droplets of water. Since they were all soaking wet, one could hardly complain, but Val gave him a flat look.

Sindari gave *her* a flat look. *The nefarious evil-doer?*

That way. Val drew her gun and pointed it toward a gap between the rock wall and the edge of the waterfall.

Was it Arwen's imagination, or did a hint of black mist flow out of it, creeping along the ledge toward them? The sensation of magic behind the water made her nerves crawl. It was dark-elven magic. No doubt. It had permeated the tunnels where she'd been born.

Will your bullets fire after being soaked? Arwen readied her bow, saving the dark-elf arrow until they saw Harlik-van, but the burn on her hand made gripping the weapon painful.

Yup. They're magical. This isn't my first soaking. Trust me.

I do.

Val stepped past Sindari and led the way. Arwen was on the verge of offering to go first when Val's charm flashed green three times. A faint pulse of magical energy came from a disk mounted on the rock.

Val fired three times at it, bullets sparking orange when they struck. The device tumbled from the wall, spat sparks, then bounced into the water. Smoke wafted from it before it floated under the waterfall and disappeared.

I'm at the I-don't-give-a-shit-if-he-knows-we're-coming stage of the incursion, Val said.

I don't think silence matters at this point but camouflage, perhaps. They'd been hidden before falling, but the beams and swimming had broken the spell. Arwen dug her hand into her soggy pocket, relieved the charm hadn't fallen out.

Might as well, but he's going to know where we're coming from. There's only one door. Despite the words, Val also activated her charm. *And it's covered in creepy mist.*

I see.

Water sprayed them as they crept between the rock and the waterfall. Val held her gun *and* her glowing sword, making Arwen feel under-armed as she trailed with her bow.

The mist thickened, curling around their knees. The place had definite Halloween vibes. Arwen wouldn't have been surprised by a black cat sauntering past but doubted they would face anything so benign.

They remained close enough to see each other, and Arwen benefited from the light from Val's sword. It illuminated a cave matching the one in the photo the dark elf had sent her father, with a great pool as large as the one outside, this one less turbulent. The placid water appeared deep, but it was impossible to tell.

The dark-elven magic Arwen sensed emanated from below the surface, and she eyed the pool warily. It wasn't strong, but it reminded her of the ritual caves of her youth, the demons her mother's people had summoned.

She stayed well back from the water as she peered into the rest of the cave.

I don't see Mark. Arwen had told Val about the photo on the way up. *Or Harlik-van.*

Me either. Val paused, crouching as she scanned the darkness, her gun pointing in the same direction as her eyes. The light of her sword didn't penetrate into the depths of the cave.

Arwen reminded herself how good Harlik-van's camouflaging

magic was. He might be aiming a weapon at them that very second. Did Val have armor under her shirt?

Arwen was about to ask when the mist thickened like a dense fog and a sizzle sounded in the air above the pool. A smell like burning hair filled the cave, and a bubble formed on the surface, then popped.

The magic in the pool intensified, registering much more strongly to Arwen's senses. Something powerful had arrived from another world. No, another dimension.

"What is that stink?" Val shifted her aim toward the pool.

"A demon," Arwen said with grim certainty, memories from her childhood flooding her mind. "A lesser water demon, I think."

Barely visible through the mist, ripples moved the water outward in concentric circles. Arwen aimed at the center with her bow, though they couldn't see anything yet.

"Any chance *lesser* means it's not that powerful?" Val asked.

Arwen shook her head. "The lesser demons aren't as intelligent as the greater and usually serve masters instead of taking servants of their own, but they're plenty powerful. Sometimes, more so than those who summon them expect. Even experienced dark-elven priests have been killed by them."

"I'll be sure to direct it toward the guy we're looking for."

Water splashed upward with a tremendous *whoosh* as an entity with mauve flesh erupted from the center of the pool. The thick black mist dulled their visibility of the amorphous body, but they had no problem picking out eight appendages like tentacles that thrust into the air, each thicker than Arwen's waist. Like an octopus, the tentacles were lined with suckers.

Watch out for those, Arwen warned telepathically, pointing her bow at the creature, though it had neither eyes nor a mouth, so she didn't know where to aim. *They're not just for grabbing onto things but for extracting a victim's soul.*

Will it sense us through our camouflage?

Probably.

Using magic rather than the tentacles, the demon propelled itself toward them.

"Shit," Val said.

31

"MAGICAL WEAPONS WILL WORK ON IT, RIGHT?" VAL ASKED.

"I hope so." Arwen aimed at what might have been a head angled out of the bulbous body like a giant wart, but she didn't know if demons had brains and would be vulnerable there. Anatomy hadn't been covered in her summoning lessons.

The tentacles waved ominously in the air, almost in invitation. Dark magic pulsed off the demon, making the black mist ripple similarly to the water. When the pulses hit Arwen, she winced, each bringing pain even though she didn't feel a physical blow. She staggered back while attempting to erect a mental defense to protect her vulnerable mind.

Val grunted in pain but, instead of backing away, sprang with Sindari to the edge of the pool. "That's about enough of that."

She fired at the demon with her gun, but the bullets passed through and disappeared into the waterfall.

"What the hell?" Val demanded. "Is it an illusion?"

One tentacle slapped at the water, spraying a wave into her eyes.

"No," Arwen said. "But it's not fully in our dimension."

"Just fully enough to kill us?"

"Yes."

Val jammed her firearm back into its holster and gripped her sword with both hands. "Get over here, ugly, and let's see how you like Storm."

As if it understood, the demon propelled itself closer to the edge. One of the tentacles swept toward Val.

Before it reached her, Arwen fired at it, alarmed at the idea of the demon draining her soul.

With adrenaline surging through her veins, she forgot about the injury to her hand, but a twinge made it spasm, throwing her aim off. Her arrow only skimmed the tentacle, slicing through one of the suckers. That didn't keep the demon from swinging toward Val.

Another pulse of power—a mental attack that brought a sharp stab of pain to the mind—accompanied the blow. Wincing, Val almost missed defending against the tentacle. Sindari sprang at it, his powerful jaws snapping for the mauve flesh. Unlike with the bullets, the magical tiger's fangs and claws sank into the demon, but the tentacles were so strong that he couldn't pull it down. He hung in the air like a cat caught in a curtain.

Val recovered and slashed at another tentacle that swept in, trying to grab her so it could crush her and extract her soul. Her glowing sword cut into it, spilling purple ichor that looked nothing like blood, but even the blade's great magic wasn't enough to halt the attack. The heavy limb continued toward her. She leaped back, but the tip flicked, extending and clipping her, and knocked her into a spin.

The tentacle that Sindari gripped jerked up and down as the demon sought to fling him away. When that didn't work, it wrapped around him, suckers plastering to his fur.

"Get out of there, Sindari," Val barked. "That thing's going to hoover up your soul."

The tiger snarled but wouldn't let go of his hold. He hung half in the water, half in the air, as his jaws remained attached, the tentacle grasping him.

Once more, Arwen fired, gritting her teeth against her injuries and the demon's ongoing mental attacks. Her arrow sank deep into the head.

A faint shudder went through the demon. Maybe it *did* have a brain in there.

Its grip loosened on the tiger, but it didn't release him fully. Its other tentacles continued to swing about.

Val ran into the water to help Sindari. Though shallow near the edge, the pool grew deep quickly. She stopped when she reached a drop-off and was just close enough to hack into the tentacle that held the tiger.

"Let him go, you oversized squid!" Taking her pain and frustration out on the demon, Val swung numerous times, pausing only to defend against another tentacle that swept toward her from the side.

With all four paws, Sindari raked his claws through mauve flesh, and the demon finally released him.

As Arwen nocked another arrow, a whoosh of magic came from the back of the cave. Dark-elven magic. It hammered into Val's back so hard that it knocked her forward into the pool. She didn't release her sword and managed to swing it up to defend against another tentacle, but it took her a moment to claw her way back to shallow water.

Arwen spun toward the source of the magic but still couldn't see or sense Harlik-van. How did *his* camouflaging magic remain in place even when he ran or launched attacks? She clenched her jaw, tempted to fire toward where she thought he might be, but she only had so many arrows in her quiver.

Give me your word, Harlik-van spoke calmly into her mind in Dark Elven, *that you will never attempt to remove that tattoo, and I will release my hold on the demon and let you walk out of this cave. I will stop killing those with the power to remove magical marks.*

"Did you kill the other artist?" Arwen demanded. "Mark?"

Frustrated, she loosed her arrow, trying to let his telepathic voice guide her to his location.

Val glanced back at her voice, but she was too busy defending to say anything.

Arwen's arrow disappeared into the darkness at the back of the cave before clattering off a rock wall. She'd hit nothing, as she'd feared.

I'll kill all those you seek out if you do not vow to leave your tattoo be. Harlik-van sounded like he'd moved.

Arwen fingered the shaft of Imoshaun's arrow, the one meant for dark elves. Dare she risk taking another wild shot? No. She had to figure out where Harlik-van was, if only for a second.

"You would take my word that I would leave it alone, and you'd go back to your people?" Arwen asked skeptically.

More tentacles slapped down as the demon battled Val and Sindari, and water spattered the rocky shoreline.

Too bad Harlik-van wasn't close to the edge or Arwen might have picked him out by where the spray didn't hit the ground. But maybe she could track him if he wasn't paying too much attention.

The demon pulsed more mental attacks at them. One almost brought Arwen to her knees with an intense blast of pain, and she had to use her bow like a staff until she could recover.

"This guy is pissing me off," Val growled.

Arwen eased behind a boulder, ostensibly using it for cover, but she also crouched, resting one hand on the cool cave floor.

It's true that I don't know you well, Harlik-van replied, *and whether you would value your word is a question, but I grow weary of this tedious assignment. Watching the mongrel spawn of She Who Leads is as stimulating as harvesting nightwater fungi.*

Nightwater fungi. That was one of the ingredients in the

recipe. He was taunting her, letting her know he'd read both halves of the page.

Another magical attack from Harlik-van smashed into Val's back, again making her stumble.

"If you could keep him from piling on," she yelled, "that would be great!"

Again, Val recovered in time to block a tentacle, even managing to slash off the tip, but the demon continued to assail her and Sindari.

"Sorry. I'm trying!" Hoping Harlik-van was distracted by throwing attacks at Val, Arwen let her soul-tracking magic flow into the ground.

As usual, her vision altered, the already dim light growing weaker as her eyesight shifted. The faint bioluminescent-green glow of footprints on the cave floor appeared. Not surprisingly, a heavy concentration ran back and forth from the entrance. They traveled straight toward two boulders in the gloom. Was his camp behind them? Was *he*?

Arwen rubbed her camouflaging charm again and left cover to creep along the back wall of the cave. She pointed her nocked arrow toward the two boulders and squinted, hoping to spot movement or sense him, if only for an instant.

Sindari roared, swimming under a tentacle that swept toward Val and slashing his claws toward the body of the demon.

"Yeah, take that, bitch," Val snarled.

Something splatted to the ground three feet in front of Arwen, startling her. The tip of a tentacle, still twitching, ichor oozing out. Smoke wafted from the dark liquid. She skirted it.

In the pool, a bunch of slender green tentacles joined the fray. Those didn't belong to the demon, too, did they?

No, those were vines. Elven vines. Val must have created them, the tendrils growing up from the bottom of the pool and attempting to grasp their enemy.

The demon surged about, breaking the vines with its huge body, but they distracted it. Val plunged her sword into a slow-moving tentacle waving in the air.

Will you attack me if you get the opportunity? Harlik-van asked dryly. *When I have not harmed you?*

Arwen wanted to point out that he'd harmed—*killed*—numerous people around her, but she worried he would pinpoint her location by her telepathic voice. She reached the back of the cave, and his camp came into view, a few books in a stack, a pot, a backpack, and a blanket on a sleeping pad. Was Harlik-van in the middle of the camp now? Crouching and facing Val? Preparing another attack?

Arwen aimed at the spot where he might be, but she longed for verification. She wanted the special dark-elf arrow to have a chance.

A tingle ran into her hand from the arrow, startling her. Its magic seemed to beg her to fire, promising it would hit him. Would it?

That is the Ruin Bringer, isn't it? All of our people want her dead. She Who Leads will reward me if I'm responsible. Her death is not forbidden—it would be praised. Yes. His last word was almost a snarl.

For the first time, Arwen sensed a swell of magic, not from in the camp but from atop one of the boulders. She shifted her aim and fired.

The arrow sped away, flashing silver in the dark air. The scrape of a boot on rock sounded—Harlik-van jumping off. But a grunt of pain escaped his throat. She'd gotten him.

Harlik-van appeared in the air, falling and rolling when he hit the ground. Arwen's arrow clattered away. It hadn't been a direct hit. She'd only grazed him. Either that or his magic had protected him. Yes, she sensed a barrier around him.

Yanking another arrow from her quiver, Arwen ran around the boulder to target him again.

He tore a dagger free and leaped to his feet, his hood falling back to reveal a mane of hair as white as his skin. Instead of whirling to attack Arwen, he sprinted toward Val—toward her back.

With Sindari's help, she'd lopped off three tentacles and damaged others, but the demon kept attacking her.

"Look out, Val!" Arwen fired again.

With his eyes locked on the hated Ruin Bringer, Harlik-van didn't see Arwen's attack coming. The magical barrier slowed it down, but, with the remains of Starblade's power in Arwen's bow, the arrow had the power to pierce his defenses. It thudded between his shoulder blades as he sprang for Val.

She'd heard Arwen's warning and leaped aside. Harlik-van's slashing dagger missed her, and, with the arrow jutting from between his shoulder blades, he tumbled into the water.

The demon must not have recognized its summoner—or maybe it did and hated him as much as the intruders—for it slammed a tentacle down on his back. A second one swept in from the side, knocking the dark elf flying. He tumbled into the waterfall, its power catching him and pummeling him. Soon, Harlik-van disappeared into the froth.

Arwen readied another arrow and crept to the edge of the pool, not trusting that they'd defeated him. She might have gotten him in the heart, but she wasn't sure. That thick cloak and his magic could have kept the arrow from plunging deep.

From the water, Val raised her blade, prepared to defend further against the demon.

But with Harlik-van's hold released, it had no reason to remain in this dimension. Drawing its remaining tentacles close to its body, the demon returned to deep water and sank below the surface. A new swell of magic formed, and it swam through a portal to return to its home.

Sindari limped out of the water, and Val joined him on the edge as the mist and the stink in the air faded.

"Did that kill the dark elf?" Sword in hand, Val eyed the waterfall. "I can't sense him, but I couldn't for *most* of the fight. Just at the end, after you hit him and he was rushing me. Can you believe that bastard wanted me more than you?"

"They haven't forgiven you for ruining their plans to take over the world. Twice."

"We only ruined their plans for that once. The other time, Zav and I interrupted a sacrifice."

"An equally heinous act."

When the water didn't stir again, Arwen headed for the camp, hoping one of those books held the rest of the recipe. She hadn't agreed to Harlik-van's demand, and she intended to remove her tattoo as soon as she could. If possible, she would heed Imoshaun's advice and have it done on another world, one where that telescope couldn't spy on her. She shivered at the idea that he'd watched her every movement for weeks. At least.

"Remind me to destroy that telescope on the way out," Arwen said.

"Good idea." Val pointed at the exit with her sword. "Sindari and I will check outside for him."

"Okay."

Arwen picked up the books in the camp, recognizing them from the troll's parlor, and flipped through one. Yes, there was the other half of the page that had been ripped out. She clutched the book to her chest and collected her arrows, lamenting that she'd lost one. Unless they found Harlik-van outside, floating face down in the pool with it sticking out of his back.

The first arrow she'd fired at him had a smear of blood on the tip. She didn't wipe it off. Maybe the heritage device would like samples of dark-elf blood.

After checking the rest of the camp to see if it held anything else useful and finding little but survival gear, Arwen joined Val outside. She stood on the ledge, gripping her chin as she gazed at the frothy pool, the inexorable waterfall continuing to plunge into it.

"No sign of him?" Arwen reached out with her senses, checking above as well as the depths below, but she didn't detect anything.

"No." Val's phone buzzed weakly. When she pulled it from a wet pocket, water dripped from it. The screen didn't come on. "That's going to need to go in the sauna for a while to dry out."

Arwen checked hers, though she expected it also wouldn't work. Surprisingly, the screen came on for a moment, a message from Willard popping up.

Tell Thorvald to get her ass back to Seattle and do something about all these dragons.

Alarm flashed through Arwen as she remembered the confrontation going on at Green Lake. She wanted to call Willard, but she wasn't able to turn on the screen again.

"I'll show you where I get mine fixed after battles." Val sheathed her sword and started up the rock face.

After a long last look at the pool, Arwen followed her. It might have been wise to stick around and make *sure* Harlik-van was dead, but she worried about Starblade. They had to find out what was going on back in Seattle.

32

THE MUSCLES IN ARWEN'S BATTERED BODY STIFFENED UP ON THE ride back to Seattle, leaving her fantasizing about the rejuvenation pool in Starblade's refuge. His *former* refuge. Unless the dragon confrontation they were driving toward changed something, he still wouldn't be able to linger on Earth.

"It doesn't sound like there's any more fighting going on." Off and on, Val had been in telepathic contact with Zavryd, who was engaged in a negotiation. "Which is good because Sindari has used up the time his magic allows him to stay on Earth in a given day."

Ah, that explained why he'd disappeared from Arwen's senses as they'd been tramping back over the dark mountain toward the Jeep. She'd been too exhausted after the battle and climbing back up the cliff to ask questions or even talk much until they'd plopped down in the Jeep. If not for her concern for Starblade, she might have dozed off once they'd reached pavement and the ride had gotten smoother.

"He also threatened to gnaw off my foot if I called him forth again for such an unappealing battle," Val added.

"He doesn't like fighting demons? Or dark elves?"

"Oh, he enjoys combatting all manner of challenging opponents. The *unappealing* part was having to jump off a cliff into a pool and being sprayed by a waterfall."

"I would have thought the tentacle wrapped around him would have been more offensive."

"No, water pummeling a tiger's sensitive eardrums is worse. Or so he says."

As they turned off the freeway at the Green Lake exit, Arwen sensed dragons—a *lot* of dragons—and worried the "negotiation" was failing.

She leaned forward in her seat, peering toward the dark sky. "Is it going okay? I was surprised you stopped at Imoshaun's workshop instead of driving straight here."

Imoshaun had also been surprised when they'd knocked on her door at midnight.

"It's fine, and I had a hunch you wanted to drop off that blood sample right away for analysis." Val gave her a sidelong look.

"A hunch you haven't yet explained." Arwen had only shared some of what Harlik-van had said during their encounters, so she didn't know how Val could know more about him than she.

"Let's just say that I find it odd that he never went after you, instead targeting those around you."

"I assume my mother told him to keep me alive because she has plans for me."

"We'll see."

Arwen scowled at her forearm but also hugged the elven recipe book, reminding herself she was a step closer to being able to have the tattoo removed. She would find the ingredients and someone who could do the deed soon. She *hoped* she'd taken out Harlik-van, but, even if she had, she couldn't count on her mother not sending someone else after her.

"That reminds me..." Arwen pulled out her phone, hoping it had dried out and would turn on.

It bleeped indignantly at her, then heated in her hand as the display lit up. Not certain how long it would work, she hurried to text Willard, asking if her agents could find out if Mark was alive. There'd been no evidence in the cave to suggest that he'd ever been there. She hoped Harlik-van had used illusion magic to take the photograph that he'd sent to her father.

As Val turned onto her street, the auras of multiple dragons overwhelmed Arwen's senses with their power. Some were centered around Val's and Matti's houses, and others perched in the park around Green Lake. Arwen recognized the auras of Starblade, Yendral, and Zavryd, but not the female or male dragon also at the end of the street with them. One of the dragons in the park was the same who'd harassed them near North Bend.

"Should we camouflage ourselves?" Arwen caught herself whispering.

"Nah. Our side outnumbers theirs. And I sense Matti and Sarrlevi are home."

"Are they established dragon fighters?"

"Oh, yeah. Sarrlevi has killed at least one that I know of, and there's nothing more dangerous than a mamma bear with cubs. Or expecting cubs."

"Is that Matti?" Arwen didn't know how the half-dwarf enchanter would like that analogy.

"Yup."

When Val parked the Jeep, three dragons looked down at them from rooftops of different houses. Zavryd and his family members Val had identified earlier.

Presumably, Matti didn't mind that the lilac dragon occupied her roof, and Zavryd was perched on the tower portion of Val's Victorian house, but did the owner of the third house have any idea that a black-scaled dragon with gray around his muzzle sat on the slate roof, his tail curled around the chimney?

Starblade and Yendral were in their elven forms on the lawn of Val's house near a collection of magical mushrooms that Arwen had noticed before. She didn't know if it was an active fairy ring and could take one to another realm or not.

Across the street, Matti and Sarrlevi sat on their porch swing, holding hands, as if they'd come out to stargaze. Their weapons leaned close, however, promising they could leap into battle if needed.

Starblade nodded gravely at Arwen when she opened the Jeep door and stepped out with her weapons. Yendral grinned and waved at her, nothing grave about him.

An angry roar came from the direction of Green Lake.

The gray-muzzled dragon roared back, then released the chimney to stick his tail in the air like a flagpole, twitching the tip twice. Arwen had a feeling that was the dragon equivalent of giving the middle finger.

You taunt them, Uncle Ston'tareknor? Zavryd asked.

Every chance I get. Their clan conspired to afflict me with that horrible illness and locked me in a stasis chamber for ages.

Stasis chambers are most unappealing, Starblade said telepathically.

Yes, my progeny, it is better to die heroically in battle than be ignobly interred so, Ston'tareknor said.

Had you died in battle, Zavryd said, *you would not currently be enjoying your new fae female who feeds you salty fish eggs after mating activities.*

Caviar, yes. They are delicious. She is delicious. The older dragon showed his fangs in what might have been a smile.

"Uhm, progeny?" Arwen left the Jeep to stand beside Starblade. "Was he talking to you?"

"Yes," Starblade said. "The results of the heritage detector prompted Zavryd'nokquetal, at his mate's urging, to question Ston'tareknor, who seems to be a less uptight family member than some. Zavryd'nokquetal found out that Ston'tareknor not only gave blood for the half-dragon experiment but that it was voluntary. Well, somewhat voluntary. I gather there were bribes of food and, ah, elven maidens. I trust he shifted into a less scaled form to enjoy their companionship."

Even as the lilac dragon roared and also did the middle-finger tail gesture toward the park, Arwen allowed herself fledgling hope. "Does that mean they'll..." She stopped herself from saying *protect you,* not wanting to prick Starblade's pride again. "Consider you an ally and offer the benefits of... clan membership?"

"Clan membership?" Starblade asked. "It is not a—ah, what was mentioned in the Study of Manliness?—Masonic lodge."

"No secret handshake, huh?"

"There may be tail slapping."

From his deadpan tone, Arwen couldn't tell if he was joking.

Starblade touched her hand. "I do wish to thank you for intervening, because I do believe the Silverclaws will not openly come after me now, at least not as long as I stay in the area of Zavryd'nokquetal's domicile on Earth." Only a quick lip curl suggested he might resent having to stay in Zavryd's shadow for protection. "They've made it clear that if they find me on another world, they'll be within their rights to attack and slay me. They blame me for Darvanylar's death, fairly, I suppose, though it was self-defense. They also blame me for the death of one of their clan members in our battle on Veleshna Var, though the dragons were attacking *us* unprovoked."

"So... you *have* to stay here? On Earth?" Arwen knew he wouldn't be pleased, even if he had earlier resolved himself to learn how to fit in with the natives, but she couldn't keep from smiling. "There'll be time then for me to make you that dinner. And the items on Yendral's list."

"Yes. And for me to build your rejuvenation pool."

"I bet that's the *real* reason she's been trying to keep him around," Val said from the Jeep.

Matti had joined her, leaning against the door, and nodded in agreement.

"I'll look forward to that," Arwen said, ignoring them. Starblade was still touching her hand and gazing at her. She bit her lip, barely resisting the urge to kiss him on the cheek. Or maybe somewhere more intimate.

Val's phone rang, breaking the spell. Starblade withdrew his hand, clasping it with his other behind his back, and looked toward the park. Judging by the ongoing growls and tail twitches from the dragons, their telepathic negotiations continued.

"Is Yendral also that dragon's, uhm, progeny?" Arwen asked.

"No. If Yendral is interested in learning who his progenitor is, he will have to find a number of samples for the gnome's device. Or ask *you* to do so, since your arrows are an effective method of gathering blood from dragons." Starblade's eyes glinted. In approval?

She smiled again.

The mongrel Yendral has no tie to our clan, Zavryd said haughtily from the roof. *I suggest you seek the Starsinger Clan. He oozes their foppish hippiness.*

"I'd be insulted," Yendral said, "but he's letting me stand within the protective wards of his property while his uncle gives tail taunts to our enemies."

"Yes," Starblade said. "It would be wise for you to hold your tongue."

Yendral nodded agreeably.

Arwen's phone rang. Since Val was reporting to Willard, she pulled it out, wondering who would call her so late. So few people had her number at all.

"Yes?" Arwen asked.

"It's Imoshaun."

Oh, that made sense.

"Did you already run the dark elf's blood?" Arwen guessed.

"Yes, I did."

A flutter in her belly made her realize she was nervous about the results. Val had seemed certain they would have some significance, but how many dark-elf blood samples could be in the heritage detector?

"Did you say you killed the owner of this blood?" Imoshaun asked.

"I shot him in the back, and he fell into a waterfall."

"Given how powerful dark elves are, that's not as definitive an answer as you might think."

"I know. We didn't see the body, and we had to return to the city for—"

An indignant roar loud enough to make the ground shiver came from the park.

"—reasons," Arwen finished.

"Well, according to the heritage detector, that dark elf is or was your brother."

"I... what?"

"*Half* brother, I'd guess, though the results aren't precise enough to be certain of that."

It took Arwen a long moment to digest the news. Did it change anything? She wasn't sure.

She might be in more trouble than she would have guessed for killing another of her mother's children, but Arwen hadn't even *known* her mother had other children. She supposed she might have guessed that her imprisoned father hadn't been her mother's only sexual partner over the years—for all Arwen knew, her mother might be centuries old—but she'd never pondered the possibility before. Since she'd never seen Harlik-van when she'd been growing up, at least not that she remembered, she couldn't have been expected to treat him differently from any other dark elf who'd inserted himself into her life and killed people.

"You look like you licked Yendral's foot," Starblade said, watching her. "Are you well?"

"Yes. But I think I may be in trouble."

"More trouble?"

"Yeah."

Starblade offered her his arm. "You may need an enchanted hidden sanctuary as well as a rejuvenation pool."

Arwen leaned against his side. "I have no doubt, but the dark elves already know where I live."

She remembered that Harlik-van had sent a messenger to her father at the farm, and shuddered.

"I will help you stave them off," Starblade said. "I now owe you another favor."

"Are you sure? I think we might be even now. I did shoot you in the leg."

"I have not forgotten. Due to the magic of your arrow and bow, the wound aches even though it has healed. I will need to soak it in your new rejuvenation pool once I build it."

She was about to ask him what was wrong with *his* rejuvenation pool, but he was gazing at her through lowered lashes, his handsome face appealing, his arm around her shoulders comforting.

"I'd allow that," Arwen said.

"Magnanimous."

Her senses picked up a swell of magic at the park—a portal forming. One after the other, the Silverclaw dragons departed, the familiar one pausing to share last words: *Do not think our clan will forget your crimes, mongrels. If you leave this world and the wake of those Stormforge tails, we will hunt you down and slay you.*

"I suppose it is good that I continue to practice human ways to fit in," Starblade said.

Arwen thought about mentioning that he could ditch the high-school letter jacket, but he'd defended her wardrobe to Amber, so she wouldn't tease him about his. "Yes," was all she said.

She worried about what the future would bring, but at least Starblade could stay on Earth.

EPILOGUE

"Is it hard to find parking in the city for such a large vehicle?" Arwen sat in the passenger seat of Nin's food truck as it navigated through Fremont toward the Coffee Dragon.

"The barista who opens in the morning sets out cones for me when I plan to bring it to the shop. As long as goblins don't steal them to use as materials for a project, there is a place for me." Calm, even-tempered Nin honked three times at a bakery van backing out of a driveway without looking. "That is your competition."

Arwen touched a hand to her chest and raised her eyebrows.

"A bakery run by a quarter-orc that offers burnt coffee with their dry scones and donuts. Their drinks are inferior, and the baked goods that I have sampled from your kitchen are much better, but... ogres, trolls, and goblins *do* love donuts." Nin eyed Arwen as she swung the lumbering truck around a corner. "Can you make donuts?"

"I have recipes, but I don't have a deep fryer. Also, I prefer to make desserts that use the fruit from the farm. That's where the magic is." Literally. Arwen knew how to make healthy bushes and trees that grew delicious fruit. She didn't know how her power might infuse a scone to improve the taste.

"Can you not make fruity donuts?"

"I suppose there is such a thing as apple fritters."

"Yes. Americans *love* deep-fried desserts. And apples too. Please consider adding *fritters* to your offerings." Even with an accent, Nin's English was always crisp and precise, but the way she said fritters implied she hadn't encountered the word often. "Your very delicious offerings that I am eager to add to our shop." She waved toward the back of the truck where they'd stored Arwen's strawberry shortcake fixings along with her first blueberry pies of the season.

With as much as Arwen had going on, it had been a challenge to find time to fill Nin's order, especially since she was working on *Yendral's* order, too, but she hadn't seen any dark elves for a few days and dared hope that Harlik-van was gone and her mother's people had decided to leave her alone. For now at least.

"I'll look into commercial deep fryers," Arwen said, "but I'm limited by the size of my father's home. I've already usurped what used to be the dining room to expand the kitchen."

"Perhaps I could order a Donut-O-Matic for the Coffee Dragon, and you could make them there. Since we remodeled, the building is reasonably spacious. Have you been to the mini-donut shop at Pike Place Market? People *love* watching conveyer belts carrying blobs of dough into powerful ovens to create finished desserts in front of their eyes."

Arwen imagined taking Starblade to that donut shop to witness the machine in action. The only problem was that he would want to improve it with Gnomish parts. She doubted the owner would care to be advised on how to give his donut maker more *equine* power.

"Too bad such a machine is quite expensive," Nin said. "I have priced them before."

"Maybe the goblins could save you money by building you one from scratch."

Nin slanted a horrified gape in her direction, possibly imagining a Donut-O-Matic made from recycled beer cans, hubcaps, and mattress springs with two stolen cones perched on top.

"Or maybe the company offers financing," Arwen added.

"Yes, that would be more logical to consider."

When Nin pulled up to the curb in front of the Coffee Dragon, there weren't any cones, but two ogres with clubs on their shoulders stood to claim the parking spot. One saw the truck coming and rubbed his belly.

"I see I will have to fire up the grill and rice cooker right away," Nin said. "Our patrons are already waiting."

Arwen wondered if any other eateries in the Seattle area had eight-foot-tall *patrons* who waited with clubs for their meals.

"You will wish to visit the new tenant working in the loft before coming out to construct your strawberry shortcakes." Nin nodded toward the front door of the two-story coffee shop. "Do not take too long, however, as the ogres—and those trolls and half-orcs coming out and lining up—eat their meals faster than wolves. Admittedly, some of our customers *are* wolves." Her next nod was toward a shifter couple walking hand-in-hand up the sidewalk toward the truck. "They will very soon be ready for dessert."

"I'm prepared to start anytime."

Arwen didn't know who the tenant was that Nin wanted her to see, but she sensed Matti and Val in the coffee shop and wanted to invite them to the dinner she was planning for Starblade and Yendral. Though she hated crowds, and she didn't know where she would seat that many people at once, the idea of having a meal with only Starblade and Yendral made her nervous. *Starblade* was no problem, but since Yendral had talked about her *squish* and referred to her as *our female*, Arwen would prefer more people be around for the dinner. Even though she could take care of herself in most situations, her naïveté made her uncertain how to handle men who had an interest in her. She doubted even a half-dragon would do anything untoward with the Ruin Bringer and her huge tiger at the table.

"Very good," Nin said. "I appreciate you coming. If this works out well, perhaps we could always have you here on Wednesdays to serve desserts. That would not interfere with your farmers market days, correct? I believe you will earn much more here than there. If you smile and flirt with the male customers, they will tip well." Nin waved at one of the better-looking half-orcs in the line.

Uncertainly, Arwen tried a smile. It was hard to keep an edge of panic from creeping into it. More and more beings were stepping into line, and she feared this would grow more crowded than the farmers market. She mentally braced herself to pass them and go inside but ended up with a death grip on the door handle and her smile frozen in a painful rictus.

"Perhaps—" Nin eyed her rigid lips, "—you should not smile."

"Sorry. I'm not very good at... people."

"You can stay in the back of the truck while I serve the items."

"That would be ideal." It wasn't that warm today, but Arwen had to wipe sweat off her brow. "Thank you."

"I will smile for both of us and split the tips with you."

"You're a fair business partner."

"Certainly."

The front door of the Coffee Dragon opened, and Amber stuck her head out. With so many full- and half-blooded magical beings inside, Arwen hadn't detected her.

Amber spotted Arwen right away and waved for her to come in.

After opening the door and hopping out, Arwen told herself to walk calmly past the boisterous line of customers, like a professional businesswoman, but too many of them looked at her, their expressions everything from curious to suspicious to lascivious. An ogre whistled and commented on her ass.

Arwen bolted for the front door.

"Don't be rude to women, meat paws!" Amber yelled to the ogre.

Arwen sprang past her and put her back to the wall beside the door.

"Look," Amber told her, "I get that you don't like crowds—and that's a super *sketch* crowd—but if a guy is rude and whistles at you, you should correct his behavior, not flee."

"I'm not sure how to correct an ogre's behavior." Arwen grimaced at the idea of confronting a stranger in a crowd, especially on proper social etiquette, a subject she was *not* an expert on.

"Shooting an arrow into his balls would do it."

"That's not an overly aggressive response?"

"Nah. Magical beings heal quickly. But for at least one day, his whistles would be really high-pitched." Amber pointed toward a table that was—thankfully—in a corner less busy than the rest of the bustling shop.

Before they reached Val and Matti, both of whom were sipping carbonated waters instead of coffee, a shirtless goblin ambled down the stairs. He turned toward tables of other goblins while flexing his biceps to show off not his modest muscle but a tattoo featuring a glowing trio of cogs on his green skin. It must have been new, because his buddies oohed, ahhed, and drew wrench-shaped salutes in the air.

"This is the strangest coffee shop in the greater Seattle area," Amber said. "And that's saying a *lot*. There's a place in Ballard that only has bean bags and yoga mats to sit on while you're admiring cityscapes made from *moss* hanging on the walls."

"I'm surprised to see you here," Arwen said. "Did you come to spend time with your mother?"

"As if I'd come to the weirdo menagerie during my summer break to hang out with Val." Amber looked frankly at Arwen. "When will you start serving the strawberry shortcakes?"

"Ah. Soon. Nin wanted me to meet her new tenant. Do you know who that is?"

Amber shrugged. "No idea, but I don't think there are any extra rooms unless you count that little library back there. Or the restroom that the goblins *improved*."

Arwen hadn't yet needed to visit the Coffee Dragon's facilities. Amber's nose wrinkle suggested she didn't want to.

"Hey, Arwen," Val said. "Willard wanted me to let you know that Markyseel, the half-troll tattoo artist, is alive and well, but I guess you already saw."

"I did?"

Only as Val pointed to the shirtless goblin, who was now on top of a table so he could show off his tattoo from a greater height, did Arwen grasp the meaning. She scanned the crowd with her senses, the auras of dozens making it hard to pick out one person, but she finally detected Mark in the loft, heading for the stairs. Raucous goblin laughter floated down ahead of him, and two fist-size dice ricocheted down the steps. One plinked into a patron's coffee mug, resulting in a prompt call to the barista for a refund.

"I thought he was in Tacoma," Arwen said.

"Tacoma." Amber wrinkled her nose with the same distaste she'd had for the goblin-improved restroom.

"You think this is a better place to do business?"

Amber considered that as she eyed the eccentric magical yard art on the walls and in cases around the shop. "There's a big customer base to draw from, if they don't mind dice hitting them in the side of the head while they're being inked."

"I'm not sure an ogre would even *feel* dice hitting him in the head." Matti sipped her water, then rested her hands over her abdomen. She looked like she could deliver her twins at any moment.

"That's the truth," Val said. "More good news for you, Arwen. The troll clan in Lynnwood no longer wants me to kill you."

"They figured out I wasn't responsible for Star Inker's death?"

"You can thank Willard for that somewhat, but I understand Mark is pretty active in the troll community, despite his pointy ears." Val waved toward the stairs where the also-shirtless, green-skinned tattoo artist was descending. "Apparently, he told them you were cute and would never murder an innocent troll."

"Uhm."

"You could do worse," Val said. "He's a lot more appealing shirtless than the goblins."

"That's not saying much," Matti murmured.

"No? He has nice muscles, and the tattoos are kind of intriguing," Val said.

"Are you allowed to admire other men when you're mated to a dragon?" Matti asked.

"Only when he's not around to get huffy about it. Besides, I'm only looking for a friend." Val lifted her water toward Arwen.

"I'm relieved the trolls don't want me dead any longer." Arwen didn't comment on Mark's appearance, though he was heading for their table.

Maybe she *should* consider dating friendly men who weren't troubled by her dark-elven blood, but did she have an interest in Mark? She couldn't help but remember Starblade touching her hand in the kitchen and wrapping his arms around her after the dragon battle. Wasn't it possible he would one day realize that he *liked* her? And didn't only want to help her with her problems because he felt obligated?

"Any word from Willard about the dark elves?" Arwen asked when she realized Matti and Val were watching her. What expression had she worn as she mused about Starblade? She hoped neither of them were mind readers.

"They haven't been seen since the incident in Bellevue, and when she had her favorite operative—" Val touched her chest, "—fly out to check the waterfall lair, there was no sign of your new brother."

Arwen winced at the term. "I'm not sure if that's good or bad. If there had been a body, we'd know for sure that he died."

"Yeah, it's probably telling that there wasn't. I kind of doubt the local goblins carted it away for parts. *Zoltan* might do that, but goblins prefer the mechanical to the biological."

"Hello, Arwen, the beautiful lady who kept a werewolf from killing me." Mark rested a hand on his flat abdomen, the tattooed tendrils of some mythological creature circling his navel, and bowed.

"Hello, Mark. I'm glad you're well."

"Very well. Despite repeated blunt-object trauma this morning." Mark rubbed the side of his head and looked upward as another round of laughter echoed from the loft. "I didn't realize how passionate goblins were about their gaming sessions when I agreed that a corner up there would be nice until I get my shop fixed up."

"The trebuchets and catapults that they use to launch their dice weren't a clue?" Matti asked.

"In retrospect, they should have been. Especially given their size." Mark took a breath and faced Arwen. "My lady archer, would you like to get a coffee one day?" When more laughter sounded and another die pinged down the stairs, he added, "Perhaps in a less *busy* establishment."

"Uhm." Not sure how to respond, Arwen waffled. "Let me think about it, please." Her phone rang, and she pounced on it, relieved for the interruption. "Hello?"

A goblin in the doorway announced that the food truck had

opened and was serving meals, and a stampede of customers left their tables to rush out. Mark looked like he might wait and try to entice Arwen with another possible dating activity, but his nostrils twitched at the scent of cooking beef, and he wandered out.

"Something arrived at the farm this morning," her father said.

Fear clutched Arwen's heart. "From the dark elf?"

She hadn't yet told her father that Harlik-van was her brother, and didn't know if she would. She was conflicted over having possibly killed him.

"No, but it came via the same goblin messenger, so I *was* concerned when he pedaled up the driveway. But he removed a box with Gnomish writing on the side and gave it to me before holding out a hat made from bicycle chains and asking for a tip. The *first* time, he didn't do that. Like he knew he was delivering something awful."

"Gnomish writing?" Arwen asked.

"I think so. I'm not positive what I'm looking at, but I think it might be the part your half-dragon friend mentioned. A *flip*-some-thing. There's a brochure with diagrams that show how to install it on different wheeled contraptions. One kind of looks like a tractor, except for the plate armor and spikes. Are there worlds where farm equipment needs to be outfitted like a siege engine?"

"I have no doubt." Arwen's fear faded, but she didn't know what to make of the gift.

"Will he be by to show me where this would go in Frodo?"

"I... have invited him and his friend for a dinner."

"All right, good. Frodo doesn't *need* more horsepower, but it's hard to resist upgrades. Very hard." Father was always gruff and never *delighted* by things, but he sounded pleased by the delivery. "I'll show it to you when you get back. Be careful in the city."

"I will be."

After hanging up, Arwen looked to Val, who had her eyebrows up, probably wondering if the call signaled trouble. Arwen was tempted to ask her opinion on something. A woman-to-woman kind of thing. Matti had gone out to check on the line for the food truck, and Amber had taken her seat and was texting. Since she wasn't paying attention, maybe Arwen could have a private discussion with Val.

"Val," Arwen said quietly, "have you ever had a man say he doesn't like you romantically but then do things to suggest that maybe he *does* care in some way?"

Amber, proving she wasn't as engrossed as Arwen had thought, lifted her head. "Like by getting you jewelry?"

"A gnomish tractor part," Arwen said.

"Oh, it's not the guy who looked under the hood of my car, is it?" Amber stood up. "You can do *much* better, Arwen."

"Better than a half-dragon? He's powerful and can fly." And he was handsome, especially when shirtless, and he kept doing nice things for her...

"The shirtless tattoo guy is cute," Amber said. "Green skin and quirky, sure, but you're quirky too. You ought to like that."

"Why don't you get some lunch, Amber?" Val made a shooing motion with her hand.

"I'm old enough to talk about romance and adult things," Amber said. "And I'm not leaving without Arwen. She needs someone to guide her safely to the food truck to make my shortcake."

"Your noble selflessness in helping a friend is admirable."

"I'm an admirable kind of girl."

Arwen waved to indicate that Amber staying for the conversation was fine.

"You don't want to take dating advice from Val, anyway," Amber said. "Her husband is even nuttier than the half-dragon."

After giving her daughter a flat look, Val told Arwen, "Some men aren't mature enough to express their feelings honestly."

"Starblade is hundreds of years old," Arwen said.

"Maybe there's another issue."

"Yeah," Amber said, "like he could be married on seven worlds and have twenty-six kids."

"I doubt that's it," Arwen said. "Especially when he was locked in that stasis chamber for centuries."

"Something else, then," Val suggested. "Maybe he's getting over another relationship."

"Sure," Amber said, "he could be *divorced* on seven worlds."

Val snorted.

Arwen started to wave dismissively but remembered what Starblade had said—or *not* said—about Gemlytha, the dark-elven half-dragon. Could that have something to do with it?

"Give him some time," Val said.

"Or have coffee with the quirky elf guy," Amber suggested. "He seems fun."

"You *could* use some fun in your life." Val nodded in agreement. "You're rather grave for someone so young."

"I'll think about it. Thank you."

"You're *very* welcome." Amber linked arms with Arwen. "This way. My future strawberry shortcake is calling you."

"Noble selflessness," Val repeated.

Amber gave her mother a thumbs-up as she led Arwen out of the shop. The ogre who'd whistled earlier eyed Arwen but didn't say anything. Maybe Amber *was* a decent guide.

THE END

Printed in the USA
CPSIA information can be obtained
at www.ICGtesting.com
LVHW041549221223
767232LV00001B/51